HITTING THE SAUCE
by Lisa Shiroff

Tasfil Publishing, LLC
New Jersey, USA

DEDICATION

It's cliché, I know, but I dedicate this book to my wonderful husband, Glenn. It's because he tolerates my bad puns, suffers my recipe experiments, and never wavers in his faith and support for me that I am able to do whatever it is I do, including write.

CONTENTS

JUST ANOTHER MONDAY

I stepped into the shower and stood there for a few minutes, letting the water wash over me. With eyes closed against the needling spray, I tilted my face into the stream and mouthed the words *Today is the day*.

I wasn't trying to drown myself before work. The mantra was yet another attempt to finally make good on a New Year's resolution to put my life back together. It'd been six weeks since I'd made that promise to myself, five months since my life had fallen apart. Ever optimistic, I approached each Monday as a new beginning, with a new theory to apply, a new therapeutic tool to use, and a new method to fix what might prove unfixable.

Nothing had yet to work. I was now down to positive affirmations and hope.

"Today is the day," I said aloud and reached for the shampoo bottle.

I paused, thinking I heard an alarm somewhere. Poking my head out the shower door, I learned I was right. An alarm *was* blaring. My burglar alarm, to be exact.

A bolt of adrenaline shot down my spine. Being naked and alone when someone breaks into my house was yet one more thing I was ill-equipped to handle.

All too aware of just how defenseless I was, I shut the shower door and inched back to the wall. The tiles were jarringly cold on my skin despite the steamy water in front of me. I pressed hard against them anyway, wanting to get as far from the fogged-up door as possible. That knife-wielding hand silhouette from *Psycho* played in my memory, which was weird because I'd never seen the movie.

My imagination didn't stop there, though. I could easily envision masked men scurrying through my house. Looking for what or who,

I hadn't a clue; I just knew they were intent on doing horrible deeds and probably doing them to me.

I found myself cringing, sliding down, and crunching into a ball, waiting for my demise. Then I waited some more. And still I waited. After a few more minutes waiting, my shoulders grew tired. I dropped to the floor and sat, straining only my ears.

The siren continued its shrill yell. I remained immobile in the shower, listening, until I noticed the water wasn't quite as hot as it had been and was coming out colder and colder.

"Ugh. I just did it again." I rolled my head back, bumping it on the tile. "C'mon, Lucy. Today is supposed to be the day!"

I stood and turned the water off. Wrapped in a towel, I stepped out of the shower, opened the bathroom door to my bedroom, and of course, no one was there. Obviously, the alarm had scared the person off, and I'd wasted all the hot water behaving like a cornered Chihuahua instead of taking control of my life. Again.

Inside the bedroom door, I punched my code in the alarm pad and hit *off*. The siren quieted.

"Hello!" A man shouted from downstairs.

I slammed the door and locked it. Then I realized serial killers probably didn't shout pleasant greetings before striking.

"Who's there?" I called.

"Officer Stanley Cooper, with the Atlantic City Police Department!" he yelled back.

I opened the door and leaned out far enough to see down the stairs. At the bottom was a familiar face. Officer Cooper had arrested my son last fall.

"Hi, um, I was in the shower. I'll be out in a second," I said.

He nodded. "We'll be down here in the kitchen. Looks like that's where someone attempted to break in."

I let the police do their thing and inspect my house for evidence while I did my best to get ready for work, which included extra deodorant. I could hear my mother psychically nagging me from 1,200 miles away: *You could have at least washed under your arms while you were sitting there, doing nothing in the shower.*

I pulled my hair back into a curly ponytail, tugged on a pair of black slacks, and buttoned up a white blouse. In the mirror, I thought I looked drab but also somewhat utilitarian. Like I was the kind of person who got things done, solved problems, had her life together.

"Today is the day," I said to my reflection. "Today is the day I take life by the horns and shake some sense into it. Yes. Today is the day, damn it."

Downstairs, I served coffee to the same officer I had yelled at back in September when he had politely waited for my son to put on his sneakers. I was nicer to him for this visit, and he was even more polite with me.

Someone had definitely broken into my house. Someone had entered the mudroom door without damaging the lock, rummaged through the food in the kitchen, and was too lazy to shut the cabinets when he was done. The only person I could think of doing that was my soon-to-be-officially-ex-husband, Lester.

"He doesn't know your code?" Cooper asked.

"I put in a new alarm system when he left."

"Does he have a key?" Cooper's partner, Officer Bryant, asked.

"No. But it's entirely possible I forgot to lock the door last night. I've been a little absent-minded lately."

"Is he considered dangerous?" he asked.

"He's considered stupid." I tried to pour myself a cup of coffee, but the pot was empty.

"Look," Cooper said. "You do live in a nice section of AC, but still, no neighborhood here is nice enough to leave the doors unlocked. You might want to be more careful in the future."

"We can't file this as a domestic dispute," Bryant said. "But if you seriously suspect your ex-, we can call him in to question him."

"Thanks, but I don't think that's necessary." I gathered their empty cups and put them in the dishwasher. "Lester had our kids for their first weekend with him. He probably just realized he had nothing to send to school with my daughter for lunch. She refuses to eat the school food."

"Really?"

"Yes. She's quite the picky eater."

"No. I mean, do you really think that's what he wanted?"

I nodded, which meant I was lying to the police, something I was pretty sure was supposed to be illegal. But I didn't want them getting involved in my divorce battles. Today was the day I would take charge and handle things for myself. I would get even with Les.

Bryant frowned at his partner and stood. "How would you like us to proceed from here?"

"I'll deal with it," I said. "I hope this didn't take you away from more serious problems this morning."

"Serious problems in Atlantic City?" Cooper laughed. "Never."

I called Les from my cell as I sped to work. His line went directly to voicemail.

"I don't get it," I said after the beep. "Were you hungry? I'm sure you don't have much to eat at your place. Your skinny girlfriend probably needs all the cupboard space for her Diet Coke and cigarettes, right? But was that really necessary? And you still can't shut a freaking door, can you? What the hell is the matter with you?"

And now I was going to be late for work on a Monday. It was a bad sign that wouldn't be missed. I'm the activities director at the Atlantic City Community Center for Seniors. I'm surrounded by mental health professionals who, while specializing in the concerns and care of the elderly, were still trained to perceive late Mondays as a sign of someone with a weekend drug or alcohol problem. And weekend drug or alcohol problems often become workweek drug or alcohol problems. Or at least good fodder for gossip.

I pulled into the parking lot at the center, found a spot, and whispered my new motto as I ran-walked to the building. "Today is the day I begin putting my life back together. Today is the day I get it all in control. Today is the day I take charge." I crossed the breezeway, yanked open the center's doors, sped through the common area, and wound up in reception a little short of breath.

"Here she is," the receptionist, Gayle, said instead of greeting me. "Lucy," she waved her hand toward a man on the other side of her desk. "This is Enzo Fabian. He said he had an appointment scheduled with you for nine o'clock."

"Oh, I'm so sorry," I panted. "I had you down for nine-fifteen."

"Regardless, it's nine-thirty now, and I've been waiting." He replaced a brochure on Internet dating services in the wall rack behind him.

"Yes, again, I am very sorry. I, uh, had a meeting before work this morning that took longer than I expected." I extended my hand. "It's so nice to meet you, Mr. Enzo."

"It's Fabian." Ignoring my hand, he tugged on the ends of his jacket sleeves, one at a time, before looking at me.

"Well then, call me Lucy."

"No, it's *Mr.* Fabian." He pulled at the lapels of his jacket.

"Excuse me?"

A snort of laughter came from Gayle.

"My name is Enzo Fabian, not Fabian Enzo." His nonsmiling face assured me he found no humor in the situation. He was stern and polished: olive skin, slicked back dark hair with a touch of gray at the temples. He wore shiny shoes and an almost equally shiny suit. He was a stereotypical Italian, complete with an I've-got-connections squint to his eyes. New Jersey is full of men who look like that; most of them are of Irish or Russian descent.

"Once again, I'm sorry, Mr. *Fabian.*" I cleared my throat. "Of course. I remember now. We spoke on the phone last week. Why don't we go have a seat at my desk?"

He nodded and followed me through administration. I did my best to keep my eyes averted from the die-cut hearts and Cupids taped to everything that didn't move as I led him through the maze of cubicles. If it weren't for Stacey, from human resources, I would have made it to my desk untainted by the phony displays of affection. But as I rounded the last corner, she pounced on me and shoved a pink-and-red paper in my face.

"Only four more days," she crooned.

I took the paper and looked at it. It was an invitation to a singles-only Valentine's party.

"Shouldn't this be against company policy?" I tried to give it back to her.

"Of course not." She wouldn't take it from me. "It's a personal thing, at my house. You *must* come, Lucy. I've got just the man for you-oo!" She ran off before I could trip her.

I refrained from asking Enzo Fabian if he had a lighter. Instead, I wadded the paper into a ball and marched to my cubicle.

"I'm sure there's fresh coffee in the break room," I said. I threw the invitation in the trash under my desk and picked up my cup. "Could I get you some?"

"No, thank you." He sat in a client chair, crossed his legs, and ran a hand down his trouser shin, smoothing a slight crease, before looking at me again.

"Okay, right to business then." I gave him an acquiescing nod and took my chair behind my desk. "Judging by appearances, you are not the one in need of our services, correct?"

"Correct."

I waited for him to continue. He didn't.

"So, are you looking here on behalf of a parent?"

"Yes." He gave me a closed-lip smile. "My mother passed away a few months ago, and my father is having a hard time adjusting to living here as a single man."

"I'm sorry to hear that. So, they were not local?"

"What do you mean?"

"Did he move to this area *after* her death? When you said 'adjusting to living here,' I thought perhaps—"

"Oh, no. Actually, yes." He frowned. "Yes, he moved here...from Philadelphia."

"I see." I realized I was caressing my coffee cup.

"What do you see?"

"I see why you would like him to join us here." I pried my fingers from the mug and opened a file drawer to retrieve the intake forms. "So that he could meet people in the community and perhaps make new friends."

He paused as if to think about what I'd said. "Yes, yes, that's exactly right."

"Well, joining our center will certainly encourage him to develop friendships with people around here as well as help him learn how to live as a single man." I tapped the papers on my desk to line up their edges. "I have to ask, though, was it his idea to enroll here, or do you just feel he is in need of it?"

"Why do you have to ask?"

"He isn't here. Often, that's a sign the senior is unwilling to be a part of our community."

"Oh." He bit his lower lip. "We didn't think of that."

"I'm sorry?"

"We uh, I didn't realize that was the normal thing to do."

"Yes, usually, an interested senior wants to be part of the whole process of joining. Are you sure he knows you're here to enroll him?"

"Yes. He.. uh...he had a project he needed to take care of this morning. So he sent me instead."

"But he's interested in what we can do for him?"

"He's very interested in you."

"Me?"

"Your services." He re-crossed his legs, smoothing out his trouser shin again. "But would you be the one working directly with my father?"

"That would depend on what it is he needs or wants from us." I found a clipboard on my credenza. "I mostly preside over group meetings as a facilitator, but I do substitute whenever I'm needed in the classes."

"Is that *all* you do here?"

I let the clipboard clack loudly on the intake forms. "I do quite a bit behind the scenes, Mr. Fabian. Is there something specific you or your father wants from the senior center?"

"We specifically want to know who will be working with him."

"That would depend on which class or group he chooses to join. I can give you biographical information on all of our associates."

"That would be good. Can I see yours?"

I dropped the clipboard, opened another file drawer, pulled out the brochure listing the experience of everyone who works at the center, including me, and handed it to him in silence.

He looked it over. "Yes, here you are. Lucinda Womzak. Right. Yes. I think you're the one."

"I don't understand. Is there something particular you're looking for? Does your father have a special need?"

"What do you mean?"

"I was inquiring as to whether he was suffering from a professionally diagnosed physical or psychological disorder."

"Does he need one to be a member here?"

"No."

"I don't think he has a problem like that. Can you handle a normal man?"

I sucked in on my lips to keep from saying I'd yet to meet one. "What would your father like to get from our center?" I asked after taking a long inhale.

"He would like…safe companionship. Can you offer that?"

"Safe companionship? I'm not sure I understand."

"He needs to find someone he can be comfortable around, to talk about anything with."

"So you think he needs someone to be his friend, his confidant?"

"Confidant. Yes. That's not something *you* would do, is it?"

I leaned back in my chair and took another long inhale. I couldn't blame him for not wanting *me* near his dad. I didn't exactly start off on my most professional footing with him. However, if he didn't have such a snobby attitude, I'd probably be handling the whole meeting better. Also, I'd certainly be on my game if I'd had a little bit of coffee in my system. But it was all his fault that I didn't have a fresh cup of the electric juice in front of me.

I exhaled, and instead of taking another calming inhale, I lost control of my tongue. "I'm not sure what you're getting at, Mr. Fabian, but I've been working in this center, dealing with seniors, for more than ten years. I have yet to lose one. I have yet to accidentally or even intentionally poison one. I have yet to have one commit suicide on my watch. I—"

"But will you spend one-on-one time with my father?"

"Again, that would depend on what he needs from the center. He may not ever see me here. Now then—"

"Do you do that frequently, though? Spend alone time with your clients? Do you try to get close to them?"

"Often I—"

"How close?" He tilted his head in such a way that I got what I thought was his point. I exploded with laughter so hard my belly bounced. He remained unamused. His eyes were so dark I couldn't see their pupils. They were so emotionless it was hard for me to believe the laugh lines extending from their corners were well-deserved.

"Forgive me." I took a tissue and dabbed my eyes. "It's been a long time since someone mistook me for trophy-wife material." I laughed again and blew my nose at the idea. Even if I were a hot honey, there's no way I'd get back into the dating market on the arm of an over-seventy stud-muffin on Viagra. I pulled myself together and looked the man in his humorless eyes. "I have no intentions of becoming romantically involved with any of the seniors here. Now then, has your father made his move to the area?"

"His what?"

"His move from Phila—"

"Oh, that." He ran a finger along the inside of his shirt collar. "Yes."

"Good, then perhaps you could have him complete this paperwork." I removed the pages from the clipboard and handed them to him. Ordinarily, I like to have the intake forms completed in person because that tends to make potential clients more committed to joining. But I couldn't wait any longer for coffee. "Send it in, and then we'll arrange for a tour of the facilities. If he still wishes to join afterward, we'll process everything."

"How long will all that take?"

"That would depend on him. When he returns the paper—"

"I could have it to you tomorrow."

"He should probably tour the center, maybe stop in on an open class or two."

"When do they happen? Do you have a schedule? Can he do it today?"

In slow motion, I pulled a schedule from the wall file. Something felt off to me, very off. The whole meeting with the man was a little off, but it was getting even further away from the path of normalcy, and I was beginning to suspect it had nothing to do with my clean coffee cup. "Here is—"

He snatched the printout from my hands and looked it over.

"As you can see," I continued, "there are plenty of group therapy sessions dealing with grief and life changes. The ones highlighted in yellow are ones I facilitate. They are open groups, meaning they're not confidential, and anyone can attend. The other classes, the ones where we teach seniors to use webcams, or the cooking or hobby classes, might give you a good idea of exactly how my associates would interact with your father. And of course, depending on his needs, we can arrange for private, more personal thera—"

"Very good." He stood, shoved the papers into his breast pocket, and tugged at the ends of both sleeves again. I wondered if he had something hidden inside them. "You will see us soon." He smiled a smile so bright and wide that if it were possible, I'd swear he stole it from someone else.

IS IT TOO EARLY FOR A DO-OVER?

I headed straight to the break room and poured a cup of sludge before making a new pot of coffee. Once it was ready and I was armed with a fresh cup, I was able to summon the courage to face my e-mail.

The last thing I had read on the previous Friday was a message from Mona, the center's Director of Administrative Operations. It was a confidential memo letting me know the center's holdings had taken a hit and we were in dire financial straits. Our budget gurus were intent on examining everything we were doing, and it was very possible, if we didn't find a way to cut costs and increase funding, the place might have to close its doors before the end of the year.

We were a private organization funded by a philanthropic donation from a little old lady who literally hit the jackpot. Her name was Mildred Mae Gold, and she took her lottery winnings in one lump sum, which, after taxes, left her more than seventy million in cash. She built a new animal shelter, funded a foundation that spays and neuters stray cats, and, when she realized she still had plenty of money in the coffers, she decided to spend it on older people. She said she'd always wished there was someplace she could go and learn something new or just be around people her age without having to move into a home. She set up the foundation for the community center, refusing to have it named after her as she didn't want people to think she was vain, and died a few months later.

Her start-up money went a long way but not long enough. And now, according to Friday's e-mail, rather than appealing to the government for aid and assistance, which would take away our flexibility in how we ran the place, what we charged, and what we offered, the center would begin asking for donations from the general population, and we would be upping our membership fees.

In the interim, I needed to put together a "sound and reasonable" justification for each group and class. I would need to prove that we were using our associates' time and skills as efficiently as possible. If it should be discovered that I had "excess staffing measures in occurrence," I would need to eliminate the positions involved and merge activities. I was also to do a census for each class and group to determine whether we could make changes to raise our staff-to-senior ratio without upsetting our members. And, if I had time, maybe I should pray for a miracle.

I sat at my desk with the fresh brew in hand and read the follow-up Mona had managed to produce that morning. It wasn't a retraction. Instead, there were sign-in sheet attachments I was to use with each group and class, and an Excel form in which I was to input the group names, member names, and rationale for existing.

I printed a sign-in sheet, made the sign of the cross over it, and headed to my Monday morning eleven o'clock group.

"Why are you taking names, Lucy?" Mr. Schwartz asked. He stood at the card table where I'd placed the sign-in sheets next to a bowl of dairy-free, wheat-free cookies. "Who are you going to give this information to?"

"It's just for me, Mr. Schwartz." I smiled at him as I helped my intern, Rachel, arrange the chairs into as perfect a circle as we could make. "I'm trying to figure out exactly how many people we're working with in all the programs we run here to make sure we're using our time to *your* best advantage."

"But why do you need names?" He bent over and inspected the cookies at close range.

"I thought it would be easier. The cookies are safe. They are gluten-free and wheat-free."

Satisfied that the members would think the chairs were evenly spaced, thus no one chair was in a more prominent position, hence more important, than another, I retrieved my precious coffee cup from my own seat and sat.

"Who else will see these papers?" Mr. Schwartz picked up a cookie, scrutinized it at close range, and took a sniff. "Why does anyone need to have proof I was here?" He braved a nibble.

"Actually, no one does. If you'd like, you may put 'anonymous' down on the line," I said, even though I knew that now all the attendees would list themselves as *anonymous* and the sheet would be worthless to Mona.

My Monday morning group was an odd bunch who didn't fit in anywhere else at the center or anywhere out in the world. I had slowly pulled them together over the years as I realized none of them had their own safe place. I believed everyone needed that one special place where, even if you were not unconditionally loved by everyone else there, you were unconditionally accepted. A place where you knew you were safe to be yourself with no inhibitions. A place where you could say what you wanted, dress the way you wanted, act in whatever way you were comfortable, and no one would hold it against you—for long anyway. Most people have that place at home; others find it at work or in their church, and still others get it with their fellow card players in the casinos. The folks who made up this group didn't have that place until I gave it to them.

This group would be the hardest to justify to people looking to cut economic corners. On the schedule, it was listed as "Misc." *from 11:00 until needed.* It had never been clearly defined for anyone. Nor were any specific goals or themed rationale routinely applied to it. My only intention every Monday was to give the members an opportunity to simply be themselves. I was sure number-minded people would put the group first on the chopping block to improve the center's time use. Though I felt it was the most in need of existing.

Although I never insisted on a point for our meetings, I always showed up with notes or discussion ideas covering topics I thought they could use a little help with. For today's meeting, I had hoped to encourage them all, particularly Mrs. Elliot, to keep their medical appointments. It had seemed to me that as the winter had progressed, Mrs. Elliot's left shoulder had grown noticeably larger than her right, and I knew she had *a hatin'* (as she called it) on her doctor.

However, inspired by Mona's memos, I switched gears. I thought I'd get the group to help me come up with a name for them. I wanted to see how they viewed themselves and why they were there. Perhaps their perspective would help me define and rationalize them in my new reports.

"Hey, Lucy," Rachel took her place beside me. "Do you think we can meet sometime?" she asked. The seniors continued to file in, stop for cookies, and glance at the sign-in sheets before inspecting the chairs.

"Of course. Is everything okay?"

"My parents told me last night I was going to have to support myself this summer. I need a real job. I'm hoping you could put in a good word for me. You always said I would like it here if I'd just give it a chance."

"You actually want to work here?"

She had changed her major from Child Care and Support Services to Gerontological Social Work right before interning with us. Recently, I suspected she would go back to school to study engineering.

"Anywhere."

Given our financial situation, the center was probably a no-go, but I had a lot of local connections. I scribbled a note on my steno pad to remember to ask around for her. "Let's figure out a good time to talk when there are no ears around, sound good?"

"Sure," she said, staring over my shoulder.

I craned my head around until I heard something crack in my neck. There, in the doorway, stood Enzo Fabian with a man who looked older than he, but not quite old enough to be his father. Nor was there a family resemblance. The other man was taller and had a bulkier build. He wore a similar suit, but he was obviously more comfortable in it: Enzo kept pulling and tugging on his jacket.

It'd been only about an hour since the man had left my cubicle. He must have immediately gone to get his friend before returning to the center.

"This isn't good," I muttered, wishing he had taken his time.

"You know them?" Rachel asked.

"The shorter one is doing a test run to see if he should sign up his father. Maybe the other is his brother?"

"They look like extras from a mob movie. Think they're packing guns?"

"Maybe, but don't let anyone else in here think that."

I stood to greet them. Enzo gave a slight, almost imperceptible shake of his head. I returned to my chair while he and his brother, his hired thug, or whoever the henchman was, took their places, standing with their backs against the wall just inside the door.

Really, I should have been happy to see them. Certainly, it would be good for the center to have another paying customer. And really, I would have been happy to see them if they had shown up at any other time. This was the worst group possible for them to have picked to observe. I intentionally lost control of these people every week. It's one of the things they needed: a safe, controlled loss of control. Outsiders watching might not understand. They might even think I was negligent and incompetent.

"Good morning," I said to the group. I received a few grumbled greetings in response. No one sat. I turned to Rachel and winked.

"So your folks want you to get a job?" I asked in a loud voice.

"Well, it's damned time she supported herself," Mrs. Elliot plopped her large rear end into a chair. I eyed up her shoulder. It was still swollen. Mr. Schwartz slipped into the chair next to her.

"Oh, you poor thing," Mr. Hanson scurried over and sat next to Rachel. He put his magenta-nailed hand on her arm. "I know it can be scary to forge out into the wilderness. But you are smart, honey, you can—"

"It's a parent's duty to be sure each child is well equipped for the future," Mr. Moffat interrupted with a slight German accent. He sat his very trim, well-groomed self next to Mr. George, who was on my right. Mrs. O'Leary, who always wore rain boots despite the weather and never made eye contact with anyone, quietly sat beside Mr. Hanson and pulled out her knitting needles and gray yarn.

"Parental duty!" Mr. Thomas shouted as he sat next to Mrs. O'Leary. "Parental duty. That's what's wrong with America's youth today." He wagged his finger around the circle. "Everyone thinks it's their parents' duty to do everything for them. When I was a child, just out of primary school, I was supporting myself with a job—"

"Oh, were you? Ha!" Mr. Moffat retorted. "I guess you were lying then when you said you were recruited by the Phillies just out of primary school." He pushed round, wire-rimmed glasses up his nose. "You did *nothing*."

My comment had worked. Everyone, except Mrs. Dimiccio, had taken a seat in a hurry. The rule of the room was that you could not speak beyond *hello* until you sat, regardless of whether you found the perfect chair or how opinionated you were on the topic. Mrs. Dimiccio, who seldom knew what we were talking about, always sat last in whatever chair was available, as she could never remember that there were no assigned seats.

"We'll discuss Rachel's future at another meeting," I said. "Today I'd like to talk about naming our group. After that, maybe we could continue the discussion we started last week about speaking honestly with our doctors. I think—"

"I ain't saying nothing else to that man," Mrs. Elliot said.

"I understand," I replied. "But doctors are important so we'll get back to them in a minute. Right now—"

"There are strangers in the room!" shouted Mr. Schwartz. He pointed at Enzo and his friend.

"Actually, they are not strangers to me." I straightened in my seat. "They are observing me in action to evaluate my skills."

I could tell Mr. Schwartz wasn't sure if he believed me. He glanced around the room for support and almost found it in Mrs. Elliot.

"Who says you ain't got skills?" She turned in her chair to shout directly at our visitors. "She got skills, man! What you think—"

"Mrs. Elliot, thank you, honestly, thank you," I said over her shouting. "It's not whether or not I *have* skills, it's how well I *use* them." I faced Enzo. "Perhaps this is not the best group for you to observe."

He wiped dust motes from his arm before answering. "I think it is," he said.

"Well then," I turned back to my seniors. "If you feel uncomfortable or if there is something private you wish to discuss with just the group, perhaps you could hold it off until next week." I touched Rachel's arm. "Would you be kind enough to take some notes?"

"Take notes?" Mr. Schwartz cried. He gripped his chair as if to keep seated. "Take notes? Why are you recording what I'm saying?"

"I'm not. Mr. Schwartz, please. Give me a minute to explain." I breathed in deeply and thought about adding a few more minutes to my walk that night so I could have a cookie. But on the exhale, I remembered how they tasted and changed my mind. "Right now, on the center schedule, this time slot is marked as *miscellaneous*. And, aside from being just not a nice way to describe all of you here, it is a term that our new computer system is rejecting." I tried to elbow Rachel without anyone else seeing. I hate to lie to my seniors, but if I explained to this group that their place was in danger of going away from them unless I justified it with facts and figures, the room would erupt into chaos, paranoia, tears, and even fainting spells. "So, I was hoping we could work on a name for us, and maybe even a fun acronym."

"An acro-what?" Mrs. Dimiccio asked.

"An acronym," I said louder. "You know, like PATCO stands for Port Authority Transit Corporation?" I assumed they were all familiar with the train system, PATCO, as it was the line that serviced Atlantic City.

"Port what?" she asked.

"Port Authority."

"Did you go on a cruise?" Mrs. Dimiccio wanted to know. "I didn't realize you'd been gone."

"I didn't go anywhere. I was just trying to give you an example of what I meant. But we don't need to use an ac—"

"Well, why were you at the port?"

"I wasn't. I was just trying to use an example—"

"Example shmample. Why are you recording our meeting?" Mr. Schwartz asked again.

"We need a name for our group," I explained. "I thought we could brainstorm together and Rachel could take notes."

"Oh." Mr. Schwartz crossed his arms and frowned into space, presumably thinking up a name.

There was a lull for a few minutes until Mrs. O'Leary made a suggestion.

"How about SOS?" she asked as she knitted the same project she brought each week: a very, very long, gray swath of something very, very gray and long.

"Sauce?" Rachel asked. "As in spaghetti sauce?"

"That would be gravy," Mrs. Dimiccio said. "You put gravy on spaghetti."

"No, S–O–S SOS," Mrs. O'Leary said. "It could stand for Seniors Out of Sync. We could also use S-O-O-S, SOOS. I saw a TV show about Out-of-Sync Children. That's what made me think of it."

"I don't understand why people on TV say you put tomato sauce on spaghetti," Mrs. Dimiccio said.

"Only people in New Jersey call it tomato gravy, honey," Mr. Hanson offered. "Everyone outside of Jersey calls it tomato sauce."

"Oh, is that where Lucy went?" Mrs. Dimiccio asked.

"Yes, yes, it was," I said. "Good, so there's a start. S-O-S, SOS.

Seniors Out of Sync. Anyone else have an idea?"

"It'd sound better as Out of Sync Seniors." Mr. Thomas tightened his crossed arms, ready for battle.

"Then that would be O-S-S, OSS, or O-O-S-S, OOSS," said Mrs. O'Leary. She turned her long, gray thing around to knit in the opposite direction.

"Either way, that sounds nice," I said. "Any other ideas?"

"Osssssssss. Oooooooosssss," purred Mr. Hanson.

"O-S-S?" Mr. Moffat said. "How underhanded!"

"I don't understand." I looked at him. "What is underhanded?"

"The O-S-S spied on the Germans," Mr. Moffat leered at Mr. Thomas. "He's digging at my race again."

"Osssssssss. Oooooooosssss," repeated Mr. Hanson in the background.

"I don't think that's the case," I said. "I'm sure Mr. Thomas was just trying to be helpful. Does anyone else have a suggestion?"

"Osssssssss. Oooooooosssss," continued Mr. Hanson.

"What you wearing under that blouse?" Mrs. Elliot demanded of him.

Mr. Hanson's eyes were shut, his lips puckered as he made the sounds: "Osssssssss. Oooooooosssss."

"Mr. Hanson!" Mrs. Elliot yelled. "Leo!"

"Huh?" His startled legs jerked, and his arms flailed.

"Under your blouse!" Mrs. Elliot shouted. "Is that a black bra?"

"It is." Mr. Hanson unbuttoned his shirt. "It's new. Want to see?"

Mr. Hanson needed to be able to show off his women's clothes without anyone making him feel awkward. He got that from the group. But a quick glance at Enzo Fabian's appalled face told me he didn't realize what was going on.

"You can't wear a black bra under a white blouse," Mrs. Elliot said. She wasn't attacking him. She was in the group because she needed a place where she felt valued and validated. She was trying to help him.

"Why not?" Mr. Hanson asked. With his shirt completely open, he arched his back, giving us all a good view of his white chest hairs sprouting over the padded black bra.

"It's not right," Mrs. Elliot said.

"She's correct," Mrs. O'Leary confirmed. She was there so she could have a place where she was seen and heard. "You can't wear a black bra under a white blouse."

"But she does," he said, pointing to Mrs. Elliot.

"Yes. Because I'm black," Mrs. Elliot explained. "If I were white, I'd wear a white bra under a white blouse and you should, too."

"Actually, dear," Mrs. O'Leary corrected with knitting needles clacking. "He should wear a beige or a tan one under a white shirt."

"And he should put gravy on his pasta," Mrs. Dimiccio added, probably making it quite clear that she was in the group because she had no idea where else to go on Monday mornings.

"But I want to wear a black bra!" Mr. Hanson shouted. "I wanna be a black lady today."

"Has anyone ever noticed how much of your behavior is based on you wanting to be someone you aren't?" I offered.

"I'm not that way at all," Mr. Moffat replied. "I find I'm perfectly brilliant and well-rounded. More people should be like me."

"Perfectly brilliant? You're insane!" retorted Mr. Thomas. He and Mr. Moffat argued in this room because they couldn't do it at home. They had married twin sisters. Both were now widowed but stuck in their decades-old habit of pretending to get along. They let loose only in this room. "If everyone were more like you, the world would be full of loud, blathering know-it-alls! The world could do less with—"

"You!" Mr. Moffat charged back. "The world doesn't need—"

"You know," I said loudly, yet calmly. "I think the world is a beautiful place in that there are so many different kinds of people. I was just commenting because I often see people unhappy because they wish they were someone else or some*where* else. For example—"

"I wish I were on Broadway singing right now," Mr. Hanson said. He broke down and sobbed into his hands. Mrs. O'Leary dropped her knitting to rub his back with loud tsk-tsking. "I can sing." He leaned his head onto her lap, in dangerous proximity to the points of her needles. "You should hear me. I should have been on Broadway."

"Do you realize how dangerous the streets of New York are, man?" Mr. Schwartz asked. "You're lucky you're here. Sing now. Sing here."

Perhaps if Enzo Fabian's father were a drag queen, or had delusions, or exhibited some other eccentric behavior, he would realize what he was witnessing. Another peek at his shocked face, though, assured me I wouldn't be passing a check from him to Mona in the near future.

Regardless, I let Mr. Hanson perform and receive the validation that he was an acceptable member of the human race that he so desperately needed. He wiped his tears and, with his shirt still open and bra showing, he stood in the center of the circle and belted out a tune I'd never heard before.

He finished on a shaky high note and buttoned his blouse while we applauded. I glanced over to where the men were standing and caught Enzo's backside. He took his jacket off as he followed the other man out the door. Mr. George said something as I watched them leave.

Mr. George is one of my favorite seniors. He's rumored to be the son of one of the few African American Prohibition-era bootleggers. He's always reserved, and nothing ever riles him. Quiet, yet seemingly amused, he'll sit and smile a smile that tells you he understood more than the rest of us and that he knew exactly how absurd the world really is.

"Excuse me?" I asked, bending closer to him while Mr. Thomas and Mr. Moffat argued over who wrote the song Mr. Hanson sang.

"MOFs," Mr. George whispered into my right ear, leaning hard on his cane. "That's what we should call ourselves. M-O-F, MOFs."

"And what would that stand for?"

"Messed-up Old Fucks."

HOPE SPRINGS ETERNAL, SOMETIMES

Les didn't return my call all day. I was going to try him again as I drove to pick my kids up from high school that afternoon, but my doctor called me first. I saw the name of his practice on the caller ID and eagerly anticipated bad news.

"What do you mean there's nothing wrong with me?" I asked into my minivan's Bluetooth. "How is that possible?"

"Looks like you take good care of yourself, Lucy," he said.

"But I'm sure I have a thyroid condition. Did you test that?"

"Yes. It tested normal. Why would you think otherwise?"

"I was on WebMD. I have all the symptoms."

"Can I tell you how much I hate that website? Many conditions share similar symptoms."

I pulled up behind a Toyota in the school's car line and put the van in park. "You don't understand. I *have* to have a thyroid problem."

"Have to?"

"Yes! Fixing my thyroid would fix so many other problems. Don't you get it? A verified thyroid condition is a fat woman's wet dream." I leaned my head against the steering wheel while he laughed. "Really, what else could be wrong with me? What else can you look at?"

"What kind of problems are you having, Lucy?"

I sat up straight again. "Let's start with all the weight I've gained. Why is that happening?"

"Actually, you've lost weight since you were here in October."

"Because my sister has been forcing me to power walk every night. But I'm still fatter than I used to be when I never exercised at all."

"It's perfectly natural as a woman ages for her to put on a few extra pounds *and* for it to be harder to lose."

"You know, that's an almost nice way to tell me I'm getting old."

"You of all people should know there's nothing wrong with getting old."

I huffed a sigh. "Well, what about my hair? Is that from age? It's coming out by the handfuls. And my brain! My attention span has shrunk to the size of a microchip—without giving me the same processing power, mind you. And it's getting harder to remember who that woman is I see in the mirror every morning. According to WebMD, those are all signs and symptoms of a thyroid problem. How else can you explain it?"

"Honestly, Lucy?"

"Only be honest if you think a lie would hurt me more."

"You're overstressed," he said with another laugh.

"I know that." I waited for him to continue. He was more patient than I. "And?"

"And that's it."

"That can't be it."

"Stress can easily cause hair loss, weight gain, fatigue—"

"But there's no cure for stress!" I shouted. "There's no pill, no—"

"Yes, there is."

I thought maybe he was on the verge of prescribing an antianxiety medication, and wiggled my rear in my seat with a new sense of hope. "What is it?"

He paused before answering. "You've been a patient of mine for so many years, I feel I can speak to you as I would a friend. Can I do that?"

"Again, only if it's less painful than the alternative." I gazed across the roofs of the cars lined up in front of me, wishing I'd never gone to college. People often assume social workers are immune to ever being anything other than calm, rational, and analytical. As if a degree made you less human, less emotional. If Dr. Munoz was about to tell me I should already know how to handle my world falling apart without being stressed, he might experience firsthand how very wrong he was. He might get to be an audible witness to me ramming my minivan into the first unmovable target I could find, which unfortunately meant the Prius parked in front of me would be trounced by a gas guzzler.

"I realize there is plenty going on in your life that you don't like and you cannot control," he said. "However, I know you. In the past, you have always been able to focus on what you could control and on finding the good in situations. Think back to when I sewed up your daughter's head after she'd hit it on the board during a bad dive. Do you remember what you said to Joy then?"

"I barely remember lunch."

"I remember it well because I thought it was such a perfect piece of advice that I have rephrased it for many other patients since."

"What was it?"

"Remember how angry she was? She was upset because she had messed up the dive, not because she had hurt herself. You told her the accident was done and over with. She couldn't undo it and being angry about it only wasted her energy. You told her it was time to heal. You said if she insisted on staying upset and angry about what she couldn't control and what had happened in the past, it would only make the trauma last longer and the healing more difficult."

"Are you sure I said that? That seems uncharacteristically wise."

"Ha! You are wise," he said. "And now I think you need to take your own advice."

"Taking a pill seems much easier."

He laughed again. "I'm so glad you've kept your sense of humor through everything, Lucy. Use it on yourself. Let go of the past. Make the best of whatever you can control now and stay focused only on that."

We clicked off. I was tempted to call my insurance company to see if I could get a new doctor, but then I saw my daughter, Joy, emerge from the school. *Today is the day*, I reminded myself.

While the kids were at their dad's for their first partial-custody visit over the past weekend, I had prepared a speech meant to motivate them to work with me to fix our family. I had originally planned on being able to say, "The doctor is prescribing a medicine to help get me back to normal so I can lead us." Unfortunately, it now looked like I was going to have to improvise.

It was hard to believe, as I watched my daughter trudge to the van in a cloud of anger, how we used to be a happy, positive, and cohesive family unit. I had been one of the lucky few who had everything a woman could want: a kind, stably employed, and faithful husband, two well-adjusted kids, a lovely home with a great kitchen, a satisfying job, and even a nice dog in our yard.

Then one day, the Tuesday after Labor Day, Les informed me he was leaving me for another woman; Joy informed me she had called the police on her brother for selling marijuana; and the groomer called to inform me my dog had been killed in a freak accident.

Yes, in one day, my life turned into a country and western song, and serendipitously, I'd discovered a new kind of information overload.

Looking back, that was actually a good day. I was too numb to think and feel. The next day, Wednesday, when all the emotions and thoughts walloped me, was the worst day of my life. The following five months were spent in a dazzled state, fighting with lawyers, fighting the juvenile justice system, and fighting back the tears as my children became increasingly distant from me. We now seldom spoke, and they did their best to leave whatever room I was in. They didn't even eat at the kitchen table with me anymore. I often felt like I was living with two secretive boarders.

But that was then. Today would be the day I reconnected with them. Today would be the day we rediscovered our loving bond. Today would be the day we begin the trek back to the life we used to have. I sat taller in the seat. *Today is the day!*

Joy opened the van door.

"Hi, pumpkin!" I squeaked.

"God, Mom." She climbed in and sat in the seat behind me. "Do you think you'll ever get, like, a real car? It's *so* embarrassing having to ride in a minivan all the time."

"Seems to me minivans are popular in the car line at school."

"Whatever."

Although I wasn't looking, I knew beneath all the black liner, she was rolling her eyes. Joy was once a bubbly, cheerful, popular, and pretty girl; a champion on her high school swim team. She was now a Goth queen, who swam only on occasion. The transformation happened the week after Labor Day. Joy had said her newly dyed black hair, black nails, black lipstick, and swollen, pierced tongue all resulted from her simply being ready for a change and that it had nothing to do with her dad. Les had said he believed her. I still thought they were both lying.

"Where's Ash?" I asked. The name Asher is Hebrew for blessed or happy. It was suggested by my Jewish obstetrician, and it seemed like a good idea when I gave birth to the twins. I was on the receiving end of a multitude of painkillers that day.

"How would I know?"

Instead of answering, I thought about what I'd make for dinner. Joy should have known where her brother was because they were in the same grade, with the same teachers, with the same circle of friends, with nearly identical schedules, and with lockers next to each other. But I couldn't control what she thought she knew. So I followed Dr. Munoz's orders and focused on what I could control: dinner. I wondered whether I had enough green pepper at home to make a decent meatloaf.

"Yo," Asher greeted us. He climbed into the van, flopped onto the far backseat, where he immediately pulled out his cell phone and started texting.

Technically, we lived far enough from the high school that my kids should have been riding the bus. But Joy feels the bus is beneath her, and Asher had to be picked up by an adult as part of his probation requirements. Usually, I was glad to do the ride. As tense as it was, it was guaranteed time I'd have alone with them, and I could pretend we were still a loving, fully functional family.

But today, their actual, physical presence in the van was a bit demoralizing and dampened my resolve to reconnect. I had hoped they had missed me over the weekend and that they'd be glad to see me. Their less-than-enthusiastic greetings only reminded me of how I was, and had been, failing at this mom stuff.

Not only was I failing, but I was running out of time to fix whatever I'd done wrong. Within two years, my kids would be adults, supposedly ready and able to fend for themselves—something Les and I, as parents, were supposed to teach them.

Over the weekend, I realized the depths of my responsibility, *my personal* responsibility now that I was a single mom. Not only did I need to reconnect with my children and do so soon, but I also needed to help them lift themselves up to become whatever good human beings they could still become. I needed to prove to them I was the right person for the job of stable parent. That I was capable and strong. That I knew what the hell I was doing. I needed to convince them, even if I wasn't so sure I could do it myself.

In silence, I inched the van to the front of the car line and waited until it was safe to exit the lot and merge into the traffic on Albany Avenue. I couldn't find a segue to begin an inspiring speech, but as I turned onto the street, my usual post-school questions, as if by physical memory, popped out of my mouth.

"Everyone have a good day?" I asked.

"Ugh," said Joy.

"Anything exciting happen?"

"Mm." I think it came from Ash.

"Much homework?"

"Mm," from Joy that time, Ash grunted.

I braved a new question: "How were things at your dad's?" I held my breath while I waited for their response. *The girlfriend* happened to live at their dad's new place, so really, they'd just spent the weekend with her, too. *The girlfriend*, I'm sure, has a name. I just can't ever remember what it is. I do remember she is only slightly younger than I am, much skinnier, and has sleek platinum-blond hair. I had no idea whether she was the kind of woman who was great with kids or had ever successfully dealt with sixteen-year-old twins on the road to self-destruction, so I wasn't sure whether I was jealous of her parenting abilities. Though I had to admit I admired her dieting skills.

They took their time contemplating their answer and eventually murmured "okay" in stereo.

I almost asked if they knew why their dad had stopped by our house that morning, but I wasn't sure I could ask in a nice way, which meant the question could fall under the *pitting your child against the other parent* category we'd been warned about in court. Instead, I went back to my old routine.

"Do I need to take anyone somewhere tonight?"

"No," from both

"Who will be home for dinner?"

"Me," said Ash.

"Any friends coming over?"

"Maybe," said Joy.

Silence ensued.

Today is the day, I repeated in my head, today is the day I connect with them.

"Hey, remember when I had a doctor's appointment last week?" I started.

No one responded. I glanced in the rear-view mirror to make sure they hadn't put on headphones. All ears were unadorned except for jewelry. Ash's small gold hoops glinted in his dark hair, and Joy's giant, pointed, harpoon-looking things jutted from her earlobes. They almost grazed her shoulders. If her neck were any shorter, she wouldn't have been able to turn her head without slicing open her school uniform.

"Remember how things used to be?" I tried again and refocused my eyes on the traffic.

They sat mute. Perhaps they were thinking about my questions.

"Well, so...I've been noticing that I've been changing." I stopped at the light in the turn lane to go north on Atlantic Avenue. When I had rehearsed this talk with them in my head, they had responded much more quickly, compassionately, and eagerly than they were now.

"I mean, I know there have been a lot of changes in our lives over the past year, but I think maybe you two had noticed how your mom had been changing, too. Have you?"

"Christ, Mom," Joy finally said. "TMI okay? I mean, really, no one needs to hear about you going through menopause."

"That's *not* what I'm talking about! I'm only forty years old, you know."

She didn't respond.

When I got the green, I accelerated up the long track of Atlantic Avenue, where there are more traffic lights than necessary and none of them are timed well. I took advantage of the frequent stops to assess the ineffectiveness of the opening to my inspiring talk and to devise a new one. Glancing around me, I marveled, as I always did, at how the street went from slums to paradise without even an inch of real estate separating the two, and I realized Atlantic City was a metaphor for my life.

I stopped at the light by Caesar's Palace Casino, the home of my father's favorite blackjack tables, and thought: *here is proof.*

"Did Pop-Pop ever talk to you about when he and Grandmom moved here?" I asked them. No answer. "He once told me that when they first moved to Atlantic City from Philadelphia, he immediately fell in love with the place because of its promise of potential. Do you know what he meant?"

Silence. I continued anyway, after all, they weren't saying *no* to.

"AC was going through what some consider a renaissance period. A bunch of old buildings were renovated, and new ones were built." I paused, thinking I heard something. But apparently Joy had just shifted in her seat to glare out the other window. "Anyway, that's when I was born. And you know what? AC is doing it again, right? I mean, Hurricane Sandy was just a couple of months ago, and there has been so much going on. People are moving on with their lives, their businesses, and...and, you can start to see shiny spots in the ghetto, right?"

Crickets would have been louder in my van.

"I think it's inspiring. And I hope you do, too, because we have the chance to do it, too. We can start a new chapter in our family's history. Beginning now, tonight. We can round the final turn and enter the homestretch to become the happy, positive family we once were."

I paused to glance in the rear-view mirror. If I didn't know better, I would have thought an invisible sound barrier separated us.

"Granted, your father will be absent from future family portraits," I continued. "But you and I, we can get our old lives back. We can find a way to, to, to re-create a clean and beautiful new life. We can and will climb our way up out of the ruins!" I banged the steering wheel not only for emphasis, but because I realized I believed in myself. "I mean it. Despite everything, we can do it." A glance in the mirror, though, showed me they didn't share my optimism.

"I can do it, anyway. I know I can." *Today is the day.* I wasn't going to let their silence make me retreat. We were still a family after all. Dysfunctional, broken, and non-communicative, but we were still a family. "Beginning today. And you know what else? What I started telling you before, you know how I've kind of become an overweight, fuzzy-thinking, lost, and unorganized person?"

Silence.

"Well, Dr. Munoz checked me out. The good news is I'm in great health."

More silence.

"Which means you have me to count on again. I know it seems like your mom has turned into this confused, chubby woman who occasionally forgets to turn off the kitchen stove." I thought my voice sounded as though it was wavering. I cleared my throat. "Dr. Munoz said all that was from me not dealing with stress that well. So, I promise you, I'm taking care of that, too, and I'm recommitting myself to our family, to you."

I turned left at the light for New Hampshire Avenue and drove as slowly as my fellow Jersey drivers would allow without shooting me. I needed more time with my kids. Our ride home was almost over, and they were no closer to being happy or hopeful than they were when I had picked them up.

Didn't they miss our old life? Didn't they want the stability they used to have before everything went to hell? They had to want stability, didn't they? They didn't even know where they would be living in a month. For all they knew, their next home, aside from every other weekend spent with their dad, could be under the boardwalk. Didn't they care? Didn't they want to hope for something better?

I turned right onto Main Avenue and crept toward our soon-to-be-former home on the inlet.

"Ash, Joy," I started. My voice caught.

"Oh God! She's, like, crying," Joy said.

Ash looked up from his cell and locked eyes with me in the mirror.

"S'up?" he asked.

"I'm not crying." I tried to force back the tears so I could tell the truth. "Really. I'm the happiest I've been in a long time. I just found out I'm healthy. It's just been the stress in my life that's made me gain weight and feel confused. But I'm going to deal with it. I'm going to make things like they once were."

"Huh?" he asked.

"God," Joy huffed. "She's saying it's not her fault she's fat."

"I'm saying." I shook my head as if that would force everything that came out of my mouth to make sense. "I'm saying, I'm healthy enough that I'm ready and able to, to recommit myself to you, to us as a family, to help us all get back to where we once were. To get our old lives back."

"Cool." His head bobbed up and down, possibly to the music that was playing in the background.

"Whatever," Joy said. Ash's head continued to bounce.

I approached our home, thinking about green peppers and meatloaf. But my thoughts stopped cold when I saw the garage. The door was open midway up, and when I clicked the remote in my van, it wouldn't budge.

I got out and took a closer look. Someone had forced his way into my garage, breaking the door in the process.

Today is the day Lester had better have an alibi.

SURPRISING FINDINGS

E nzo Fabian was waiting for me in my cubicle when I returned to it after the staff meeting on Tuesday morning. I wasn't surprised. Gayle had alerted me as I walked past reception, saying he said he felt uncomfortable waiting out there.

"Good morning, Mr. Fabian." I sat and pulled open the belly drawer of my desk to look for my stash of Band-Aids. My thumb had continued to bleed through each bandage I had put on it after cleaning up a vase Joy had thrown the night before. I still didn't know the details of what had happened. I was down in the kitchen, on the phone, yelling at Lester for breaking into my house twice that day. He had insisted it wasn't him but had agreed to pay the garage door repair bill anyway, which sounded to me like an admission of guilt.

I had run into the hallway immediately after hearing the crash and found Joy standing outside her bedroom door, fuming, staring at the broken pieces at the top of the stairs.

"S'up?" Ash had asked, appearing at the same time as I did.

"Every. Fucking. Thing," Joy had said. "If you'd take your head out of your ass sometime, maybe you'd notice." She slammed herself behind her bedroom door. Ash quietly retreated into his room. And I cleaned up the mess, slicing open my thumb in the process.

There was a positive in the situation. I had to work long and hard to find it, but I did. She had thrown a cheap vase. It came with a bouquet of flowers that Les had given me over the summer. I took her choice as a sign that she was at least thinking a little before she acted. She could have chosen the expensive Lalique one my sister had given me that was sitting next to it on the shelf.

I finished wrapping a new bandage over my thumb while Enzo returned a brochure on STDs in seniors to the holder on my desk.

His hand ran down his arm, smoothing his sleeve. He was in another good, but not an overly expensive, suit. It was a suit you bought from Lord and Taylor's, not from a private boutique.

"I didn't realize you'd had enough of an opportunity to determine if your father would like spending time here," I said.

"Yes, well, we figured it out yesterday. I'd like to complete his paperwork as quickly as possible so that he can join in that meeting."

"Oh, which one?"

"The one we observed you in yesterday." He met my eyes.

"I see. Well, um …."

"Or is he limited to which groups he could join?"

"No, of course not." I paused. My gut told me not to trust him. My brain told me I might just be being defensive—he was a good-looking man and, aside from my friend Nico, I had sworn never to trust a good-looking man again. "The thing is, that particular group is, well, sometimes it takes them a few meetings to warm up to strangers. There may be an adjustment period where your father might not feel welcome."

"It won't be the first time he didn't feel welcome somewhere." He smiled a surprisingly kind smile. A smile that made me rethink the worthiness of the lines around his eyes. I almost reconsidered that antitrust policy against good-looking men, too. Almost. "But I misplaced the papers you gave me yesterday. Could I get another set and bring them back later in the week?"

"That would be fine." I opened the file to retrieve new intake forms. "But would he like a tour first to see all the amenities?"

"Hmm," Enzo ran his fingers along the inside of his shirt collar, pulling it away from his neck. "Would *you* do it?"

I got the feeling he was afraid I'd get lost in the building.

"I could."

"Then, yes, maybe that would be good, too. Could we do it Friday morning?"

"Sure." I turned to my monitor and pulled up my computer calendar, glad to have a shift in focus. I didn't understand why I was having such a hard time reading the man. "How about eleven thirty?" I took a business card out of the holder, noted the time for the tour on the reverse, and handed it to him.

"Why is the name marked out?" he asked.

"Oh!" I took the card back. "Sorry about that." I threw the card away under my desk. To subdue a rage while on hold with Lester's attorney once, I had scratched out my married name on all the business cards in my holder. I opened my drawer to find the box of extras for a clean one. It was empty. I opted for a Post-it. "Again, I'm sorry." I wrote down the date and time for a tour.

"But you are Lucinda Womzak, correct?" he asked.

"Um, well...yes." Flustered was an understatement.

He sharpened his eyes at me. "You don't sound sure. Who are you?"

"I'm sorry." My face warmed with a flush. "Why don't you just call me Lucy? Everyone does."

"Lucy, it is important that I know exactly who my father will be dealing with."

"You are so right. I understand. You need to be sure I'm a stable human being." I leaned back in my chair and pretended I was the trained professional I used to be. "I am Lucy Womzak. I'm also in the middle of a divorce and have been thinking I may want to go back to my maiden name. I'm sorry if my cards confused you."

"Oh, I see." He buttoned then unbuttoned his jacket. "I would change my name if I were you. Womzak isn't all that appealing."

He petted his lapel, smoothing the nap before looking up to smile at me again. His actions reminded me of a girl in high school who'd bought an expensive dress only to return it to the store after wearing it to prom.

"Right," I said. "I'll see you Friday."

He left. I shot an email to Mona, telling her I needed new business cards and asking what I should do if I wish to change my name on them.

Les's abrupt departure was a complete surprise to me. Within four days of his announcement that he was leaving, he'd taken all his personal belongings out of our house and moved them into his new home, the home he now shared with *the girlfriend*. I didn't have much time to prepare for the divorce, but his attorney had been quick and efficient. Mine was on the lethargic side and seemed to think his primary responsibility was to remind me it would hurt my custody battle should I hit *the girlfriend* over the head with a frying pan. His opinion shouldn't have surprised me. He'd refused to concede that smashing her face with a serving platter was a good idea, too.

I hadn't had a chance to fully contemplate what to do about my name. I didn't feel comfortable being a Womzak anymore, but I wasn't sure if it would upset my kids if I made that change.

But now I needed new business cards. I needed to order little squares of cardstock with my name on them, *my* name. And despite how weird or snobby Enzo Fabian's manner was, I could trust his judgment on one thing: Womzak wasn't an appealing name. Certainly not as appealing as my maiden name. I had traded in one of the best names in the world for Womzak. I was once Lucy McCool. And I could be her again.

Today is the day. Well, it would be if my kids were okay with it.

When lunchtime came, I drove to meet my friend, Nico, at Teplitzkey's Diner. My sister Angie had walked over and arrived when I did. Angie and I are Irish twins: she's eleven months my senior. We like to say we were conceived in the one year our parents got along.

Angie is also my opposite. She is tall, thin, and blond, at the far end of the spectrum from me, with my somewhat short, chubby frame and curly brown hair. And she is happily childless. While my hero, having remained independent and never bothering to marry, had always been a disappointment to our mother. I went to college after high school, met Les, and married the summer after we received our degrees. Having twins soon afterward completed the trifecta of a good little girl in my mother's opinion: college, husband, kids. She tolerated my continuing to work because she had Angie to complain about.

Angie had opted for massage therapy training, which would have sat just fine with Mom if she'd used it to snag herself a husband. Instead, she succeeded in building a private practice and now owns quite the successful day spa. Mom still didn't approve, but I loved it. She provided me easy access to all the wax I needed to keep my facial hair under control. We're half Italian and half Irish, and the Italian part of our ancestry was quite furry.

Angie lived in a two-bedroom townhouse overlooking the bay and had graciously offered to have the kids and me live with her until I found a permanent home. But that would mean Joy and Ash would have to share a bedroom. I had refused her offer on the grounds that if nuclear warfare was frowned upon, we certainly couldn't let my kids share a bedroom. Though as yet, I had nowhere else to go and needed to be out by March first.

Nico had recently suggested he had the perfect place and said we could move in immediately if we wanted. Nico had a lot of connections in AC, but on both sides of the legal fence. If it were, indeed, the perfect place, there might have been a catch or two to go along with it. I agreed to meet him at lunch today to discuss in front of Angie so that she could keep me from doing something potentially stupid.

Nico was already at the restaurant when we entered. He sat on a barstool reading something on an electronic tablet.

I had met Nico through Les. He is in the security business, which has a loose definition in Atlantic City, and he had known Les for years; their relationship was both professional and personal. Nico and I had developed a great friendship over the past decade based on our love of good food and drink. He and Angie were at my soon-to-be-former house for dinner almost as much as Lester was. Actually, over the past couple of months, their presence at my dining room table was more of a constant than that of my own children's.

Most people in Atlantic City know Nico, know *of* him, as a tough and somewhat mysterious man. People who really *did* know him knew he had a surprising side. Not only was Nico a foodie, but he was also a lover of the arts. He was as likely to be reading a nineteenth-century Russian masterpiece on his tablet that day as an e-mail about facilitating a shipment of counterfeit watches.

"Lucy." He stood to greet me with a kiss on the cheek. "Glad you could make it. You too, Ange." He pecked her cheek. "I didn't realize you'd both come today."

"Do you mind?" Angie asked.

"No. Not at all."

We sat in a booth by a window overlooking Chelsea Avenue. It was a glorious, sunny, but cold and windy day.

"I hope they still have that Portobello mushroom sandwich," Angie said, picking up the menu. Another offense to our mother is that Angie is a vegetarian.

"Ew," Nico grunted. "Luce, tell me you're getting something better."

"I'm thinking of the spinach salad without the pecans."

"That's almost as bad. Did I tell you this was my treat?"

"Yes, but the calories will go to *my* hips."

"What do you really want?" He pulled down my menu to look me in the face. "What would you get if you were as skinny as an anorexic?"

"Hm," I glanced at the menu, "probably, if I were guaranteed not to gain any weight, I'd get a starter of those mini-soft pretzels, the smoked short ribs, and a chocolate-tini."

"Is that what you're ordering?" the waitress asked. She placed three glasses of water on the table.

"Oh God, no! Just the spinach salad, hold the pecans, please, and coffee."

"I'll have the Portobello sandwich and Pellegrino," Angie said.

"And I'll have the Monte' Cristo," Nico said. "We'll share an order of the pretzels."

"Absolutely no way, Nico," I said.

"I'm paying." He winked at the waitress. She took our menus and left.

"You know I have no willpower," I said to him. "Angie, please force me to add a mile to our walk tonight for each pretzel I eat."

"Thanks, Nico. Now I'll have to postpone my date," she said. "Unless you walk her."

"Work out with me instead, Lucy," he said. "My uncle's gym will do you better than a walk."

"I'm *not* up for that." I leaned back in my booth, remembered *today is the day,* and added: "I'll keep it in mind for when I am, though. But, you know of an apartment or something?"

"I think I have the perfect place for you to live."

"Where?"

"Here in AC. Where else?"

"Where in AC?"

"Before I go there, there's a little backstory as to why it's available." He paused while the waitress placed our drinks on the table.

"Is this the part where you tell us you really called her here today because you need an alibi?" Angie asked after the waitress left.

"I'd love to know what you hens say about me behind my back."

"It would only swell your ego," I said. "But I have to agree with Angie. It sounds a little fishy."

"Not fishy, really. Just different." He sipped his water. "I've a client who owes me a large amount of money, a very large amount. He was also in the process of getting a divorce. He owned a condo that his wife didn't know about and needed to unload it. So he offered it to me as payment. It was worth about 125 thousand more than what he owed me, though. So I paid him the extra 125 Ks for it, and we were even." He sipped again. "You following me?"

"No. Why didn't he just sell the condo and pay you from his proceeds?" I asked.

"Because, again, his wife didn't know about it. He needed to sell it before the final settlement went through, otherwise she'd get half of what the condo was worth."

"Sounds like a real winner," Angie scoffed.

"Don't think this means I'll stop complaining about Les," I said.

"You shouldn't." He grinned. "Anyway, the thing is, Lucy, I think the place would be perfect for you. And, I happen to know what your half of the settlement was on *your* house with your divorce."

"How?"

"I got all kinds of contacts, babe." His grin broadened into a smile. "So I know you can afford this place."

The waitress set a platter of small, hot, soft pretzels on the table alongside a ramekin of honey-mustard. Nico picked one up, ripped it in half, and dunked part in the sauce before reaching across the table to hand it to me.

"Well?" he asked as I chewed those delicious carbs as slowly and thoroughly as possible.

"The pretzels are divine. Probably even worth an extra mile."

"I'm serious. You're walking with her tonight, Nico." Angie ate a whole pretzel without the mustard.

"But what do you think about the condo?"

"I'm not sure. Why don't you live there?"

"I'm fine where I am. Besides, your *casa* is *mi casa*, right?" He popped the other half of my pretzel into his mouth. "Anyway, like I said. It's perfect for you. There are three bedrooms, three baths, and an amazing kitchen."

"And it's all legal?"

He laughed. "Lucy! Do you really think I'd sell you a place I don't own? Honest, it's legal. You can have your idiot attorney look over the paperwork if you want. I'll sell it to you at the same 125 thousand I bought it for."

I bit off a tiny piece of another pretzel and took a sip of water while I thought it over.

"Why are you doing this?" I asked.

"Why wouldn't I?"

"Because it makes no sense. Why don't you flip it for a profit?"

"Luce, you've always been there for me, right? There has always been food at your house for me, right?"

"Yes. But that's not the same as—"

"You take care of everyone."

"But—"

"Don't you think it's time someone took care of you?"

"He's got a point," Angie said, eating another whole pretzel because nothing ever makes her fat, ever.

"So what do you think?" Nico asked.

"Nico, I appreciate your friendship, really, I do."

"Good, because I've decided you get me in the divorce," he said.

"What?" I laughed.

He waited while the waitress brought the rest of our food.

"When couples split, their friends don't always stay friends with both of them," he explained. "I'm choosing you. Les behaved like an ass."

"Amen!" Angie said.

"Oh, thank you, Nico. I hadn't even thought about the division of friends. I'm still working on the dishware." I munched on my salad. It was boring without the nuts.

"Well, when you figure out which dishes belong to you, you'll know which ones I'll be eating on. And I think you should be piling those plates up with food in that condo."

"I was thinking of just renting somewhere for a while. It's a big decision to make. Maybe I could rent it from you?"

"I don't wanna be a landlord. Why don't you just take a look and see what you think? Huh? We can go right after lunch if you have time."

I didn't have to be back at the office until two thirty when the Loss, Grief, and Bereavement group met, and Angie had a few minutes, too. We ate, then let Nico pay the tab before following him out to Chelsea Avenue.

"Should we take the same car?" I asked. "Where is this place?"

"Right here." He started across the street with Angie, and me a few feet behind.

"Here, where?"

"Here, up." He pointed up alongside the wall of a high-rise on the boardwalk, taking the entire block between Montpelier and Chelsea Avenues.

"I can't afford here!"

"Yes, you can. One-twenty-five, remember?"

"Really?"

"Really. Come in and take a look."

He used a key fob with a security tab to electronically open the main doors, bypassing a doorman and a valet driver. He then walked us to the elevator.

"This place is great, Lucy," Angie said as we went up. "I looked here when I bought my townhome, but couldn't afford it at the time. What on Earth did you do for a client to make him owe you so much money, Nico? Who is it?"

"Sorry, Angie, I can't divulge personal details. People trust me for a reason."

"Not even a hint?"

"Client confidentiality, sweetheart," he said. "That's all I'm saying." The elevator stopped on the fifteenth floor. "Anyway, Lucy," he continued as we stepped out of the car. "There's garage parking, and the ground floor has storage facilities available for your beach supplies, making for an easy trek out to the beach."

"Ash would like being so close to the beach," I said as we walked down the hallway.

"The building was once a hotel, so you'll find a few extra amenities here, too. Like on the sixth floor, there's a workout facility and an indoor pool. The pool is available year-round."

"An indoor, year-round pool? God, Joy would love that," I said.

Nico stopped before the last door in the hallway. "So Ash would be happy with this. That would make Joy happy." He put a key into the lock. "What would make Lucy happy?"

"To have everyone around me be happy." I followed him into the condo.

He stopped short just inside. I bumped into him. Angie somehow managed to avoid making us collapse.

"Seriously, Lucy." He turned and stared directly into my eyes from just a few inches away, his hands on my shoulders. "Do you have any idea what would make you, just you, happy?"

I took my time answering him. That was something I'd never really thought about before. I'd spent my life being happy because everyone around me was happy. It had worked out just fine until the day after Labor Day.

"I'm still waiting for an answer," Nico said. He turned on his heel and walked toward the interior of the apartment.

"I think…" I slowly followed him. "I think…" I stopped and stared out the sliding glass doors. "Oh my God!"

I expected the view to be decent, but my expectations fell far short of reality. I couldn't say anything as I walked up to the doors. Nico opened them, and we stepped out onto the balcony, into the cold wind and sun. I could see all the way down the south end of the boardwalk toward Ventnor. I could see the stretch of beach beside it, and I could see out for miles over the ocean. The sun sparkled off the dark blue of the Atlantic. There were a couple of clam trawlers and a few other boats on the horizon. I knew there would be hundreds more in the summer, including beautiful personal luxuries sailing over the water.

I walked around the side of the balcony, where I could look out over the southern part of the town. From up there, the city, *my* city, was clean and healthy, vibrant and full of life. It was a shining, hopeful city.

"I think looking at this every day would make me happy," I said.

Nico gave me his set of keys. We went down to the business office. He introduced me to the women who worked there as the next owner of the unit, and then he and Angie left. One of the women gave me a complete tour of the facility and a magnetic tag for my car that would allow me into the parking garage.

My head was spinning from all the information and the excitement—and from the worry that maybe I'd behaved too impulsively. Who agrees to buy a home so quickly? And does so based on the view? What if I don't like it on a stormy or even snowy day? What if the closets are small? I didn't even look at the bathrooms. Angie was supposed to prevent me from being too rash. What happened to her?

I went back up to the condo to call my mother from my cell and give her the good news.

My mother's approval of me only lasted until Les left. Not that she was ever a fan of him. She was just of the mindset that a non-church-going-casino-general-manager husband was better than none. And if her daughter couldn't even keep a non-church-going-casino-general-manager husband, then there was something inherently wrong with her.

She started lowering her opinion of me the second I told her Les had left. I was now almost as bad as Angie.

Thankfully, she had gone to Florida for the winter. She left the day after Christmas and was due back the day before Mother's day. She was a woman with priorities.

I stood looking through the sliding glass doors, staring out over the ocean while she destroyed my excitement.

"I know that building well," she said. "Marcy Goldman lived there. She was in my card group."

"So you know we'll be safe here," I said.

"Safe, yes, you'll be safe," she conceded. "But what about your woolens?"

"What?"

"Your woolens!" she yelled. "You have no place to lay your woolens out flat to dry. What will you do with them?"

"I've never had room to lay woolens out to dry." I knocked on a wall to see if perhaps it was strong enough to hold up under the pressure of my banging my head against it. "I don't own any woolens."

"Of course you don't," she said. "But Lester does. How did you take care of his clothes?"

"I sent them to the cleaners, Ma."

"That's probably why he left you, you know," she said. "If you had taken better care—"

"You know, Ma, I'm sorry, but I gotta go. I have a meeting. I just wanted to give you the good news that your grandchildren would not be homeless come next month."

"You know you could always move in with me," she said before I clicked off.

I went downstairs and walked over to my van on Chelsea Avenue. I got in, turned on the ignition, and checked to ensure the street was clear before I pulled out. I thought I recognized the profile of someone in the car parked illegally on the opposite side of the street. A closer look showed me it was Enzo Fabian. He was sitting in the driver's seat, examining his fingernails. He never looked up to see me, but I had this sick sensation in my stomach telling me he knew I was there.

ST. FRIDAY

"Mail call!" Charlie from the mailroom met me outside my cubicle. "And happy Valentine's Day!"

Lucky for him, he was quick. He put a stack of mail in my hands before I had a chance to smack him.

"Thanks, Charlie. And, uh, just so you know, I prefer to call it Friday." I sat at my desk and glanced through the pile.

There was a large Priority Mail envelope on the bottom. I pulled it to the top and froze: it was from Lester's attorney.

Taking long, calming breaths, I told myself I was stronger than I believed I was. *Today is the day. I can handle whatever they're throwing at me now. I can do it.*

I turned the envelope over, ripped open the perforated tab, and pulled out several sheets of paper. They were my divorce papers. I knew they were coming. In fact, I was expecting them. I was just expecting them to go directly to *my* attorney, who would subsequently give them to me. I also expected to receive them on a day other than Valentine's Day.

I set the pages on my desk, directly in front of me, and read the words in extra-large, bold print on the top page: ***Final Judgment***. They sucked the air out of me, and for a few, very long moments, the world around me seemed perversely quiet and deathly still. I, too, was quiet and still. I'm not sure I even breathed. My vision tunneled until all I saw was the page in front of me. All else seemed to fade into blackness.

Things were final now, at an end, officially, for my marriage.

Meanwhile, the rest of the universe was still spinning and

making noise, something I noticed when Enzo Fabian grabbed my arm and jerked me out of my chair.

"Are you all right?" he asked. "Did you have a seizure?"

"What?" I stared at him, unable at first to recognize who he was. Around the same time I realized who stood before me, I also noticed he wasn't alone. Enzo had entered my cubicle with the man who had accompanied him to the Miscellaneous group meeting earlier in the week.

"I was talking to you," Enzo said. "You just sat there all spacey. Do you need a doctor?"

I shook my arm free of him, leaned back against my desk, and ran my hands over my face, through my hair.

"I'm fine." I made myself turn around and pick up the papers. My gut wrenched, and I dropped them again. "I just uh…" I leaned my hands on the desk and took a big inhale. Today *is the day.* "I'm fine." I turned to face him with a fake smile.

"You look very pale," he said. "Do you need some water? Or coffee? You like coffee, right?"

"Thank you, Mr. Fabian, thank you for your concern. That is very nice of you." I shook my head. "I just got some bad news, that's all."

"Looks like divorce papers," said the other man. He was leaning over my desk, looking upside down at Lester's mess.

"Right, ummm." I scooped up the judgment, tapped the pages on my desk to align their edges, and tucked it back into the Priority Mail envelope. Tapping papers is usually a soothing exercise for me. That whole sense of creating order is stress-relieving. Usually. But I needed more. Like, maybe I should dump out all the recycling bins in the building. "Again, thank you for your concern."

"Divorce papers on Valentine's Day. That's just not right," the other man said. "That should be rectified."

"Yes, well, it's all part of the process," I said, though I had no idea what either of us meant. "So, you are...?"

"I'm Aldo, Aldo Fabian." The man smiled at me. "I'm Enzo's

father."

Despite still being in recovery from seeing my final judgment, I was cognizant enough for my bullshit radar to blip a red light in the warning zone. Aldo looked nothing like Enzo and was only about ten years older, at a stretch. Granted, he could have been a stepfather, a much younger partner to Enzo's mother. But that didn't feel right to me, either.

"Nice to meet you, Mr. Fabian," I forced out and sat in my chair. "Did your son give you the intake forms to complete?"

"These?" Enzo carefully pulled an envelope out of an interior jacket pocket. "Yes, he completed them. But first, can we get that tour?"

If Aldo Fabian had been a wheelchair-bound man of ninety-seven and Enzo was next in line to be the Pope, I might have been able to pull myself together enough to take them on a tour. But, they weren't. And I was too undone from the Priority Mail package to deal with whoever they were.

"You know, actually, I'm really not feeling so great right now," I said. "Would you mind terribly if I had someone else take you? I'm sure Rachel, the woman who assisted with Monday's group, would be glad to—"

"No, that's not necessary," Enzo said, looking at the other man.

"Right," added Aldo. "We'll just come in on Monday for that group therapy thing. And if there's time and you feel better, maybe you could give me a private tour afterward."

Enzo handed me the envelope. "Here is that paperwork along with a year's worth of membership dues, in cash." He placed it next to the Priority Mail envelope on my desk. "We'll see ourselves out."

They left. I looked at the paperwork and counted the money. It was all there. Everything appeared to be in order until I looked closely at Aldo's personal information.

I texted Nico, asking if he could meet me at my soon-to-be-former home on Maine Avenue, and then I texted Angie, telling her I needed help staying sober until I had to pick my kids up from school.

Nico was the first to arrive. He let himself in and found me in the dining room. I'd put all the leaves in the table to make it as big as I could, and was rolling out the many balls of pasta dough I'd mixed. There were no eggs, nor any flour left in my house. Pasta was something I could control.

"What's going on?" he asked as he approached the table.

"I'm trying not to drink," I said. "I'm doing my best to keep my hands busy, so I can't lift a glass."

"Why not just have a drink?"

"I don't think I'll stop with one, and I need to pick the kids up from school soon."

"Why have a drink at all?"

"My Final Judgment came today."

"Directly from St. Peter?"

"Directly from Haneman, Jacobvitz, and Haneman." I paused to smile at him. "I'm officially divorced. On Valentine's Day."

"Ouch." He pulled me into a sideways hug. "Sorry to hear it, hon. But look on the bright side."

I gazed up at him.

"You still got me." He winked before letting go to take off his jacket. I went back to rolling out the dough with my grandmother's marble roller. It was heavy in my hands. I felt capable of doing anything in the world with that roller, including smashing Lester's face, *the girlfriend's*, too, Jacobvitz's, both the Hanemans', and maybe even my own attorney's.

"You can have a drink if you'd like," I said. "There's an open bottle of wine in the kitchen."

"Thanks. Maybe in a few minutes." He took a seat at the dining table. I continued to flatten the dough. "You just wanted my company? Or is there something I can do for you?"

"Both, actually." I checked how thin the dough was.

"You want me to take care of Les?"

I laughed. "I should have thought of that before." I formed the dough into a long, jelly-roll-style tube and wiped my hands on my apron. "I'll be right back," I said and went to get my purse.

Before leaving the center, I took Aldo Fabien's intake forms and the cash for a year's worth of membership dues to Mona's office, making a detour through the copy room. I knew I was breaking privacy rules. And I knew it was an offense that wasn't only illegal, but one that would cost me my license to practice social work in the state if I got caught. But, I felt that if there was one person on the planet I could safely share private information about a client with, it would be Nico.

"You know everyone in AC, right?" I asked when I returned.

"Everyone who is anyone."

"What about an Enzo Fabian, who is supposed to be the son of Aldo Fabian? They're from Philly."

"No." He leaned back in his chair and shook his head. "I never heard of them. Why?"

"Here's the deal." I sat next to him. "You know how you couldn't say who the client was that you got the condo from?"

"Because it was confidential."

"I work the same way. I could get fired and lose my license to practice as a social worker if anyone knew I was showing you what I'm about to show you. Promise me you won't say anything to anyone?"

"I promise." He pointed to the pasta dough roll. "You cutting any of that on the wide side?"

"I can."

"Good. You do that, and I'll do anything for you." He smirked, then his face changed. "You know I'll always do anything for you, though, right? Not just for the pasta."

"Yeah, I know." I pulled the copied pages from my purse. "I appreciate it, and that's why I wanted to talk to you about this. A man who calls himself Enzo Fabian comes to the senior center to enroll his dad. I meet with him, and he's...off."

"Off like nuts?"

"No. There's just something that isn't right. He doesn't ask the right questions, says the wrong stuff, acts...well, just weird. Then, he shows up with this man who looks only a little older than he is, but is supposed to be his dad. They observe me with a rather eccentric group of seniors and leave." I paused to get my wine. I poured him a glass while I was in the kitchen.

"So you need my help, how?" he asked as he accepted the wine.

"I'm not sure," I sipped. He took away my glass. "Thanks. That group where they watched me is so strange and odd that most sane people casually observing it would probably want to keep their parents as far away from it as possible. But, Enzo comes in and tells me not only is his 'dad' enrolling in our program, but he wants to be part of that group."

"Okay."

"Oh, wait. I forgot a part."

"Good thing I took the wine away from you."

"It's not the wine, it's stress."

"What?"

"Nothing. Remember when I stayed at the condo on Tuesday after you left?"

"Yeah."

"Well, Enzo first shows up in my office on Monday morning, then watches that group a little while later. Tuesday morning, he comes in and says he wants to enroll his dad. Then, Tuesday afternoon, when I walk out of the condo and get in my van, I see him in a car parked across the street, just sitting there like he's waiting for someone."

"Hm." Nico sipped his wine and stared at me. "That's something of a weird coincidence. But this isn't a big town. It could simply be a coincidence."

"That's what I tried to tell myself. But there's something that's just not right with these two men." I handed him the papers. "Look. Do you see that address? That's supposed to be where the dad lives."

"Miss America Way?" Nico met my eyes. "No one lives there."

"Right. I double-checked on my way home today. The convention center is there, and that's pretty much it. And look here." I pointed to another spot on the page. "See how the Social Security number is illegible? And they put 'not-applicable' for the driver's license number."

"I see."

"Don't you think that's suspicious?"

"Ordinarily I'd say 'yes, this kind of thing is suspicious,' but..." he drank again. "They're just trying to get a senior enrolled in a club of sorts. Why would anyone falsify documents to do that?"

"I don't know." I looked at the dough and picked up my knife. "How wide?"

"At least a half inch."

I cut the wide noodles, wondering what he'd do with them. I thought they'd be good in a butter-garlic sauce. "Something just isn't right," I insisted after a few slices. "The one who is supposed to be the dad doesn't look at all like he's old enough to be a senior. Oh, and they paid for the full year's dues in cash."

"How much?"

"Fifteen hundred dollars."

"Cash, not a check?"

"Cash." I like cutting pasta noodles. It has that same calming effect on me as tapping stacks of paper. Seeing the definite, straight lines once the dough is cut makes the world seem like an orderly and safe place.

"Again, I agree that would seem suspicious," he said. "But only if they were buying one-way tickets on a plane. Do you suppose they just don't want anyone knowing the old man is going to the center?"

"It's possible." I glanced up at him. "But, seriously, he doesn't look old enough to be a member. And, I think the Enzo guy, the supposed son, is wearing borrowed suits."

"What?"

"Look. They're up to something that has nothing to do with what they're posing as. I can feel it in my gut."

"Your intuition is that good?" The question made me look at him. I knew he was thinking about Les cheating on me.

"It's good," I said. "My intuition doesn't always show up when I need it, but when it does, it's as accurate as my meat thermometer. I always trust it."

"So what do you want from me?"

"I was hoping you could nose around a little. Find out something, whatever you can, about these guys. The father wants to join a group that could be really vulnerable. I don't want them doing damage to any of my people."

"That's my Lucy," Nico laughed. "Always looking out for her people." He stood, grabbed his jacket, and tucked the papers into a pocket. "I'll see what I can find, deal?"

"Deal."

"So how long until you have to pick the kids up?"

I leaned back so I could see the clock in the kitchen.

"I have about an hour. Why?"

"I was supposed to be somewhere this afternoon. I just need to tell my guys how much longer I will be here." He tapped a text on his cell phone.

"Don't." I smiled at him. "I'm fine, Nico. Honest. Go. Do your thing."

"Are you sure?"

"Yes. Angie should be here any minute, anyway."

He looked at me as if he didn't believe me. "All right. But, will you do me a favor?"

"Anything."

"Start looking out for yourself the way you do for everyone else, will ya?"

"I'll do my best."

"Good." He slipped into his jacket. "Now, when should I come by to pick up the noodles, or are you going to cook them for me, too?"

"Come by anytime tomorrow for raw ones. Then I'll serve them in a delicious butter-garlic sauce when you give me good news that I have nothing to worry about with these Fabian men."

"Will do." He kissed my cheek. "You got a mover lined up for next weekend?"

"I do."

"Good. See you around, babe." He let himself out.

WHAT'S IN A NAME?

The one called Aldo tapped on the edge of my cubicle door at ten-fifty-five the following Monday morning.

"Hello, Mr. Fabian," I said. "I just need a minute." He sat in the client chair. I quickly sent an e-mail to Gayle reminding her to give me a heads-up before sending people my way. "Are you alone today?"

"So far." He was in another suit similar to the ones Enzo wore–nice, but not overly expensive–and had a trench coat draped over his arm.

"We only have a few minutes before the MOFs begin." I stood. "Why don't we go on down?"

"So you settled on a name?" he asked as we headed toward the common area. Group therapy took place in the classrooms on the other side of the building.

"It's still in the works," I answered. "I'm surprised your son told you about that."

"I was at the meeting, remember?"

"The meeting?"

"Last week, when the group was trying to come up with a new name."

"Oh, *that* name!" I laughed. "Forgive me. I thought you were referring to something else. Anyway, yes, Rachel, my intern, and I thought one of the suggestions, MOFs, was a good one. It stands for Memorable Older Folks."

"Interesting."

It really stood for Marginalized Outcast Faction. That's what Rachel and I considered a good euphemism for Messed-up Old Fucks, as really, that name seemed to fit the group best. Marginalized

Outcast Faction was also a name that would look important on my internal reports and communications, and it gave me a variety of ways to describe them. It would also probably scare the members of the group, so as far as they were concerned, they were Memorable Older Folks.

I stopped outside the classroom door. "Mr. Fabian, I really don't mean to be presumptuous, honestly."

"You know, people only say that when they are about to be."

"Yes." I smiled. He smiled in return, the smile of a shady used car salesman. The kind he'd use to assure you the sunroof didn't leak or that the knocking sound was just simply because the car had sat too long on the lot and would eventually work itself out. "I don't know why you want to join this group, but I feel I must warn you, they can be a little...well, it might just be best if you stayed on the quiet side today and let them get used to your presence before you start introducing them to your personality."

"My thoughts exactly," he said, which I suspected had a double entendre I didn't get. "Beauty before age." He stepped aside, allowing me to enter the room first.

Rachel and I went through the ritual of setting up the chairs in a perfect circle before we sat and watched the others come into the room.

Aldo chose a seat opposite me. His smile made me glad I wasn't wearing a skirt.

"Lucy!" Mr. Schwartz yelled in my ear. I was sure he thought he was whispering. "I need to speak with you privately."

I followed him out to the hallway.

"Is something wrong, Mr. Schwartz?"

"That man in there." He pointed a bony finger back toward the room. "He was here last week. You said he was observing you. Why is he here now? Who is he observing today?"

"He's no longer observing anyone." I gave him the most assuring smile I could muster. "He and his son were satisfied with my level of service, so he decided to join your group."

"He can't just do that, can he?"

"Actually, he can now that he has enrolled in the senior center."

"And the center allowed him in?"

"There was no reason not to." And there were fifteen hundred reasons why they would do it without following up on the information on his application.

"He doesn't look old enough."

"Just between you and me, Mr. Schwartz, I think he had plastic surgery."

"You feel he's safe?"

"I do." I hoped.

"Oh, well then, I guess we should go back inside before they start talking about us."

Mr. Schwartz's fears were exaggerated as far as the group talking about us went. They milled around, inspecting the circle of chairs, casting glances at Aldo, and didn't seem to notice we weren't there. It was the same folks as the previous Monday.

"Has anyone heard from Harriet Millers?" I asked when I returned to my chair. "We haven't seen her in a couple of weeks."

"Oh, she dead," Mrs. Elliot said. She paused to watch Mr. Moffat move a chair the tiniest bit, and then sat in it before he could.

"She passed away?" I asked. "I wonder why the family hasn't notified the center. Are you sure?"

"That's what that woman said in the bad eatin' class," Mrs. Elliot said.

"Where?"

"The damned cooking class where they won't let you use salt," she explained. "That crazy, skinny woman who runs it told us old Harriet done gone and died on us on account of her poor eating."

"Edna said that?" I made a note to look into the situation. Edna had been becoming more disgruntled with her job every day, which meant there could be a paid opening for Rachel if she could work for less money. Edna wasn't a registered dietitian. The one cooking class she taught adhered to the guidelines given to us by the folks over at Meals on Wheels. I could help Rachel with that if necessary.

"I don't understand why people keep telling us how to eat," Mr. Thomas said, his face frowning across from Mrs. Elliot. "I've been eating salt all my life, and now some underweight, pushy thing tells me I shouldn't have any."

"It's not that you shouldn't have any," Mr. Moffat sneered at him. He inched his chair forward. "But, if you would pay attention, you would understand that a lifetime of eating too much salt will cause you to have an early death."

"Harriet was older than me. I don't call that early," Mrs. Elliot said. She leaned back in her chair, left shoulder up high, and looked over at Aldo. "You still observing?"

"Yes, yes, I am," he answered her, staring at me.

"And what exactly you looking for?"

"Answers," he said without having to stop and think about it. His eyes were glued to mine.

"If you want answers, you should try the Internet," Mrs. O'Leary told him, her knitting needles already bobbing. "My grandchildren are learning everything from that machine. They don't need people to tell them anything anymore."

"Your daughter should keep her children away from those things. They're dangerous, I tell you. Dangerous," Mr. Schwartz warned her.

"Well, I think everyone is seated, or almost," I said as Mrs. Dimiccio took a chair next to Aldo. She beamed at him as if they were old friends. "Let's get started."

"Aren't introductions in line, Lucy?" Mr. Hanson asked. He batted his eyes at Aldo. "I think we have a newcomer!" he sang. "Tell us, handsome, what's your name and where you from?"

Today, Mr. Hanson sported men's brown-and-black tweed pants and a tan Oxford-style button-down shirt, with white patent-leather women's pumps. His fuchsia lips contrasted with the dark stubble on his chin, but somehow went well with the giant silver hoops swinging from his ears.

Aldo looked alarmed and cleared his throat before answering. "My name is Aldo Fabian, and I am from New York City."

I caught my breath. Rachel heard me and shot me a look. I swallowed and gave a tiny shake of my head at her. I may have been close to the DTs from caffeine withdrawal that morning, but I clearly remembered Enzo saying his father had moved here from Philadelphia.

"It's good you got out alive," Mr. Schwartz said. "I'm Frederick Schwartz."

"I'm Delilah Dimiccio," Mrs. Dimiccio said.

"No you ain't," Mrs. Elliot corrected her. "She's Orella. Orella Dimiccio. And I'm Addie Elliot."

"Well then, who's Delilah?" Mrs. Dimiccio asked.

"I don't know! You'se the one who said it."

"Perhaps she is your sister," I offered.

"Yes, that must be it," Mrs. Dimiccio said. "Is she here yet?"

"She called to say she couldn't make it," Rachel redirected her. Mrs. Dimiccio didn't have a sister. "And I'm Rachel. As for everyone else, starting on my left, we have Frances O'leary and Robert Thomas. Next to Mrs. Dimiccio is Leo Hanson, Mrs. Elliot, of course, then Gunther Moffat, and finally Reggie George." While she spoke, she held her notebook so only I could see. She'd written a note on it: *U OK? Ur pale.*

"Thank you, Rachel." I nodded to her. "Let's get started. Now, a couple of you have had unfortunate experiences with pets. I thought it would be helpful and maybe even healing if we could discuss what we've gone through. And perhaps we can talk about ways to plan for our pets' futures."

I smiled around the group. Aldo was looking at me as if I were naked and had *the girlfriend's* body. "Maybe you would like to begin, Mrs. Elliot? I believe you currently have an unusual circumstance going on in your home concerning pets, yes?"

"Unusual circumstance?" She crossed her arms over her ample bosom. Whatever was going on with the shoulder didn't impede her arm movements. "Yeah, I guess that's what you could call it. Unusual circumstance. Hunh!" She scratched her neck before continuing. "My sister done passed away—"

"Oh, sweetheart!" Mr. Hanson leaped from his chair and knelt before her, pulling her hands into his. "I'm so sorry. Honey, are you all right?"

"I'm fine. Now get your fool ass back in your seat before you get in trouble," she told him. "She died a couple year ago. Anyway, she had this parrot. One of her kids took the parrot when she died, but it kept biting him. So he gave it to his sister, my niece. Well, wouldn't you know? My niece done moved in with me, as if I have all the space in the world for her and her kids. And she brought that damned parrot into my home."

"A pair of what?" Mrs. Dimiccio asked.

"A pair of nothing. It's a parrot." Mrs. Elliot said. "A damned big bird who shits all over his cage and then flaps about spraying that shit all over my house. It's loud too."

"You should call the police on her," Mr. Thomas said, his eyes were slits in his face. "These young people today. They have no respect for their elders. She shouldn't be allowed to come into your house and make a mess and a bunch of noise."

"You can't call the police on a bird," Mr. Moffat interjected with guttural, almost spitting, hard Cs. "If you'd pay attention, you would know she needs help training that bird."

"Oh, I thought it was clothing," Mrs. Dimiccio said.

"Actually," I said, "I brought it up because it's something we should all be thinking about. For those of us with pets, we need to think about what would happen to them should we have changes in our lives."

"You mean when we die, dear," Mrs. O'Leary said, staring at her nonstop needles. "What will happen to our animals when we die?"

"Well, there's that," I said slowly.

"I have my dogs taken care of." She paused to count the gray stitches lined up on a needle.

"I didn't realize you had any pets," I said.

"I have six dogs. That's why I always wear rain boots." She resumed her knitting.

"Excuse me?" Rachel asked.

I remained silent, not wanting to make the connection between dog ownership and boots.

"I have everything explained in my will on how to take care of them," Mrs. O'Leary continued.

"Yes," I said. "Wills are important, but that is just one area to think about. What about if you need to go into the hospital for just a couple of days? What happens to your dogs then? Have you made arrangements for someone to take care of them should you find yourself in a hospital for a day or two?"

"What about the rest of your belongings, Lucy?" Aldo asked. "Did your older family members ever entrust you with their belongings or their contacts? Maybe you could help the group by telling us what worked for your family?"

"I, uh, well, let's stick to one topic here at a time," I stumbled through my answer. That *contacts* word threw me off my game. I got the feeling he was talking in some kind of code that he expected me to understand.

"My grandmother left instructions in her will for her cats," Rachel offered. "But no one knew what to do with them when she had to go into the hospital. They were alone in her apartment for three days before anyone remembered them. After that happened, she and a neighbor agreed to take care of each other's cats if one of them should be laid up like that again."

"My cats can take care of themselves for a few days. But the litter box smell would be awful," Mr. Hanson said as tears rimmed his eyes. "My Johnny was always a hater of the litter box smell. I guess it's a good thing he died before I did after all."

Mrs. Elliot pulled an old-fashioned, white cloth hankie out from between her ample breasts and handed it to him. He dabbed his eyes.

"I realize this can be a difficult subject," I said. "But, again, it's something important you need to have prepared ahead of time, in case of an emergency or a sudden change."

"You mean sudden death, dear," Mrs. O'Leary said.

"Who else has pets?" Rachel asked.

I glanced around the circle again. Aldo continued to leer at me. I crossed my legs tighter and held up the folder with my notes in front of my chest.

"I got me an old hound dog," Mr. George said after a few quiet minutes. He stared directly at Aldo. "He'll probably die before me, but if not, I guess I should talk to my son. Maybe he could take care of him. Though my son can barely take care of himself."

There was another long pause in the conversation, which put me on the edge of my seat. That group seldom paused and certainly never for long. They didn't feel as safe as they used to.

"I've never trusted an animal enough to have one in my house," Mr. Schwartz eventually said.

If I had hackles, they would have raised. I was like a mama wolf sensing whatever eats baby wolves was outside her den, looking for a way to get to her pups. Aldo was the only change in the room. He was the one making my seniors and me feel off. He was up to some kind of no good. I knew it, and I got the feeling my seniors did, too. On any other Monday, Mr. Schwartz would have ranted about whatever danger he could imagine from having a pet in one's home. And Mr. Moffat would have been explaining why he was an expert in animal husbandry. And Mr. Thomas would have been challenging Mr. Moffat.

"Mr. Moffat," I tried. "What about you? Don't you have a dog?"

"Yes, I have Butch, my poodle. He is well trained, of course," Mr. Moffat announced, but without force.

"I suppose that means it can take care of itself when you pass?" Mr. Thomas said, but not in a taunting way.

"I just meant that it could easily adapt to another family if need be," Mr. Moffat answered. "Truth be told, I worry more about dying and no one noticing for a couple of days. Butch will probably try to hold his bladder waiting for me to let him out. He will be confused and in pain. What will happen to him while he waits for someone to find my body and let him outside to relieve himself?"

"I read in the paper once that a dog in a similar situation ate his owner," Mrs. O'Leary said.

"But where did it relieve itself?" Mr. Moffat wanted to know.

"I'm not sure if they mentioned that," Mrs. O'Leary answered.

"Well, Mr. Moffat, that's a very good point," I tried to cheer him on.

"Of course it is. Otherwise, I wouldn't have brought it up."

I smiled. "Yes, so, now that you did bring it up, do you have any ideas about how to alleviate your fears?"

He stayed quiet for a minute before answering. Then he simply said: "No."

"Then that's probably a good place for us to start brainstorming."

Before continuing, I peeked at Aldo again and noticed, with relief, he wasn't looking at me. He was peering beyond me, toward the door of the room. I "accidentally" dropped my pen and bent down to look for it. At the door, I saw Enzo, standing in the hall, flattening his jacket lapels.

"So, of course, you need to start with a frank, open discussion with your doctor so that you know what is going on with your own personal health," I said when I sat up. "We're all on good, speaking terms with our doctors, right?"

They had turned into my children and did not answer me.

"You know," I tried, and looked pointedly at Mrs. Elliot. "I just recently went to the doctor and told him all sorts of things that I wasn't sure if he could help me with. But, because he's my doctor, I knew he needed to know exactly what was going on in my life." I let my eyes circle the group. The only ones willing to meet them belonged to Aldo.

"I prefer to tell my good friends my secrets," he said. "Or my family."

"I wasn't talking about secrets," I insisted. "I was—"

"Yes, but who do you tell your secrets to, Lucy?" Aldo asked. "Everyone tells you their secrets, right? I bet your parents even told you their secrets. Did they?"

It was my turn to be quiet. The silence was almost loud for an uncomfortable minute.

"My old hound dog's name is Ben," Mr. George eventually said. He grinned widely at Aldo. "You got yourself a dog? You can tell them anything."

The group floundered after that. We ended early because few were willing to speak.

"I need to get that man out of this group," I whispered to Rachel while we gathered our things.

"Who is he?" she asked.

"I honestly don't—"

"Are we still on for our tour, Lucy?" Aldo asked. He touched my arm.

"Sure. Right, Rachel?"

She looked puzzled but nodded.

"Great. Mr. Fabian here would like to tour the facility. I'm so glad you have time to come with us." I glanced up at his face; his smile was clearly forced now. "She's new and needs to learn how to do these kinds of things."

During the tour, I shot Nico a text, asking if he'd found anything out about the Fabian men. He replied, saying he'd be in Trenton for a couple of days, and if I cooked anything he really liked, to save him some leftovers. But he mentioned nothing about the Fabians.

SIGNS OF THINGS TO COME

Les was surprised to learn where I would be living.

"Which floor?" he asked when he picked up the kids the following Thursday night.

"Fifteenth." I finished boxing the last of the prepackaged foods in the kitchen, pretending like it didn't kill me that he'd brought *the girlfriend* with him. As if *the girlfriend* was needed to take our teenage children out of our former home.

I sought refuge in the mudroom. He followed me. I opened and shut the empty cabinets as if I had a purpose in there and left as quickly as I could. The mudroom was too small and intimate for me to be in it with Les. As well as letting you out into our tiny backyard, it housed our washer and dryer. It was the one room in the house that had, that used to have, a little bit of each of us in it at all times: everyone's clothes and shoes, the kids' backpacks, Les' grill accessories, the dog's leash, our beach chairs. It was the true family room in our house, our house that now belonged to someone else, because Les was an ass.

"What unit number?" He was on my heels as I headed to the front room.

"1509." At the stairs, I yelled: "Ash! Joy! You about ready?"

"Uh, how did you manage to get that?" he asked.

I turned toward him and screwed up my face to look bitchy. "Actually, Nico found it for me." To my satisfaction, he flinched.

"There you are," *the girlfriend* crooned to Joy as if she were talking to a puppy. "We were waiting for you."

I looked at Joy to make sure she rolled her eyes. She did. She immediately went into the kitchen to put her shoes on, though she was carrying them in her hand and could have put them on in front of us.

Ash, as usual, was the last to arrive. I watched his long and lanky, very lean, and perpetually relaxed body lope down the stairs. I couldn't help but wonder how he managed to stay in slow motion when the drug tests kept coming back negative.

"Hi!" yelped *the girlfriend*. Ignoring her, Ash stepped into his hi-top sneakers and shuffled to me without tying them.

"Bye, Mom," he said, kissing me on my cheek.

"Bye, hon. I love you."

Joy prowled back in the room. Like a wound-up, short and powerful bobcat on amphetamines, she stood next to her sloth brother and glared at me.

"I love you too, Joy," I said. "And don't worry about your crabs. I'll follow the instructions to a T."

"I know," she said as a way of saying *thanks*. She had printed a page of instructions for handling her hermit crabs when she went to her father's the first time. She'd added two more for me to use during the move this weekend. Apparently, the little critters get stressed easily. It was important that I kept them happy.

I followed everyone to the door and locked it behind them.

God, it felt good making that bastard flinch.

It was pretty quick work for the moving crew the next morning. Over half of what was in the house was going to a charity organization that my realtor would let in the following week. By three o'clock that afternoon, Angie and I were in the condo, unpacking. By six, we were close to done.

"I'm meeting Nico for dinner soon. Wanna join us?" I asked from the kitchen. "Or are you going out with Ted?" I could see her on the other side of the pass-through, standing in the combined living and dining rooms. The building's business manager called that part of the condo the living area, a phrase I hated because it suggested to me we had a dead area somewhere, too.

"No, thank you, and no," she collapsed on the couch.

"What and what?" I walked around the partial wall and joined her.

"No, thank you. I don't want to join you and Nico. And no. I'm not going out with Ted. I broke up with him."

"What? Why?"

"Let's just say I don't want to be involved with a man who

explains uncomfortable situations by saying he has a long story with his ex-."

"He really said that?"

"Yes."

"What'd you say?"

"That I didn't want to be a subplot."

"I love it!" I laughed and slapped her thigh. "But why don't you join us? Nico and me."

"I don't want to be a third wheel, either."

"Are you nuts? Since when were you ever a third wheel? What does that mean anyway?"

She flicked her hair over her shoulder. "I just get the feeling Nico would like to have some alone time with you."

"What would make you say that?"

"There's something in the way he's been looking at you lately. I don't think he'd like me interrupting when he finally has you to himself."

"You're imagining things." I checked my cell to see what time it was. "You know what Nico likes. He's always got a tall, leggy cocktail waitress hanging on him. That's not me."

"He hasn't been around with anyone for a couple of years, now. Lots of women have noticed. Haven't you?"

"No. Though now that you mention it, I guess it has been a while since he's brought a member of his bimbo-of-the-week club by the house." I got up to pile the flattened boxes into a neater stack. "Are there any more empties?"

"One more." She stood and squished another box. "What's up with you and him, then? And why is he asking you out for dinner instead of inviting himself over like usual?"

"He knew I was moving today, so I wouldn't be cooking, as you probably guessed. Anyway, he's helping me with a project for the center. I'm sure he's going to update me on that." I took the box from her and added it to my pile.

"Nico Mancuso is doing social work?"

"No." I picked the stack up. "There's something odd about a new client. I asked him to investigate."

"Sounds mysterious."

"I guess. Can you get the door?"

She jogged past me to open it. "Sounds like maybe you two could snuggle up together on a stakeout."

"Come on, Angie!" I stopped in the hall to look at her. "I just got divorced."

"And your ex is already shacking up with someone else. There's no grace period. You're not in mourning."

"Please. Nico is simply doing me a favor. I'll be back. I'm just dropping these by the recycling bin down the hall."

Angie was putting on her jacket when I returned.

"Give me a call tomorrow if you want to grab a bite to eat or something for dinner, okay?" she asked.

"Sure."

"Unless you're tucking in with Nico." She ran out too soon to see how well I could imitate Joy's eye-rolling.

Nico had suggested I meet him at a restaurant on the boardwalk at the bottom of my building. I'd never been there, but had seen the sign with the giant shrimp on it numerous times. He claimed the shrimp were excellent and that the vodka-lemonades the place was famous for were just as good.

The boardwalk was dark and cold when I got there. It was also pretty dark in the restaurant, but it was toasty warm. I was wearing a new sweater that Angie had given me for my birthday. It had a large scoop neck, so large that I probably should have worn a tank top under it. I took off my coat when I entered, making the sweater slip off my shoulder and down my arm, revealing a bra strap. A hand pulled it back up. I jumped and slapped the hand away before I realized it was Nico.

"Jesus! You scared me," I said to him.

"Sorry about that." He kissed me on the cheek as a greeting. "Next time, I'll let you expose yourself."

"Only do it if you think it'll get us a discount." He led me to a table in the center of the room. "So are the vodka-lemonades really good?" I told myself all the lifting and bending required for the move meant that I could allow myself a few extra calories.

"That's why I'm a regular here."

"I thought you were a regular at my place."

"I'm a regular wherever the food is good. So do you want the shrimp, too?"

"Not if it's fried." I looked over the menu. "How are the salads?"

"They're salads. Get something with flavor, like the fried shrimp."

"Sounds yummy, but I think I'll do a salad with grilled chicken."

"Did you forget how to live, Lucy?"

"No. But I haven't forgotten how to be fat, either." I set the menu down. "I'm in a new sweater and, while it's slightly smaller than what I was wearing a couple of months ago, it's still not the size I want it to be."

"And you look great in it. But you gotta enjoy life, too. How about I get the shrimp and share a little? You got access to a full gym now. Work it off there if you need to."

"You should have started with that. I'll eat *your* shrimp. I just don't want any of my own." I gave him a lopsided grin.

He blew out an exaggerated sigh and went up to the counter to place the order.

"Thank you for inviting me out. I didn't realize I needed a break," I said when he returned with the drinks.

"It's my pleasure." When Nico smiles, the creases around his eyes tell you whether he means it. That night, he meant his smile, and knowing it made my stomach flutter. I'd never had flutters around him before. It had to have been Angie's fault.

"Did you invite me here to give me an update on my mystery men?" I asked, in part, to chase away the flutters.

His smile fell. "Yeah, I have an update. And a confession of sorts."

"I'm only interested in the update. But we can find you a priest afterward if you want."

"I might need it when I'm done here tonight."

"What does that mean?"

"I may need someone to give me my last rites."

I leaned over the table. "Who are these men?"

"I don't know. But I do know, they are not who they described on your paperwork. Those men do not exist in AC or Philly."

"The one called Aldo, just this week, said he was from New York."

"I'll look up there. But here's the interesting part. There have been a couple of strangers around town, who fit the description you gave me, who have been asking questions."

"About?"

He raised his eyebrows. "About Les and you."

"Oh." I took a long drink. "I wasn't expecting that. Do you think they're the same men?"

"I can't be one hundred percent positive. It's just *really* coincidental."

"Yeah." I leaned back in my chair and looked hard at him. "There's something else, though. I can see it on your face. What are you not telling me? And should I call for that priest now?"

"Maybe, but," he paused while a waitress put our food on the table. He portioned out some shrimp on an extra plate and gave it to me. "Remember, I was the one who gave you the krill. Hopefully you'll like it enough to go easy on me."

I bit into a shrimp and ripped off the tail. I was glad it was dark in the restaurant, so no one could see. The shrimp were so good, I may have drooled. "They'll serve for penance."

"Good. Now, here's the confession." He reached across the table and put his hand on my arm. "Remember how you felt uncomfortable showing me those enrollment papers? It violated some kind of confidentiality agreement?"

"Please tell me you didn't show those to anyone."

"I didn't. That's not my confession." He ran his fingers down my arm until he grabbed my hand. "I work in a similar way. I don't always have contracts, but my clients know they can trust me not to say anything about our business relationships or about what I know of their personal and professional lives to anyone. Even family. Does your policy include not talking to family?"

"Yes."

"So, if a wife comes in and you work with her and she tells you she doesn't want her husband to know what it's about, can you tell the husband anyway?"

"Not unless she signs a waiver." I didn't like the tone of his voice. I tried to pull my hand away, but he held strong.

"Then you'll understand." His grip tightened. "Your condo—"

"I don't think I want to hear this, Nico," I whispered.

"You need to. The condo belonged to Les."

My stomach lurched. That's why the little shit flinched. But Nico lied to me?

"Well, I guess I betrayed you. So we're even." I pulled harder; he held tight. "Almost."

"What do you mean?"

"When Les came to pick up the kids yesterday, he asked how I got it." I yanked my hand free. "I told him from you."

"That's all right. I figured you'd tell him."

I looked at my salad. It made me nauseous. "Why didn't you tell me, Nico? How could you keep that from me?"

"I just explained why."

"But—"

"It was a confidentiality issue with a client. Les is a client. You are my friend. I felt guilty as hell. But I also felt that the condo rightfully belonged to you. I was waiting to tell you this later, when I could figure out how. I'm not keeping that 125. I put it into a trust for you."

"What?"

"The money you paid for what should have been yours to begin with. It's in a trust for you."

"I can't...I can't process that now." I pressed my fingertips into my forehead. "Let me get this straight. Les owned...He sold...Oh my God! Is that where he met up with her? *The girlfriend?*"

"No, he didn't use that condo for that." He scratched the back of his head. "He needed it for...well, for business associates."

"He lets players stay free at the casino all the time. Why a condo?"

"That's not the kind of business associates I'm talking about."

He took a sip. I drank, too. And as I swallowed, his earlier words echoed inside my head.

"Wait!" I slammed my glass down. "You said 'he didn't use that condo for *that.*' What does that mean?"

"What?"

"By saying 'that condo for *that,*' you kind of make it sound like there was another place somewhere for *that.* For *the girlfriend.* Was there?"

"Lucy, really, we don't need to go there."

"I do."

"No. You don't. Let's get back to what—"

"Stop!" I yelled and stood. He stood too and grabbed my arm.

"Sit down," he said through his teeth. "There's something important I need to tell you." He stared hard into my eyes. "What Les is or was doing with that woman doesn't matter right now. What matters is that when I sold that condo to you, I may have unintentionally put you in the middle of something. *That's* what matters."

"I don't understand."

"Then let me explain."

I returned to my chair. He came around the table to sit next to me.

I noticed everyone in the restaurant had their eyes averted from us. There aren't many places where a conversation can happen in public when a woman yells *stop,* then a man grabs her by the arm and makes her sit, and everyone around them ignores it. Atlantic City is one of those places. People like to pretend they don't see what's going on around them here. It keeps them out of trouble.

"Just tell me first, did he have another place? For her?"

"Seriously, Luce, that doesn't matter." One of his hands was on my back, the other was on my arm.

"It matters to me." I leaned into his shoulder. "Did he, Nico?"

"I think so," he said after a long pause.

"How long? How long has he had it? How long has he been with her?"

Nico didn't answer. I could feel his breath on the side of my head, and his hand rubbing my back. He cleared his throat.

"I don't know, really. I found out about your condo a couple of years ago when he needed my help with a contact. I was under the impression he had another place, but I wasn't sure until he filed for divorce. And I'm still not sure why he had that one."

I twisted around to look at him. "He said, when he came clean the day after Labor Day, he said he'd only met her in the summer. I mean, it could have been another lie, but were there others before her?"

Nico paused again. "I think so, Luce. *Now* I think so. I suspected it for a long while, but I wasn't sure."

I felt numb and unable to move, but as I stared at the shrimp, I realized it was probably getting cold and should be eaten soon. Fried shrimp should never go to waste. Salad was a different story.

"So, he had a few extra places." I chewed. "One for business. One apparently for pleasure. And to think I always bragged about how hard he worked. Even I didn't know."

"Well, if it helps, he kept everything very discreet." Nico moved my salad to the empty table next to us and started eating the shrimp, too. Perhaps he realized he was in danger of not getting any. "People weren't saying 'oh, poor Lucy' behind your back or anything. As I said, *I* only found this shit out a couple of years ago."

"But you did know, and if I'm such a good friend..." I snapped my head back to make him look me in the face.

"Listen, if you told Les you knew, it was very possible he'd be pissed off enough to make sure everyone knew they couldn't trust me. Things could get ugly for me, you know?"

I snorted.

"I could lose my life if people thought they couldn't trust me. Do you understand?" He put his hand on my cheek. "I've been trying hard for two years to figure out what to do as I hated like hell keeping you in the dark. It's been killing me. I never wanted you to be hurt by anyone, not even by that shit of a husband you had. But my hands were tied. Do you understand?"

I took my time answering him. He continued to hold my face and gaze into my eyes while he waited.

"I understand," I finally said. He let go of me. "I just don't want to understand."

"I'm sorry. I really am, but back to your place."

"Back to my place. Though I'm not sure I care."

"You need to, I think. See, Les, had...First, did you know he was an associate?"

"Of who?"

"No. Not that kind of associate." Nico blew out a stream of air. "You know how he's connected to your Uncle Sid?"

"What do you mean?"

Nico glanced around before continuing. "I'm talking about how Les and your Uncle Sid are," he leaned closer to whisper, "involved with the mob."

"With what? No way, Nico. Les? Uncle Sid?" My mother's brother was literally my godfather, and he was the sweetest, nicest, most clean-cut old man around.

"Yes, Les. Your Uncle Sid.

"You can't be right."

"I can, and I am."

"For how long?"

"Sid, all his life. Les, I think since he was in college."

"No! I knew Les then. That's when we met. He was a hardworking, blue-collar, good guy from northeast Philly."

"He was a poor kid from Philadelphia with aspirations. You were an Italian girl with connections."

"Irish-Italian, and *so* not connected. My dad was a cop, remember? And you can't be right about Uncle Sid." He used to live in Philly and ran a candy store on the boardwalk during the summer season. He was now retired and lived full-time in his house down the Jersey shore in Avalon. Uncle Sid had always been one of my favorite people since I was a little girl. After my dad died last year, he was there with support and advice. He was there again when Les left. He was the one who paid for my mom to spend the winter in Florida to get her away from me.

"Lucy, honey, your Uncle Sid was made."

"Uncle Sid? How do you know?"

He cocked his head at me.

"How could I not know?" I asked.

"Well, it's probably not talk around the dinner table when your dad's a cop. I'm sure he kept everything on the up-and-up in front of his sister's family."

"But Les? Are you sure?"

"That's how we met," Nico leaned back in his chair. "I helped your Uncle Sid with some security work one day when Les was around."

"So Uncle Sid kept that from me, too? Who else knows?"

"Your uncle was probably just protecting you. Les, too, by not mentioning anything."

"I wonder if Daddy knew." I ate another shrimp. "He never liked Les. Marrying Les was the one time in my life I didn't listen to my father. He tried to talk me out of it. Can you believe that?"

Nico smiled. "Well, you got two good kids from him, anyway."

"Have you forgotten what my kids are like these days?" I slumped in my chair. "I feel like such a fool, Nico."

"Don't, babe." He relaxed in his chair. "When people have secrets they need to keep, they keep them. There was no reason you would have known."

"Yeah, well," I picked at the shrimp tails left in the basket. "So what has any of this to do with the condo?"

"It's possible that it has nothing to do with your condo."

"You're kidding me, right? You just put me through hell—"

"I mean," he put a finger on my lips. "It could be another coincidence. But here it is. Your guys are not on record as being real anywhere. And, a set of men who fit your description are walking around asking questions about Les and you. One of the people I spoke to said those two mysterious men even mentioned your father."

"My father?"

"Yeah. It's not making sense right now. But it has me wondering if these two guys are trying to get to Les somehow. Maybe they know you were married to him, and now that you've split, maybe they think you'd be more likely to tell them something about him. It's possible they had dealings with him at the condo, which might explain why you saw one of them outside it. Maybe he was looking for Les there."

"But my dad?"

"There was a definite inquiry into is Lucy Womzak Sean McCool's daughter?"

"Weird. Who told you that?" I smirked. "Or is that client confidentiality?"

Nico grinned. "I will tell you it was the owner of a pawn shop. That's all."

Nico paid the tab, and we left the restaurant. Outside on the boardwalk, the wind blew hard into our faces.

"Hey, listen," he said, huddling close to me against the wind. "I'm going into Philly tomorrow to see the Picasso exhibit at the art museum. It'd be nice to have some company. Would you like to come along?"

"I don't know. I still need to unpack the kids' bathrooms."

"First, the kids are old enough to do that themselves. Second, teenage boys don't want their moms going through their bathroom shit. Teenage girls probably feel the same way. Third, Lucy gets to take a break now and then. C'mon, Luce, do something *you'd* enjoy for a change. Would you enjoy going to the museum?"

I thought about it. I haven't managed to come up with a new theory or slogan for two weeks now. I'd hoped to do it this weekend. But I was starting to like my *today is the day* concept. And, I hadn't been to the art museum in years. "Yes," I said. "I would enjoy going to the museum."

"Good. Then I'll pick you up in the morning." He kissed me on my cheek. "See you around, babe."

Before he could take a step away from me, I spotted Enzo passing under a lamp on the boardwalk, heading in our direction.

"Nico," I grabbed his coat.

"You canceling already?"

"No! It's that man, Enzo. Enzo Fabian is here."

"What? Where?"

We stepped close to the wall, in the shadows of the shrimp bar. Nico put his arms around me, as if we were in an intimate embrace, and turned us around so I could look over his shoulder. I was about to tease him for pulling a cheesy TV trick, but when I felt his hands slip under my jacket and I realized how close my face was to his neck, I almost kissed him instead. Perhaps I shouldn't have had a vodka-based drink.

"He's wearing a long, gray coat and a white scarf," I said, forcing myself to take a step back. "He's not wearing a hat."

We froze in place until Enzo passed by. "That's him," I whispered. "Now what?"

"Now I think that's one coincidence too many. I don't like that he's so close to your building again. I think I'll follow him around for a while. Hopefully, he's heading to a casino or someplace where I might know someone he knows."

KINDS OF PEOPLE

Not sure what one wears to an art museum, I opted for an oversized, long-sleeved, velvety tunic with a giant V-neck and a lacy camisole peeking from underneath. I tugged on a pair of leggings and turned around in the mirror, excited to see how I looked. The outfit wasn't new. It was from last summer when my weight was going up, and I needed something warm to wear in the over-air-conditioned building at work. I had ballooned to the point where I couldn't wear it anymore by October. And now I was in a size I almost liked again, and it fit me once more. There was still room for improvement, but things were heading in the right direction.

I stuck in a pair of dangly gold earrings and wished I had perfume. Les hated perfume, so I never wore any. I was going to have to get some now that he was sniffing *the girlfriend*.

Nico came up to check out how the condo was looking before we left.

"God, that's a great view," he said, staring through the sliders. He turned on his heel to face me through the pass-through. "But you look just as good."

"Thanks." Nico flirts with everyone, so I didn't take it personally, though I couldn't help but notice part of me wanted to. "Having second thoughts about selling the place?" I measured out a scoopful of protein powder and dumped it into the cold coffee in the bottom of my cup.

"I never considered myself the rightful owner. It should have been yours the moment you two split. No, it should have been yours from the beginning." He came to the pass-through. "What are you doing?"

"I know it looks disgusting." I whisked the powder until it dissolved, then added fresh, hot coffee to the cup. "But, it's low cal and keeps me from getting hungry before lunch."

"How's it taste, though?" He came into the kitchen.

"It's not as bad as you might think. I use chocolate-flavored protein powder and tell myself it's mocha. Wanna taste?" I held up the cup, expecting him to refuse.

He sipped from the cup while it was still in my hand. I wished Angie were there to see it. I was fairly certain this wasn't the kind of behavior "just friends" engaged in, but I wasn't sure. It'd been too many years since I did anything resembling dating. Not that I thought we were on a date. Maybe I just wished we were.

"Not bad," he said. "I do the protein shake thing in the morning, too. Never thought of putting it straight in my coffee.

"I just wish someone would invent a Bailey's-flavored protein powder. Wouldn't that be even better? Or Kahlua?"

"I love the way you think." He grinned at me. "Now slug that down. We've got a long drive."

I waited until we were in traffic before I interrogated him about the night before. Obviously, he didn't have juicy news for me, or he'd have mentioned it himself.

"So whatever happened last night?" I asked as he merged into the traffic on the Atlantic City Expressway.

His eyes bounced between the highway and the rearview mirror before he answered me. "I followed your man Enzo up the boardwalk and into the Tropicana. He was at a blackjack table for a while. But his eyes weren't just watching the cards. I got the feeling he was waiting for someone."

"Anyone show up?"

"Yeah, but it was someone who wanted to talk to me."

"What? Who?"

Nico took his eyes off the highway long enough to grin directly at me. "Your ex saw me and asked if we could chat."

"Really?"

"Really." Nico slowed as we went through the EZPass toll booth. I studied his profile, noticing how much he'd aged in the years I'd known him. He'd once told me his mother had named him after the actor, Nicodemo Mancuso, hoping he would be as handsome. And he had once been a gorgeous man. Now he was handsome, albeit tough and rugged-looking.

He'd entered his adult life as a professional boxer trained by his two uncles, who owned a gym. He was good enough to make decent money in the ring and had quit when he was still in his twenties and only had his nose broken three times. He became a bodyguard and grew his business with other strong, able-bodied men from the gym. Somehow, the bodyguard business expanded into the realm of alarm systems, security cameras, private investigation, and from there into ombudsmanship, as Nico says, and then he always winks and defines that as *helping two parties see eye to eye.*

After the fighting career and other injuries he'd received in the line of duty, his face had taken on a hardened look. He was still good-looking, but scarred, and now laugh lines ran deep and long, and his full hair that curled away from his face was streaked with white.

But his body remained firm and strong-looking. Nico took great care of his body. We women, or hens as he called us, used to stand on my deck when I'd host summer barbecues and admire the rear of his physique while he spoke to the men in the yard.

He waited until we were back in the faster traffic before he spoke again. "Les was worried about what I might or might not have said to you about the condo."

"Yeah. I guess he would be." My eyes didn't want to stop staring at the round, sensual curve of his shoulder. "What'd you tell him?"

"Well, client confidentiality prevented me from telling him everything, you know." He smiled outright. "But I did tell him the truth without getting either of us in trouble. I said I felt you deserved the condo, so I sold it to you without telling you who sold it to me. That's how the original deal went down, right?"

"Right." I laughed. "He believed you?"

"I think so. I changed the subject and talked business with him."

"And?"

"Les is worried about something. He asked me where my loyalties were regarding him *and* you."

"Your loyalties?"

"Yeah. I told him I considered you my friend and he a business associate."

"Was he upset with that?"

"No, he seemed to be okay with it. But, he said he might be in need of my services again, soon."

"Oh, now that's interesting."

"Unfortunately, by the time we were done talking, I'd lost Enzo."

We rode silently for several minutes. We went past the closed-for-winter farmers' markets and onto Route Seventy-three before something sank in deep enough to bother me.

"Wait a minute! Wait just one Goddamned minute." I turned in my seat to face him directly.

"You want me to pull over?" Nico glanced at me.

"No, that's not what I meant." I ran my hands through my hair and worked my jaw before continuing. "Was *the girlfriend* at the Tropicana, too?"

"Not that I saw."

"So, he gets his kids, who he sees for a couple of days every two weeks, and when they're at his house, he leaves them, possibly with *the girlfriend*, and goes out to a casino?"

"Kind of looks that way."

"What kind of a father does that?" I folded my arms in front of me. "Christ! It's like I didn't even know who I was married to."

"Sweetheart, I suspected that for a long time."

"You always surprise me," I said to Nico as he tucked his museum membership card into his wallet. He handed me a building map as we headed toward the exhibit. "Tough man Nico Mancuso is a proud member of the art museum?"

"So I appreciate the finer things in life. Something wrong with that?"

"Not at all." We took the stairs to the exhibition floor. "It's just that, you know, most manly men don't care about art and literature."

"You trying to hint at something?" He stopped midway up the stairs and cocked his head at me. "I'll prove to you right here, right now, on these steps how manly I can be."

"I'm sure you could, but I came to see the art, not get arrested." My face warmed as a brief, but vivid, picture of Nico, naked, on top of me on the stairs, flashed through my mind. "And that's not what I meant. You're, you know, on the rough-and-tumble side. It's not like you have a job selling fine clothes or expensive jewelry."

"I have a job protecting the people who wear that stuff. Maybe it rubs off." We continued up the steps. He stopped again at the top. "One of my first clients was an art gallery owner from Philly. He'd bought this huge house in Sea Isle and needed the place outfitted with an intense alarm system. When I did the work, I kept stopping to look at all the art that he'd brought in. I asked him what it was about. He told me. He was an old man, you would have liked him."

"Probably."

"Anyway, he taught me a lot. Then later, he had me redo his system in his Philly store, and that got me hooked on the museums here."

"I see. Anyway, I wasn't being negative. I think it's great that you like the finer things in life. It's just something that, if I were looking at you on the surface, I'd never expect it."

"We need to go this way." He led me to the exhibit opening. "Here's the thing. I've seen enough ugly shit in my life. Maybe that's what's reflected on the surface of me. But think about it, if I didn't balance out that ugly shit with art, with beauty, what kind of person would I turn into?"

"That makes sense, I guess. But tell me, these paintings, do you think they are beautiful? They don't seem so to me. Not all of them anyway. In fact, many of the Picassos I'm familiar with seem too angry or sad to be beautiful." We stopped in front of a large painting. "Look at this one."

"Well, first of all, this isn't Picasso," Nico told me. "It's Juan Gris. He was a contemporary of Picasso and a fellow cubist."

"See? You amaze me!" I squinted at the plaque beside the painting. He was right. It was called *Still Life Before an Open Window*.

Nico smiled at it. "You find this angry or sad?"

"A little sad." I stood before it. "The colors are beautiful, I'll give you that. Those shades of blue and purple make me want to touch them. But they are melancholy colors. And it's a lonely scene."

"Can you see what's in the picture?"

"A bottle, a newspaper…"

"It's your typical still life combination: the bottle and paper, and there's also a book, some fruit, and a glass on a table before a window. Do you see it all?" He waited while I looked it over.

"I think so, yes."

"Now, look at the contrasts in how he painted the lighting. There's moonlight coming in from outside the window and electric light inside. Can you tell?"

"Yes…I think I see it." I squinted at the painting.

"See how Gris played with the lighting to show each object in different ways? It's the same thing: one bottle, one book, but they are presented in a different light, and you can see the difference, right?"

"Yes." I could tell exactly what he was talking about now.

"Now, imagine walking into a room lit by a lamp of some kind, and there was moonlight coming through a window behind a table set with those things. Now imagine walking back out of that room and remembering what you saw." He paused, as if to give me time to process it. "When it comes back to your memory, do you see it as you originally did, or do you see separate parts of it in the various ways the light hits it?"

I closed my eyes to figure out the answer.

"I see separate parts of it in different light."

"Ah, very good. Look at that painting again. It may not be a beautiful piece that matches your sofa, but isn't it a beautiful thing that Gris could capture a concept like that?"

I looked again at the painting, then turned to him and almost swooned. "I think it's a beautiful thing that you could make me see that." And I vowed to slap Angie the first chance I got. Surely I wouldn't have felt like swooning if she hadn't got me thinking maybe Nico had more than a friendly interest in me. Unless, of course, we were on a date. How was I to know?

He grinned at me. "Honey, you ain't seen nothing yet."

We went through the exhibit slowly, enjoying every last bit of it like we would a platter of linguine alfredo.

"You should become an art critic," I said to him when we finally got to the few actual Picasso pieces in the show. "You're so good at this."

"I'm even better at what I do. I like to keep this as a pleasure, not work."

"Oh my God!" I stood before a painting I knew very well.

"What is it?"

"I know this one. Picasso's *Three Musicians*. Right?"

"Right. How do you know it?"

Tears welled up in my eyes, and I couldn't speak. Nico took me by the arm and led me to a small bench.

"Would you believe my dad liked that painting?" We sat. I looked through my purse for a tissue. "God, that's so crazy." I wiped my nose.

"I never pegged him to be an art lover," Nico said.

"He wasn't. That's the funny thing." I looked down at the tissue clenched in my lap. "When he retired from being a cop, it was like he didn't know what to do with himself."

"How old was he when he retired?"

"Fifty-five. He had to. It's mandatory when you're a cop in New Jersey. Have to retire at fifty-five, if you make it that long."

"He didn't want to do part-time security or anything?"

"He tried. But he got bored with it pretty quickly. He started wandering then. That's what I called it. He'd wander around town looking for something to do. Sometimes he'd come to my house looking for something to fix. It was always good when he'd have to search out a solution, find the perfect tool or part or whatever. It used to drive Les nuts. But it seemed to give him purpose."

I pinched the bridge of my nose, regretting the furtive, whispered conversations with Les. He kept saying I should get Daddy a full psychiatric workup, maybe even get him medicated. I kept insisting I knew better.

"Then one day, I was taking the twins to the beach. They were around ten, maybe. I stopped by my parents' place because Joy was upset about leaving something there that she wanted. When I pulled up in front, my dad was lying on the sidewalk. I panicked."

"What was wrong?"

"Nothing. He was just lying there. He said he was looking at the grass from a closer angle. Said he was tired of looking at it from above."

"That's really odd." Nico reached out and took one of my hands. I stared at his hand, unable to remember him touching me so much. Could Angie have a point? No. He called me his friend, didn't he? Did I want more than that? His hand did feel good on mine. Possibly too good. "What happened?"

"It was God-awful hot," I said, grateful to get my head focused on something else. "I thought maybe he had had a heatstroke or was on the verge of one. I made him get in the car. I was going to take him to the hospital, but he insisted he was fine. I didn't know where to go or what to do. He said my mom went to the bookstore, but he didn't know which one, and the only one I knew of was the discount bookstore down in Ventnor." I smiled at him. "Turns out, she had told him she was going to the Bookman's. Their friends Miriam and Joseph Bookman had just come from Hammonton and had blueberries for her."

Nico grinned back at me and squeezed my hand.

"Anyway, I took him to the bookstore. Obviously, my mom wasn't there, but it felt good in the air conditioning, and he seemed okay. Not only that, but he was having fun shopping with the kids, so we stayed for a while. Asher found this book, an art book for children called *An Introduction to the Great Masters* or something like that. He and my dad sat at a little table to look at it. They were so cute together. You should have seen Daddy sitting with his knees almost up to his chin because the table was child-size."

Again, the tears welled up. I wiped them away with my free hand. "I think I'd just met you back then, so I don't know if you remember, but Asher was one of those kids who never sat still. It's hard to believe now, I know. But I used to joke he was faster than the speed of sound. He'd run down the hall to greet me, and I swear I'd feel his body slamming into me before I heard the sound of his feet. I remember looking at him that day, amazed that my father had him sitting so still, looking at that damned book." Nico scooted closer on the bench, his other hand moving to the small of my back. I felt a little part of me melt. I might have leaned into him more.

"My dad wanted to buy the book for Asher, but he asked if he could tear out the page with that painting on it." I continued mostly to stop thinking about Nico's intentions in touching me so much. "He took it and kept it on his refrigerator door."

"Wow. Yeah, that's really odd. And cool at the same time," Nico said.

I inhaled as his hand moved up to my shoulder.

"I don't remember him seeming like the wandering type," he said. There was no longing in his voice. He was simply comforting a friend with his touch. I needed to get over it. "He seemed normal to me."

"I know. The wandering lasted for years, though." His hand was cupping where my neck and shoulder met, touching my skin, making me want to press into him. "Then, something happened, and he was his old self again, the self he was when he was a cop. That's probably when you spent the most time with him. It was just the last year or so of his life. I can't help but think maybe he had a form of depression for a while and snapped out of it right before he...he..."

"I know," Nico said.

I still couldn't say the words. I didn't think I could ever outright say that my father had killed himself. That he had voluntarily taken himself away from us.

Nico pulled me to him and kissed my forehead. "Christ, you had one hell of a year, babe."

I inhaled the smell of him. It wasn't a smell I could name, as it wasn't cologne or scented deodorant. I picked up a hint of leather from his coat, and...just Nico. Just warm and strong, Nico. Too warm and strong. I pulled away and stood. I had to before I made a fool of myself.

"Yeah, well, I made it through." I smiled at him. *Today is the day.* "Right?"

"Right." He stood, too. "You hungry? They got an awesome restaurant here."

"I am, but are you going to give me grief if I order a salad?"

"No, you had fried shrimp last night. You want a salad today, you can have a salad."

We headed back toward the stairs when my cell phone vibrated. I took it out of my purse and looked at the caller's name.

"Oh hell. It's Asher's probation officer. This can't be good."

UNLIKELY PAIRS

I could never figure out why Asher was allowed to live. Back on that fateful day, the day after Labor Day, I was in the kitchen. I had just gotten home from work and the kids from school. I stood leaning against the sink, staring out the window without seeing anything. My mind just couldn't process any external stimuli. All its resources were tied up trying to figure out how to tell Joy and Ash that not only was their dog dead, but that their father and I had a brief conversation on my lunch break, and now he wouldn't be living in our home anymore.

Joy had bounded in, opened the refrigerator, took out a soda, and said: "The police will be arriving soon. But don't worry, Mom, I explained how the whole operation is Ash's and has nothing to do with you." She popped open the top of her soda can and left the kitchen.

"You what?" I said, going after her. She headed up the stairs. "What are you talking about?"

Before she could answer, there was a loud, urgent knocking on my front door. I knew it was never a good sign when people pounded on your door instead of ringing the bell, but I opened it anyway.

The police confiscated an assortment of paraphernalia from Ash's bedroom and the crawl space in the attic above it. Then I had the privilege of watching my son get handcuffed and hauled off to juvenile detention. He was charged with selling marijuana, and that was back when the state wasn't even considering making it legal for medical conditions.

I had enough social worker friends with enough connections that he got off with nine months' probation. I didn't think that even qualified as a slap on the wrist, but I didn't care. I had to keep my baby out of jail. What I never understood, though, is why his dealer-supplier never came after him or suspected him of snitching. After my eye-opening conversation with Nico, I began to wonder whether Les had more powerful connections than I did.

As it turned out, Rick, Ash's probation officer, was a really likable guy who agreed with me that Ash was just experimenting a little too much and was an overall good kid. Apparently, his daughter, Gabi, liked Ash, too. They went to school together. Rick had called me at the museum to ask if I was okay with Ash dating his daughter. He was okay with it.

"So, let me get this straight," Angie said, the following Wednesday evening after I explained everything to her. She rolled her head to the side and rested it on the edge of the hot tub, and looked at me. "Your son's probation officer called to make sure it was okay with *you* that your son was dating *his* daughter?"

"Yes. Rick was worried I would think there was some kind of conflict of interest."

"Still, shouldn't that have been the other way around? Shouldn't *you* be asking him if *he* was okay with it?"

"One would think," I laughed. "But you know Asher. When he makes an effort to open his mouth and talk, he can charm the pants off anyone." I choked. "Jesus! Did I just say that about my own son?"

"But it's true," Angie laughed with me. The timer on the tub buzzed, and the water stopped moving.

"Ugh. That means it's time for me to get showered and dressed so I can go pick him up. He's at their house now." I climbed out of the hot tub. "I'm just glad he's talking to someone. Rick thinks he's got quite the sense of humor. I know he used to, but I can't seem to get more than two syllables at a time from the kid."

"He's a teen boy." Angie wrapped herself in a towel. "I don't think they're supposed to talk to their moms that much at his age."

"And Joy's not supposed to want to be in the same room as her mom?" I asked. "Is that normal?"

"It was for me." Angie grinned.

Instead of power walking, Angie and I had worked out in the condo's gym that week for forty-five minutes each night and then rewarded ourselves with fifteen minutes in the hot tub. Meanwhile, Joy had started swimming laps in the pool, which was right beside the hot tub. As soon as we would get settled in the steamy water, she would get out of the pool, dry off, and leave. After all, we were in the same room as her.

However, she always gave me a "See ya" before heading upstairs, which, for her, was a pleasantry. I liked the fact that she was swimming again. Granted, it was only the third day she lived at the condo, but she had swum every evening, which meant she hadn't been loading up on the eyeliner when she was home. And, I overheard her tell a friend on the phone that she was going to stop dying her hair black because the chlorine would make it look green. I knew there were shampoos to help counteract the chlorine, but I saw no reason to point that out to her.

Joy was on the house phone when Angie and I made our way back to my unit. It had to be my mother. She's the reason we still have a house phone. We can't seem to get her to call a cell.

"Okay, Grandmom," Joy said into the phone, holding her hand up to stop me from speaking. "I'll tell Mom you called when she gets in." She turned her back to me and listened. "I know...I won't...Love you, too. Bye." Joy clicked the phone off and returned it to its receiver before looking at me.

"Trust me, you didn't want to talk to her." She went to the sofa, plopped down, and turned the TV on. Either she thought I was going straight to the shower, or there was something else going on. And why had she done something kind for me? She could have easily handed over the phone and left. Something was wrong.

"Was she in a mood?" Angie asked, going through her gym bag on the dining table.

"Oh yeah, and uh, Mom? It's not my fault, but, like, you gotta throw her a surprise party when she gets back." She held the remote up, scrolling through the guide on the TV.

"A what?" I asked. Slowly, I eased into a chair. I felt like a snake hunter trying to blend in with her environment so as not to scare off the rarely seen Joy-species sunning itself on the sofa-shaped rock.

"She kept going on and on about some lady in Boca who just had a surprise party for her seventieth birthday. I guess all her family was there, people from South America and everything. So Grandmom made me promise to tell her what kind of dress she'll need to buy for her sixtieth. She said she knew you were probably already working on it, and she wants to be prepared."

"No!" I shouted. Angie burst out laughing. "As if that's what I need on my plate right now."

"It's not my fault!" Joy yelled.

"Pumpkin, I know it's not. I didn't mean it that way." I rubbed my sweaty forehead. "Ange! What the hell am I going to do?"

"Sounds like you're going to throw a party. And I'm going to get in the shower now." She headed into Joy's bathroom.

"Joy, I really am sorry if you thought I was upset with you," I said, wondering if I should be worried because she still hadn't left the room, though I was still in it. "She's a good grandmother to you, I know. But as a mother, she drives me nuts."

"Yeah."

"Are you thinking you know the feeling?"

She smirked.

She must be doing drugs. I peered down at her, unsure if that would be so terrible. After all, she seemed almost close to being near the proximity of contentedness in my presence. Maybe there was a legal equivalent I could get prescribed for her.

We watched a TV show for several minutes, an activity that should have brought me great relief as it was the first time in months that we'd spent any time together. But it only made me worry.

"Uh, Mom?" she eventually said, but continued to look at the TV.

"Yes." My stomach twitched.

"Like, there's something else." She flicked through the channels.

"What pumpkin?" Something was definitely wrong.

"There's uh…" She refused to make eye contact with me. "I need to tell you something."

I panicked.

"Oh my God! You're pregnant." I cupped my face in my hands.

"Jesus Christ, Mom!" She threw the remote on the couch and stood. "I'm not that fucked up!"

"Don't say 'fuck' in front of me!" I yelled and stood with her.

"Why the bleep not?" Her hands were clenched into fists by her side in a way that brought me back in time to when I used to watch Angie and our mother fight. Angie used to stand like that and, like her, Joy was cute when she was mad.

"I don't know, pumpkin. I almost said because my mother told me never to use that word in front of her." I started laughing. "Oh God! I'm turning into her! Maybe I'm the one who's fucked up." I crumpled back in the chair, laughing.

"What's so funny in here?" Angie came out with wet hair.

"My mom's losing it," Joy said.

"Good thing you got me, kid." Angie picked up her cell phone and read something on the screen. "Though you know what? I think I'm going gay."

"Despite the fact that you're born gay and you can't 'go' gay, I might support you on that one." I wiped my eyes.

"Just might? I thought we sisters stuck together."

"It depends on whether it's considered homicide when your news kills our mother."

"Ha. But really, she might prefer that over the shit I'm attracting with online dating. Look what they let out of the psych ward in the three days I've been on this site."

I took her phone and scrolled through the profiles of the men to give Joy and me a minute to recover from my lunatic accusation. "Wow, yeah, slim pickings."

"All I want is someone with stable employment, or at least who's employable, and nice, and attractive. Is that so hard to find?" Angie took the phone back.

"Go pick up Asher for me."

"What?"

"Yeah, Aunt Angie!" Joy had been heading toward her room. She stopped and turned to face us. Her eyes were wide and she was actually smiling. "His probation officer is hot."

"How hot?" Angie asked.

"He's, like, Latin," Joy said. "Dark hair, dark eyes, dark skin, *really* good teeth. Muscular. Kind of tall, but not too tall. He's got really broad shoulders and—"

"And he's divorced," I interrupted. Joy's enthusiasm and apparent close observation of her brother's forty-plus-year old probation officer disturbed me.

"Employed, hot, and divorced?" She raised her eyebrows. "Nice?"

"He's good to my kid."

"Do I have time to dry my hair?"

While she finished getting ready, I called Rick to tell him who was picking up Ash. Joy locked herself in her room for the night, so I picked up the phone again to call my mother, all the while worrying about what my daughter wanted to talk to me about.

Angie called my cell when I was in the break room on Friday morning.

"Oh, my, *God*," she said. "Not only is he nice, good-looking looking and employed, but he's funny too."

"Does this mean you spoke to Rick again? Already?" I poured a cup of coffee.

"Yes. He just called. We're going out tomorrow night."

I sat at a table. "How'd he get your number?"

"I gave it to him on Wednesday. Have you totally forgotten how to date?"

I sipped my coffee and apparently took longer to answer than she thought was appropriate.

"You have, haven't you?"

"It doesn't matter, anyway. It's hard to date right now. When am I supposed to squeeze it in?"

"What are you doing this weekend?"

"My kids both have a bunch of friends coming over to watch some movie tonight. Can you believe I'm hosting a coed sleepover? I'm scared shitless."

"That's not what I asked. What are *you* going to do tonight?"

"I can't leave them alone. I'll be in my room watching something else on my TV with the volume turned down so I can hear everything *they're* doing." I took a long swig of coffee.

"Why don't you call Nico and ask him to join you in your bedroom?"

I spit my coffee back into my mug.

"I can't do that!"

"Why not? Wasn't he just all touchy-feely? Isn't that how he was at the museum?"

"Well, yeah, but I'm not sure what his intentions were," I said as Rachel entered the break room. She raised her eyebrows at me. I blushed.

"Then find out. My money is on him being willing to take it up a notch," Angie said.

"If that's true, then he'll let me know. I couldn't ask him out."

"Why not? It's been the twenty-first century for over a decade now. Women can and do ask men out."

"Yes, but not my generation."

"We're from the same generation, remember? Girls did it when we were in high school."

"Fast girls did it."

"Hey! I did it."

"Exactly my point," I laughed. "Anyway, I have to go." I ended the call and tried to focus my thoughts on Rachel. We were meeting to discuss her future at the center.

I had to admit, I missed Nico. He had dropped me off after the museum, kissed me on the cheek, and, as usual, said: "See you around, babe." It's how we folks in Jersey greet and say goodbye. We kiss and say something meaningless. He'd been saying good-bye like that to me for years, and I kept reminding myself he always referred to me as his friend. But, while his friendship meant the world to me, it was getting harder for me to admit I only wanted to be his friend.

"You okay?" Rachel asked, sitting opposite me at the table.

"What?"

"You looked like you were somewhere else."

"I'm thinking maybe it's time I get a new dog."

"Really?"

"Yeah, you know, for companionship."

"Aren't dogs a lot of work?"

"Well, yes, particularly when they're puppies, but…" I slugged back the last of my coffee. "I still miss my dog." Sure, puppies are a lot of work, but training one would give me something else to focus on besides how good Nico smells.

"Dating might be less work."

"You sound like my sister. I just hung up on that conversation. I'm not ready for dating yet." I fumbled with the files on the table. "Anyway, I have good news for you. Or at least I think it's good. You might not."

"If it means I get a paycheck, it'll be the best news."

What a relief for me. Edna had given notice. We still had to go through the legal motions of posting ads as if we were really recruiting, but Rachel had the job if she wanted it and would take a much lower pay rate than Edna had worked for.

Rachel wanted it and apparently had cheap rent.

"Thanks," I said. "That's such a load off my back."

"No problem, just one thing?"

"What?"

"Can I still assist you in Monday's MOF meetings? Those guys are growing on me."

"That would be great. You've grown on them, too. We'll definitely figure it out. Besides, you know it's not good to make sudden changes with them."

"Yeah there's that and…" she put her hand on mine over the files. "There's something up with that new member. I don't feel comfortable leaving him alone with you. I don't like the way he looks at you."

I smiled at her. If I were a true professional, I would have said something to allay her worries. Instead, I'm human.

"Thank you so much. I can't figure out what's up with him either. I really appreciate you having my back."

"Good. I mean, I think dating might be good for you if you want companionship, but not him, okay?"

"No worries, there!" I laughed.

We sorted the files, divvying up the ones she'd need for her classes and groups. Her cell dinged. She glanced down at it and giggled before sending a text in reply.

"That's someone *I'm* dating," she grinned and picked up the files I'd set aside for her.

"Hey, Rachel." I scratched my head. "Can I ask you something woman-to-woman?"

"Sure." She was young, very pretty, and smart. I figured she'd be a good one to ask.

"Do you ever ask boys out?"

"No. I think that'd be illegal," she smirked. "But I have asked guys my age, you know, *men*, out."

"Really? How do you do it?"

She laughed again. "How well do you know this guy?"

"Really well. I mean, we've been friends for a long time." I could feel the heat emanating from my cheeks. "I can't freaking believe I'm having this conversation. This is insane! I'm too old for this."

"I'm glad you're doing it. The people I call my parents are really my mom and step-dad. The smartest thing my mom ever did was date after my dad left. My step-dad might ride me hard about being responsible, but don't ever tell anyone I said this, I need him to ride me hard that way."

"Well, I've been out of the dating world for a long time. And when I was in it, I didn't date much. I married when I was twenty-two."

"Really? Why?"

"I'm not sure anymore. But you know, when you're young, you think you have all the answers."

"I don't think that. All I know is I want to have as much fun as possible before I'm too old to have any."

"That's a much healthier attitude than mine was." I drained my coffee cup. "So, what do I do? I mean, I don't even know if he'd want to be more than friends."

"How often do you talk to him?"

"I don't know. Usually once or twice a week. He'll either pop into my place or he'll text me to meet him somewhere. Last Saturday, he took me to Philly, to the art museum."

"Then why is it hard for *you* to call *him* up and say 'hey, let's have dinner tomorrow'?"

"Because I'm a girl! It's not the way I was raised. Ugh!" I hit myself in the forehead. "It's like every day, I find myself turning into my mother more and more. I don't want to be that woman."

"Then call him, now."

I waited for her to leave before I picked up my cell phone. I had just scrolled to Nico's name and was about to press the call button, but then Stacey and the whole HR team entered the room. I barely had the nerve to say the words out loud to him; there was no way I could do it in front of all of them. But if I waited until I got back to my cubicle, I'd probably talk myself out of it.

My kids don't like my chili cuz I put 2 much garlic in it, I texted him and gathered my cup and files. That was a safe thing to say, I thought. That sentence could have many meanings. Well, it could have only one meaning, but I could segue it into several different topics. I chewed on my lips all the way back to my cubicle, worrying about how he would interpret the sentence.

My phone beeped with his reply as I sat at my desk.

No such thing as 2 much garlic.

That's what I think. But it's hard to make enough for just 1. I held my breath as I typed.

When u making it? His response was immediate.

Tomorrow? My heart was pounding, and I realized I was smiling.

Time?

6:30ish.

C u then.

Wow. I'd just asked a boy out on a date for the first time in my life. I wasn't sure if the boy knew I had asked him on a date, but that was okay with me. Better than okay. In fact, I was tingling all over the way I did when I was sixteen and hunky Kevin Flynn asked me for my number. Only this time, my dad wasn't there to forbid me from going out with him. He was a bad egg, Daddy had said about Kevin, and he was right. The man wound up in jail with a life sentence before he was twenty-one.

MORE THAN CHILI HEATING UP

Nico walked in, without knocking, just a few minutes before 6:30. I had put his name, along with Angie's and probation officer Rick's on a list with the doorman downstairs, saying they could come up at any time. However, Les would have to wait for the doorman to buzz me and be given my permission. I'm sure it was a sadistic pleasure, but I didn't care. I liked the power that little tidbit gave me over him.

"Mmmm, smells good," Nico said by way of greeting. He kissed me hello, on the cheek, the way a friend does. "I could smell it all the way down the hall." He handed me a bottle of wine and turned to take off his coat. I took the wine into the kitchen, thinking maybe I should look into that online dating business. Angie and I were opposites after all. If it didn't work for her, that probably meant I stood a chance of it working for me.

To accompany the chili, I'd made garlic bread and a salad of mixed spring greens, walnuts, and bleu cheese. I pulled the strawberry vinaigrette I'd put together out of the refrigerator and went to the counter, where the salad was waiting to be tossed with it.

"You need to eat quickly?" Nico searched through the drawers in the kitchen.

"You're not hungry?" I handed him a wine bottle opener.

"Thanks." He took the opener. "I'm a little hungry, but why don't we just sit for a few and relax, huh? Where are the kids?"

"Joy's sleeping over at a friend's and I have to pick Ash up at eleven." Asher had gone to the movies with a bunch of friends, probation-officer-daughter Gabi among them, and then they were all going out for pizza afterward. More pizza. It seemed so unfair to me. Two nights in a row, those kids were eating pizza. And not a one of them was overweight.

Rick had picked Asher up and took him and Gabi to meet the others. I was to get them afterward. Rick looked embarrassed when he came to the door. I could tell he wanted to say something to me about Angie, but he didn't know what. I knew how he felt. My sister was dating my son's girlfriend's father; it almost sounded like incest.

"So we have time," Nico said. He'd found the glasses and was about to pour the wine. "Oh, wait, I guess this needs to sit, right? Since it's red?"

"What kind of Italian are you?" I smiled at him. "Of course, it needs to sit. Would you like a beer while you wait?"

"Yes, because that's the kind of Italian I am. The kind who likes an Irish ale while he waits." He opened the refrigerator and pulled out two bottles of Guinness.

"But it's a good wine." I looked at the label. "It should go well with the chili."

"We'll save it for dinner, then." He went into the living area and sat on the sofa. I followed him, but instead of sitting next to him, I ambled over to look out the sliders. Outside, the ocean was a dark, purple-blue color. The not-quite-full moon shone a streak across the water toward us. Lights were on down below, and despite the fact that a cold front was coming through and it was below forty degrees with strong, gale-force winds, there were a number of people strolling down the boardwalk.

"Looking forward to eating out on your balcony?" Nico's voice was close behind me.

"Yes, I am." I took a long inhale, wishing I was brave enough to lean back far enough to find out how close he was.

"I'm looking forward to you barbecuing out there," he said. "Summers aren't summers without Lucy's barbecues." He put his hand on the small of my back.

"Barbecues might be off." I gave a small laugh. I don't know why. "I'm not sure I'll be doing them this year."

"Why not?"

"Well, for one thing, Les always manned the grill." I felt his thumb rub back and forth on my back. I wanted to close my eyes and rest against him so badly that I knew for sure I could never invite him up again, at least not when the kids were out. In fact, maybe I needed to put some distance between us somehow until I could take being just friends again.

"You don't need Les. I'll man your grill."

If only, I thought as an energy buzzed up from my womb to my breasts. I cleared my throat. "Anyway, I can't get a grill. It's against fire code to have them on the balcony here."

"Really? I didn't know that." His hand slid up to my shoulder. I caught my breath. "If I'd known, I would have found you a different place." He gave my shoulder a squeeze, a good-natured, friendly squeeze, and went back to the sofa.

"I thought maybe I'd still do a party of some sort anyway." I slowly turned to him, trying to control my breath. "I haven't been too social since the split. I think it's time I get back in the swing of things, you know?" And maybe find someone else to man my nonexistent grill.

I dallied at the table. Unable to say anything, I pretended to move the place settings around.

"You okay?" he asked.

"Yeah, why?"

"I don't know. You don't seem yourself."

"Oh, sorry. I'm fine." Still standing, I took a swig of the beer.

I stared into my bottle as if it would channel my father's energy. He never had a problem talking, particularly when he had a Guinness in his hand. But then again, he probably never struggled with his feelings for Nico.

"Come here." Nico patted the sofa beside him.

Too willing, I complied. I sat next to him, actually leaned against him. It was his fault. He had put his arm around my shoulder. What else could I do? A fresh-baked soft pretzel would have been easier to resist.

When did he start doing this? Had he always touched me so much? My body buzzed. The moment could have been delicious. I could have just closed my eyes and sunk into him, but I was too caught up in trying to figure out what was going on. It certainly wasn't normal behavior for us. We'd never snuggled on the sofa. Never. Had he interpreted my message as an invitation for a date? Or was that wishful thinking?

"When was the last time you just sat and relaxed?" he asked, his voice soft and comforting. "Doesn't this feel good? I know I needed it. Thanks for inviting me over."

"It's my pleasure." So very much my pleasure that I can't ever do it again, unless it was his pleasure, too. How was I to know if it was his pleasure too? And who said I was relaxed? I was near panic.

"You look settled in. You happy here?"

"I think so. Still something of an adjustment." Yes, Internet dating could be good for me, I thought. Maybe being around strange men would help me remember what normal behavior is.

"As it should be." He took a long drink of his beer. "Listen, I have to be in Trenton for breakfast tomorrow morning."

"Trenton?" I turned to look at him, which made his arm fall off me and gave me a topic that wasn't related to me, to us, to focus on. "What time are you getting up?"

"Too early," he smirked. "It's a breakfast security gig for a pretty important client."

"You know, most normal people only worry about the eggs Benedict being dangerous at breakfast." Yes, that's what I needed, for him to let go of me.

"I don't deal with most normal people," he laughed. "I love how you always make me laugh, Luce. Really. It's been a tough week, and I appreciate it." He touched my face with the back of his hand. I clenched my jaw to keep my bottom lip from quivering. I needed to tell the man to keep his hands to himself. I just couldn't figure out how to make my mouth work when my skin was in contact with his. "I stayed in town all week," he continued, "you know, in case you needed me or something." He dropped his fingers from my face and took hold of my empty hand. My other one had a death grip on my beer bottle. "I should be back by early afternoon. I know this sounds shitty, but do you think you could stay inside until I text you that I'm back in town? I just don't want you to be out walking in the morning and bump into the Fabians when I can't get here."

I took another drink and found my voice.

"You know, I'd been telling myself they were a non-issue all week." I tried to will my hand to move out of his. "There haven't been any more surprise visits from Enzo. And Aldo didn't show up at group therapy on Monday. He hasn't been to any of the other classes, either." I grinned. "Except for all of Dave's classes."

"Did you see him?" Nico let go of me to turn more toward me on the sofa. I took advantage of the break to completely bar myself from him touching me. I faced him, with both my feet on the sofa, my beer in my right hand up on my knees, near my chin, and my left hand tucked between my stomach and thighs. I wasn't comfortable, and I probably looked awkward, but he couldn't naturally, easily, touch me.

"No, I didn't see him. He wasn't really there." I sipped the Guinness. "There's been a bunch of budget cuts at the center, and more are in the works. Everyone's trying hard to make themselves look more important than everyone else. Apparently, Dave Blumenthal happens to be someone who really needs his job. All his classes were filled to maximum capacity. Aldo Fabian was on the sign-in sheets for all of them, as well as a few people who came back from the grave."

Nico laughed. "I haven't heard you talk about your job in a long while. Tell me about some craziness. I need some laughs."

So we were friends all evening. We laughed, we ate, we drank, we cleaned up. It could have been Angie with me, except I never longed for her touch to mean more than it did. Eventually, I was able to just relax into being around him, the way I used to, and I stopped obsessing over his intentions. I even forgot to worry about Enzo and Aldo until something clicked in my brain when I had to go get the kids, and he was leaving.

"If you want me to stay indoors tomorrow morning," I said as I locked my condo door behind us. "Does that mean you think they could be a problem for me? The Fabian family?"

We went down the hall to the elevators before he answered me.

"I wish I could say for sure, but I don't know. Les wants to meet with me tomorrow afternoon, though. And you don't know that, okay? You know nothing about that."

"I got it."

"He said he's having a problem. Been hearing about people snooping around on him. He's hoping I could look into who it might be. If they are totally different from your guys, I'll rest a little easier."

We went down the elevator to the parking garage floor in silence. Nico walked me to my van, and then my friend bent down, kissed me on the cheek, and said: "See you around, babe."

I smirked at him and bit my lip. Disappointment washed through me. My breath was too shaky for me to reply. I silently willed him to turn around and walk away.

Our eyes locked in the fluorescent light of the garage. He stared so hard into me I couldn't look away, though I was embarrassed knowing he could see what I was feeling, what I was wishing would happen.

I swallowed, struggling for the strength to turn around and open my van door. He reached up and put his hand on my cheek. He held it there briefly, then slid it around to the back of my head and pulled me in to kiss him, on the lips, softly, sweetly.

We stood, foreheads pressed against each other's, while my heart tried to beat into his chest. My hands found their way to his shoulders. After a long moment, he kissed me gently again and wrapped his other arm around me, holding me in tight. I held equally hard to him.

"Luce," he whispered, his lips moving to my ear. "Oh, Lucy, baby. We gotta be real careful, okay? I mean, really careful. We can't just...just...I mean, we can. Yes, we can. I think there's this...this great thing in front of us. It could be incredible. It could be perfect. But we have this great friendship that we could destroy with it, too. I don't want to lose you in any way." I could feel him inhale deeply. "You know what I mean?" He pulled away from me and looked in my eyes again.

"Yeah. I know exactly what you mean."

We were more than friends, and he didn't know what to do about it, either.

STRANGE RELATIONS

"Enzo Fabian is here to see you," Gayle called through the intercom on Monday morning.

"Thanks, Gayle. You can send him back." I grabbed my cell and texted the news to Nico.

"Good morning, Mrs. Womzak," Enzo said as he entered my cubicle. This time, he was in a white mock-turtleneck and black jeans, carrying a black leather jacket over his arm. "Is it still Mrs. Womzak?"

"Yes." I had yet to clarify with my kids how they'd feel about me switching back to my maiden name. I hadn't been able to have an actual conversation with them yet, aside from when I questioned Joy about her menstrual cycle. "Is your father all right?"

"Oh, he's fine." Enzo sat comfortably. He didn't pull at his clothes or smooth out wrinkles. He didn't pretend to be interested in a brochure on my desk. Apparently, he'd decided he needed to give me a new approach. "In fact, he'll be in that group thing this morning. I was just hoping I could talk to you about him." His voice had a more relaxed manner, too.

I glanced at the clock on my phone. The MOFs would start in seven minutes.

"We only have a few minutes. Is there something in particular you're concerned about?"

He grinned. "My father has some secrets that the rest of the family almost knows about, you know what I mean?"

"No. But he sure does seem obsessed with them."

"What do you mean?"

"Nothing, really. He brought up secrets the last time he came to group. Would you know what he's talking about?"

"We know he's hiding something from us. And we would like to encourage him to tell us about it. You know, let him get it off his chest."

I waited.

"I understand that sometimes people don't tell all their secrets to family members for a number of reasons," he continued. "But if you had the feeling your father was hiding something from you that he felt, I don't know, maybe guilty about hiding? Maybe you'd want to let him know that he could tell you anything and that you'd love him no matter what."

"Perhaps. But I'm of the belief that you should let people know that, regardless of whether you think they have a secret." I thought of Les and what he'd hidden from me. "If, of course, you really love them."

"True." Enzo glanced at his watch. "But maybe exposing the secret would give him peace, you know? So I was wondering, what would *you* have done to encourage your father in a similar situation? Did you ever think your father kept secrets? Did he tell you some? Or did you ever encourage him to confess, maybe to someone else like a therapist or a good friend?"

Referring to my father in the past tense was one coincidence too many.

"Actually, Mr. Fabian, my father kept a lot of secrets from me. In fact, I *never* knew what Santa would bring."

"Ha! You're a funny woman, Mrs. Womzak."

"Sorry, I'm late, Lucy," Rachel entered my cubicle with her head bent over her phone. She looked up. "Oh, sorry again. I didn't realize you had someone in here."

"No apologies are necessary, Rachel. This is Mr. Fabian's son." Her face registered disbelief. I wondered if Enzo saw it as clearly as I did. "He was just leaving as it's time for us to set up group therapy."

I made sure Enzo left the cubicle in front of me. We went through administration together and entered the common area just as Nico waltzed in. Instantly, he wrapped his arms around me.

"Hey there," he said, kissing me on the lips. "I was hoping you had a few minutes for coffee."

"Oh, I'm sorry," I said to him. "I'd love to, but I'm about to go into group therapy now."

"Can we do lunch, then?"

"Sure."

"Text me when you're out." He pulled me into a tight hug. "Is that him?" he whispered into my ear.

"Yes."

"See you around, babe." He kissed me on the lips again and walked away.

I turned to find Rachel and Enzo staring at me.

"Excuse me," I said. "He's a little exuberant."

"Looks as if you rectified things," Enzo said before leaving.

"Soooooo, I guess that means you asked him out," Rachel said as we arranged the chairs.

"You guessed right."

"I guess that means you'll do it again?"

"I hope that means I won't *have* to do it again." I took my seat. She sat beside me.

"That serious that quick?"

"Not that quick. I've known the man for years. And it's not serious." I didn't think so, anyway.

I'd repeated what he'd said to me in the garage to Angie, and then I'd repeated it over and over and over in my head all day on Sunday as I chauffeured the kids to every nook and corner of Atlantic City. Trying to figure out what kind of relationship we now had was such a giddy, heady, and nerve-racking experience. I was glad I wasn't a teenager. I didn't want the delicious feelings to be normal.

Rachel and I watched the seniors enter the room and go through their chair-selection processes. Last week, when Aldo was absent, we had a follow-up on the pet talk. The seniors behaved like their typical selves, fully expressing whatever they wanted, however they wanted. Mr. Hanson, who had on blue nail polish, very red lipstick, and a white George Washington wig in honor of Presidents' Day, announced he'd made arrangements for his nephew to take care of his cat should he have any problems. Mr. Moffat had told us that his housekeeper would call every morning to be sure he was still alive and that she would take Butch, his poodle, should Mr. Moffat die first. However, if Butch should be the first to go, he would be freeze-dried and kept in a glass case until Mr. Moffat went. They would then be interred together. No one was able to continue the pet conversation after that.

This week, I was intent on getting back to the topic of

communicating with our doctors.

I didn't know if it was because Enzo had brought up my father, but I kept thinking of him while I watched my seniors finagle a chair. He was like many of them after he retired, though he was young compared to the ones in the room with me. He wandered around, not quite knowing why he was still alive and not quite sure what to do with himself. But then, he snapped out of it. I'd even mentioned to Angie that it seemed as if he had found a reason to live. For over a year, he was his old self: full of jokes and funny stories, always ready to lift a beer in toast, the life of the party, the one with strong shoulders and good advice. Until one day, he was found dead. It didn't make sense, but his note assured us it was suicide.

"Lucy?" I heard Rachel say.

"What? I'm sorry, I was lost in thought."

"Thinking about your new man?"

Mr. Hanson dashed to the seat next to me.

"You're seeing someone new?" he asked. "Tell me about him. What's he look like, honey?" He sat, clad in a sparkly black, very tight, long-sleeve T-shirt and black dress slacks tucked into red women's cowboy boots. He'd crossed his skinny legs and dangled his clutched hands over his knees. He wore bright-orange nail polish and too-thick mascara. I couldn't help but think he was proof positive that not all gay men have good fashion sense.

I started laughing. "Mr. Hanson! I am not here to tell you about my private life."

"Why not? We tell you about ours," Aldo chimed in. He sat in the chair opposite me again.

"Because this is your dime." I looked hard at him. "It's my job to listen to you and help you."

"Oh, but honey, you have real exciting news," Mr. Hanson wiggled my hand.

"I'm glad she got an exciting life," Mrs. Elliot said, sitting next to him. "Someone around here need to." I liked how she looked out for Mr. Hanson. He had lost his Johnny less than a year ago and was still grieving him hard. They'd been together for close to fifty years. Mr. Hanson wound up crying nearly every week, and either Mrs. Elliot or Mrs. O'Leary, or both, would make sure to sit next to him when he needed comforting.

By now, all the other regulars had seated themselves, I was sure, to grill me about my exciting life.

"Well," I said. "I hate to start today's meeting this way, but I do have some sad news for you."

They gazed at me, silent.

"Do you remember when Mrs. Elliot mentioned a couple of weeks ago that she believed Harriet Millers had passed?"

No one answered me.

"She was in the hospital at the time," I continued. "And I'm sorry to say, but her family called to tell us she has been moved into hospice. If any of you would like to contact her or send a card or note, her daughter has given me permission to give you her information. Just see me after the group."

"Was it the salt?" Mrs. Elliot asked after a few quiet seconds.

"No, I don't think so. As we all know, Mrs. Miller had a host of health issues she'd been dealing with for many years. I think they all finally took their toll."

"Which is why I am in the utmost, perfect health for a man my age," Mr. Moffat said. "The better you take care of yourself, the longer you will live. It only makes sense."

"Unless you get hit by a bus," Mr. Thomas said. "I dare you to walk in front of a moving bus and see how well you survive that."

"Well then," I interrupted, "let's use Mrs. Miller's experience as inspiration, shall we?"

"Inspiration to die, Lucy?" Mr. Schwartz's mouth was wide open. "Is that what you want us to do? How could you?"

"No! Goodness, Mr. Schwartz, that's *not* what I'm saying."

"She wouldn't have a job if we all done up and died," Mrs. Elliot said.

"There are plenty of other seniors to take our place," Mrs. O'Leary said as she knitted.

"Everybody," I worked hard not to laugh. "Everybody, please. I do not want any of you to die. And it's not a matter of job security. I love you all. Honestly."

Mr. Hanson threw his arms around me. "And you mean so much to me, honey." The tears rolled. The sobbing began. "You all do. I don't know how I would have gotten through this year without you. And you, Rachel." He stood to give her a hug. "And you, Freddy." He hugged Mr. Schwartz, and Mr. Schwartz hugged him back with stiff arms. "And you—"

"Yes, we have a lovely, supportive group," I said. "But we need to be in our seats, Mr. Hanson."

He returned to his place beside me, wiping his eyes. Mrs. Elliot took him by the chin to clean the black streaks of tear-diluted mascara running down his face.

"What I meant by letting Mrs. Miller be an inspiration to us is that she was always open and communicative with her doctors." I looked around the group, waiting for someone to say something.

"I know, when I'm at the doctor," Rachel offered. "Sometimes I have to remind myself that he is there to help me and that it is his professional duty not to be judgmental."

She would have received more communication from fish.

"Have any of you felt like you couldn't tell your doctor something?"

"I don't know any Dr. Something," Mrs. Dimiccio said. "That's a funny name. Is he new here?"

"She's wanting to know if you're keeping something from your doctor," Mrs. O'Leary explained.

"Mrs. Elliot," I went for the direct approach. "What about you? Do you think it's possible you're letting your opinion of your doctor prevent you from getting the best health care he can offer?"

"Is my doctor here, now?" Mrs. Dimiccio asked. "Why?"

"Your doctor ain't here now," Mrs. Elliot told her.

"Then why are you talking about him?" Mrs. Dimiccio wanted to know.

"I think he's a good one," I told her. "It's important to have a good doctor, one you can tell anything to."

"I find wool yarn to be itchy these days," Mrs. O'Leary said. "Do you think that's the sort of thing I should tell my doctor, Lucy? I never used to think it was itchy. But now I must buy cotton." Her long, gray swath puddled at her feet. It had to be nearing ten feet, and while it was all gray, you could see differences. You could tell when she had changed yarns, presumably after she'd finished a skein.

"You could be developing an allergy to it," I offered. "But yes, that is something like what I mean. If you notice any changes at all in your body, you should definitely discuss it with your doctor."

"I usually have no problems discussing things with my doctor," Aldo said. "My family is another story. Lucy, did your older relatives easily talk to you?"

"What?" My arms prickled with goose bumps, but I wasn't cold.

"Anyone here have problems talking to their family?" Aldo asked the group, but he continued to stare directly at me.

"Good Lord, yes," Mrs. Elliot said. "My niece, who lives with me, doesn't listen to nothing I say. And her kids! They're even worse."

"That's what's wrong with America's youth today," Mr. Thomas said. "They never listen to their elders."

"Maybe because their elders don't know what they are talking about," Mr. Moffat replied. "At least some of them don't."

"Some of the youth listen to us," Mr. Fabian suggested. "Right, Lucy? You listened to your elders, didn't you? Did they tell you their secrets?"

"I don't think I'd be considered today's youth," I said after blinking several times in silence. "At any rate, we were talking specifically about health issues and our doctors."

"Yes," he said. "But sometimes our issues are with our family members. Sometimes, maybe we feel we need to keep something from our loved ones. Sometimes, maybe, as we get closer to dying, we're stuck telling them things we'd been keeping inside for a long time. Perhaps you've had an experience like that. Maybe with a parent?"

I swear the man was looking right through me. I felt a rushing in my ears, as if I were about to faint. I reached out and grabbed Rachel's arm in case I fell over.

"You know," Rachel said. "I think I am considered America's youth. And I am a little insulted that you all here think I don't listen to you." She made eye contact with me. I smiled a *thank-you* to her.

"Honey!" Mr. Hanson yelled. "I am *so* sorry! We all are."

"You a good one," Mrs. Elliot nodded to her.

"Well, let's get back to the point," I said with my insides trembling. "Specifically, you, Mrs. Elliot, have you spoken to your doctor lately?"

"You know," she sulked in her chair, "talking to her doctor ain't keeping Harriet alive right now."

Nico sent me a text while I was still in with the group: Interesting turn of events. Meet me for lunch at Teplitzky's?

He was waiting for me in a booth.

"Hi." I approached him.

He stood, pulled on the front of my jacket, making me bend over the table, and kissed me on the lips. I liked our new version of friendship.

"Hi yourself." He sat. "I took the liberty of ordering us some pretzels."

"Thanks. But what will you eat?" I grinned as I slid into the booth.

"Coffee?" a waitress who seemed to have materialized out of thin air asked. She held a carafe in her hand.

"Sure." I let her pour some into the cup already on the table. She refilled Nico's. "So you had something interesting happen to you," I said after she finished. "I had something interesting happen to me. It's been an interesting day all the way around." I paused to sip the too-hot java. "But you go first, did you follow Enzo?"

"I did." He grinned. "I tailed him all the way to the end of the Trump Pier, where he sat down and watched the eleven o'clock fountain show. Guess who he sat with."

I thought about it and could only come up with one person.

"Les?"

"The girlfriend."

ANOTHER TURN

Nico couldn't get close enough to hear what Enzo and *the girlfriend* spoke about. And unfortunately, nothing new came up regarding the Fabians for the rest of the week. But as far as Nico and I went, things bubbled along nicely. As the days passed, we quickly slid into a closer and more physically intimate relationship.

Monday evening, he kissed me on the lips as a greeting in front of the kids. He didn't suck my face in or anything; he just pecked me on the mouth instead of the cheek. Joy raised her eyebrows. Ash bobbed his head.

I didn't see him on Tuesday, but on Wednesday, he stayed for dinner, after which he sat on the sofa with his arm around me. I held my breath waiting for Joy to yell or complain, but she actually sat at the other end. She didn't make conversation with us, but when he left, she gave him a pleasant "see ya." Ash fist bumped him *hello* and *goodbye*. I decided they'd given us their blessing

Les was early to pick the kids up on Thursday, and this time he came alone. I had just heard Joy's shower shut off when the doorman downstairs asked if he should be allowed up. Ash was in his room finishing homework.

I let him in and immediately searched for something to do to keep myself occupied.

"Place looks good." Les followed me into the kitchen. He leaned against the sink counter. Because it is a galley kitchen, it was hard to maneuver in there without accidentally touching him. I retreated to the living area, sat on the chair, and pretended to read a magazine. He came in and sat on the ottoman in front of me.

"Lucy." He touched my hand.

"Mm?" I kept my eyes on the pages in front of me.

"I know this is going to sound strange, but I need a favor."

I gave a short laugh. "Really, Les? You need a favor from me?"

"I know you don't owe me anything. But, I was wondering if maybe you could let me into your parents' place."

I dropped the magazine to look at him.

"Why?"

"I think maybe I left something there."

"What?"

"Nothing important, just a couple small things. I'm not even sure. But if I could go in and take a look…"

I couldn't remember Les ever saying he was taking anything to my parents' place. I couldn't even imagine a reason why he would need to, especially something small. Our house was much bigger than theirs.

"I don't think I can, Les. I don't have the keys to get in." I lied.

"Oh, I thought maybe when your mom went to Florida, she gave a set to you."

"She gave them to Angie, and I know what *she'd* tell you." The idiot must have forgotten I had a set for our entire marriage.

"Lucy." He was on the edge of the chair now, too close to me, and touched my chin, gently. "Can we talk, please?"

I could hear Joy's hair dryer and prayed she wasn't pulling her hair straight. That could take a long time.

"We don't have much to talk about, Les." I jerked my head away. "Unless it's about the kids." I tried to stand. He grabbed my arm and kept me seated.

"Please. It does have to do with the kids."

I stared into his eyes.

"In a way." He took my other arm and leaned into me. "Look, it's just…it's just that I miss you. I really do." His face was inches from mine. He reached up and wrapped a curl around his finger. "Your hair looks nice like this." He smiled at me. "I messed up. Big time."

I twisted my head away from him again. I couldn't let him do this to me, and I knew it would be unbelievably easy to give in. He was the man who took my virginity. Aside from my obstetrician, he was the only man ever to see every private inch of my body. He was the only person I'd curled up next to in bed for the last eighteen years. He was the man I'd always thought I'd be with for the rest of my life. I had built a definite sense of compatibility and comfort with him that I wasn't sure I'd ever be able to replicate with anyone else because he was also the man who'd hurt me more than I thought I could bear.

"You're right about that, Les." I braved eye contact again. "But I've moved on. You've moved on."

"Does it have to be this way? I want to move back. I want to be back with you." He pressed closer. "Please, Lucy. God, I'm so sorry." His hands moved to my face. He tried to pull me into a kiss.

I straddled my legs over the arm of the chair and lunged off. Joy's hair dryer silenced.

"Just tell me." He stood. "Tell me what I can do to fix things. Tell me what I can do to make us a family again."

"The thing is, Les." I backed away from him. "I'm happy right now. I'm in a good place. I don't think there is anything you could do."

He caught me against the wall. His hands planted on either side of my head. This wasn't the Les I'd ever known. My Les was always mild-mannered and calm. He would never pin me against a wall.

"Nothing, Lucy? Are we beyond hope?"

"I received the Final Judgment on Valentine's Day." Tears built up in my eyes. "I had to deal with your girlfriend coming into *our* house to take *my* children to the place *you* share with *her*. You pretty much killed any chance of hope." I put my hands against his chest, ready to push him away.

"But do you really think that's what's best for the kids?" he asked. He inched his face closer. "Wouldn't it be bettèr if we were in one house again, all sitting around the kitchen table? As a family?"

I thought he was going to kiss me again. I closed my eyes and turned my face to the ceiling.

"ASH! JOY! YOUR FATHER'S HERE!"

"Everything okay?" Nico had come in when I was yelling.

He had a grocery bag in one arm. With the other, he removed Les's hand from the wall and pulled me sideways to him. This time, when he kissed me, his lips were parted. I felt the tip of his tongue touch mine. I didn't know whether it was for Les' benefit or simply because Nico wanted to kiss me like that. But it didn't matter. It made me a little weak in the knees.

"You two look chummy," Les said.

Without replying, Nico went into the kitchen, opened the refrigerator, and stocked it with the food he had in the bag. I wondered if Les realized Nico was claiming his territory. I went into the kitchen to help.

Ash and Joy appeared. Ash's feet were in hi-tops that weren't laced. He fist-bumped Nico and kissed me on the cheek. "'bye, Mom," he said, making eye contact with me. "Love you."

"'Bye, sweetie, I love you, too." I looked at Joy. Her kohl black liner was so thick and heavy, I could easily imagine it straining her eyelids when she blinked. She had on black lipstick and wore black stick things in her ears for earrings. I wasn't sure what she had done to her hair with the dryer. She had it pulled into spiky bunches that almost looked like pigtails, only they were angular, pointing in different directions.

She presented me with her cheek to kiss. I did. I wouldn't want to mess up that lipstick, after all.

"Love you, Mom," she said.

"I love you too, pumpkin."

"Nico, make sure she has a good weekend, 'K?"

"'K," he said.

"So the Goth look was to punish her father, not me," I said to Nico after they left. "You have no idea how relieved I am to know that."

"What was going on when I came in?" Nico handed me a beer and went to the living area.

"I'm not sure. Les was weird tonight."

"Weird? He had you up against the wall, and you just call it weird? Looks to me like he wanted something." He turned on his heels and faced me. "Looks like he wanted you."

"I'm not sure."

"About what?"

"About Les."

"Do you want him to want you?"

I took his free hand and went to the sofa, where I kept a hold of him, making him sit next to me.

I took a minute to look him over, blatantly look him over. I'd never allowed myself to do that unless it was in jest with my girlfriends, and I certainly never did it in front of him. Maybe I was staking my claim.

He was lean and muscular. There was a raw masculinity to his body that was echoed in his face. His jaw line was angular and his cheeks thin. A faded scar slanted over his right cheekbone and another slanted in the opposite direction on his bottom lip. He could look deadly tough if he wanted to. But when I looked in his eyes, I saw the beauty of him, the tenderness he was capable of expressing, the joy he was willing to feel when he allowed himself to feel it. I wanted him to feel it right then.

"Nico, aside from him being my kids' father, I don't want anything to do with Les anymore." I smiled into his deep, dark eyes. "What I meant was: I think he was trying to seduce me as a last resort. *That's* what I'm not sure about." I kissed him then, forcing his mouth open to accept mine. He didn't resist.

"Good." He held my head against his and gently bit my earlobe. "I've been waiting for you for a long time. I was willing to wait even longer if you needed it to settle into us being together. But seeing him that close to you tonight…" He inhaled. "I hope you don't mind me making sure he knows I'm on the possessive side."

"As long as you don't harm him so much, he can't take the kids every other weekend." I laughed. "It's nice to be alone together, isn't it?"

We fell back against the sofa, with me tucked into his arm.

"Does that mean he and *the girlfriend* broke up?" Nico asked.

"I don't know." I sipped the beer.

"Then what did you mean when you said 'last resort'?"

"Oh!" I sat up and turned to face him. "Jesus! See what kissing you does? I totally forgot to tell you."

He laughed. "Tell me what?"

"When he first came in, he wanted to know if I could let him into my parents' place. I refused, and that's when he started coming on to me."

Nico's eyes narrowed. "He wanted what?"

"Me to let him into my mom's place."

"Why?"

"Said something about how maybe he left something there."

"Do you think he did?"

"No. That would be something he'd ask me to do. He didn't have that kind of relationship with my parents."

"Interesting." He paused to sip his beer. "*Can* you get into her place?"

"Of course."

"What do you say we take a ride over there and nose through it?"

My mom still lived in my childhood home in Venice Park, the closest thing to a suburb Atlantic City has. On the western edge of town, it is a neighborhood that actually has yards surrounding the homes, not the postage-stamps of green grass or sand pretending to be lawns as in the city proper. The roads are ramrod straight and form blocks as urban roads do, but they are not as narrow, and the houses are not crammed as tightly. But, unlike a real suburb, there is no mall and no family restaurants. Citizens of Venice Park have to make do with the Cedar Foods Market and the Old Waterway Inn.

We made it over in about ten minutes and immediately learned we weren't the only ones interested in the house. As soon as Nico turned down the street where I grew up, I saw a van in my mother's driveway.

"Who could be there?" I asked.

He drove past a short way, turned right onto a side street, and went down another block. He killed the lights and turned around before going back up to my parents' street and stopping.

We could see people with flashlights walking around the house.

"Your mom still have the alarm I put in?" Nico asked.

"Yes."

"Will the service call her in Florida if it goes off?"

"No, she set it up to be me while she's away." I peered into the darkness. It was impossible to see any faces, only black forms of three people moving around the house.

Nico reached behind my seat and pulled a black bag to the front. He took out a set of binoculars.

"These should help me see better. They're night vision."

"You're like a Boy Scout, huh? Always prepared?"

"It's my job. Write this down." He trained the binoculars on the car and said the license plate number to me. I punched it into my cell phone and immediately e-mailed it to him.

"Now what do we do?" I asked.

"We wait to see what they do. If they break in, they'll stay until the alarm goes off. We stay here to see if they take anything when they leave. When the alarm company calls you, tell them to call the police. We'll drive off a couple of blocks, so it looks like we show up right after the police get there. At that point, we'll have a legitimate reason for going through the house: to search for anything stolen. Got it?"

"Got it."

"We should probably hear the alarm from here. Didn't she want the loudest siren I could get?"

"I believe her words were 'it better wake the entire eastern seaboard.'"

"Gotta love Ma McCool." He resumed watching the house.

"You know, this is a weird time to bring it up, but while we're waiting," I leaned against the door. "What do you think about me going back to my maiden name?"

"I don't like you being a Womzak, and McCool is probably the best name on the planet. But," he paused and refocused the binoculars, "it doesn't matter what I think. It only matters what you think."

"I'm worried that it might be upsetting to the kids. Do you think so?"

"It doesn't matter what the kids think. It's your name. You should have the name that makes you happy."

"But—"

"What name would make you happy?"

"But—"

"What name would make you happy? Oh! They're in."

I held my breath until I heard the alarm go off. A few seconds later, the van zoomed down the street past us.

"Did you see them?" I asked.

"Not their faces. And I'm not sure, but it looks like they had something small in their hands. It could have been tools. They were all carrying something."

I answered my cell phone and told the alarm company I had no idea what was going on.

After the police made sure the premises were vacated, they asked me to walk through to see if I noticed anything missing. Nico went with me.

"Cleanest robbers I've ever seen in my life," one of the officers said. "We'll have someone dusting for prints in a few minutes. Try not to touch anything."

The house had changed very little over the years. My mom was something of an anal retentive control freak. Once something was put into place, it stayed there unless an act of God moved it, and then God better apologize.

Nico immediately went up the stairs. "Professional robbers know they usually have between thirty seconds and a full minute before the alarm company will call the house owner," he said, heading up. I followed him. "Then they know they have a couple more minutes before the police show up. Usually, they go right to the bedrooms looking for jewelry. Unless they want electronics, then they head straight to the living room. Where does your mom keep her jewelry? The good stuff?"

"I'm not sure. This is her room." We walked into her bedroom. I couldn't remember the last time I was in my parents' bedroom. I felt like an intruder and had to resist the urge to tiptoe. Nothing appeared to have been touched.

He pulled a sleeve over his hand to open her closet. "Nothing looks like it was disturbed in here."

We went down the hallway to the room I once shared with Angie. My parents had kept our old twin beds but had painted the walls and updated the carpeting for their occasional guests. I could tell immediately that no one had been in that room for a long time.

Back in the hall, I stopped at the top of the stairs.

"Something missing?" Nico asked.

"Huh?" I was staring at a picture ledge housing the photographs from my and Angie's confirmations. Mother was beaming in mine, frowning in Angie's. Our father was equally proud and happy in both. There were no photos of Les.

"Everything there?" he asked.

"Yeah. I guess so."

Downstairs, we looked around the living and dining rooms. The only room that looked like anyone had been in it was the kitchen. All the cabinet doors were open.

"Oh my God," I said.

"What's the matter?"

"This is just like what happened in my house on Maine Avenue, remember when I thought Les…"

"Shh." Nico nodded to the policeman in the dining room.

"Do you think someone was looking for food?" I asked the young cop as he entered the kitchen. I trusted Nico's instincts not to say anything about my break-in. "Maybe it was someone hungry."

"People that hungry can't afford professional kits to break locks," said the officer.

"What does that mean?" I asked.

"Where is your mother?" he asked, ignoring my question. "When is she coming back?"

"She's in Florida for the winter. She won't be back until May."

"How long has your mom been away?"

"Since December."

"Why?" Nico asked him.

"You're sure the lock was locked?" the officer asked.

"Absolutely. Since December."

"Then it was definitely picked," the officer said. "Looks like a professional job. Barely scratched it."

"What does that mean, though? How do you know it wasn't some hungry kid good at picking locks?" I asked.

"The fact that the TV and the jewelry are still here and the lock was picked so cleanly suggests that whoever broke in was looking for something specific," another officer said as he came into the room. "Would you know if your mom had anything that belonged to someone else?"

"No! My mother doesn't steal!"

"Officer, do you know whose house this is?" Nico asked.

Their faces were too young to have worked with my dad.

"Her father was a retired cop," Nico said. "He was Sean McCool. Ever heard of him?"

"Yeah," said Officer Number Two. "Isn't he the one who—"

"I'm wondering if it was someone he'd arrested a long time ago," Nico interrupted. "You know how it is when you're a police officer. Sometimes you make enemies when you're doing your job, right? Maybe someone just got out of jail and was looking for him to get even."

"Who are you?" Officer Number One asked.

"Nico Mancuso. I'm an old family friend, and it was my security company that installed the alarm system here."

The officer's radio squawked. "Don't touch anything," he warned again and left the room, heading toward the front of the house. We waited in the kitchen. I stood still and watched Nico pry through everything in the kitchen, using a paper towel to prevent his fingers from leaving prints.

"What are you looking for?" I asked him.

"An empty space."

"Versus one full of stuff?"

He turned to grin at me. "I'm looking for a space that looks like something should be there but isn't."

"Hey. We said not to touch anything. That includes the cabinet doors," police officer one said as he reentered the room. "You can wait outside until we're ready for you to relock the place."

"God, Nico," I said. "Please don't let me forget to come back and make sure everything is perfect. The last person who needs to know her house was broken into is my mom." I stopped before the refrigerator and looked at the picture of Picasso's *Three Musicians*.

"It's still here." I touched the picture. "Not that anyone would want it, but still. I'm glad it's here."

THE CALM BEFORE BREAKFAST

Nico slept over in my condo that night—on the couch in the living room, as he said he was working and did not want to get distracted in case someone wanted to visit my kitchen in the middle of the night. Frankly, I was fine with that. I was scared out of my wits and wanted him to be working. Not that it mattered, I slept poorly anyway.

I made a full pot of coffee the next morning.

"Didn't sleep so well?" he asked, massaging my shoulders as I stared at the pot waiting for it to finish.

"No, did you?"

"Not bad." He ran his hands down my back and wrapped his arms around my midriff. I tried to suck in my gut without him noticing and leaned against him.

"It's funny, Nico. If you had told me ten years ago that I'd be standing here on a Friday morning with your arms around me, I'd never believe it."

"Ten years ago, neither would I." He nuzzled my neck. "But five years ago, I would have said it was something I hoped would happen. Two years ago, I would have told you it deserved to happen, and I was just waiting for it."

I wondered why I never thought of him as anything more than a friend. I'd never been tempted to stray in my marriage. Not even with a gorgeous man I fed frequently. How could Les cheat on me?

Nico let go of me and picked up the paint chips I'd gathered at the hardware store on my lunch hour the day before.

"What are you painting?"

"The kitchen." The coffee was finally done. I poured out two cups.

"Orange? You're painting the kitchen orange?"

"No, not orange. I like this one. It's tangerine sunset. This is also nice: mandarin sorbet."

"They're both orange. You can't paint the kitchen orange."

"Yes, I can. And it's your fault, so you have to like it." I handed him a cup.

"Why do I deserve that?"

"Because when you took me to see that Picasso exhibit. I really loved the orange he used."

"Picasso was famous for a blue period, not an orange one."

"I don't care. I like the way he worked with orange. I want the same orange from the *Three Musicians* on what little wall space I have in here."

"It's freaking orange. You can't have an orange kitchen."

"Why not?"

"What's wrong with white?"

"Nothing, except when there's too much. Look at this place. The walls are white. The countertops are white. The cabinets are white. The appliances are white. It's sterile. It's as cold as a hospital kitchen."

He sipped his coffee and looked around.

"You gotta point." He frowned. "But orange?"

"It would make me happy."

"Aaah!" He gave me a loud, smacking kiss. "Yes! Then paint it orange."

Nico stayed over again on Friday night. I had bought clams on my lunch hour from Barbera's Seafood, but I was too tired to cook, so we did take-out shrimp and vodka-lemonades from the bar I dubbed *the shrimp place*, as I couldn't remember its name.

We sat on the floor in the living area because I missed sitting on the floor with Dasher. I still missed him. We'd had Dash for close to fourteen loyal years before a hairdryer exploded and gave him a heart attack.

"What do you think about me getting another dog?" I asked Nico.

"Do you really want another dog?"

"I'm not sure. I really miss Dash. And I think the kids do, too."

"So, does it matter what I think about you getting another dog?"

"It does. I think. Maybe." I threw a small, decorative pillow at him. "I guess I'm the one who's not sure if she wants another dog."

"That's what I was thinking."

We ate on the floor, then snuggled on the sofa afterward. And then I went to bed in the next room while Nico spent the night in the living area, again.

I slept better that night, but I woke wondering why he was still staying out there. Granted, I'd been out of the dating world long enough that perhaps I had no idea how long it would take before he'd want to share sheets with me. But he'd said he'd been waiting for me for a long while. If he really was all that into me, he'd at least hint at sex, wouldn't he? Unless he was waiting for me to send a signal.

The fact that I was tempted to do so surprised me. And I wasn't sure if I had the gall to follow through on the idea. *Could today be the day* for that?

"What do you think about brunch this morning?" I asked him. "Instead of a protein shake?"

"I think I like brunch." He stood barefoot and shirtless in a pair of jeans, looking out the sliders. "God, it's almost cruel to have a view like that when it's so damned cold outside."

"It's even more cruel from my viewpoint," I said from behind him.

He turned around."Oooo, Lucy McCool getting sassy." He tackled me. We tumbled onto the sofa. "I like it. I've never heard you be so forward before." He rolled on top of me.

"I don't think I've *been* so forward before." We kissed. "You must bring it out of me."

"I can bring out more." His lips ran over my chin and down my neck. "You know, it's daylight. I could take a work break. Hmm...let's see what else I can bring out. Maybe something out of this shirt."

He pulled up the hemline of my T-shirt and began kissing up my stomach. I wanted to push him off, embarrassed by the fat still there. I didn't. His tongue made its way to my bra line. He slipped his hands under me and started unhooking it.

"I know! That was so funny!" Angie said.

Nico and I froze in place. I looked toward the door and watched Angie shut it, laughing with her cell phone pressed against her face. She glanced up and saw us on the sofa.

"I gotta go, Rick." She powered off the call and placed a hand over her eyes.

"Don't mind me," she said. "I'll raid the fridge and be back later to work on Mom's party."

"Shit! I forgot," I said.

Nico pulled his head out from under my shirt and sat up.

"Forgot what?"

"You did it again."

"What did I do now?" Grinning, he ran his hands through my hair.

"Made me forget what I'm doing." I kissed him lightly on the lips and wiggled my bra back in place. "I'm supposed to be planning my mother's surprise birthday party, she decided I was giving her."

Angie came into the living area with an apple, a coffee travel mug, and a cereal bar in her hands. "I'm out of here. Call me later?"

"Stay, Ange," I said. "I think I was going to make brunch. That's what I was going to do, right?" I asked Nico.

"Right. And I'm going to shower." He stood. "That way you two hens can discuss what Angie just saw without me in the room, 'cause I'm staying for brunch and you won't be able to talk about it in front of me."

He left the room.

"Aack! So what's it like sleeping with that muscular bod?" Angie asked as soon as he was out of earshot.

I opened the refrigerator door. "I don't know. We were interrupted." I pulled out eggs, onion, a red pepper, and mozzarella and parmesan cheeses. "Can I put bacon in the frittatas?" She's a lacto-ovo vegetarian, so she'll eat cheese and eggs. I didn't understand how bacon could be that much worse.

"So that wasn't a good-morning tryst on the couch? And no bacon in the eggs."

"He slept there last night, and the night before." I found a package of frozen spinach in the freezer.

"And you're being such a prude because?"

"It was his idea." I peeled the onion. "He was working."

"I don't understand."

I told her all about the break-ins at my old home and at our mother's house. I hadn't said anything to her about my house on Main Avenue before because I didn't want her to go off on Les about it. Now that I was pretty sure it wasn't him, I thought I should warn her in case her house was next on the hit list.

"This is all too bizarre," she said as the three of us sat down to eat. "But do you know what? I think someone broke into my house yesterday, too."

"Just think?" Nico asked.

"Yeah." Angie flipped her napkin out and smoothed it on her lap. "I was on my way to work when the alarm company called. When I went back home, the police were there. We weren't sure if someone had broken in or not because the lock wasn't damaged. But all the cabinet doors in the kitchen were open."

"Why didn't you tell me?" I asked.

"I didn't want you to worry. The police didn't think it was a big deal."

"Shouldn't they have seen a pattern forming?" I asked. "My house, Angie's, my mom's. All the same kind of thing, right?"

"Right," Nico said. "But, you didn't make a report at your old house, so unless the same cops showed up at Angie's, no one would have made the connection. And since Angie's and your mom's place happened on the same day, the police might not have had time to put two and two together, yet." Nico sipped his drink. "This isn't just OJ, huh?" he asked.

"No, it's a mimosa."

"Oh, Luce, I'd love to partake, but you're not my only client right now." He went to the kitchen. "Was anything missing, Angie?" he asked through the pass-through.

"No, that's the crazy thing." She sipped her drink. "I'm glad you're working, Nico. These are good."

"You'll make it up to me, right, Luce?" He returned to the table with a glass of plain orange juice.

"Of course." I smiled at him as his hand squeezed my knee. Part of me wanted to scream to the world from my balcony, telling everyone that Nico squeezed my knee in front of my sister, but if I did, he'd have to let go of me, so I stayed put.

"Are you sure you didn't leave the cabinet doors open, Angie?" Nico asked her. "Maybe from making breakfast?"

"Nico, you're not the only one who relies on Lucy for real food, you know." Angie held a forkful of frittata in the air. "I get coffee to-go from the convenience store on my way into work. That's my breakfast."

"And she's a vegetarian because it's healthy," I said.

"I have some other clients who need my services today." Nico took his plate to the kitchen. "Can you two hens hang together? I don't think I want either of you alone until I know what's going on."

"Yeah," Angie said. "We were planning on it anyway. But do you really think we're in danger?"

"I don't know what to think." He returned to the table and stood behind me, his hands on my shoulders. "But, I don't want to take any chances."

"I'll be here all day," Angie said. "It should take about that long to plan this damned party. Got plenty of champagne, Lucy? Can you make more of these?"

"Not nearly enough. But there's still a full bar of other forms we can abuse." I chewed my last piece of bacon.

"I don't get it, Luce." Nico put his jacket on. "You love to throw a party. Why not this one?"

"First of all, it's the week after Memorial Day weekend. I really wanted to do a big, summer-opening Memorial Day non-barbecue. Similar to the parties I used to have. I don't want to do two big parties."

"But why can't you combine—"

"Memorial Day with my mother's birthday? Out of the question!" I laughed and sucked down the remaining mimosa. "It wouldn't be good enough for her. She has never behaved like the wife of a working-class cop, you know. Besides, now that I'm on her bad list, I'll have to work extra hard to keep the complaints to a minimum. No matter what I do, it won't be perfect. I could get a cardinal to do the blessing, bring Liberace back from the dead for the music, channel Julia Child for the food, and she will still find something to bitch about and rip apart. It's going to be an awful lot of work, and the end result will be a stressful evening for me, and she still won't be happy. I want Memorial Day to be fun."

"Then why do anything at all for her?" he asked.

"Because my mother expects it of me. I have to."

"No, you don't." He stood. "You could hire it out."

"Right," I gave him a half-smile.

"Call her favorite restaurant and book a room for the night." He winked at me. "You got plenty of money in an account just waiting for a use. Let the restaurant handle it. You have enough to do. When she complains—if she complains—tell her the truth: you're not Martha Stewart and that you don't even play her on TV." He glanced at his watch. "I need to go, babe."

FINDING JOY

I gotta tell ya, Lucy," Angie said as we cleaned the brunch dishes. "I like the way Nico thinks. Why not a restaurant? Where were you thinking?"

"The sixth floor here has a huge room with kitchen facilities. I could do the food and hire freelance caterers to help."

"Which means you'll spend the entire evening working the kitchen and supervising the servers."

"It sounds better the way I said it."

"It doesn't matter how you say it, the truth is you'll be leaving me to spend the evening at the table with her without you as a buffer."

I laughed and filled the dishwasher with detergent.

"What's so bad about a restaurant?" Angie asked. "We'll invite everyone she knows. Do you really think she'll hate it?"

"I really don't know what she'll hate." I shut the dishwasher and turned it on. "I do know I owe you a huge apology."

"For what?"

"All our lives, I always thought you exaggerated the way Ma treated you. And that if you had just given her some slack, maybe she'd have given you some. But I don't give her any grief, and she's piling it on me these days like she always has on you."

"You mean this party?"

"The party, by way of Joy, mind you, she has yet to speak to me about it. When I'm talking to her, all I get is harping on my divorce, the condo, everything." I went into the living area and sat on the floor beside the coffee table.

"The condo?" Angie followed me and sat on the sofa. "What could she possibly say about this place? It's perfect!"

"She's still going on about how I have no place for woolens."

"What kind of person actually uses that word?"

"I don't know." I paused and leafed through the tablet where I'd written notes on what to do for her party. "And now she wants to know where I have a proper dinner since I no longer have a formal dining room." I set my elbows on the coffee table and leaned my head into my hands. "She's convinced Les would have come back to me by now if I had found a place with a proper dining room." I laughed again, maybe to keep from crying. "I'm sorry, Ange. I really am. I never saw it before because I never experienced it directly."

Angie slid off the sofa and picked up the notepad.

"No apologies necessary, Lucy. You stood up for me plenty. I'm just glad to see I've rubbed off on you to the point where you call a sweater a sweater and you don't need a formal dining room." She threw the tablet down on the table. "And you know what? I really think Nico has a great idea with this restaurant thing. I mean, if you can't handle hand-washing a bunch of knits for a shit husband, how could she expect you to handle a party for a bitch mom?"

"Angie!"

"Am I wrong?" She stood. "Come on."

"Where are we going?"

"I think we need to treat our worthless selves to a manicure and new clothes." She pulled me up by the hand. "I want something vampy for my date with Rick tonight, and you need something sexy for when you get Nico off the sofa and into the bedroom."

We had manicures done at her spa, then headed to the mall at the Trump Pier. A woman with artificially straight, very dark hair walked out as we walked in. She wore tight black pants tucked into stiletto-heeled black boots, an even tighter leopard-print shirt, an open, shiny black leather jacket, giant designer sunglasses, though it was misting and cloudy out, and a black patent-leather newsboy hat. Completing the look was jewelry large enough to fit the Statue of Liberty. She must have had a steel rod implanted in her neck to support it all.

"Oh my Gawd!" she shrieked when she saw us. "Angie!" She air-kissed my sister's cheek. "I was just saying it's been too long since I've had a massage." She pronounced *massage* like ma-SAW-ush.

"Here." Angie pulled a card out of her purse. "Have one on me."

"You're FABulous! Really!" The woman tucked the card into her purse. "Anyway, I gotta run!" she practically yelled as she toddled off in her stiletto boots.

"Sometimes it's good to see people go," Angie said.

"Why'd you give her a card?"

"That's why she stopped to say hello. Besides, while she's there, she'll have much more done to her than that half-hour massage gift card. She's loaded."

"She's our age, right?"

"Yeah."

"Wow! She's such a stereotype, I hate to admit it, but she looks great."

"She's had a lot sucked out of her and even more injected into her. We'd all look that great if we'd been to the doctor that much." Angie led me to the up escalator. "And even with all that work, she's friendless and lonely. She's in a real shit of a marriage, too. You're better off being you."

"Divorced and fat?"

"Divorced and involved with a guy who's had the hots for you for years."

"Do you really think for years?"

"Did you really think he kept coming over for free meals?"

"Yes."

"You're hopeless."

"C'mon, Angie. It's Nico. And I'm me. Fat."

"I think the right word is 'sensual.'"

"I'm short and a size ten."

"With serious boobs and curves." She stopped before a boutique. "Let's go in here and see what we can find to show them off."

We entered the store, and Angie started going through the racks. I mimicked her with no serious intent to buy anything. I still had some pounds I wanted to lose first. But then I saw a display of T-shirts I thought Joy might like. They were mostly black and decorated with sculls, daggers, and other graphics that apparently appeal to some teen girls, though I thought they were better suited for pirates, thugs, and people who sacrificed squirrels. I headed over and stopped immediately when I recognized the back of a sleek, platinum blond head. I ran back to Angie.

"No way, Ange," I whispered. "I can't shop here."

"Why not? Look at these jeans. I think this retro, distressed style would look good on you."

"It's not the clothes," I whispered, tugging on her arm. "Look! It's *the girlfriend.*"

125

Angie looked up. An evil smile spread across her face.

"Oh yes, you *can* shop here, and you will. In fact, you're going to be waited on hand and foot. It's the least you deserve."

We waited for another customer to leave before going up to *the girlfriend*.

"I didn't know you worked here," Angie said.

The girlfriend looked at Angie, then at me, then back to Angie.

"Is there something I can help you with?" she asked my sister in her squeaky voice. Apparently, having a throat that thin restricts your larynx.

"Why yes." Angie handed her a pair of jeans. "Can you show me the full line from this designer, in sizes four and ten? I think that's a good place to start." She looked around her. "We'll wait for you in the fitting rooms. You can bring us some coffee, too."

The girlfriend glanced at me. I gave her a sweet smile and followed Angie to the back of the store. Another sales clerk brought coffee and tiny muffins, which reminded me exactly why I love the boutiques in AC: they take good care of you. If it had been evening, they would have had wine, so it was probably good we were there in the morning. My mouth tends to run ahead of my brain when I drink wine. Me, wine, *the girlfriend*...things could get ugly.

I tried on seven pairs of jeans, decided on two, and let Angie talk me into some racy pullover tops that were all about showing off cleavage. *The girlfriend* started out being strictly business with us until she came into my booth when I needed help figuring out how to properly button and snap a wrap-around tunic kind of thing. She explained that it could be worn in two different ways, and connected it in the first way, which crisscrossed over my boobs.

"You probably want to strangle me with this, don't you?" She made eye contact with me in the mirror. I wasn't sure if the comment was about Les or because I looked like a dominatrix the way that tunic wrapped around me.

I saw, for the first time, the worry lines coming from the corners of her eyes and the crease between her brows. Her very pale blond hair betrayed dark roots, and she sucked nervously on her lips. The wrinkles around her mouth suggested she was either a smoker now or had been a heavy smoker in the past. Somehow, I felt sorry for her. She looked scared and insecure.

"You know, it's crazy, but I don't want to strangle you. I don't hate you. Really." I turned to look at her directly. "I think I'm happier now than I have been for years."

"Oh, well, good." She broke eye contact and went on as before, showing me the other way to wear the top. I didn't buy it.

"So do we go for shoes now?" Angie asked.

"Sounds good. I liked the boots that woman was wearing, the ones you ran into earlier. Think I could find some similar ones with a lower heel?"

My phone rang. I handed Angie my shopping bags while I fished through my purse. It was Joy.

"Mom! Can you come get me?" Her voice shook as if she were crying. "I need to get away from Daddy. Please? Can you come get me?"

If it hadn't been misting that morning, we would have walked down the boardwalk to Angie's spa and then to the Pier. Instead, we had taken Angie's two-seater car. So we had to go back to get my minivan before we could pick up Joy at her father's townhome on the bay. It took us about twenty minutes, and by that time, the mist had become a steady rain. Joy was standing outside in the cold, completely soaked, as if she'd been waiting there since she called.

"Does he know where you are?" I asked her.

"I don't know, and I don't care." Joy settled into the backseat. "I hate him, Mom. I really do. He's such an ass."

"Joy! He's your father."

"He's a fucking racist pig!"

"Joy!"

"What?"

"You can't talk about him like that." I looked at her in the rearview mirror. "He deserves more respect than that."

"Why?"

"Because...because he's your father."

"Mom, I've had sex ed, remember? I know all it takes to be a dad is sperm. Just about any twelve-year-old boy could be a dad. Does that mean I have to respect them all for it?"

"She has a point," Angie said.

My phone rang. This time it was Lester.

"Joy is with me," I answered.

"Yeah, I watched her get in your van. She's got one hell of a mouth on her."

"So I've heard."

"What are you going to do with her?"

I looked at her again in the rear-view mirror, a drowned rat in my backseat. We were still parked in front of his townhome. The shit couldn't even come out of his house to give his daughter an umbrella while she stood in the cold rain.

"I'm going to take her shopping." I clicked off and turned around in my seat to look at Joy. "Aunt Angie and I were shopping when you called. Wanna go back to the mall with us?"

Judging by the look on her face, she suspected my body had been taken over by an extra-terrestrial species. "Um, okay."

I pulled out, and we headed to the Quarter at the Tropicana.

"Actually, Mom," Joy said after a few minutes. "I do kind of need something."

"Yeah? What?"

"It's why Daddy and I were fighting."

"You were fighting about going shopping?"

"No! God!" I'm sure she paused to concentrate on rolling her eyes. "We were fighting because I need a dress."

I didn't understand what she was talking about, but I couldn't figure out a response that wouldn't make her mad at me.

"What do you need a dress for?" Angie eventually asked, twisting around in her seat.

"Remember when I said I needed to talk to you, Mom, and you accused me of being pregnant?"

"What?" Angie asked.

"Look," I said. "You began the conversation with 'I need to tell you something.' Every time someone has ever said 'I need to tell you something' to me, it's been bad, no, horrible news. That's how your father told me he was leaving. How the Pets With Panache guy told me Dash died. How…" I broke off.

The first time those words meant bad news was when I read them in a note. My father had taped a small, green piece of paper to my refrigerator the day he was found dead in an alley. He'd written on it: *Lucy, I have to tell you something.* I shook my head. "Anyway, please don't *ever* use that phrase with me again, okay?"

"Okay," Joy actually laughed. "But I need a dress. That's what I wanted to talk to you about. Justin asked me to the cotillion."

Justin was one of the boys who had come to the coed sleepover. I thought that meant my pregnant comment was justified, but I knew enough to let it go. Besides, he was a perfectly normal-looking teenage boy: no out-of-the-ordinary piercings, no grommets in his ears, no tattoos, no hair dye. I was delighted Justin had asked her to go to the cotillion.

"And your dad was mad because?" I braved asking.

"'Cause he's, like, half-black. Do you have a problem with that?"

"No." I tried to look at her in the rear-view mirror. "Did your dad really have a problem with it?"

"Duh! Why do you think we were fighting?"

So there was something else I never knew about Les.

We shopped, without anything even resembling an argument, all afternoon. I got boots with heels almost too high for me to walk in, a slinky nightgown, and new bras that made me feel like my boobs were up to my chin. We also found a dress for Joy that, although it was black, had no rips, studs, spikes, or other potentially dangerous decorations. It needed a few alterations to fit correctly, though. Angie was going to pick it up on Wednesday, as she was getting some slacks hemmed, too.

We went back to the condo, and I told Angie to go home. I was sure Nico would be back soon—it was close to dinner time—and she needed to get ready for her date with Rick.

By seven o'clock, I'd fed Joy and myself pasta with turkey meatballs. There was no sign of Nico. I was beginning to worry about him, but I couldn't let on to Joy.

She immersed herself in the task of cleaning out her hermit crab cages while talking on her cell with headphones on. Eventually, she went into her room to watch TV and Skype Justin on her laptop. I paced around the condo until my phone beeped with a text message.

At blackjack table with Enzo. B home L8.

In case *home* meant my home, I left the pillow and blanket on the sofa and turned on the hall light. With the inaugural wearing of the new nightgown postponed, I put on an oversized T-shirt and went to bed.

I woke and looked at the clock: it was one-twenty-seven in the morning, and someone was in my bed, touching me.

I gripped the side of the mattress. Tried to pull myself out of bed.

But an arm pinned me down.

"It's me," Nico said. He slid under the sheets and spooned up against me. "You left the hall light on." He nuzzled into my neck. I reached back to him and ran my hand down his side, over his hip. He was naked.

"I didn't want you to trip," I said. What was wrong with me? Nico was naked. Sexy Nico was *naked,* in bed with me, and *that's* what I said?

"That was so nice of you. But the light made me want to see you." His mouth took in my earlobe, and his hand slid under my T-shirt, sending fireworks sparking up my belly. "Then seeing you made me want to touch you." I let him roll me onto my back, his hand moving up to my breast.

"Oh, Luce." His lips traveled up my neck to my mouth. "My sweet Lucy."

"Wait." I panicked. Ever the romantic, I tried to wriggle away from him. "I need to brush my teeth."

"No." He was on top of me now. "No, please. Don't go anywhere." He tried to kiss me again.

"But I taste like sleep."

"Let me taste your sleep." He gently bit my lower lip. "I want to taste your sleep. I want to taste all of you." His mouth opened mine, and I tasted him: a little peanut, a little whiskey, all Nico. He broke off the kiss. "I want to experience all of you." I let him pull the T-shirt completely off me. He kissed me again and started slowly down my front with his mouth.

"Mmmm, Lucy." His tongue found a nipple. He paused there, and breathing was almost impossible for me. "My Lucy. My Lucy, who turns the hall light on." He continued kissing, working his way to bury his face in my cleavage. Champagne bubbles tickled up from my core, out of my breasts. "My Lucy, who's proof there's good in the world." His mouth traveled to my stomach. I forgot all about the extra fat and submitted to the warmth and sensation of him. "Beautiful Lucy, who reminds me there's love in the world. My Lucy." He continued going down and down with his mouth on my body. His tongue traced my C-section scar and went all the way down to where no tongue had ever gone before. Les had never been that adventurous with me, not that I even thought about Les that night. I could barely even think. I could only feel.

After making love, we fell asleep tangled up with each other, exhausted and satisfied. I remember thinking my world had never felt so peaceful and happy as that moment when I drifted off. It was a great way to fall asleep. And probably would have been a great way to stay sleeping all night long. Even a great way to wake up in the morning. But around four thirty, the fire alarms in the building went off. An electronic voice came through the intercom insisting that the building be evacuated.

RUDE AWAKENING

M OM!" Joy raced in my room and flipped on the light. Nico and I ripped up the sheets.

"What do we do?" Her eyes were wide, panicked.

"Get dressed," Nico said calmly. "Shoes and coat. We'll be out in a second. Everything will be okay."

She ran out of the room, and we jumped out of bed.

"Listen," he said as he pulled up his jeans. "I'm sure they'll want you to go through the lobby, but I want you to go down to the parking garage and leave the building. Go to my place, got it?"

He handed me his keys. I had slid into leggings and a sweater.

"What are you going to do?"

"Surveillance from your balcony." He stepped into his shoes. "This alarm is yet another coincidence that I don't believe is really coincidental. I have a feeling someone is trying to get in here and couldn't get past the doorman, so they found a way to do it while making sure you're not home. But I don't want you around. I don't want anyone to see you. Wait at my place until I call."

"Will you be all right?"

He grinned at me before looking down at his cell phone. "This is the kind of stuff I do best. Don't worry about me. I'm turning off the alarm at my place with my phone now."

I didn't move. Joy ran back into the room.

"I'm ready," she said.

He took my face in his hands. "You know what to do?"

I nodded.

"I love you, Luce." He kissed me.

"I love you too, Nico."

"Good." He kissed me again. "Now go."

I took his keys and flew out the door with Joy while the building alarms continued to blare in the halls.

We ran down the stairs and joined several other residents. We were the only ones in a hurry.

"Mom, I'm, like, really freaking out," Joy gripped my hand tight. "What if this is, like, a nine-eleven thing and the building collapses or something?"

"It's nothing to worry about, doll," said an older woman taking her time on the steps. "These happen every couple of years."

"Yeah," said the man walking with her. "Something about the fire alarm in the elevator. When dust piles up on it, it goes off. Just never seems to happen during the day."

Their comments slowed our pace, even though I doubted their accuracy.

We were not the only ones to exit the stairs in the parking garage. Many residents had stopped there to discuss where to meet for coffee while waiting for the fire trucks. Our emergency was a social activity for them. I followed Nico's orders and went directly to his apartment, which was a tiny one-bedroom place above the Mancuso Security Office storefront on Arctic Avenue.

"You been here before?" Joy asked as I let her in.

"Yes," I said. "I brought him chicken soup last year when he was sick."

She stepped inside and looked at me. "So he was just waiting for dad to fuck things up, huh?"

"I don't know." I clenched my jaw so I couldn't scold her over the F-word.

"I always pictured him living in a luxury condo." She turned a circle in the room. "This place is kind of dumpy."

"I guess so." I relocked the door behind us. "But he spends most of his time at a luxury condo these days. Is that okay with you? That he's at our place all the time?"

"Yeah. I like him better than Dad." Joy turned on a lamp as if she were instantly at home, then dropped onto the sofa.

"I do too." I sat beside her. "But I want you to like your dad better."

"Whatever. Why didn't Nico come?"

"He said something about wanting to talk to security in the building. I'm sure if he thought there was a real problem, he would have."

She found the remote and turned on the TV. I looked about the apartment. While not exactly dumpy, it was Spartan, with only the bare essentials: a sofa, a TV on a stand, and a tiny dinette with two chairs. I found it odd that he enjoyed the art museum so much when the only decorations were the many stacks of books piled up along the walls.

When I brought him the soup, he apologized for how it looked. Said he never had a gift for making a place a home, and that's why he loved my house so much.

I realized Joy was right. He had been waiting. He was a patient man. He must have known it was a matter of time, which bothered me on a level I was too tired to work through. *How could he have known Les better than I did?*

"I think I'm going to try to sleep some more," I said, standing. "What about you?"

"I don't know."

I went to the equally bare bedroom. The bed was king-sized.

"It's a big bed, if you want to sleep next to me," I said from the door.

"Sleeping with my mom in her boyfriend's bed? God, Mom." Joy rolled her eyes and settled in on the sofa.

I dozed off and on with my cell phone on the pillow next to me.

He called at seven-forty-five.

"You had visitors," he said. "And it was what I suspected: Enzo was here with two friends. I'm guessing one is Aldo. I don't know who the other was."

"What?" I sat up in his bed.

"Look, there's a lot I gotta get you caught up on. But first, Les and I are to meet for breakfast, and I can't get to him until you come home with my keys."

"Oh, right. We'll be there in a few minutes."

Joy's not a morning person on a night when she gets enough sleep. I got only a grunt and a snort on the way back to the condo. She immediately went to her bed after giving Nico a snarl.

"She's tired," I said.

"That's probably good." He handed me a cup of coffee. "We can talk while she sleeps. Listen, is your head clear?"

"Ha!" I sipped the coffee. "But this will help. What the hell is happening? You were at the blackjack table with Enzo, and then he comes here?"

"Yes, but let me back up. The license plate numbers, the one from when I tailed Enzo to the fountains and the one from the van at your parents' place, belong to cars registered with addresses in Newark. One to Enzo Finarelli and the other to his cousin Aldo Finarelli."

"Another interesting coincidence." I curled my fingers into air quotes on the last word.

"Indeed." Nico grinned and cheered me with his cup. "My contacts up there dug around and found out what kind of guys they are."

"And that is?"

"Freelancers, of sorts."

"Writers? Photographers? Accountants?"

"Perhaps insurance claims specialists is most applicable."

"I don't get it."

"Let's say, you have a big debt you owe someone. Not the kind with a promissory note or a credit card agreement, but the kind of debt you have with someone who does physical harm if you don't pay up."

"Are they thugs for hire?"

"I'm sure that wouldn't be below them, but that's not it. Sometimes people get in trouble and need to get cash quickly without anyone else knowing. They can do that by a convenient insurance payout when their jewelry or their sports memorabilia collection is stolen, but somehow the heirloom silver or a favorite fur coat is left untouched."

"I see, I think."

"Enzo and Aldo can make that kind of theft happen as long as they get to sell what they stole and keep the proceeds."

"And this applies to Les, me, or my parents, how?"

"I'm not sure. You ever have a burglary on Maine Avenue?"

"No. We never had a claim on our homeowner's insurance. And I don't remember my parents saying anything."

"That's the missing piece." Nico drained his coffee. "So I played a couple hands with Enzo. He recognized me from the senior center, and I could tell he wasn't sure what to do at first. When the seat next to him opened up, I went over, introduced myself, and asked if he remembered me. He did. We went for a walk.

"I asked him point-blank what he wanted from you; he tried to assure me he wanted nothing to do with you."

"But you said he was here in the middle of the night."

"Right. I didn't say I thought Enzo was telling the *truth*." He stretched, arching his back. "I think he thinks you have something that should rightfully be his. Or something that he was hired to find and retrieve for someone else. I watched them through the blinds on the balcony. If Enzo had been alone, I would have confronted him. But I was outnumbered."

"I'm glad you stayed safe."

"Yeah, well, it doesn't help us much because we still don't know what they want. Clearly, whatever they are looking for is kitchen-related. They went through everything in your kitchen and didn't touch the other rooms. I didn't get a clear view of them, but I think they took something because they had bags, like small duffel bags, with something in them when they left. I looked through your cabinets, and it looks like there are empty spaces. But I'd like you to take a peek."

I went to the kitchen. He stood on the opposite side of the pass-through and watched me. I opened all the cabinets.

"I'm not sure, but I think something is different."

"How?"

I stared into the pantry. The top shelf had baking supplies: flour, sugar, powdered sugar, baking powder, powdered cocoa, and more. Nothing seemed to be missing. The next shelf down was the kids' snacks, and it didn't look like it'd been touched. The middle shelf, the shelf that held the staples, appeared to be emptier.

"I don't know, Nico." I moved a few items around. "I mean, this shelf looks like something's not right. But I don't know. It could just be that I need to go grocery shopping." I looked at him through the pass-through. "I'm sorry."

"No apologies. Nothing is making sense to me either." He stood. "Interestingly, perhaps coincidentally? Les wants to meet with me. Maybe he can clarify a few things. I'm going to have breakfast with him now."

"Here?"

"No, Gilchrist's." He brought his coffee cup into the kitchen and rinsed it in the sink before putting it in the dishwasher. I liked that he did that. Les never rinsed out his coffee cups.

Sleep was out of the question. I left Joy a note and went down to the gym to work out. She was in the shower when I came back up. Nico texted me: *Done with Les. Researching now. B in touch soon.*

I showered and found Joy in the kitchen. She was a little less surly, so I offered to make us my special grilled cheese sandwiches.

"When are you going to tell me to call Dad and apologize to him?" she asked when we were eating.

"I'm not. The fight is between you two. If I were he, as the more mature person, I would be reaching out to you."

"And if you were me?"

I smiled at her. "I don't know how to answer that, pumpkin. Maybe you should call Aunt Angie. I'm only now beginning to fight with a parent. She has more experience." I refilled my water glass. "Here's the thing, though. You're stuck with him. No matter what happens, he's going to be your father for the rest of your life." I paused, wondering how I would handle it if it turned out Les was involved in organized crime on a dangerous level. Is that something I could use to file for full custody? "Anyway, you're supposed to be with him next weekend, too, remember?"

"No! Isn't that your weekend?"

"You'll be back with me for two weeks in a row after that," I said. "He's taking you and Ash to Philly for the weekend. Your cousin's Sweet Sixteen is on Friday."

"Oh, that's right." She chewed and wrinkled her nose. "Thanks for getting me two nice dresses. I guess you could have made me wear the Sweet Sixteen one to the cotillion."

"I've been looking at you dressed in spikes for too many months to turn down the opportunity to buy a pretty dress for you." We smiled at each other. "But what I'm trying to tell you is this: you two are going to have to figure something out. This is your home, without a doubt, but he's legally your father, and you're going to be with him again and again, beginning with this Thursday coming up."

Her cell phone rang in her bedroom. She disappeared to answer it while I cleaned up the lunch dishes.

"Dad's downstairs," she said, coming back into the living area. "He wants to talk."

I smiled. Les finally did the right thing. "And what was your answer?"

"I said he could come up," she said as the intercom buzzed. "Is that okay?"

He came in looking pale, tired, and unshaven. Les always shaved.

"You look a little rough." I shut the door behind him.

"It's been a rough couple of days. I don't know if you're interested, but Kay left."

"Who?" He tilted his head at me. "Oh, her." *The girlfriend* had left him. "Gee, am I supposed to say I'm sorry?"

"No." He sat on the sofa. "No, I'm the one full of apologies today." He looked at Joy, still sitting at the dining table. "Can I speak to your mom privately for a minute first?"

Joy went to her room. I didn't feel comfortable being alone with him. I still felt weak around him when it was just the two of us. We had been together for so long. He might have been a worse husband than I had any inkling about, but what I did know about wasn't bad. Actually, it was pretty good. He was by my side for two decades. And he had faked marital happiness with me well enough that I'd believed our family really was happy, that I was really happy.

"What's this about?" I stood with my arms crossed, leaning against the bar at the pass-through.

"Joy, for one. You, for another."

"Let's start with Joy."

"Have you heard the language that comes out of her mouth? What the hell is up with that?"

"It's the language that comes out of just about everyone in this town, teens especially."

"That doesn't make it right."

"It doesn't make it wrong, either."

"Her brother doesn't talk like that."

"Her brother barely talks. He grunts and says 's'up.' Which, I think, is short for 'what's up?' but I'm not sure."

He smiled at me. "I love you, Lucy."

I pretended I didn't hear him and picked at my cuticle.

When he got tired of waiting for a response, he continued. "I think Joy owes me more respect than to talk to me that way. I'm her father for Christ's sake."

"As Joy explained to me, any twelve-year-old could be a father. Does that mean she has to respect them?" I forced a laugh. "Besides, think about how you're respecting her these days. It's a two-way street, you know. Give her a little leeway. She's a young woman, whether or not you want her to be. She's in the process of defining who she is, and there's no law that says she has to define herself according to what you want her to be. And since when did you become a racist?"

"What? Look where I choose to live! Ninety percent of the people in this town are African American. I'm not a racist, you know that. Is that what she said?"

"Isn't that why you were arguing? You didn't want her dating Justin?"

"Because I'd never met the kid. *That* was my only objection. Shouldn't I at least get a chance to meet some boy before I spend money on an expensive dress and let him take her out until God knows what hour of the night? He's got a driver's license. I just wanted to meet him first."

"Okay. You win that one." I smirked at him. Our eyes met and briefly, against my will, the old comfort and ease I used to have with him crept into my stomach. I walked over to the sliders and looked at the ocean.

"So how do you handle that mouth?" he asked.

"I try to ignore it."

"How's it working?"

"She's not fighting with me these days."

Les sighed. I glanced over my shoulder. He was resting his head on the back of the sofa.

"I can't handle this father shit without you." He looked at me again. "Turns out, I'm not good at handling life without you."

My stomach churned. I needed to call Joy out of her room, but couldn't make my mouth open yet. I may not have ever been wildly, passionately in love with him, but I'd been content. And content had been pretty damned good. I'd never believed in the fairy-tale kind of love other girls did anyway. Nor the man-sweeps-you-off-your-feet kind of passion. I had wanted stability in a husband, stability and children. That's what he gave me. He had fulfilled my expectations, and I had been comfortable, content.

Yes, I'd been comfortable and content in a life that was a lie. And now I was paying the price. A big mystery was at the center of my life. Two strange men wanted something from me. They wanted it so badly that they were willing to break into my apartment and the homes of the people closest to me. They were willing to try to get information from me at my job. And those men knew me, most likely, because of Les.

Aside from that, there was whatever I was cooking up with Nico that was pretty damned close to him sweeping me off my feet. The passion I'd felt the night before was such an extreme, it was like nothing I ever thought could be real.

"Les, it's too late for that now." My voice was flat, sounding to me as if it belonged to someone else. I couldn't tell if he believed me. "You are not the person I thought I'd married. You killed that trust. I don't think I could ever feel safe with you again."

"And you feel safe with Nico?"

"I feel...I feel a lot of things with Nico." I smiled at him. "And safe is only one of them."

"But we share children. That's something I gave you. He would never do that."

"Which is fine with me. I don't want any more, remember?" I'd tried to convince him to get a vasectomy, but he'd refused. So I had my tubes tied.

Les stood and rubbed his face with his hands. "Just, please," he said, looking at me again. "Please promise me you'll think about us. How we were. What our life was like. I'd do anything to get that back again, Lucy. I really did love you. I still do. I was just caught up in a crazy lifestyle for a while. But I'm willing to give that up if you would just be back by my side. We could have our old life back."

Interesting. He was offering what I had promised to give to my kids a couple of weeks ago: our old life back. Was that still a good idea?

I went to Joy's door and knocked.

WHAT ARE THE ODDS?

I grabbed my coat and headed downstairs. A cold rain shower fell, and the wind seemed intent on drilling it into me. The sky was so gray and the air so thick, I could barely see the ocean beyond the water's edge. I crossed the boardwalk and went onto the sand anyway. As the only one fool enough to be walking on the beach in that kind of weather, I could easily pretend I was all alone in the world.

The wind plastered the rain sideways against my head. It trickled down my cheek, my neck, and inside my coat, chilling me to the core. If it had been my kids out there, I would have been pitching quite the fit for them to get their asses back inside where they'd be warm and dry. But I needed to be out there. It cleared my head.

So that's how Les explained it: he was caught up in a crazy lifestyle. What was wrong with the lifestyle we had? We had a great life before he left. We were all happy. Weren't we?

I trundled down the shore thinking about the life Les and I actually had. I had grown up wanting nothing but to be married, have a couple of kids, and get a dog. I got it all, but it wasn't enough. I realized I wanted something else: a career. I went back to work and realized I missed out on all the partying and fun I could have had as a single woman, so I quit doing one-on-one therapy, took the job at the senior center, where I could work fewer hours and have more of a social life. I became known as the queen of summer barbecues. But I could never relax. I always had a project that needed my attention, something to make our house, our lives, better. Looking back, I realized none of it really mattered—finding the right drapes for the living room, coordinating the right after-school activities, researching the right swim coach, buying the right something or other. None of it kept our family together.

I had constantly looked for ways to make everything right, perfect, to make sure all needs were met before they were felt. In other words, I was exhausted all the time because I was caught up in some kind of lifestyle. Apparently, he'd been doing the same thing too; he just got more sleep than I did. Could I really hold it against him?

But could I go back to him? What would my life be like with him again? What would my life be like without Nico? Nico was right that night in the garage. We would kill an excellent friendship if we didn't work out as...as whatever we were now.

Nico and I were more than friends, yes, but we weren't in a committed relationship, a marriage. Nico and I were happy with whatever we were. Was I happy when I was with Les, truly happy? Or had I been telling myself I was because I was supposed to be? After all, everyone around me seemed happy, so didn't that mean I should be, too?

But were they happy? Really? Was Asher's part-time job choice a decision made because he was enjoying his life? Where did Joy suddenly find all the Gothic makeup and clothing? Was she keeping it hidden from me somehow? Who was really happy?

Les had acted happy. He had behaved as if he was genuinely satisfied throughout our marriage, until the day he left me. And I truly believed Les loved me. I never suspected he was seeing anyone because he was always so good to me. He supported me in everything I did or wanted to do. He good-naturedly tolerated my sense of humor and frequently told me how much he appreciated everything I did. He always remembered my birthday and our anniversary, and he listened to me tell him everything that went through my mind. What had happened?

He did work a lot of evenings and weekends, as all people in his position do. Naturally, he would sleep late in the mornings when I was at work. Our sex life had dwindled to what I'd called, only partially in jest, perfunctory sex: those two evenings he had off from work, and an occasional weekend morning when neither of the kids needed to be driven somewhere.

Was that it? Did we fall apart? Did he stray because he needed more sex? He was never one to demand it. He never pressured me, and he never stopped approaching me the way he did the first time we were together, when neither of us really knew what we were doing. He was always timid in bed. Would that explain why he was too timid to ask me for more?

And when I thought it through, I realized our sex life dwindled even more to become very rare occasions last spring and almost stopped over the summer. It decreased in frequency as my weight increased in girth. The added pounds arrived when I learned I could survive my father's viewings, wake, and funeral by eating my way through them. Is that why *the girlfriend* was so skinny? Did he love me, but not my fat?

I paused on the beach. The rain had picked up, slashing through the air like wet bullets. The ocean crashed beside me. I stood still as the constant motion of the world around me came into focus.

Everything was in shades of gray. The sand was the color of mussel shells, the ocean was slate with light-ash hued waves. I couldn't see beyond the dune to the land, but the sky was tarnished pewter. Mrs. O'Leary's gray swath sprang to mind, her passive-aggressive outlet for the rage eating away at her. I understood that rage. I had a lava flow of ire burning in my stomach. I was about to explode in my gray world.

Les fucked up our family to have sex with a skinny bitch.

I stomped closer to the dunes. The sand was looser there and harder to trudge through. But the rain was so dense I couldn't see an entrance to the boardwalk unless I was up there. I was ready to go back and face that shit I had married against my father's wishes.

The wind changed direction and splattered me in the face. Perhaps it was nature's way of giving me a good slap. Les wasn't the only problem. I was the one who let herself go. He didn't help, but I'd started it. And now what was I to do? How was I to fix it? Did I owe it to him to try again? To myself? To the kids?

I found a walkway to the boardwalk, climbed it, and looked inland. Having traveled south on the beach, I didn't recognize any of the buildings I saw before me, as I seldom go that way. I wasn't sure how far I'd roamed, but I did know it was impossible to get lost if you stayed on the boardwalk. I turned around, putting the ocean on my right so I knew I was heading north, and headed home. My teeth chattered, my nose ran, and my head spun.

Did any of this matter now? Did it matter why he left? Les was involved in organized crime. My father would have been yelling, "I told you so!" if he were alive. I stopped on the boardwalk as I realized another coincidence that may not have been a coincidence after all: my father tolerated Les for our entire marriage up until around a year before his death, which happened to be around the same time that Nico had learned about the condo. My dad had returned to his old self that last year of his life, but had treated Les worse than ever.

Did Daddy know, too? How?

I tried to stomp off the wet sand that clung to my shoes and pants. Everything on me was soaked, and my body struggled to fight the pull of gravity. The wind belted my face, cutting my breath short, and my coat was ineffective. As I continued north, thinking about my father and his feelings toward Les, I became more and more suspicious, but of what, I wasn't sure.

The rain slowed as I approached Montpelier Avenue, the street that runs along the side of my building opposite Chelsea. I heard my phone ring and dug it out of my pocket. I had to turn around to shield it from the rain to read Nico's name on the screen.

"Where the hell are you?" he yelled.

"On the boardwalk."

"Jesus Christ! I've been scared shitless!"

"Why? What happened?"

"Didn't you get any of my texts? I think I sent about a dozen, and you didn't respond. This is the fourth fucking time I called your cell phone!"

"Oh God, Nico, I'm sorry. I didn't hear any of it."

"My guys are tearing this city apart looking for you. Where have you been?"

"Walking on the beach."

"It's raining!"

"I know. And it's windy, too. I guess that's why I didn't hear my phone. I'm sorry I worried you."

"That's okay." His voice calmed. "As long as you're okay, that's all that matters. You are okay, aren't you?"

"I will be. I'm almost at my condo. Where are you? I need—" I coughed as I realized I was about to say *I need to tell you something.* "I have to talk to you," I said.

"I need to talk to you, too. I'm pulling into the building now. I'll wait for you in the lobby."

He was true to his word, wrapping his arms around my cold, wet body when he saw me.

"What the hell were you doing out there? You're soaked." We got on the elevator.

"I needed to give Les and Joy some alone time. He came over to talk to her about their fight. But listen, I think—"

"Is that why she was here last night? They had a fight?"

"Yes."

"So you had to go out on the beach and risk pneumonia so they could kiss and make up?"

The elevator doors opened. We stepped out on my floor and headed down the hall.

"No, not really. They needed privacy so…" I stopped before my door. "I don't know." I leaned against him, just to feel his strength. "But that doesn't matter now. I think…I have an idea, but I'm not sure if it makes sense."

He opened the door. Les was still there. He was sitting at the dining table with Joy. They were drinking hot cocoa.

"Good, glad you two are warm, dry, and happy. It's time for you to leave," Nico said to them as he pulled me into my bedroom. "Get dried and changed. I'll make cocoa for you."

"But—"

"No buts."

I did as I was told, slowly. I shivered so badly I could barely make my fingers work.

When I came out of the bedroom, Nico was the only one in the condo. He had two cups of cocoa on the coffee table before the sofa. He wrapped the sofa throw around me as we sat.

"Where'd they go?" I asked.

"I sent them to Les' home, where they are supposed to be this weekend. Where you should have sent them instead of sacrificing yourself to the elements."

I sipped the cocoa and felt its warmth all the way down to my stomach.

"Thank you," I said to him.

"You need to tell me something?"

"Yes." I blinked slowly. "I think whatever is going on involves my dad."

He put both hands on my cheeks and kissed my forehead. "Yeah, I think so, too."

A DAD ALWAYS KNOWS

Y ou go first," Nico said.

We settled on the sofa with cocoa cups in hand.

"It doesn't make complete sense. It's more a feeling than anything fact-based."

"I trust your intuition. It's only been wrong as far as Les is concerned."

"Well, like I said, this doesn't make sense." I sipped and set the cup on the table so I could curl my legs under me; my feet were still cold.

"Let's hear it." He rubbed my thigh.

"Daddy died about a year ago, right?"

He nodded.

"And it was about a year before *that* when he started acting like his old self again." I paused and wove my still-cold fingers into his warm ones. "That was around the time you found out about Les' other life."

"Mmm."

"Did my dad know about it, too?"

"I think so."

"Well, that's all I got. That's the only connection I could make, but my gut is now telling me there's something more to it. Daddy knew something, and I hope to God that whatever it was had nothing to do with his death. If Les is in any way responsible—" I inhaled sharply through my nose and reached for my mug of cocoa. "Anyway, why do *you* think all this has something to do with my dad?"

"It's a long story." Nico drank a sip.

"You're my only date, you know."

His eyes crinkled at me over the top of his cup.

"When I met Les for breakfast this morning, he was a wreck," he said. "He and Ash went out for dinner last night. While they were gone, someone broke into his house but stole nothing."

"Oh, you know, I was kind of thinking maybe Les was the third man."

"Good deductive reasoning. I'd been suspecting that too." Nico sipped. "I didn't mention anything about your condo being searched, but I did tell him you got a call from the alarm company about your parents' place being broken into."

"Did he say anything about that?"

"He didn't want to, but I pressed him. I made him feel guilty by suggesting you could be hurt because of him. I told him to tell me everything, or I'd have to personally get even should anything happen to you." Nico gave me a lopsided grin. "Les is a little afraid of me, you know."

I laughed. "Did your threat work?"

"It was a promise, and yes, it did. But let's backtrack a couple of years." Nico paused to put his mug on the table and kiss my free hand. "I hate telling you this stuff. I really do."

"You'd rather keep secrets from me?"

"I'd rather you not have to go through any of it. I'd rather me never knowing anything about it to begin with. But then again, if I hadn't, we wouldn't be here now, like this, on the sofa."

I smiled. "I know you're contrite, Nico. I'm not upset with you."

"But you have every reason to be."

"I understand client confidentiality."

"Right." He kissed my fingertips. "Here goes. A couple of years ago, Les called me to ask if I could connect him with someone who was good with gold and gems and that he could trust to be confidential."

"What does that mean? Like an underground jeweler?"

"I guess you could call it that." He twisted his body sideways to face me. "I connected him with Rocco Laurent in Philadelphia. He's an antiques dealer, specifically an antique jewelry dealer."

"So you gave Les a contact for a legitimate business?"

"Rocco had a legitimate business on Jeweler's Row in Philly, yes, but he also had a gift for altering or redesigning jewelry."

"Why would Les need that?"

"Apparently, he lost something he shouldn't have," Nico smirked and ran a hand along the inseam of my leggings. "He asked me to bring Rocco to him here; that's when I learned about this condo. And the day I brought Rocco here, we had just handed my keys to the valet guy downstairs when your father came by."

"My father was just, dare I say, *coincidentally*, strolling through the valet area?"

"Exactly. And, not only was that a coincidence, but he and Rocco knew each other. They exchanged a few pleasantries, and your dad walked away."

"Well, he was born and raised in Philly. It's possible they knew each other from back then."

"It's possible."

"What did they talk about?"

"Nothing that stood out to me at the time. I asked Rocco how he knew him, and he said your dad did business with him a very long time ago, and your dad had recently, as in just a week or so before, contacted him about making a repair."

"He left Philly before I was born, so I could see the long-time thing. But I don't know about repairing good jewelry. I'm sure I'd remember my mother complaining about something being broken if she'd had something nice enough to get repaired. That part doesn't sound right."

"Well, there was something about how your dad just showed up that morning. I got the feeling he was waiting for someone." Nico shifted on the sofa.

"You think he was waiting for you and Rocco?"

"Maybe. I don't know. But Rocco and I came up here. I introduced him to Les and went back downstairs to give them privacy. I spotted your dad over by the back door to Lou's."

"Where?"

"The shrimp place."

"Oh. What was he doing there?"

"Standing by a column. Behind it, actually. I only saw him because I'd crossed over that way heading to Lou's, where I was to wait for Rocco." Nico paused. "Your dad was clearly looking for someone. He was positioned very carefully. He did *not* want to be seen by anyone coming in or going out of this building."

"Did you say anything to him?"

"No. The man was on a stakeout. Why would I interfere?"

151

"Do you think he was spying on Les?"

"I do now." He was quiet for a minute. The only noise I could hear was the heater humming and the rain splattering on the windows. "Your feet warm?"

"What?"

"Are your feet warm?" He tugged my legs out from under me, put my feet in his lap, and massaged them.

"Thank you," I smiled at him. "But there has to be more."

"There is. I just wanted to make sure you were comfortable. Is this good?"

"Mmmm." His thumbs pressed into the arches of my feet. "So good *I* may have to get even."

"I'll be sure to make you pay up," he grinned. "But back to business. Are you ready?"

"No, but go ahead anyway." I leaned back against the arm of the sofa and let him knead away at my feet.

"So this morning, Les reminded me of that meeting with Rocco."

"Did he mention anything about my dad?"

"Yes. He—"

"Did he say my dad had been following him?"

"No, actually, he was confused by your dad's involvement."

"What involvement?"

"If you'd let me finish." He smiled. I pretended to zip my lips. "Les told me he had needed Rocco's services that morning to re-create some kind of medallion that had been stolen by accident."

"Stolen by accident?"

"Yes," Nico paused and held my eyes. "Does the name Sal Pulsoni ring a bell?"

"No. Who is he?"

"He's a 'made man' in Philly. He's also your Uncle Sid's former brother-in-law."

"Uncle Sid's..." I stopped to think what *former brother-in-law* meant. "Oh, is he the one who married my mom's twin sister?" My mom's sister died shortly after she'd married. Angie was a baby, and I hadn't been born, so we'd never met her. I wasn't even sure what her name was. My mother never spoke about her. "How would you know who he is?"

"Les told me."

"How would Les know him?"

"Your Uncle Sid introduced them." Nico stopped and waited. "Isn't this when you say 'why would Uncle Sid introduce Les to him'?"

I laughed and tried to tickle his stomach with my toes.

"I'm sorry! This is all a bit much! *I* didn't even know the man's name." I leaned my head back and looked at the ceiling. "Make it all make sense, Nico." I looked at him again. "Please?" I stood, reluctantly taking my feet away from him, but the need to cook, to do something where I was in control, hit me hard. "What do you want for dinner?"

"Whatever you feel like cooking."

"Linguine with clam sauce? I bought some fresh clams on Thursday. If we don't eat them tonight, they'll go bad."

"Love linguine with clams. How are you doing them, red or white?"

"Does it matter?" I went to the kitchen.

"No, I was just curious." He leaned into the pass-through. "I like them both."

I opened the cabinet door.

"Oh, looks like I'm out of tomato gravy up here. I have more down in storage, but let's just make it easy and have white." I opened the refrigerator and pulled out the clams I'd bought at Barbera's. I put the shells in the sink to scrub them, but they were pretty clean and didn't need much from me. "Les, Dad, Uncle Sid, his former brother-in-law, Sal Somebody, Enzo, Aldo...Put them all together for me, please, while I put together this meal."

"Let's go back a few years," Nico said. "Here's the reason I introduced Les and Rocco. Sal needed cash. Sid connected him with Les who made arrangements for a robbery of jewelry done by the Finarelli cousins, Aldo and Enzo."

"One of those insurance things?" I set the clams aside to peel an onion.

"Right, an insurance thing." Nico paused and watched me cut the onion. "There was a catch, though. Sal didn't want everything stolen. He had a few things that had sentimental value to him."

"Aw, a sensitive mobster." I scraped the onion into a pan of olive oil and broke apart a head of garlic. "I take it a lot of garlic will be good for you?"

"I've been keeping a toothbrush here. Have you noticed?"

"I did."

"Do you mind?"

"Not at all." But I did wonder why his shaving kit was by the sink. He repacked it every day. I couldn't understand why he didn't just leave everything out and tuck the kit under the sink.

Nico came into the kitchen and took a bottle of wine out of the refrigerator. "Well, Les followed orders, but either he neglected to mention what was to stay, or Enzo and Aldo forgot; no one knows, but everything was stolen, including a medallion for St. Cecelia that Sal wanted to keep." He poured two glasses of wine.

"St. who?"

"St. Cecelia. Sal was not happy and ordered Les to find it. Enzo and Aldo had sold everything to a variety of pawnshops throughout the AC area. Les went to them all, and when he finally found the right shop, the owner had already sold it."

"I guess that was another fashion statement I missed." I added the garlic to the onion, and the kitchen filled with the delicious aroma of the sauté. I sipped my wine and filled a pot with water for the linguine. "I didn't realize St. Cecelia medallions were that popular. Think they made earrings for her?"

"I like it when you wear big earrings."

"I do too." I grinned over my shoulder at him. "But that was two years ago." I added red pepper flakes to the garlic and onion and opened a jar of parsley.

"You're not using fresh herbs?"

"None to be found in the market this time of year." I sprinkled on the parsley, then added clam juice from a jar, a bit of the wine, and stirred before looking at him. "So I'm waiting. That was two years ago. What has that to do with anything now?" I dumped in the clams, put a lid on the pot, and set the timer.

"Sal became impatient, so Les tried to have another medallion made."

"Enter Rocco." I leaned against the counter, waiting for the water to boil.

"Enter Rocco." Nico stood opposite me, leaning against the sink. "Rocco made another medallion according to the directions Les provided. Les sent it on to Sal, but Sal had had a stroke and was in the hospital, so he didn't get it. He was in intensive care for a while, then in an assisted-living facility for a long time, where he relearned how to walk and talk. He got out about three weeks ago and went home." Nico sipped his wine. "The first thing he did was look for his medallion, and that's when he learned it was a fake."

"How?"

Nico grinned at me. "Les must have never been an altar boy."

"What? Why?" My water was boiling. I dumped the linguine in and stirred, then lifted the lid to stir the clam sauce.

"St. Cecelia is the patron saint of music. Are you familiar with what her symbols look like?"

"No."

"Well, sometimes she's depicted with a harp, at others with a piano-looking thing. I think it's called a pianoforte. Anyway, there isn't one specific image that is always used with her. But Les didn't know that. He just said, 'Make a medallion for St. Cecelia and put it on a rosary chain with ruby beads.'"

"Real rubies?" I asked as the timer went off.

"Real."

"Wow." I opened the clam sauce lid and stirred again, looking for any shells that hadn't opened. They all looked perfect. I moved the pan to the back burner and took the butter out of the refrigerator.

"Rocco made the medallion with St. Cecelia at the piano thing, and apparently the original had her at a harp. Sal wants his original medallion back so badly that he wants to kill Les over it."

"What?" I froze with my face in the steam of the linguine water.

"He gave him thirty days to find the original one." Nico drained his wineglass and set it down. "Should I set the table?"

"Sure." I made my arms move to take the colander from the cabinet and put it in the sink. With my stomach in knots, I wasn't sure I'd be able to eat dinner, though I'd made one of my favorite meals. "Does Les know where it is?"

Nico stopped arranging the placemats on the dining table to look at me through the pass-through.

"No. But he knows who bought it from the pawn shop."

"Who?" I stared at him.

"Your father."

I was sure he misspoke. "What? No way! What would he have done with it? My mother didn't wear anything like that." My hands shook as I piled our plates with linguine and clam sauce. His was stable when he refilled our wineglasses.

"When Les found the right shop, the owner said it was old Officer McCool who'd bought it. The man knew your dad from his days as a cop. Les couldn't go to your dad and ask for it back. He was sure your dad would have him arrested."

"Or worse," I said and sat at the table. "So what's going to happen now? Do you think the Fabian, or Finarelli, or whoever guys want the medallion too?"

"Well, what happens now is that Les has until Friday to find the medallion. That's what he wants my help with. And I have no idea about the Finarelli men. If they were looking for a medallion, why only search in kitchens?"

"Right. I don't get it." I tucked my napkin on my lap. "What happens if Les can't find the original medallion?"

"Sal will be a very unhappy man."

GOOD GRAVY

Linguine and clam sauce, linguine and *fresh* clam sauce, is so divinely good it can make you forget you ever had a problem, even the problem that your ex-husband might be in danger of losing his life. And following that main course by making love with Nico, almost gave me amnesia.

I waltzed into work the next day, convinced all was right in the world and that it would stay that way from now through eternity, or at least as long as Barbera's continued to get fresh clams.

But not all my MOFs ate as well as I did the night before. Mr. Schwartz must not have. He didn't show up to group, and his absence worried me. He'd never missed a day. I was sure he was staying away because he felt Aldo had invaded us.

Unlike the other meetings he had attended, Aldo was not the first in the room for group that morning. Mr. George was. And he managed to snatch the chair opposite me in the circle, forcing Aldo to sit next to him. Mr. George gave me a nod and a smile that suggested he knew what he was doing and that he, too, had linguine and fresh clam sauce for dinner the night before. I smiled back at him as I reached into my pocket for my cell phone.

It wasn't there.

My heart shot to my throat. I'd left the phone in my cubicle. I couldn't get up to get it. When I leave the seniors like that, they freak. Granted, Mr. Schwartz would be leading the freak-out episode, and he wasn't there, but I had a feeling they would all interrogate me as to why I had to leave, and then Aldo might even get suspicious.

My mind scrambled until I realized I could send Rachel out. She often ran errands for group members and me.

I scribbled a note, slid it into a manila folder, and handed it to her.

"Do me a favor," I said. "Will you try to contact Mr. Schwartz right away to make sure he's all right?" I bugged my eyes at her, then tried to roll them toward Aldo before looking down at the folder. "You'll find all the contact info in this file."

"Sure, Lucy," she smiled at me. I held my breath while I waited for her to look in the file. She shifted in her seat and opened it while sipping her coffee. I saw her eyes scan the note telling her to get my phone from my cubicle and send a text to Nico saying Aldo was here. "I'm worried about him too," she said as she stood to leave the room.

"Who are you worried about, dear?" Mrs. O'Leary asked.

"Mr. Schwartz," I said. "He has never missed a group meeting. Has anyone heard from him?"

"I'm worried, too. Freddie is a dear, dear friend of mine," Mr. Hanson said. We waited a moment for tears, but none came. He looked to be wearing Joy's black eyeliner. I hoped he could hold tough for the entire meeting.

"Well, maybe he just has out-of-town visitors. I'm sure Rachel will let us know about him."

"About who?" Mrs. Dimiccio asked.

"Mr. Schwartz."

"I knew a Schwartz once. Henry Schwartz. He lived on the floor above me."

"That ain't the same Schwartz," Mrs. Elliot said. "She be talking 'bout Freddie. Freddie ain't here."

"Right, well, I'm sure Rachel will find out," I said.

"Did Freddie eat a lot of salt?" Mrs. Elliot asked. "Think they put him in with Harriett?"

"I'm not sure what's going on with him," I said. "But I am sure Rachel will get to the bottom of it."

"Maybe you're right," Mrs. Dimiccio said. "Maybe my Schwartz lived on the bottom floor, not above me."

"It ain't that Schwartz!" Mrs. Elliot yelled at her.

"Yes, well..." I was lost, completely rattled, and couldn't quite figure out how to get myself back together. Aldo's face was angry, and I was clearly his target. I glanced at my notepad to see what I'd planned to talk about. It said: doctors and schedule changes.

I went the easy route first and explained that, while they may notice changes to the rest of the schedule, our meeting would continue at the same time in the same room every Monday. We'd been assured we could have uninterrupted group meetings every week. What I left out was that Mona had told Rachel and me we were geniuses with the name of the group. She said the budget gurus thought *Marginalized Outcast Faction* sounded like a group that would be too dangerous to mess around with. My rationale on keeping them together wasn't even needed, which was good because I had yet to get around to writing it.

Rachel returned before I could start speaking with our doctors.

"Did you find Freddie, dear?" Mrs. O'leary asked her.

"I had to leave a message," Rachel said. "Lucy," she handed me my phone, "you left this in my cubicle. I thought you might want it back."

"Thank you." I tucked the phone in the pocket of my slacks. "I was wondering where it was."

"You should be careful about all the radiation pouring out of that phone, Lucy," Mr. Moffat suggested. "There are all kinds of studies proving they cause cancer in rats."

"Does she look like a rat, man?" Mr. Thomas challenged.

"No, but anyone with a grain of intelligence would realize that if something could hurt a rat, it could hurt a human." Mr. Moffat retorted.

And they were off.

My seniors were off in their own world of real and imagined fears, trying to find a way to express themselves. Aldo remained silent. His continual glare at me was his only contribution. We were eventually able to turn the cell phone and cancer conversation into one about speaking to our doctors, and, with a little gentle coercion, Mrs. Elliot agreed to make an appointment with her doctor.

Aldo sat mute until it was time for everyone to leave.

"Lucy," he said as the others put on hats and coats. "I was hoping I could have a few minutes of your time." His eyes slid to Rachel for a nanosecond. "Privately."

"Of course." I prayed Nico had made it to the senior center by now and was somewhere on the grounds.

Mr. George approached me, cutting in front of Aldo to lean into my left side.

"He's no good," Mr. George whispered in my ear. "You want me to stay with you? I know how to use this cane right."

"Thank you, Mr. George." I smiled at him. "But I think I'll be fine."

"You have a gun on you?"

"No! I'm sure that's not necessary."

"I hope not. He has one." He nodded his head toward the door. "Don't you let him take you outside, now."

"I won't." I swallowed hard. "Thank you. I really appreciate your looking out for me."

I hate the way TV portrays people from New Jersey. If you believed what you watched, you'd think the state was filled with Italian descendants who were either shallow and stupid or mob-connected. Truth be told, I used to say I'd never met anyone like the people I saw on television. And then Nico told me about Uncle Sid, and then I learned what kind of people Enzo and Aldo were. Now I suspected there may be some facts behind the stereotypes. And my new opinion, coupled with Mr. George's warnings, made me even more fearful of Aldo.

He waited until everyone left the area before looping his arm in mine.

"Lucy, Lucy, Lucy," he said. "I'm so disappointed in you." He walked me toward the common area.

"Why?" My heart pounded in my ears. "Is there something you need from the senior center?"

"No. But there is something I need from you."

We reached the common area. I expected to see Nico, but no one was there. We don't hold classes between noon and two o'clock, so no one would be coming or going from the front doors unless it was a coworker heading out to lunch, but most people on our payroll only go out on Fridays. Yes, there were security cameras that would recognize Aldo's face, but where would I be or what would be left of my body by the time they figured out who he was? I stopped walking.

He slid his arm out of mine and gripped my biceps tight as he dragged me to the door.

"Please! You're hurting me." I tried to wiggle away from him.

"No, I'm making sure I have your attention."

"Why are you doing this?"

He stopped just outside the doors, spinning me around to face him.

"I want to take you to lunch." He still gripped my arm tightly. "Enzo and me, we want to have a sit-down chat with you. All private, like." At that moment, the van that had been in my parents' driveway pulled up. Aldo slid the side door open and shoved me inside.

"Where are you taking me?" I asked from the rear of the van, where I sat on a box.

"Like I said, to lunch." He sat on another box, removed a gun from his jacket, and pointed it at me. "We don't want to hurt you, Lucy. This thing here is just to make sure you don't do something stupid."

The gun didn't look real to me. But then again, I'd never looked at one from the perspective of it being pointed at me. Lacking anything of substance to base my opinion on, I decided not to experiment by pushing my luck.

"I promise you, I won't do anything stupid." I swallowed. "I, uh, I would like to know where we're going for lunch."

"Angelo's. Ever been?"

"On Fairmount?"

"Yes. Is there another?"

"No, not that I know of." And yet another true coincidence: the last name of the people who run Angelo's is Mancuso, but Nico is not related to them. Was he expecting Nico to be there?

"They have real good food, don't you think?" he asked.

"Um, yes. Real good." I continued to stare at the gun. "But I've never been taken there at gunpoint. You could have just made reservations, you know."

"Ah, Lucy. You do have quite the sense of humor." Aldo smiled at me. "I like you, I really do. But, you wouldn't let me get close to you, Lucy. I tried at that senior center. To get close to you. I thought maybe you'd open up to me and talk freely like. The way you do with those crazy people in there. You work with some loony old people, you know."

"Yeah, seems I always have crazy people around me."

"But you didn't let me in. If you had, maybe we could have gone for walks or something."

"Is this a date?"

"Ha! Now that your divorce is final, you're playing the field, huh?" He winked at me. "Good for you. And maybe when you're done with that other Italian, you can give me a call. But for right now, we got some business to take care of."

"Business? You need a gun for business? You need to kidnap me for business?" I couldn't believe how brave I sounded. I thought I might have even sounded cocky. I've never been cocky in my life. A little sarcastic, maybe, snarky for sure, but not cocky. I wondered whether that meant I'd actually found something positive in being taken hostage.

"Don't use that word," he snapped at me and jerked his gun. "We're not in the kidnapping business. Believe me, Enzo and me, we don't want to hurt you. So if you just talk nicely to us, I'll be dropping you back at the old people place, and you can keep on dealing with those crazies. Got it?"

"I think so." I sat quietly, trying to casually glance out the small rear windows of the van. I saw no sign of Nico, but there was plenty of traffic. If I could bust out the back doors, there would be several witnesses to see me get attacked by Aldo should he follow. But those witnesses would have to be willing to step forward after they most likely ran over me.

I stayed put.

The driver stopped in front of Angelo's. Aldo grabbed me by the arm again, pulled me close to him as he stepped out of the van, and walked with me, almost pressed up against him, into the restaurant. I felt the gun poking me in my kidney area.

Enzo was sitting in the far back corner. Several plates of food littered the table before him. Aldo made me sit next to the wall on the opposite side of the table from Enzo and sat close beside me.

"Just so you know, we're not alone," Enzo said. "We got a couple friends eating lunch here right now. So even if you did manage to break away from the table, one of them will catch you. Got it?"

"Got it." I looked around as much as I could. They had me sitting with my back to the entrance. The only people I could see without turning completely around in my seat was Enzo and Aldo. "Look, if this is about the medallion, I don't have it."

"The medallion?" Enzo asked. He and Aldo chuckled.

"No, this ain't about the medallion, honey." Enzo poured wine into three glasses. He handed me one. "Not directly anyway."

I downed the wine in one long drink. Enzo smiled and poured another glass for me. He looked up, and his smile was replaced by a frown. "You've got one protective boyfriend, you know that?"

Aldo and I turned to look behind us. There stood Nico and six of his buff men standing in the center of the restaurant. Enzo stood.

"Ah, Nico, we meet again," he said. "Why don't you join us here?" He waved his arm over the table. "Your friends can dine at their own tables. Aldo and I have several of our own friends here, too."

Nico said something to his men before approaching us.

Aldo didn't move, but Enzo sat again, directly across from me, leaving the seat across from Aldo open for Nico.

"I guess we'll need another glass." Enzo waved his arm in the air. We were clearly on familiar turf for him. He was in a black V-neck sweater and jeans, looking and acting comfortably in his attire.

"Did I miss anything?" Nico looked relaxed, too. I searched his eyes for a sign of something, exactly what, I wasn't sure. He looked calm and confident. I tried to will myself to feel that way. When I failed, I sucked down my second glass of wine. Enzo refilled it.

A waiter brought another empty glass to the table. Enzo filled it, handed it to Nico, then asked for another bottle of wine. He glanced at me. "Make that two more."

"I was just telling these gentlemen I had no idea where the medallion was," I said.

"And we were about to tell Lucy that we have no interest in the medallion," Aldo said.

"Then what do you have an interest in?" Nico sipped his wine, a tiny sip.

"Tomatoes." Enzo picked up a fork and stabbed the baked ziti. "Taste this." He handed me the fork.

I stared at him.

"Taste it," Aldo grunted. "I thought you didn't want to do anything stupid?"

"I don't. But I don't want to get poisoned either."

"If we wanted to kill you, you would already be dead."

I looked at Nico. He nodded. Enzo refilled my glass. I took a bite of the ziti, chewed slowly, swallowed, then took a slow sip of wine. Slow, but thorough. I left very little in the glass.

"Now, taste this." Enzo ripped off a chunk of bread from a loaf, dipped it into a bowl, and handed it to me.

I ate. The bowl was filled with Bolognese sauce.

"What do you think?" Enzo asked.

I finished my third glass of wine before answering. I thought they were insane, but saying that probably fell under the *stupid* category, or

163

maybe the *not nice* one. Getting drunk might fit in a different and possibly safe category altogether. "I think they're both quite good."

"But they're not as good as yours. Your sauce is much better." Enzo took a long swig of wine and leaned back in his chair. "And do you know why?"

"How do you know what my gravy tastes like?" I asked at the same moment I realized what was missing from my kitchen cabinets: my jars of homemade tomato gravy. Yes, these guys were crazy. Certifiably crazy. They'd broken into four homes looking for tomato gravy.

Aldo laughed and sipped his wine.

"Never mind," I said. "I know how you know. You stole my gravy from my kitchen. Why?"

"Your Irish father taught you how to make that sauce, right?" Enzo asked.

I stared at him, then looked at Aldo before answering. "Right."

"And he taught you to use special tomatoes, too, right?"

Again, I paused before talking. "How do you know all this?"

"Right?"

"Right! Now, how do you know all this, and why are you pointing a gun at me over it?"

"Shhhh, keep your voice down," Enzo said. He refilled my glass.

"Sorry, I get a little panicky when I feel my life is in danger," I said.

"See, Lucy, we had a deal with your father," Aldo said. "And he didn't quite keep his word."

"How did you know my father?" I took just a sip from my fourth glass of wine and ate another bite of the ziti. It *was* very good.

"Back when we were contracted by your husband—" Enzo started.

"*Ex*-husband," Nico corrected him. "He hired you to rob Salvatore Pulsoni?"

"Right," Aldo said.

"But we want to be done with that line of work," Enzo said.

"What line of work are you looking to get into now?" Nico asked. He reached his fork across the table and slowly swirled several long linguine noodles on it before putting them in his mouth. I breathed a sigh of relief and drank more wine. He'd just deliberately staked his claim on the conversation and the table. We might have been surrounded by dangerous lunatics, but Nico seemed to be capable of dealing with them, which meant I could go unconscious and let him handle everything.

"We want to open our own restaurant," Enzo said.

"That's quite the change," I offered. Apparently, the wine had hit me.

"It is." Aldo agreed. "And we have your father to thank for that."

"I'm sure he'd say 'you're very welcome' if he were here."

"How do you know Lucy's father?" Nico asked. He ripped a piece of bread off the loaf and dipped it into the Bolognese sauce. His arm went directly in front of Enzo's face.

"As I was saying, somehow McCool found out we were hired by Lucy's hus-...ex-husband and he befriended us. Even had us over to dinner one night at his home."

"What? My parents entertained you? Really?" I leaned toward him. "Did my mom like you?"

"Never met your mother. It was just your pop. Two years ago, he came up to us in this very restaurant when me and Aldo were having lunch. He introduced himself as Womzak's father-in-law and said he had a proposition for us. If we were interested, we were to contact him at his home on a Wednesday evening. At the time, I guess you could say we were interested in just about any kind of proposition. We went over the next Wednesday night, unannounced-like. But your father let us in." Enzo finished his wine and poured another glass.

"Wednesday night," I said. "My mother would not have been there. Wednesday nights are bridge nights for her. She was dealin' cards with the good women in her parish."

"There you have it. I guess that explains why your mother wasn't there," Aldo grinned and slapped me on the back. He almost knocked me into the table. "Your pop was eating dinner all by himself. He told us to pull up a couple o' chairs. We did." He grabbed me by the shoulders and propped me up better.

"So McCool invites you over. What was the proposition?" Nico asked. I noticed he was the only one actively involved in eating, not drinking. I got the feeling he was purposely staying completely sober, which was good 'cause I knew I was in no shape to drive. But then again, I didn't have a car nearby. I wondered if I was in any shape to walk.

"The proposition was, if we gave the medallion to him, he'd keep us out of jail," Enzo said.

"Didn't someone say he'd gotted it from a pawn shop?" I asked. "Or am I making 'at up?"

"You got it right," Aldo laughed. "That was part of the cover, honey."

"I don't get it." I stared into my glass. The wine was a dark red. Dark red usually goes quickly to my head. It might have made it there already since my stomach had only two bites of ziti and one chunk of bread as road bumps to slow down the four glasses I'd sucked down. Things were getting fuzzy in my thinking. It was possible I only needed one more to pass out. I hoped Enzo would refill without me having to ask him to. I didn't want to look like a lush.

"Pawn shop guys are usually easy buys," Nico explained. "I suppose, depending on who was doing the asking, your pawn broker had a different answer, right?"

"He's a smart one," Aldo said to me. He patted my knee. "He's probably a keeper."

"I think so, too," I whispered to him, trying to find my hand so I could rest my chin on it. Nico was grinning.

"So your dad gets the medallion, we skate free on the Pulsoni deal. But then we got caught for something else," Enzo continued, swirling his glass in front of him. "It was kind of related, so we thought your old man should keep us out of jail for that, too."

"I see," I said, though I really didn't.

"Right, so we figure he owes us one."

"He owed you a tomato." I nodded.

"No, he owes us a tomato source," Enzo nodded back at me.

"I think I'm the one who doesn't understand now," Nico said, and I realized I was still nodding.

"We earned time off for good behavior for being cooks in the Trenton prison. Learned some mighty fine cooking skills in that place," Aldo said.

"Right," Enzo continued. "We had a guy there, a mentor like, who taught us everything about cooking. Didn't he Aldo?"

"He did." Aldo lifted a glass like a toast. "And we learned chefs have a small world of their own. In fact, it's so small, that chef not only knew your father, but knew your father's secret."

"Secret?" Nico asked, looking at me. "Was your dad ever a chef?"

I opened my mouth to say something, but Enzo interrupted.

"Here's the thing, Lucy girl. We thought we'd like to cut into the restaurant business and stay out of jail for good. Do some real good Italian food somewhere. We like this place, and we've been eating here a lot, but we kept going back to your dad's sauce."

"Gravy," I corrected him.

"Right, your dad's gravy," Aldo said. "See Enny? I told ya that's what we should call it. It's a true Jersey thing."

"Fine, gravy." Enzo drained his glass and poured another. "You see, when your pop fed us, that was the best gravy ever. We couldn't believe he invited us to join him like that, but—"

"It a, a, a Irish thing," I interrupted. "We are obli—er, we are oblitagoried. No." I put my hand on the table to make it stop spinning. When did that start? "We are obligated—is dat de word? Yes! We's got to feed everyone who comesh into our house."

"That explains so much," Nico winked at me. I couldn't wink back without leaning against Aldo's shoulder for balance.

"Well, your dad had the best sauce, er gravy, we'd ever had. Better than my own mamma's. We asked him about it, and he said it was a secret ingredient." Enzo sipped.

"And when we were in jail, we learned what the secret ingredient was," Aldo explained. "Our head chef used to work at a place here on the shore. He was talking one day 'bout good tomatoes and how he had this special supplier near AC. We told him about your pop's gravy, how it was almost purple."

"I call it mauve," I said.

"We thought maybe saying violet on the menu," Enzo said. "Our special violet sauce."

"Lilac gravy soundsh nicer," I found myself nodding again.

"But it definitely ain't lilac in color."

"No, but violet ish close to violent, and you wanna shtay away from that, right?" I put my head back on Aldo's shoulder to make it quit nodding.

"So it has a unique color," Nico said. "And the chef knew something about a tomato that made the gravy a unique purple-mauve-violet color?"

"Oh, yeah," Aldo went on. "Our guy knew right away who your pop was. Your father was the one who made the tomato possible. But that's all our guy would say to us unless we agreed to give him a cut. He wants part of the profits from our business just for telling us

167

where to get the tomatoes. So we were thinking, since your pop didn't hold up his end of the bargain, and we got sent to prison anyway, well, we should make him pay by giving us that secret ingredient."

Enzo tapped his finger on the table. "That would set us head and shoulders above most of the other Italian restaurants in Jersey, you know? That gravy is the best in the world," he said.

I remained mute, but I had lifted my head off Aldo's shoulder to look at Enzo. I had a tough time keeping my eyes wide open.

"We been doing some experimenting since we got out," Aldo said. "After stealing your stash and that of your mother's, we think we got all the ingredients down for your gravy, except the tomatoes. Enny's got what's called a refined palate. And that's what he's telling me."

"I know it's the tomatoes," Enzo said. "I've recreated your sauce, and the only thing I haven't been able to do is find the right tomato. Your pop had the tomato connection, but you had the gravy. Your sister didn't have no sauce in her place. Neither did your ex-. Your house is where the gravy could be found. That means your pop must have given you the tomato connection."

"And you thought you had to hold her at gunpoint?" Nico asked. He was smiling, and even laughed a little. "You didn't think you could ask her outright?"

Enzo smiled back at him and leaned into his chair. I got the feeling he wasn't as drunk as I was.

"We happen to know she doesn't buy her tomatoes at any supermarket. We happen to know—"

"What was the one illegal thing was that her father did," Aldo finished for him. "And we had a feeling she wouldn't be too willing to tell us outright unless she knew we were serious about it. We tried, my friend, we tried to get her to feel comfortable confiding in us."

"That's right," Enzo chimed in. "We tried to get her to open up to Aldo and befriend him at that center. If she had been a little more friendly, he would have been inviting her out to fine places like this. They could have talked. Usually, he's pretty good with the ladies, but apparently, you're better." He clapped Nico on the back. "Because she wouldn't let either of us get to know her."

I downed my fifth glass of wine. I think it might have been Aldo's.

"So then. You're willing to make introductions for us, right?" Enzo asked, somehow looking directly in my eyes, though I couldn't get my head to stop swinging up and down. "You're willing to introduce us to your tomato source?"

"Luce?" Nico got my attention. "You have any idea what these guys are talking about?"

"Yeah," I hiccupped. "But I'ma not shure I'll remember shish convershation 'omorrow."

SOBERING THOUGHTS

W ho do you tell you're leaving for the day?" Nico asked. I leaned against him as I concentrated on making one foot step in front of the other as we walked into the senior center.

"Mona," I said. "I think."

"Hi there," he smiled at Gayle. I sat on her desk, twisted around, and attempted to smile at her too. But I must have twisted too far because I fell over. Gayle caught me.

"Where's Mona?" I heard Nico's voice and tried to sit up and find him. "Lucy just had an incident."

"Smells like an incident with a wine bottle," Gayle said. "Lucy, are you drunk?"

"I'm pretty sure." I aimed my gaze between her two sets of eyes. "I was trying real hard to get there."

"Mona!" Gayle shouted in the intercom. I ducked. "Mona, come here."

"Honestly," I found Nico. He was standing in front of me. I pressed my face into his chest. "You smell good. Wanna see my cubicle? Will you show me yours if I show you mine?"

"The cubicle might be good," Nico said. "Tell Mona to meet us in her cubicle. Do you think you can find it, Luce?"

"Like a good Girl Scout." I tripped through the administration area door.

The next thing I know, I was sitting behind my desk with images of Aldo and Enzo swirling in my head. Nico was squatting next to me, holding my chin, trying to make me look at him.

"Nico," I said to him. "You can't tell no one 'bout the 'matoes. 'K?"

"Shhh." He put his finger on my lips. "Tell me at home. After you sleep off lunch."

Sleep sounded good. I slid out of his grip and leaned my head on my desk.

Mona came in. Nico stood up.

"What is going on in here?" she asked. "Who are you?"

"Thish iz Mico, Nona," I tried to do the introduction. It was hard to enunciate with my chin firmly planted on my desk. "He'sh..."

"I'm here to take her home," Nico continued for me. "We're having a family emergency. She needs some time off. Can you make that happen?"

I turned my head sideways to look at him.

He looked fierce. If I didn't know him better, I would have been afraid. Instead, I wanted to get naked.

"Do I need to get security?" she asked me.

"No, he's shlooking out fer me," I answered, smiling at him.

"She's shnockered?" Mona asked.

"A little," Nico said. "She had a stressful lunch."

"Nico, I can't leave my old people. They need me." I smacked my lips together, and I thought I felt drool on my cheek.

"And they need you safe and well," he said, coming round my desk. He knelt beside me again. "You gotta take care of yourself before you can do anything good with them."

I leaned into him and broke down in sobs.

"She can take as long as she needs off," Mona said. "How long do you think?"

"She'll be back next Monday," Nico said.

"Monday? Just make sure she's on time. Tongues wag around here when people are late on Mondays."

The next thing I remember is waking in my bed, flat on my stomach. Nico was rubbing my back.

"Hey there," he said when he realized my eyes were open. "I think it's time to get the kids."

"What?" I rolled over to face him. "Did I pass out?"

"Yeah," Nico grinned at me. "How do you feel?"

"Thirsty." I worked my tongue. "Why's my mouth so dry?"

"No headache?"

"No headache. Just thirsty." I sat up and stretched my back.

"I'll get the kids." He kissed me on the forehead. "I just woke you so you wouldn't be unconscious when they got here."

"Yeah, that'd be hard to explain." I slid off the bed and hugged him. "Thank you for everything."

"You don't have to thank me." He sat me back on the bed. "What the hell happened there?"

"You expect me to remember?"

"No, I mean, why did you do that? You always control yourself."

I turned my head left and right, then bent my neck ear-to-shoulder on each side. "It just seemed like a good idea to be unconscious for the lunch. That way I wouldn't have to face it, you know?"

"Honey, you spent your entire marriage that way. Didn't you learn from that?"

I sighed and slumped on the bed. "I think I just did." I smiled up at him. "Thanks for waking me up."

He kissed me on the forehead. "I'll get the kids."

"You sure? I can get them."

"I don't mind."

"You could take my van if you know where my keys are."

"It'd ruin my image if I drove that van of yours."

"You hate it too? What's wrong with my van?"

"Nothing." He grinned. "It's still at the center. We'll have to get it tomorrow or something." He kissed me and walked out.

I took a shower and heard my cell phone ringing as I was stepping out. By the time I found the phone in a pocket of my slacks, wadded up on the floor by my bed, I'd missed the call from Nico. I called him back right away.

"Is everything all right?" I asked.

"Yes. Everything's fine. I'm just checking in with you. They're both bringing friends home, that's okay, right?"

I could hear the voices of the kids in the background. They were both bringing friends home. I'd have a house filled with noise that evening. Things were getting back to normal! Kids were coming over. I got dressed, thinking I should get back to normal, too. Maybe have a small party this coming Friday: Angie and Rick, me and Nico, the kids, and...Then I remembered the kids would be in Philadelphia with their dad for a Sweet Sixteen. That is, I remembered more clearly, they would be if Les were alive to take them to a Sweet Sixteen. And who knows what Aldo and Enzo would do to me if I couldn't get them in contact with crazy old Isaac Blackman about his damned tomatoes?

I called Angie and filled her in on everything while I slurped down a glass of water.

"Holy cow, Lucy! That's insane!" she said. "That's not like Daddy at all. Why would he buy a medallion like that?"

"I don't know. But Les is convinced he bought it from a pawn shop, and then my new foodie friends insisted Daddy made a deal with them over it. Have you ever seen anything like it before?"

"I'm not sure I'd recognize a medallion of St. Cecelia if it was in front of me. But it doesn't sound like anything I'd ever seen. And I'm sure I'd remember Ma having something with ruby beads on it if she ever wore it. That's not like a normal thing, is it?"

"Not for our family."

"What about the will? Did daddy mention anything in the will?"

"No, not that I remember. It just said everything went to Ma. And I don't want to talk to her about this. I want to exhaust all possibilities before I call her on it."

"Oh God, you're right. She'll freak. There will be no end to her freaking."

"I kind of feel like freaking."

"What are you going to do about the tomato deal?"

"Ange, I'm just now conscious for the first time since the conversation. I have no idea what I'm going to do. I'm stressing big time."

"So what are you making for dinner, then? I'd love to get me and Rick together with you and Nico. I think they'll hit it off well."

"I think so too, but Nico's bringing home the kids and their friends and picking up takeout from the Baltimore Grill."

"But you always cook when you're stressed."

"I know. I'm not sure what to do with myself." I refilled my water glass. "But I am sure I'll be cooking all week, as that's how long I have to find a medallion to save Les' ass, and for some reason, I think Nico said something in the car on the way home today about having that long to land a tomato deal."

"I'm not sure why you care about saving Les' ass."

"He's the father of my kids, remember?"

"Right. Every other weekend without children. Just make sure Nico knows Farmer Blackman is heavily armed. Always."

We clicked off as Nico and the kids arrived. The friends were

Gabi and Justin. Within seconds, the condo filled with the aroma of pizza and grease and teenage chatter; even Ash said, like, whole sentences, like.

"So tomorrow," I said as I went into the kitchen. "When I'm complaining about how fat I am, everyone will remember this dinner was Nico's fault?" I removed the trash can from below the sink to clean up.

"Just work out a little more, Mom." Joy brought in the used paper plates. "We're going down to go swimming."

"Nice, pumpkin," I pulled out the trash bag.

"Yeah." She grinned at me as the other kids brought in their trash. Once Ash was out of earshot, in his room with Justin, presumably changing clothes, and Gabi was in Joy's bathroom, Joy grabbed my arm. "Nico said you were exhausted and taking the week off from work. Are you okay?"

"Yes. I've just been working hard."

"And going through a lot of shit, I know." She pecked me on the cheek. "Let me know if there's anything I can do for you."

"The fact that you're socializing with your brother is more than I could ever ask for."

"Oh, that. Well, whatever." She went into her room to change.

The kids went down to the pool. Nico and I finished cleaning. He took the trash to the chute and returned to find me still in the kitchen. I was staring into the pantry where my gravy jars used to be. He came up behind me and wrapped his arms around my stomach.

"So you have more, right? Please tell me you have more," he said.

"Absolutely. I didn't have enough room here for it all. There's more down in storage."

"Ah! Lucy saves the day." He snuggled his face into my neck.

"I should go work out."

"You should get some rest." He nibbled on an earlobe.

"I just ate grease for dinner."

"And you had a liquid lunch." His hands slid over my abdomen, under my pants.

"Of about five hundred calories."

"Lucy gets a break sometimes." His tongue traveled down my neck.

"Lucy is still fat." I took his hands and placed them directly on my stomach, where it protruded the most. "Nico Mancuso doesn't date

175

women with fat like this, does he? Doesn't this ruin your image? I can't qualify for membership in the Bimbo of the Week club with a belly like this, can I?"

"The club went defunct a long while ago. And I'm not just dating you. I'm not just sleeping with you." Nico moved his mouth back up my neck and kissed my earlobe. "And I love all of you."

"But do you find me sexy?" I laughed. "And please don't patronize me."

"You wanna know the truth?" He turned me around and pounced me up on the counter.

"Yes, the truth. Tell me the truth. What makes me so attractive to you?"

"You're talking just physically here, right? Because I hope you know I love the whole package: your sense of humor, the way you're nonjudgmental and accept everyone, your—"

"Answer the damn question. What about me is so physically attractive? Huh? I can tell you all sorts of things that aren't. Let's start with the rolls of belly fat that just rested on each other when you plopped me up here. And then—"

"Stop." He unbuttoned my blouse. In an instant, his hands were inside, cupping my breasts. "First, you've got the greatest tits on the planet." He buried his face in my cleavage as I laughed. He stood straight and looked me in the eyes. "I'm serious. You've got your own sexy style, Luce. You've got curves. You bounce a little when you walk. I love it." He kissed me. "It drives me wild to watch you walk." He pulled me off the counter and led me out of the kitchen, toward the bedroom. "Come on. Let me prove to you just how sexy I think you are."

Later that evening, the friends had gone home, and Ash and Joy had showered and were ensconced in their bedrooms for the night. Nico and I were sitting on the barstools by the pass-through, drinking cocoa with our knees rubbing against each other. I couldn't believe how alive I felt being next to him. He brought out such passion in me in the bedroom, passion like I'd never felt, but outside the bedroom, he still managed to make me feel hyper alive, as if a veil had been stripped away from life and I got to see it, touch it, taste it, smell it, experience it all with heightened senses.

I smiled at him over my mug.

He smiled back and took a sip.

"I hate to dampen the good vibes of the night," he said. "But Lucy, we need to talk about today."

"You know, Dr. Munoz told me I should focus only on what I could control if I am to satisfactorily deal with the stress in my life." I sipped my cocoa. "I'd really prefer to keep all that in the can't-control column."

"But denial won't keep the Finarellis away." He reached out and touched my cheek. "I promise, Luce, everything will be all right."

"How? How is everything going to be all right?" In lieu of cooking, I paced the living area, going in circles around the coffee table. "Goddamn it! That God damned Les! This is all his fault! If he hadn't been so...so...such..."

"Such an ass, dick, bastard," Nico filled in for me. "I know, I know. But we can't let ourselves get stuck on that. We need to figure out a plan on what to do about it. I take it you want to find the medallion to save his sorry ass, though, right?"

"Yes. He's the father of my kids. You know the rhetoric."

"Right. So we have until Friday to help him get that. But that's not my main concern. My main concern is the one you refused to talk about at lunch, after lunch, and even now. What the hell was going on with your dad? What's up with the tomatoes?"

I sighed and sat on the sofa. Nico came and sat by me.

"You're never going to believe this," I said. "Not in a million years."

"Try me."

I turned sideways and rested my back against the arm of the sofa. He leaned into my bent legs and grabbed my hands. He kissed my fingertips and held my hands on my stomach. "Do you have any idea how much I love you touching me all the time?" I asked.

"I do have an idea," he said, squeezing my fingers. "Because that's how I feel. But that's not telling me anything about your dad and tomatoes."

"Think the kids can hear?"

"They each have music on. Talk tomatoes."

"Years ago, as in when I was a little girl years ago, my father befriended an old farmer out near Mays Landing. His name was Virgil Blackman."

"Virgil?"

"He was very old at the time."

"Sounds like he was born old. Isn't that a biblical name?"

"I'm not sure, but his son's name is Isaac." I grinned. "Isaac is now in charge, and he is pretty old now, too. I think one of his sons should take over. Things might be easier if they would."

"Who are his sons?"

"You have connections in Mays Landing?"

"I got connections everywhere. Who are his sons?"

"One is Zeke and the other is David, I think."

"Zeke as in Ezekiel?"

"Is there any other?"

"No idea. But go on."

"I've only met Zeke, and we've never spoken beyond 'hi, how are ya' and 'spread your legs.'"

"Spread your legs? That's the last thing I'd expect from someone named Ezekiel," Nico grinned. "So you two got close?"

"No, I got frisked the last time I went to buy tomatoes from them."

"And you think you're not sexy?"

I laughed. "Everyone got frisked."

"You know, this is really fascinating. And I hope to get the whole scoop one day, but again, you're not telling me what I need to know."

"Right, yeah. Well," I took a deep breath. "Here it is. Daddy and Virgil bonded over good tomatoes and good gravy. Virgil mentioned to my dad that he had these tomatoes unlike any he'd ever grown. You know there are literally thousands of different kinds of tomatoes, right?"

"I knew there were a bunch, but thousands?"

"Thousands. And there are people who collect species and cross species to create new ones. That was the kind of man old Virgil was. He was obsessed with tomatoes, and my dad was too, a little."

"Obsessed with tomatoes?" He kissed my knee. "This would be more fun if you were in shorts."

"Remind me to tell you crazy stories about my dad this summer." I leaned forward to kiss his forehead. "So, Virgil starts telling Daddy how he had these plant clippings brought in from Afghanistan."

"Plant clippings?"

"Tomato plant clippings."

"Tomato clippings, not poppy?"

"Heroin isn't the only thing Afghanistan perfected. They do good tomatoes over there, too." I squeezed his fingers over my stomach. "Virgil gives my dad a bushel of these special Afghan tomatoes. My dad makes the best gravy of his life. He begs Virgil for more. But there aren't any more of those tomatoes that year. My father would have to wait until the next year."

"This would be more interesting if we were talking about poppy." Nico leaned his chin on my knees.

"It gets more interesting. I promise. There are spies and intrigue and smuggling involved."

He cocked his head at me.

"I'm warning you now, this is going to sound like something from a bad movie."

"Spies, intrigue, smuggling, but no poppies? It already does."

I smirked. "Well, the next year, my dad goes out to see Virgil, who, by the way, is like in his eighties at the time. I was very little, maybe six or seven. Daddy took me. But Virgil only has about a pound of tomatoes he could sell to my dad."

"At an exorbitant price."

"Right."

"Couldn't your dad use the seeds to grow his own? Or give the tomatoes to another farmer to do that?"

"Yes, but no." I ran my fingers through his hair. "The thing is, there was something about that particular species that it wouldn't adapt well to the Jersey air or soil or water or something. Jersey might be famous for tomatoes, but not for Afghan ones. So Virgil had to rely on cuttings being imported directly to him every year to grow the plants. He'd been experimenting with amending the soil and was getting close, but he wasn't there yet. You follow me?"

"I think so. He had to keep buying new cuttings, right?"

"Right. But when Virgil explained this to my dad, it was right after the Soviet Union invaded Afghanistan. It was difficult to get his cuttings before then, and it became increasingly difficult afterward. Virgil's son, Isaac, made an offer to my dad: if he could influence customs to maybe turn a blind eye toward anything coming to them from Afghanistan, they would give him a tenth of the crop."

"Just a tenth?"

"Famous chefs along the eastern seaboard pay good money for

those tomatoes."

"Wow. So I take it they worked out a deal?" Nico's free hand found its way under my top to rest directly on my skin.

"They did. Fixing soil and testing plants takes years of work. Sometimes the plants would make it for a couple of seasons and then falter, so more experimenting would be needed. Eventually, Virgil passed away, and his son Isaac took over. He's smarter than his old man, but also a little bit insane. Meanwhile, the Soviet Union left Afghanistan, but the FDA decided that only particular tomatoes and particular plants can come from particular countries. They were worried about pests and plant diseases destroying native species here. It was now officially against the law for any kind of tomato or tomato plant to go from Afghanistan into the United States."

"Enter smugglers?" Nico leaned over to get his cocoa mug from the table and sipped.

"Enter smugglers." I nodded. "Smugglers my *dad* found for Isaac."

"Aha! Your dad, the good cop, found smugglers to ensure a steady stream of illegal plants from Afghanistan to Jersey. I get it. But I don't get why you think Isaac won't want a new customer." He put his cup back on the table and undid the top of my pants.

"I'm not done. There's more." I tried to slide down on the sofa to get under him, but he wasn't budging.

"Uh, no, hon. I'm not moving until the story is done," he said.

"Then stop touching me. It's hard to concentrate."

"But I like touching you." He spread his hand on my belly, under my clothes.

I scooted back as far as I could. "So, Isaac finally perfected the soil for the plants to thrive. He no longer needed cuttings smuggled in. But he had to keep the smugglers and my dad on the tomato payroll to make sure they kept his tomatoes secret because by now GM and Monsanto had started experimenting with genetically modified tomatoes."

"Do I need to know what that means?"

"That means companies started creating tomatoes that had their DNA intentionally mixed up."

"Why would they do that?"

"Usually, so they'd become more pest resistant."

"Sounds like a good idea." His hand caressed my stomach.

"It could be. But not everyone thinks it's a good idea. No one is sure if GMO foods can cause allergies or other health consequences. However, Monsanto and other companies are still experimenting to create the perfect tomato."

"Because?"

"Because we eat a lot of tomatoes. So, if someone can create a tomato that stays fresh for a long time, tastes fabulous, is great in sauces or gravies, is pest-resistant, was—"

"I got it. So until the perfect tomato happens, if a farmer manages to produce a really good, particular species that no one else has, he has his own niche market."

"Exactly. So some farmers get very protective. Isaac Blackman is one of them. He kept my dad and the smugglers stocked with tomatoes almost as a bribe to help keep his secret."

Nico spread my legs so he could come in and kiss my stomach. "How protective is he?"

"We're talking about hundreds of thousands of dollars in tomatoes that he wants to keep for himself." I arched my back and stared up at the ceiling, waiting for him to make the next move. But he returned to sitting the way we were: my legs back together, him leaning against them, his hands on my stomach.

"And he does that by keeping a limited number of customers?" He brought my fingers to his lips.

"Sorry, I completely lost my train of thought. It's hard as hell to talk about this with all the kissing."

"I'm trying to hurry you along."

I sighed. "Isaac needs to keep a limited number of customers because he also must be able to trust those customers not to tell anyone who their source is. He's worried about people sneaking onto his land to steal some of his Afghan-derived crop in an attempt to replicate what he is doing."

"Ah, that's where the spies come in." He stood and pulled me into the bedroom.

"Yes. Agricultural intrigue. And did I mention he's only borderline sane? He'd always been on the paranoid side, but he ratcheted that up several degrees. He strides around his farm with a huge rifle in one hand and a machete strapped to his back."

"You're kidding, right?" He stopped inside the bedroom door.

"No. And that was before the tomato crisis hit in 2008."

"The tomato crisis?"

"Yes."

"Are you still drunk from this afternoon?"

"No!" I laughed. "I know it all sounds crazy. But, remember when you couldn't find a tomato, not even in a Mexican restaurant, because they were taken off the market due to salmonella fears?"

"I remember." He grinned at me and unbuttoned my blouse. "I just didn't realize it was a crisis."

"It was! It was a huge one for tomato growers. No one could trust a tomato unless they had proof of where it came from, where the plant had grown—"

"Aha! And Isaac's were a species that no one had ever seen in this country. In fact, it had originated in Afghanistan, where we were then at war with the Taliban." His face was back in my cleavage as he undid my bra.

"Exactly. So, Isaac is scared the FDA is going to come on his land to inspect his tomatoes; he's afraid other farmers and even Monsanto are trying to infiltrate and steal from his crops!" I shrieked as he flopped me back on the bed. "I get to stop talking now, right?"

"No. I'm still dressed."

"Can I help?"

"No, I don't want you to get distracted." He grinned and climbed onto the bed, fully clothed.

"Where was I?"

"In the living room." He finished unzipping my slacks and tugged them off.

"In the story?" I asked.

"Isaac's afraid of Monsanto and the FDA finding out what he's growing." He threw my slacks on the floor.

"Yes. Seriously afraid." I flipped him onto his back and straddled him. "Listen, last year was the first time I went alone to get tomatoes from Isaac, and I promised myself I would never do it again. He now has a cell phone that you can call and leave a message saying how many bushels you want. He returns your call from an unidentified phone and tells you where to meet him. Last year, it was on an abandoned clam trawler on Gardener Inlet. I couldn't take my purse or cell phone on board with me. Just my cash in my hand—and it had to be cash. That's when I was frisked by Zeke. I made my purchase, and he told me in no uncertain terms that if I ever told anyone about my business with him, he'd have me taken care of."

THE SEARCH BEGINS

So what do we do today?" I asked Nico over our morning coffee. We were sitting on the barstools at the pass-through.

He hooked his finger in the top of my T-shirt and pulled it out. "When do the kids get up?"

"I'll start nagging at them in about fifteen minutes. But listen," I snapped the shirt out of his grip and whispered. "I've never had sex like we've been having it. I'm loving every minute of it. I can't believe how incredible it is. But my body needs a break this morning. I'm not complaining. I'm just saying there are some muscle groups that have been neglected in the gym. I need to recoup this morning, got it?"

"Got it, but I was only asking so we could plan our day." He grinned and sipped his coffee. "I think you need to put in a call to the nutty tomato man, and while we wait for him to call you back, we'll go back to your parents' place. Where did your dad hide things?"

"Hide things?" I paced. "I don't know Nico. If he hid things, he kept his hiding places secret."

"Do you think your mom knows? Would she know where he kept the medallion?"

I stopped and looked at him. He sat with his hands loosely around his cup. He looked about as relaxed as a man could look, which I realized I needed him to be because I was wired tighter than a winner at the roulette table who just decided to risk it all on one last spin.

"I can't ask her. And she's the last person we talk to about this, got it?" I stared hard at him. "Do you have any idea how much she hated my dad?"

"What?"

"She *hated* him. When Angie and I left home, we expected them to divorce, but they were committed in marriage."

"Why'd they get committed to begin with?"

"That's something Ange and I have always wondered. We had a different relationship with him from what we had with her. He was our fun parent, and she was the disciplinarian. We used to joke that between the two, we had one fully functional parent. But they didn't work as a team at all. They didn't communicate beyond 'I'll be home for dinner' or 'I'm going to so-and-so's house.' I don't think I ever heard her say a nice word to him. Even after..." I paused and clenched my eyes shut. "She doesn't miss him. How could anyone not miss my dad?" I put my hands on my hips and looked in Nico's eyes. "The only thing she said to me about his, his passing, was that it was a cowardly act. It's been almost a year since, and she has yet to even mention him. Did you notice she didn't even cry during his funeral?"

"I assumed she was medicated."

"I assumed she was relieved."

"Why did they stay together?"

"Because they were married, they had children, that's just what you do..." I stopped and stared at him. "Oh my God."

"Yeah, you're a little like her," Nico raised his eyebrows at me "You *were* a little like her. You've grown. So you don't think she would have the medallion or know anything about it?"

"I'm ninety-nine percent positive she does not have it. And it would only set her off if we told her about it." I sipped my coffee.

"Do you think your dad had a mistress?"

"I don't know." I ran my hands through my hair. "I mean, it's possible. Angie always suspected it because he never acted unhappy. But I don't remember seeing another woman grieving as much as I was at his funeral."

"Was there a will?"

"Yes. Everything went to Ma."

"Are you sure? Who was the executor?"

"I was." I rubbed my face. "I need to cook something." I found an onion in the pantry and peeled it. Nico watched me chop it.

"I take it you're making western omelets for breakfast?" he asked as I took a green pepper from the refrigerator.

"Yes. You want cheese in yours?"

"Sure. I'll go knock on the kids' doors to rouse them."

We were like a nuclear family that morning. I fed everyone the omelets while I drank a coffee-protein drink. The kids packed their backpacks, we went over after-school schedules, and then Nico drove us all to the school. He then dropped me at the senior center to pick up my unappreciated minivan.

As I drove back to the condo, I stopped at my bank and pulled out the only thing I kept in a safety deposit box: my father's will.

I'd read it only once after he died, and, because I didn't know what else to do with it and it felt too painful to keep in my house, I got the safety deposit box at the bank and put it there. I hadn't looked at it since. Given my hysterical state at the time of his death, it was possible I'd misread it the first time around.

I couldn't make myself look at it in the bank. I put it in my purse and didn't take it back out until I was safely in the condo again. I joined Nico on the sofa and handed it directly to him without unfolding it. It still hurt to see proof that my dad was dead.

"There are two versions here," I said. "A long, legal one and a short note from him on the light, green paper. They basically say the same thing."

"Short and sweet," Nico said. I paced in circles while he read the green note aloud.

To my darling daughter, Lucinda, I give you the freedom to truly love. Get the picture, Lucy. Everything else goes to your mother in appreciation of her efforts to make us a family.

He kept looking at it as if reading it silently to himself. "Do you know what he meant?"

"You mean, aside from Ma gets everything? No."

"Was this the only will?"

"There was one before it, but he changed it and created this one just a week before he, uh, you know."

"There are a couple odd things here."

"What do you mean? Isn't that like a normal will?" I stopped pacing and sat beside him on the sofa.

"Yes, the one prepared by the attorney is. But, looking at his personal message here." He held up the green note. "What stands out the most is there's no mention of Angie."

"I know. And by the way, I never told her that. It would probably hurt her feelings."

"But they didn't have problems, did they?"

"No! They always got along famously. Not like how it is with my mother and her."

"Right. So he mentions one daughter in the first sentence, then thanks your mom for making a family in the last sentence. Why would he say that to your mom if he completely left out a family member?"

"I don't know."

"Your dad was smart. He was a detective for a long time on the ACPD, and he had a reputation for being good. He didn't scrimp on details. There's a message here. He wants you to put together some missing pieces."

"What pieces?" I snuggled against him to brave looking at the green note. "There are only three sentences. That's not many pieces."

"Well, let's look at this like it contains a clue." He silently reread the will. "Listen, read it like literature."

"What do you mean?"

"If you're reading something written in a flowery, descriptive language, then the author suddenly switches to something point-blank and direct, you do a closer read to determine why there was a change in style."

"How do you know that?"

"My favorite time I was with a foster family, the mom was an English teacher. She introduced me to mystery books, got me hooked on reading, and then threw good literature at me. She taught me to appreciate it by reading it like a mystery and looking for clues. I devoured it. It became my escape when I was back at my mom's."

"I always wondered where you got the reading from. But my dad wasn't a literature buff. I don't think he even read mystery books."

"He was smart, though. And that's all it takes. So look, he wrote a sweet and loving sentence to you. He wrote a sweet and loving sentence to your mom, which he began with 'everything else.' In between, instead of something sweet and loving to your sister, is a straightforward command to you: get the picture."

"Yes, I think it has something to do with giving me the freedom to love, whatever that means."

"I don't understand that part either." Nico looked at my face. "But I think I know what he's trying to say here."

"What?"

"He wants you to get the picture. A picture. An actual picture that you would know about."

"A picture? Like maybe a photograph?"

"Maybe. Or, maybe not a photograph, but another kind of picture. One that you would know about and think of when he said 'picture' but maybe no one else would. Any ideas?"

I stared at him.

"Come on, Lucy," Nico grinned at me. "St. Cecelia is the patron saint of music...Your dad has a picture of..."

"The Three Musicians."

Nico and I raced over to my parents' place. I ran in the kitchen and snatched the picture off the refrigerator door.

"Oh hell, Nico!" I spun around to face him. "I think we were wrong. It doesn't look like anything has been changed on it."

"Turn it over."

I did, and there, taped to the back, was a small note on light green paper. I read it to Nico.

Good job, Lucy!

My gift to Asher came the day we looked at this book, and I taught him to slow down. He was always in such a hurry to see and experience everything that he missed it all. Now he understands. To my wild and untamed Asher, you will always be able to find me in your slow wandering.

Now, Lucinda, put this back where it belongs.

Tears welled in my eyes. "I guess I can't complain about Ash taking so much time to do everything anymore." I held the picture to my chest. "Okay, so now I put this back on the refrigerator. Then what?"

I looked at the appliance. Nothing else seemed to have any meaning. There was a calendar from last year, my kids' most recent school pictures, and a blank notepad connected to a cat-shaped magnet. I leafed through the notepad and turned over all the other pictures.

Nico gently pulled the note from the back of the *Three Musicians* picture.

"It doesn't belong on the refrigerator."

"It does. Once something is put in this house, it stays right there. I don't know why my mother let him put it up here to begin with. Maybe he told her it was Ash's idea. She'll have a fit if we remove it."

"Even though—"

"Oh my God! I wonder how many jars of gravy Enzo and Aldo took. I need to ask them and put some of mine in to take their place."

"Your mom's that anal?"

"She's as territorial as a cat. Trust me. Please, don't let me forget to replace the gravy." I put the picture back on the refrigerator, exactly where it had been before. "I think Joy got that anal retentive stuff from her."

"You're nuts, you know that? Come on, Lucy. Do you really think your dad, wherever he is now, really cares if your mom has a meltdown over this picture not being on the refrigerator?"

I looked at him and laughed. "I sound like a schoolgirl. Of course, he wouldn't care. But I do need to make sure I get all that powder from the fingerprinting cleaned up."

"We'll deal with that later. This came from a book, right?

"Yes."

"Where is it? I would think that's where it belonged."

"Right, but how do we know this has anything to do with the medallion?"

"We don't. My gut is telling me it does, though."

"Yeah, my gut, too. Daddy left these messages for a secret reason. He secretly bought a stolen medallion. Somehow it makes sense that they're connected, right?"

"Right. Besides, this is all we have to go on."

We returned to my condo and hit Ash's room. We should have put on HAZMAT gear before entering. Or at least stopped to buy those long poles with hooks on the end that people use to pick up snakes. I expected it to be cluttered; I don't think the kid ever put or threw anything away. I just didn't expect it to be as bad as it was. I was under the impression we hadn't lived there long enough for him to create a mini toxic landfill. But I was wrong.

Aside from the dirty laundry, there were piles of books and papers, which amazed me because I couldn't remember the last time I saw anything that wasn't an electronic in the kid's hands. Empty snack wrappers and soda cans, possibly containing science fair fodder, were strewn about the room like confetti. Basketballs that I'd never seen him play with, Boogie Boards and wet suits that were supposed to be stored in the storage locker downstairs, shoes that had to have been too small for a couple of years, and more covered the floor, the bed, and the chair.

"So when people say something is like looking for a needle in a haystack, I think we could correct them and say it's like looking for a book in Ash's room," I said.

Nico laughed.

"The kid's a lot like I was. No interest in making order, but we like it when other people do. At least we don't have to worry about covering our tracks to hide that we were snooping. I don't think he'll even suspect someone was here."

Still, as we sifted through the debris, we were careful to try to put everything back where we found it. I always prided myself on how well my kids trusted me to trust them. I didn't want to disrupt that trust. Granted, that sense of obligation I set upon myself is probably one of the reasons why Ash had been such a successful herbal trafficker, but the social workers I knew who specialize in teens all assured me I was doing the right thing. Our kids needed to know we trusted them as they went about their illicit activities and learned from their experiences, which is the way I explained it to Les.

We made it through the room, not completely confident we'd seen it all, but fairly certain the book wasn't there. I almost sat on his bed, but I wasn't sure what made the lump under the blankets. I spun in a circle, trying to think where the book could be.

"Were books packed separately when you moved?" Nico asked. "Could it have gone into Joy's room?"

"No, I don't think so. They packed their own stuff. Oh!" I grabbed Nico's arm. "We gave a bunch to the used bookstore."

"The one on Atlantic?"

"No, they were *very* particular, and I didn't want to take the time to sort through the boxes to give them what they wanted. We took them to that place over in Egg Harbor where they weren't so picky." I looked around the room again. "I hope it's still there."

We took a break to call Isaac, the paranoid tomato farmer. I had to leave a voicemail telling him I had a question about the next season. I had no idea if he'd call me back.

We ate lunch and then headed to Egg Harbor with my heart in my throat. I remembered I didn't get the feeling the woman at the bookstore was all that organized when we were dropping off the books. She didn't take any information from us, and I didn't think she'd have any idea who would have bought the book if it had sold.

"We're so far behind in checking in our inventory," she said when we explained we'd accidentally donated a book that was a family treasure just a month ago. "I don't suppose I've even gotten to your books yet. I'm still working on the ones people brought in at the beginning of the school year." She led us to a room filled with boxes in the back of her store. "Now, let's see, this stuff in here would be the oldest. As this room got filled up, I headed upstairs." We followed her to the stairs that were on the outside, at the rear of the house she used as a store, and climbed. They deposited us in an unheated, damp room with open rafters for a ceiling, bare plywood flooring, and moss growing on the walls.

She tried to determine how long the boxes had been there based on their proximity to the door and how many boxes were piled on top. Unfortunately, her system wasn't foolproof.

Nico couldn't help much, as he wouldn't recognize which books would have been in my house. He was to wait for me to find a box that I thought might be mine and then tear through it.

The work was slow going. We'd used plain, brown boxes, which looked like ninety percent of the others in the room. After about an hour of useless searching, Nico left to pick up Ash; Joy had a swim team meeting.

"S'up Ash?" I asked him when he came into the room.

"S'up?" He grinned and approached me. "Got a note?"

Nico winked behind Ash's back.

"I was explaining to Asher," he said, "how we'd accidentally found the note your dad wrote on the back of that picture and thought maybe there would be a note for Joy in his book."

"Yes," I said to Ash. I pulled the note from my purse and gave it to him.

He read it with a smile and tucked it into his jeans pocket. I cringed, wondering when those jeans would make it to the laundry or if they'd get lost in the mire of his room. I explained the store owner's filing system, and he dug in. An hour later, Nico called in a to-go order from White House subs and left to get Joy and dinner.

I'd about reached my limit. I'd been in that room for too long, digging through musty books. My sinuses were clogged from the dust and mildew. My fingers were cramping from the cold. The stress of the past couple of days was eating at my stomach. And, despite what Nico said, I was pissed off at my son for giving the damned book away.

I slammed a box of books onto the floor.

"Sorry, Ma," Ash said.

"What?"

"Sorry."

"For what?"

He stood beside me and put his arm around my shoulder. "I fucked up again, huh?"

I leaned my face into his chest, still amazed that I'd given birth to this being who stood a good seven inches taller than I did, and cried.

"It's okay, Ash," I said after a few minutes. "I told you to get rid of excess stuff. You were just following orders. You didn't fuck up." I sniffed and pulled myself away from him. "Why do you kids say 'fuck' all the time?"

He shrugged in slow motion. "It's like texting. Those four letters mean a lot."

I wiped my eyes and searched through my purse for a tissue.

"See that? There's lemonade," I said after blowing my nose. "Something good just came from me crying. My nose is no longer stuffed up."

He laughed and sat on the box I'd dropped on the floor to start looking through another.

"I think these are ours," he said.

"What?" I ran over and ripped the books out, not caring where I tossed them. The book wasn't in it. Ash started on another box of ours. I found a third. We were throwing books wildly about the room when Nico and Joy came in.

"Got it!" I screamed.

"Ugh, Mom! Do you have to be so dramatic?" Joy asked. She was in her school uniform, which was fine and sane-looking. Her eyes were lined with heavy crimson liner, and the black sticks were back in her ears. The hair was gelled into a mixture of ringlets and spikes all over her head.

"Yes, I do, pumpkin." I hugged her with my face as far from her head as I could stretch, lest I get impaled by a hair spike; they looked solid and hard. "Look! It's the book. Did Nico tell you what's going on?"

"Is there a note for me from Pop-Pop?" She sounded like a nine-year-old.

"I don't know." I leafed through the pages to see where the *Three Musicians* had been removed. There, in place of that painting, was another green note taped in the book. I replaced the picture and gently pulled out the note. I read it aloud.

My precious Joy –

To you, I gave the insight to see beauty in the uniqueness of all life. For you and me, it is easy to enjoy what most others fear and to love what many call unlovable. Never be ashamed of your individuality. I will always cheer it on in you from wherever I am. I love you, my Joy.

Lucy, I made Joy see the light.

I hoped Nico could remember the note better than I could because Joy snatched it from my hands as soon as I pronounced the "t" in *light*. I had a feeling I'd never see it again.

A BEAUTIFUL VIEW

Okay, I'm calling Isaac again," I said after I returned home from dropping the kids at school the next day. "As long as you're sure you're willing to handle the aftermath."

"Honestly, how bad can it be?" Nico was at the dining table, his laptop open before him.

"He's a paranoid man who's heavily armed. I think that means it can get pretty bad."

"You don't really believe I'd let a crazy farmer hurt you, do you? Or either of the Finarellis?"

"No, but there's only so much you can do. And—"

"And there's more that I can do that you don't know about. So relax. I already got people on Isaac and his sons. I got people following Aldo and Enzo. No one will hurt you or your family. Got it?" He focused on his laptop and typed something.

"Got it. But...um. Nico?" I twirled my key ring on my finger.

"What's up?"

"Just, um, well, I was wondering. You know how I didn't know Les was...well, are you also associated with, you know, the mob?" Not that I really wanted the answer. I just thought it was something I should know for certain. That way, I could figure out what I should do about it.

"Ha! No, babe. I'm a free agent. I don't get involved in anything directly, and I make sure whatever my part is, it's legal. I know everyone. Everyone knows me. Sometimes people need services from others that they can't get for themselves, so I help make connections. But I don't get involved in the actual deals. I have a legitimate security business that keeps the bank account filled."

"Oh, good." I kissed his forehead and threw my keys in the basket on the pass-through. "One less thing to worry about."

"What else are you worried about? Les?"

I dropped onto the sofa. "A little. Any idea what he's doing about the medallion? Do you think we should mention the notes?"

"He's hitting the pawn shops again and trying to scare up rumors on your dad. If we tell him about the notes, he'll want to get involved in finding them. Do you want that?"

"No. I don't want to give him an excuse to be near me

He sat next to me. "Call your farmer."

I dialed, got his voicemail, and left another message to call me back.

"Now what?" I asked Nico.

"Joy's room." He stood. "I want to read that note again."

"NO!" I screamed. I raced after him and barred the door to her room. "You can't go in there!"

"Why not? It has to be there. She wouldn't have taken it to school, where it might get lost or crumpled in her backpack. She's too organized for that."

"I'm sure you're right, but we can't just go into her room." I put my hands on his chest to push him away. He didn't budge. "She's not like Ash. She'll be able to tell we were in there, and she'll be so angry a hole will open up in the universe."

"We'll be careful to leave it the way we found it."

"She'll see our footprints on the carpet."

"Then we'll rake them out." He put his hands on my hips and pulled me toward him.

"She'll smell our scent." I resisted.

"Then we'll burn candles in the house to mask it." He pressed his whole body against mine.

"She'll see our skin cells floating in the dust motes."

"We can get naked and loofah in the shower first, if you want." He wrapped his arms around me and kissed me long and hard. "If you've recouped enough, we can take a break." He kissed me again and turned us around. But then the little bugger let go of me and jumped into her room.

"You can't go in there!" I ran after him and stopped cold once I was inside.

"It's right here," he said, standing before her bulletin board. The green note was tacked in the center. "See? Nothing to worry about. We don't have to touch anything."

"She'll still know we were in here. We need an excuse. I only come in here to take care of her crabs when she's at her dad's." I looked around, with just my eyes because I saw no reason to push my luck by actually stirring up her air with my presence. "The smoke detector! Yes, that's it. We'll tell her we were in here to check it out to make sure it still worked."

He looked at me. "I'll actually change the batteries so that you don't have to lie. Let's keep lying to a minimum. It'll give you less to stress about—unless you have something good in mind to bake for dessert." He smirked at me. "You sure you don't suffer from paranoid delusions? Is there something you and that farmer have in common that I don't know about?"

"I wish that were the case. Trust me. She'll know we were here. There will be hell to pay, but the battery thing might just work. What's the note say, again?"

He reread it. "He told you he showed Joy the light. That's your clue," he said.

We looked around her room. The furniture was what she'd had since she was a little girl and wanted to be a princess: a white panel bed with scrollwork on the headboard and matching dresser and vanity. Her pink-trimmed black satin quilt was a more recent buy, as were the neon-green throw pillows. The walls were covered with posters of dangerous-looking, tattooed men. I told myself they were safe and benevolent pop stars. One wall was spared the stud-filled pictures. Instead, it featured shelves loaded down with hermit crab aquariums. She called them "crabitats."

I tiptoed to the lamp on her nightstand and looked inside the black shade.

"No note here."

"What about underneath?" Nico came up to me.

"You pick it up. I don't want to be responsible for it being moved a half centimeter."

"Keep your hands here." He placed my hands around the base of the lamp, lifted it, and looked at the bottom. No note. He replaced it in my hands.

"So he didn't show her this light," I said. "She'd had it in her bedroom on Maine Avenue, too. Do we go through the house and look at all the lights?"

"Maybe." His eyes scanned the room again, eventually settling on the hermit crabs. He approached the tanks and peered in, methodically going left to right from the top down. He finally squatted and looked directly into a tank, at eye level with any crab who dared to peek out at him.

"These are usually considered unlovable, aren't they?"

"That's why she has so many." I caught myself before I sat on her perfectly made bed. "She belongs to a rescue organization. People call when they don't want their pet hermit crabs anymore. She adopts them. My father introduced her to them. That's probably what he meant in the note. He taught her how to take care of them. I think he might even be the one who made her a crab-foster-parent."

"He showed her the light, huh?"

"I guess so, as far as crabs go anyway." I approached the tanks. "They still give me the creeps."

"Do they bite?"

"I'm not sure." I bent to look at the crabitat he was fixated on. There were several larger specimens in it. "They do use their claws to climb things so they can pinch, I guess."

Each tank had small logs or netting the crabs could climb, bowls of water and food, areas of shells and rocks, and areas of shredded wood. Each was decorated according to a theme with toys and statues. The one that captured Nico's attention was set up to look like a marina; there were even toy boats in a "bay" of small blue aquarium rocks.

"I see the light." He straightened, lifted off the plexiglass lid of the tank, and handed it to me.

"Are you kidding?"

"No, but are you sure they don't bite?"

"Manly man Nico afwaid of a wittle hermit cwab?"

"Manly man Nico needs to know which hand to put in the tank. Ever notice this?" He showed me his left hand. Scars from puncture wounds marked both the back and the palm. "I'm left-handed, so it was the wrong hand to let a dog get a hold of."

"My God, Nico! What happened?"

"I was a punk-ass kid teasing a mean-ass dog. I got what I deserved at the time. But I was very, very lucky. When the doctors sewed me up, they were amazed that the teeth didn't rip my tendons. I could have lost the ability to move my fingers."

"I don't think these guys are like that," I said. "Joy never mentioned biting. She's more concerned with making sure nothing stresses them out."

"They get stressed?"

"Yes. And when they do, their legs come off."

He stared at me as if making sure I wasn't joking. "Yeah, that's lovable." He reached his hand into the tank and carefully lifted out a toy lighthouse. "Usually *these* are used to show people the light, right?" He turned it over and found nothing. "Damn! I was hoping it would be hollow." He shook it. Something shifted inside. After examining it closer, Nico unscrewed the top, exposing the hollow interior and a slip of coiled green paper.

He pulled out the paper, screwed the top back on, and carefully replaced the lighthouse in the tank. I put the lid back on it and used my shirt sleeve to wipe off any fingerprints.

"Number 159 has no name," he read.

"What else?"

"That's it."

I stared at him, unable to believe there wasn't more. He read it again.

"Shit!" I stormed out of Joy's room. "Shit! Shit! Shit!" I paced the living area. "No. That's not right. Fuck!"

"And that's different how?" Nico laughed. He went into the kitchen. "Where would I find a battery?"

"Cabinet over the refrigerator." I paced. "And 'fuck' is better because it's a short word that means so much. Ash taught me that."

"He's a smart kid, you know. Sounds like *The Prime of Miss Jean Brodie* is rubbing off on him."

"What?"

"The book by Muriel Sparks. One of my favorites. He's reading it now."

"How do you know?" I paused and watched him take a battery out of a pack.

"We talked about it." He went into Joy's room to replace the battery.

"When this is all over, I want you to tell me why you know more about the people in my family than I do!" I yelled at him when he came back. "But not now. It's Wednesday. We're two clues down with a new unsolved one in front of us. And no hint of a medallion. We could be barking up an entirely different tree. God, how I wish

Dasher were here. I don't think I ever paced when I had him to pet."

"Maybe coffee is not a good idea for you right now, huh? I was thinking of making another pot."

"Coffee is always a good idea." I was getting dizzy. I turned and paced in circles in the opposite direction. "What's up with that note, anyway? Why not a gift for someone else? The other notes mentioned gifts for people. Why not that one?"

"Maybe he's telling you how to get to the gift."

"How does that make any sense?" I shouted and stomped to a stop. "And why aren't you all worked up about it?"

"I just don't think that way." He smiled at me. "I think a little quieter. I've never seen you this agitated. You know you're cute when your face gets red like that."

"Ugh." Back to pacing. I made two laps before storming into the kitchen. I threw open the refrigerator door and let the cool air settle on me for a few seconds before I ripped open the vegetable drawer.

Nico settled on a barstool by the pass-through and watched me peel an eggplant. "How does cooking help? Not that I want you to find another outlet. And it's certainly better than you drinking yourself unconscious, but—"

"I won't ever do that again. Trust me. When you said I'd spent my entire marriage unconscious, I got the message. I'm staying alert from now on, if that will keep people from messing up my life."

He laughed.

"But, yeah, cooking helps," I said. "It gives me something I can control." I paused to look at him. He had no idea what I was talking about, probably because he'd never run into a situation he didn't think he could control. "See how I'm cutting this eggplant into even slices? It's like cutting pasta. If you pay enough attention, the pieces end up with a uniform thickness. It's soothing to me. Like at work when I line up a stack of paper. The orderliness of it is soothing. And being in control of an event, like an entire meal, is particularly helpful when I feel like I can't handle whatever is in front of me."

I tossed the eggplant with sea salt in a colander and let it sit in the sink to drain out the excess moisture.

"Good thing there's more gravy in the storage shed." I grinned at him.

"Yeah." The coffeepot gurgled the last few drops into the pot. He came into the kitchen to pour. "You feel better?"

"A little." I dried my hands. "So, 159. Do you think it could be a badge number? Like a cop badge or something?"

"Maybe. But most policemen have names." He sipped his coffee.

"Could there be one that hasn't been assigned yet?"

"Maybe. But then it wouldn't belong to anyone who could give us information."

"It could have a note taped to it."

"Maybe."

I walked back into the living area and paced in circles again.

"What about a highway? Is there a Route 159? You know, like how Thirty is called White Horse Pike?"

"Doesn't sound familiar. It's not local if there is one, but maybe."

"Can you say something other than 'maybe'?" I paced.

"Probably."

I stopped again and tried to glare at him while he grinned at me.

"You need to make something else, don't you?" he asked. "The eggplant wasn't enough."

"You're right." I inhaled deeply and thought about food. "And I think I have to do something with my hands. Maybe play with some pastry dough." Our eyes held for a full minute. "I love you, Nico. I really do."

"I love you too, babe." He nodded over his coffee mug.

"Why didn't I ever notice that before?" I approached him. "I mean, I think I've loved you for a long time, but I didn't realize it."

"You were committed to your marriage. That and you have a bad habit of ignoring what makes you happy." He put his arm around my shoulders. "Filo dough, maybe?"

"Yes! Filo dough stuffed with scallops. I can make pretty little purses out of the dough." I kissed the side of his face. "Pour that in a travel mug. I haven't been to Harbor Point deli since I moved here. I can get the dough and pick up their corned beef for Ash, and we can hit Barbera's on the way back for the scallops."

We headed out in his Land Rover with my mind obsessing over how to make scallops in Filo dough a decent companion for eggplant parmesan. That might end up being something I couldn't control. I also couldn't let go of what the number 159 could signify. I tried not to rattle off everything that was going through my head in the hopes that Nico's silent way of thinking gave us better results than my loud, blathering style.

He passed the police station on the way to Harbor Point deli.

"So you thought it was a bad idea?" I asked. "Checking police badges?"

"No, not a bad one, just unlikely." He continued down Atlantic Avenue. "Your dad was a cop for a long time, but he was retired a long time, too. He may not have had many connections left there in the administrative side of the business. Besides, since that was where he..." he paused and reached out for my hand.

"Yeah, I guess you're right. That wouldn't make sense." My father had shot himself in the temple in the alley behind the police station. His note said he did it there because they were used to cleaning up those kinds of messes, and he knew his body would be found before some kid wandered down the alley and saw his gun. As Nico said, he was careful with details.

We were in the left-hand lane to turn onto Delaware Avenue, but when the green arrow lit, Nico changed lanes and cut into the traffic going forward instead.

"Look." He pointed. And I saw it, across a vacant lot and towering above its immediate neighbors: the Absecon lighthouse. The lighthouse in Joy's crab tank was painted to look identical to it.

"Yes, the lighthouse!" I shouted. I squeezed his hand with both of mine. "Nico! The lighthouse! The steps are numbered at the lighthouse."

"Are there 159?"

"Way more than that. Over 200, in fact. My dad used to take Angie and me there every Sunday when we were little. Mom would take us to church, and then when we'd get back, he'd take us there. He'd told us climbing the lighthouse was how he liked to get close to God. Why didn't I think of that?"

"I don't know, but it sounds like a good connection."

We made our way up the avenue and into the parking lot. Nico got out and stood beside his SUV, looking up at the tower.

"You know, I've never been here," he said. "I've spent my entire life in this city and never climbed the lighthouse."

"Why not?"

"Never had the urge. Can you go outside once you're at the top?"

"Absolutely. That's what you do. Climb up. Say hello to the keeper. Step outside. Look at the horizon. Go back down."

"Sounds so thrilling," he grinned at me. "No wonder I haven't been up. Don't know if I can handle all that excitement."

We paid the donation that allowed us to make the spiraling climb.

Each step was numbered and bore the name of someone who had made a donation to the lighthouse. Step number 159 had a number but no name.

"Looks like we're here," Nico said.

The steps were made from steel mesh. You could look down through them and see the stairwell wind to the bottom floor. You could look up and see it wind all the way to the top. The walls were brick. No note was evident.

"Hell." I sat on the stairs. "Now what?"

Nico stood silent. I watched his eyes scan everything, marking the contours of the center ballast, the railings, and the steps. He ran his hands over whatever he could touch.

"Put your feet on the step, that way I don't lose track of which one it is." He walked down and stopped directly below 159.

"I should have worn a skirt," I said.

"The view would have been better," he replied. He came back up, slid his hand along the underside of the stair lip, and smiled up at me. The green note was tucked inside the hollow bull-nose stair lip.

My sweet Lucy!

You're almost there. Go on up to the top and take your time walking around the observation deck. Make the whole circumference and look at this unique, bizarre, and wonderful city from every angle. When you're done, tell the keeper your name and that there's an envelope waiting here for you."

We climbed the remaining stairs and stepped out the door onto the observation deck before I had a chance to completely catch my breath. The door opened to the east. The winds coming off the Atlantic Ocean nearly knocked us back inside. I did my best to follow my father's wishes and tried to take a good look, but we couldn't stay long, getting blasted like that. We went round the north side, where we could see the Brigantine inlet and my old house up near the Gardener's Basin area, but the wind still buffeted us. We lingered on the west side, in the lee of the wind, where I was finally able to breathe right.

It was a clear and sunny day. We could see out past the bay and swampy areas. The slums were barely noticeable from that angle, and the windmills that powered our water treatment plant stood gleaming and proud on the edge of town. Their intense whiteness struck me as hopeful and determined. I could see the townhomes on the bay where Angie has her place and all the pretty boats in the marina.

I'd never read anything where Atlantic City is described as beautiful. The casinos are called that, and sometimes the beach. Never the city proper. But from that height, at that angle, with the sun just right...my city was a beautiful and hopeful place to live.

On the south side, we felt the winds again. We stopped only long enough to make out the profile of my condo building before we ran back around to the east side to go in.

"Windy enough for you?" the keeper asked.

"I think so," I said. "I'm Lucinda Womzak. There's supposed to be an envelope for me here?"

"An envelope?"

"Yes." I looked at him, then Nico. "My father said he left an envelope for me here."

"When was he in?"

"I don't know."

"Perhaps last spring or winter," Nico said.

"I don't recall anything like that. Nope." The man smiled at us. "But here's a card."

"Thank you." I took it. It said: I SAW THE LIGHT! Congratulations, you just climbed New Jersey's tallest lighthouse, the third-tallest lighthouse in the United States. He handed an identical one to Nico. He had a whole stack ready to hand out to whoever made it to the top.

"Are you the only one who works up here?" Nico asked.

"Nope. There are two of us," the man said before turning to greet a family. "Hello there! Congratulations on the climb."

A family of three joined us: a mom, a dad, and a boy who looked to be four or five. The child sat on the floor. I guessed his legs were tired; I knew the feeling. While the father grilled the keeper on the lens, Nico snooped around. There wasn't much to look at: a placard display discussing the lens, another explaining the venting, and a table with a signature book. I leafed through the book, curling the pages to flip through them. Nothing. But when I shut it, I turned it over, and there it was: an envelope taped to the back. The words on it said: *Please give to Lucy McCool. If she doesn't retrieve it before this book is replaced, please tape it to the next one. Thank you from a deceased donor.*

I ripped it off and tapped Nico on the shoulder. We gave a quick "thank you" to the keeper and spiraled our way back down.

A NEW PERSPECTIVE

Several people were milling around the museum on the ground level. A crowd of school kids was on a field trip with their adult chaperones. I wasn't comfortable reading a letter from my dad with them clamoring around me. I expected it to be similar to the notes to Joy and Ash: inspiring and heartbreaking. And if it didn't help me find the medallion, it would also be frustrating and infuriating. I didn't want to risk inventing obscenities in front of those innocent faces, so we left to read it over lunch at the Back Bay Ale House.

The waitress led us upstairs to the dining area and put us at a table beside a window looking over Gardener's Basin. We ordered Guinnesses to drink in honor of my father while I read the note.

"I think I want to wait for the ale," I said as I pulled the envelope out of my purse. "And don't get the wrong idea. I don't want more than one. I just want that one drink while I read."

"I understand that, but I don't understand why you went by Womzak up there," Nico said.

"Habit, I guess."

"Does that mean you decided you're not going back to McCool?"

"No, I am." I smiled at him. "And I didn't wait for my kids' approval if that's your next question."

He didn't smile back at me but reached out for my hands over the table.

"What about these?" He spun my wedding rings around my finger.

"I don't know what to do with them." I took them off. "I thought about having them melted down and reworked into something for the kids."

"But?"

"But it doesn't seem right to do that. I mean, if he had died and we were happily married, maybe that would be a good idea." I held them up between us. "Is it right to give my kids a symbol of their parents' broken marriage?"

I paused while the waitress brought the beers.

"Pretty!" she said, looking at the rings. "Did those come from you?" she asked Nico.

"No." He kept his eyes level on me.

"Oh, I'm sorry...I..."

"That's okay," I assured her. "I think we're ready to order."

She took our orders with lightning speed and hurried away.

"Any suggestions?" I asked him.

"About?" He took a long drink of the beer and leaned back in his chair, still not smiling.

"The rings." I set them on the table.

"I was asking why you continue to wear them, not what you were going to do with them."

I sipped my Guinness.

"I couldn't get them off when Les left. Believe me, I tried everything: soap, cold water, olive oil. Nothing but losing weight would get those babies off." I pushed them to the side. "The fat came off, and the anger eased up, and I guess it just wasn't a priority anymore." I paused to smile at him, almost overwhelmed by how much I loved the jealous and possessive man in front of me. "I wasn't wearing them because I wanted to, Nico. Like saying my old name, it was just out of habit."

"You sure?"

"Absolutely sure."

He finally smiled.

"Good. Now read your letter," he said. "The clock's ticking, babe."

"No. Not until you tell me why you keep your shaving gear packed in the kit. Why don't you leave it out?"

"Because the rings were still on."

"Really?"

He didn't answer immediately. He continued to sit, leaning back in his chair, looking into my eyes. After a few minutes, he nodded and smirked. "Really. Now, read the damned letter."

I picked up the envelope and stared at my father's handwriting.

"You know," I said to him before reading. "I think I should call the waitress back and change my order."

"You're procrastinating."

"Maybe. But I told her I wanted the fried clams basket."

"What do you want?"

"The fried clams basket."

"And..."

"And I should have ordered a salad. I forgot that over the past two days, I had pizza with all the fat that makes it delicious and a giant carb-laden sub."

"If you get a salad, you'll still be hungry when you're done. Hungry and unsatisfied is no way to live."

"Neither is fat."

"You just climbed more than 200 stairs, and you'll be working out tonight with your sister. If you want fried clams, you should have fried clams."

"I'll have fried clams then." I laughed.

"You're beautiful, Lucy." Nico brought his elbows down to lean on the table. "I've always thought you were beautiful."

"Even when I was 169 pounds? That was in October when Angie and I started walking. Knowing that I was just one pound from 170 was quite the catalyst." I picked at the envelope, made a small tear.

"I remember October." He put his hand on mine. "I remember you trying your damnedest to make your kids happy, make your mom happy. I remember everyone around you demanding something of you, even that dick of an attorney you had. By the way, next time you need a lawyer, ask me to get one for you. He was a shit, you know that?"

"I do now."

"Well, that's what October was: you taking care of everyone and doing what everyone wanted you to do and ignoring your own needs. I'm glad you hit 169. It made you make yourself a priority. So yeah, you were beautiful at 169, you just didn't see it. And now there's a little less of Lucy, and she's happy, and the people around her need to figure out how to take care of themselves, as they should."

His eyes pierced me.

"Nico, maybe it's a mom thing, a parent thing, but—"

"No. Let me get this out." He stared so hard into my eyes that I was almost afraid. "You've spent your whole life thinking you existed to please others. And where did it get you? Alone. That's where.

Your husband left you. Your kids, up until you started getting a life of your own, didn't want to be in the same room with you. Why? Because you taught them that your happiness didn't matter. And they knew they didn't have to work to be happy because you would take care of everything."

"I love my kids, Nico."

"I know you do. And you know what? The fact that you are so passionate about the people you care about is one of the things I love about you. But Luce, there's not enough of you to go around. There's not enough Lucy for her to make everyone in the world happy. There's only enough Lucy to make herself happy. Do you get that?"

"I think so."

He reached across the table to touch my face.

"Look," he said. "This is what I'm afraid of. I'm afraid that when things calm down, you'll go back to that unbalanced life again. You need to know I can't stand by and watch you do it. I will pack up my shaving kit for good because I can't be part of your lopsided life again." He took my hand again. "I need to trust that you are with me because it makes you happy to be with me, not because you want to make me happy. I want to be the man whose body you crave when you want to make love. I want to be the man whose back you dig your nails into when you wanna fuck for a release. I also want to be the man you vent about work with, or you tell silly stories to, because you like to tell stories. I want to be the one you fight with about what color to paint the living room, and I want you to win that fight, *not* because I let you, but because you really want to paint the Goddamned living room purple." He squeezed tight to my fingers. "Do you understand?"

I nodded, tears in my eyes. "But I promise it won't be purple. That wouldn't go well with tangerine sunset."

"Good. Now read the damned letter."

Somehow I laughed. "God, I love you!"

"I love you, too. But now you're procrastinating."

The waitress brought a few people upstairs and seated them far from us. I finally ripped the envelope open and took the note out. I sipped the Guinness and looked at Nico. He seemed to know I couldn't read it.

He eased the letter out of my fingers and read it to me.

My sweet, sweet, Lucinda, Lucy Girl—

Some see Atlantic City as a filthy city, a place of slums, degradation, and vice. They might be right. But I see Atlantic City as a place of laughter, hope, and promise. A city that embraces the different, the eccentric, and the leftovers. It's wonderful you see it that way, too. Please don't ever lose that perspective. Know that each time you laugh at the obscure, each time you celebrate the odd, I'm clinking my glass in heaven to yours on Earth.

But that's not my gift to you. That's just where you'll find me whenever you need to. Sid has your gift. Ask him for it and tell him it's time to give the medallion to Angelica.

Now, go find a nice man who enjoys a good, stout ale and drink to me. Sláinte!

I was only peripherally aware of the waitress setting our food before us. I'm not sure how long it was there before Nico left his side of the table and came around to the chair next to me. He put his arm around my shoulder, and I could feel his lips press against my temple.

"You all right?" he eventually asked.

"Yeah." I looked up at him. He wiped my tears away and kissed the end of my nose.

"That Guinness there is a good, stout ale, you know," he said.

I picked up his bottle, handed it to him, then picked up mine.

"*Sláinte.*" I said, and we clinked. "So Uncle Sid has the medallion."

I left the wedding rings on the table at the Back Bay Ale House.

"Was that an accident?" Nico asked, taking my left hand as I put my key in the condo door.

"No." I squeezed his fingers. "No accident. That waitress seemed to like them. Maybe she can figure out what to do with them."

"You could call and ask if anyone found them." He followed me inside.

"I could. But I'm not going to." I turned around to face him. "Nico, I don't want the rings anymore."

"You're sure?"

"I'm sure."

"You're not saying that because I acted like a possessive ass back there, are you?"

"I thought it was cute." I smiled at him and went into the kitchen to tend to my eggplant. "Ugh! I forgot to get some gravy out of the

211

storage locker."

"I'll get it," he paused to touch my arm. "But cute? I'm not sure if I like being called 'cute.'"

"How about sweet? Endearing? Sexy?"

"I like that last one." He left to get the gravy while I sopped the water from the eggplant that the salt had drawn out. I was nearly finished breading the slices when he returned.

"Now, since I've eaten so poorly over the past couple of days." I turned the oven on to preheat. "I'm not frying these before layering them for the parmesan. I'm baking them, okay?"

"As long as it will still taste good."

"It will. I've got magic gravy, remember?"

"How could I forget?" He laughed. "But before you get lost in cooking, you need to call your uncle Sid."

"I know. I just need to get centered first. I won't get lost in cooking. I just want to ground myself. Let me get this parmesan prepped and get my brain to fully understand what and how I'll talk to my uncle."

Nico nodded and sat at the dining table to power up his laptop. I baked the eggplant and snuck in a little laundry. As I told myself, when your ex-husband's life is at risk, and you have a couple of ex-mobsters leaning hard on you, you need to be sure everyone has plenty of clean underwear to wear to the funerals.

"I had several e-mails from my men," he said after a while. "Seems as if everything Enzo and Aldo said was right. They were cooks in prison. They worked under a head chef with ties to some major restaurants in the area. It wouldn't be too much of a stretch for that chef to be aware of black-market tomatoes and the cop who made them possible." He paused and looked at me through the pass-through. "They've even deposited money on a restaurant in Cherry Hill. Looks like they're just about ready to set up shop."

"So all they need is a tomato connection, huh?" I leaned my hands on the sink counter. "But Isaac Blackman hasn't called me back. What am I going to do?"

"Call your Uncle Sid first, then call old Isaac again." Nico's eyes held level with me. "I know you don't really want to call Sid, Luce. I'm sure it'll be a bittersweet conversation, and you're more afraid of the bitter than you are of looking forward to the sweet. But I think this is going to be healing for you somehow. Maybe it will help give you better closure with your dad's passing."

"Yeah, you're probably right." I went to the living area and sat on the sofa with my cell phone. I hadn't seen Uncle Sid since his New Year's Eve party that Angie had made me go to. I had never been to one as a single woman, and I wasn't sure how to handle it. Uncle Sid never mentioned anything to me about Les at the time. In fact, during the party, I could tell he was working extra hard to make sure I was having fun and thinking about anything but Les.

He picked up on the fourth ring.

"Listen, doll," his voice was hoarse. "Is this a life-or-death emergency?"

"Possibly. But not right this second."

"Good, because I'm heading out the door to the proctologist, and that could be a life-or-death emergency. Can you call me back tomorrow? He's putting me under some kind of light anesthesia."

"Oh my God! Uncle Sid, are you all right?"

"Yeah, I'm sure I'm fine. They're just shining a light up my ass. That's what they like to do to old men like me. You've nothing to worry about, doll. But I may not be in the mood to talk later. Call me tomorrow. In fact, why don't you bring me something to eat tomorrow?"

"How about lunch? Eggplant parmesan sound good?"

"Sounds delicious, sweetheart."

"Set the table for an extra person. I'll have a guest with me." I clicked off and looked at Nico. "He's going to the doctor's now. I think for a colonoscopy."

"Ouch."

"Yeah. He'd like us for lunch tomorrow."

"Sounded like he'd prefer the eggplant parm."

"That, too." I leaned my head on the back of the couch. "Shit! Tomorrow is Thursday. I bet Les is freaking out right about now."

"He'll deal," Nico said. "Or do you want to tell him you know where the medallion is?"

I didn't answer.

"Are you worried about Les? You can admit it, you know. I won't be jealous. He was your husband for a long time. I'll understand if you want to call him."

I laughed. "Actually, Nico, that's not what I was thinking of at all." I stood. "I was thinking I need to make something else to go with the scallops in Filo dough now that I've promised Uncle Sid the eggplant." I kissed his cheek and went into the kitchen. "Any requests?"

"A salad is sometimes good."

"Finally! The man agrees that a salad is good." I smiled at him from the kitchen. "But that means I don't have to prep anything now."

"Which means you can call Isaac the tomato farmer again." Nico stretched his legs out on the coffee table. "What do you do all day at work when you can't cook?"

"Think up recipes and then cook all weekend."

"While I enjoy the food, I like the nightgown you bought last Saturday when you went shopping. Glad you took a break from the kitchen."

"You mean the nightgown you keep taking off me?"

"Don't get the wrong impression. I like seeing you in it, but when we're in bed, and it's dark, it's all about touch, you know." And I did know. He always took it off me, even the one night we didn't make love. I couldn't imagine sleeping with him when something was separating us. "What else did you get?"

"A dress for Joy. Angie's picking it up today."

"For *you*. What else did you get for *yourself*?"

"Some jeans, some funky boots, and a couple sleazy tops to wear to keep your eyes on me." I grinned. "This is one. Like it?" I arched my back to show off the clingy shirt. Nico hooked a finger into the scoop neck and pulled it out to peek in.

"I like it." He kissed my collarbone. "What do the boots look like?"

"Super high heels."

"Hmmm...I'll take you out to dinner Saturday night. We'll walk down the boardwalk. You'll wear the boots?"

"You like boots?"

"I'm picturing how you jiggle when you wear high heels."

I laughed.

"Now break time is over. Call farmer Iz," Nico said.

"Yes, sir!" I dialed. Isaac surprised me when he answered.

"Hi, uh, Mr. Blackman. This is Lucy. Lucy McCool. You remember me, right?"

"I remember you! You're calling too early in the season! I told you never to call me unless it was the right time!" I held the phone away from my ear so Nico could hear him shouting.

"I know, Mr. Blackman. But this is important."

"What? What's important? Does someone know about my plants? Did you tell someone?"

"Look, Mr. Blackman, there are some men who, uh, who worked with my father on a project. They want some of your tomatoes."

"NO! Absolutely not!"

I had to look away from Nico. His body was shaking from silent laughter, and I was afraid he'd make me laugh too.

"They're good cooks," I said. "They want to start a restaurant. They could bring you good business."

"They could be the FDA in disguise!" he screamed. "They could be spies from Monsanto! It's too risky to bring in new business. They don't know about me, do they?"

"Well, they know there are some special tomatoes and—"

"WHAT? Who told them?"

The sofa was now shaking with Nico's silent laughter.

"Look, they don't know where the tomatoes come from or anything like that. They just know my dad—"

"I DON'T CARE WHAT THEY KNOW! No! Actually, I do care! I care that they don't know anything about me, EVER! Do you understand?"

"Mr. Blackman!"

Click. Apparently, he was done talking to me.

Nico burst.

"How can you laugh at a time like this?" I pressed the heels of my hands against my forehead.

"Because that's the craziest thing I've ever heard! The FDA in disguise? Spies? Who's Monsanto again?"

"A seed company." I fell back against him. "What are we going to do, Nico?"

"Have no fear. Isaac Blackman has to have a weak point. Everyone does. My guys will find it, and we'll use it to make him talk to Enny and Aldy. Got it?" He wiped his eyes.

"You're not worried, really?"

"Not worried in the least." He took my chin in his hands. "And, tomorrow when we're talking with Sid, we'll bring this up too. I bet Enzo and Aldo know of him and wouldn't want to mess with him."

Angie called my cell, saving me from contemplating how tough my sweet Uncle Sid really was.

"How are things going?" she asked.

"Let's see, I have eggplant parmesan in the oven, and I was just about to butter sheets of Filo dough to make purses for scallops. How's it sound?"

"Like you've been through hell, and that I should probably come for dinner."

"Only if you'll eat the shellfish."

"Ew."

"I'm saving the eggplant for Uncle Sid tomorrow, who, by the way, apparently has that medallion."

"Really?"

"Yep and are you sitting down?"

"I am now."

"I think it's supposed to be a gift for you."

"That ruby necklace thing?"

"That ruby necklace thing."

"Bizarre."

"Yeah. So if you're not coming for dinner, plan on a longer workout. I need one."

We'd just finished dinner and were cleaning up when the doorman buzzed to alert us that Les was downstairs.

I looked at Nico before answering; he nodded.

"What does he want?" Joy asked. "I thought he wasn't coming until tomorrow. Mom, I really don't want to spend that much time with him."

"Why? He's your—"

"Father! Like, I know! You keep reminding me. Do you think I'll forget or something? Christ!" She stormed into the kitchen and ripped open the dishwasher.

"I thought you two kissed and made up. What's so bad about him wanting to spend time with you?" I asked, rinsing the dirty plates.

"He never spent that much time with me in the past. What the hell does he want from me now?"

"You not to swear in front of him, for one thing." I gave her the last of the plates and took the full trash bag out of the can. Nico squeezed into the kitchen to take the bag from me and left the unit to drop it down the chute.

"Oh, so, like, he can swear every other minute and I can't? They're just fucking words." She slammed the dishwasher shut and stared at me, clenched fists at her side. I knew she was waiting for me to attack her for saying *fucking.*

"I don't know, pumpkin," I said, keeping my voice calm and sweet. "Maybe you saying such fucking words makes it sound like you're growing fucking up and he's just now fucking realizing that and realizing what he's fucking missed. Think that could be the fucking case?"

"Maybe." She grinned at me and relaxed her hands.

"Anyway, Nico has been working on a project for him. Maybe that's all he wants." I put a fresh trash bag in the can and stowed it beneath the sink.

"So your ex-husband is working with your boyfriend on a project? That's so fucked up, Mom."

"You have no idea."

"I can go down and swim, then, right? I don't have to wait around here for him?"

"Sure, pumpkin. I'm going to work out as soon as Aunt Angie comes."

Joy disappeared down the hall to her bedroom as I put away the counter cleaner and the placemats.

Nico opened the door. Les followed him in, but before anyone could say anything else, Joy tore back into the living area.

"Who. The. Hell. Was in. My room?" Hands on her hips, she glared around the room before settling her fierce gaze on me.

"Your mother and I," Nico said without sounding upset, angry, or defensive, as I was tempted to be. "We switched out the batteries in your smoke detectors. Is that okay?"

"Oh, absolutely." The tension evaporated from her body. She straightened and smiled at him. "Do that anytime you want." She turned on her heels and went back into her room.

"Thanks," I said to him.

"She just needed to know that the world was safe for her right now. That's all."

"You'd think you had more experience at this father shit than I have," Les said. "You did better than I probably would have on that one."

A snort came from the end of the sofa. We looked in its direction and saw Ash staring at his cell phone, texting away like mad, as if unaware we were in the room.

"So what do you want, Les?" I turned back to him. Nico sat on the arm of the couch, at the end opposite Ash, next to where I stood.

Les's eyes darted from me to Nico to Ash and back to me.

"I was hoping to talk privately with you."

"You should have called."

Les took a few steps toward me. Nico quickly, but casually, stood and stepped between us, arms loose at his side, posture erect, shoulders back.

"Hey! I got the dress!" Angie burst into the condo and stopped. Her wide eyes bounced between Nico and Les, though it was probably difficult for them to pierce the cloud of testosterone in the room. "Jesus! Maybe I should start knocking. Never know what I'm walking into around here."

"You are always welcome to walk into my home without knocking, Ange," I smiled at her. "Always. Is that Joy's dress? She's in her room changing for the pool." I took the dress from Angie and walked past Les.

"Really, you should have called," I said to him. "I'm not available right now." I went down the hall and knocked on Joy's door. "Joy, pumpkin. Aunt Angie brought your dress."

She opened the door and actually invited Angie and me in as she tried the dress on. By the time the three of us left her bedroom, Nico and Les were gone. Ash was still on the sofa, his thumbs scrambling over his touchscreen phone.

"Um?" was all I had to say.

"Talking," was how Ash explained their absence.

TOMATO COUNTRY

I slept remarkably well for a woman with a possible death threat over her head. I guess it was easy for me, spooned up against Nico. I'm sure Les didn't sleep that well. He never did tell Nico what he wanted from me, but he did get Nico to agree to serve as an intermediary between him and Sal on Friday, should the need arise. And Nico told Les he had a lead on the medallion.

Before heading down to Uncle Sid's, I wanted to check in at work Thursday morning. Nico wanted to check out the Blackman farm, which I didn't think was a good idea. We compromised and did both.

Mona and Rachel were happy and relieved to see me. I explained I really couldn't talk about what was going on. I tried to use the excuse, "You know how messy divorces can be," and left it at that. The good news was that Mr. Schwartz didn't show up on the previous Monday because his grandson had come to town to introduce him to his fiancée.

I sat in my cubicle and called Mrs. Elliot to see if she had made her doctor appointment.

"I'll call him now," she said.

"Good. Call me back and leave a message on my answering machine telling me the date. I'll go with you if you want. That way, if he gets pushy or anything, I'll help you fend him off."

"You do that for me?"

"Absolutely, Mrs. Elliot. I'd do anything for you. Your shoulder has been worrying me probably as much as it's been worrying you."

"My shoulder?"

"Yes, your left shoulder. That's why you're going to the doctor, right?"

"Why would I talk to him about my shoulder?"

I paused to sip my coffee before answering her. "Well, I assumed you should talk to him about it."

"Why?"

"Mrs. Elliot," I sighed and closed my eyes. "I know this may be difficult to hear. And keep in mind I'm no doctor, but it seems to me there's a huge growth on your left shoulder. Have you not noticed?"

The older woman burst out laughing. I waited quietly, wondering if perhaps I should line up a psychiatrist for her.

"Good thing you ain't no doctor. That's no growth." She laughed again. "That be my fanny pack."

"What?"

"My fanny pack!"

"Your...why would you wear a fanny pack on your shoulder?"

"Cause it don't fit around my waist no more. And I wear it under my clothes 'cause it look stupid over my clothes up there."

"I see," I lied. "So why do *you* think you need to go to the doctor?"

"Honey, if your waist is so big you can't get a fanny pack around it, don't you think you should talk to someone 'bout it?"

I had her make the appointment with the doctor and told her I'd find a nutritionist to work with her, too. Relief and laughter washed through me. I couldn't believe how obsessed I was over someone else's non-issue. I shot an email to Rachel explaining the true source of Mrs. Elliot's growth. Then, before leaving the center, I sent a note to Mona, asking her how much 125 thousand dollars would help the senior center.

Around ten thirty, I drove back to the condo, packed the eggplant parmesan in a basket, grabbed a bottle of wine, and piled into Nico's Land Rover with him. Farmer Isaac Blackman and his field of secret Afghan tomatoes were about a thirty-minute drive from the condo. Nico wanted to drive by on a wide detour going down to Uncle Sid's in Avalon. We headed west on Black Horse Pike, then turned southward onto Route 40, going toward Mays Landing.

I pointed him to an off-road that cut into the pine forest, and then I showed him the dirt drive, without a marker, that divided the pines. He continued on the paved road for about a quarter mile before turning around.

"Is that a street or a driveway?" he asked.

"It's a very long driveway."

"Does it curve or is it straight?" He slowed as we went past the entrance to the Blackman farm a second time. "You sure it's a driveway? There's no mailbox."

"It's pretty straight. And I don't remember there being anything else on that drive. It dead ends in front of the farmhouse." I scooted down in my seat, trying to get my head below the window.

"You think he has telescopes trained on the street?" Nico asked before turning around again.

"I wouldn't be surprised."

"They'd have to be pretty damned powerful to look through all those trees." He squeezed my knee. "I promise you, you're safe from the tomato grower."

"It's not that I doubt you. I just don't trust crazy people."

Nico pulled to the side of the road and parked, with the truck running, about fifteen feet from the driveway. He took an iPad out of an attaché case on the floor behind my seat and tapped the screen. Pretty soon, we were looking at a satellite image of the area.

"You can't see the driveway from this image. The trees are too thick. But see that lake?" He pointed to a body of water on the screen. "It's just down this road. Let's go check it out." He handed me the iPad and drove.

"Did you forget Uncle Sid?"

"So you don't trust me, eh?"

"Nico I—"

"I can't believe you don't trust me enough to know I wouldn't forget about eggplant parmesan." With a full smile, he took my hand and held it over the center console. "Where's my laughing Lucy?"

"I don't know, Nico. Maybe I can't bring her out here. I've been coming to that farm for a long time, and each year that man gets progressively crazier. Last year on the clam trawler, he and his son were dressed in black as if they were on some covert SEAL team operation. Isaac was armed as usual, a machete on his back, a big gun in his hand. Zeke had a smaller gun on his hip."

"At least it sounds like they're legal guns. They were not trying to carry them concealed."

"And that's a good thing?"

"It means, as far as guns go, they might be careful, law-abiding citizens."

That made me laugh.

The road curved off to the right at the edge of a lake. Nico stopped again and took the iPad from me.

"I was hoping for a dirt track or trail down here. You know, where kids could go four-wheeling or ride dirt bikes?"

"Are you planning on doing that?"

"No. I'm getting hungry." He winked at me. "Not starving, though, so we can take a little walk before heading down to eat with Uncle Sid." He got out of the SUV and walked to the edge of the lake. The air was cold and damp, just a smidgen shy of misting, and it was heavy with the scent of pine.

We walked along the sandy edge, somewhat parallel to Isaac's dirt driveway, though the pines were too thick to see it or his farm. I wouldn't have seen it anyway, as I kept my head down, trying to make sure I didn't step into the water lest my brown suede boots get ruined. My mother had given me the boots at Christmas. God knows what she would think if she knew I handled suede as poorly as I did wool. I did occasionally look up to see where I was heading.

"Hey, look!" I hopped off the sand onto a large rock jutting into the lake and pointed across the water. "This must be Lake Lenape."

Nico followed my finger. "Is that another lighthouse?"

"Yeah. It's the Lake Lenape Lighthouse. I take it you haven't been there, either?"

"No. But a lighthouse on a lake? Is it that deep?"

"It's purely decorative. Cherie, in accounting, got married there last spring. It makes a beautiful place for a wedding."

From our vantage point, we could only see the top third of the lighthouse above the trees. I started to tell Nico something else about it when we heard a boat motor. Within a few seconds, a man in a small fishing boat headed around a bend and came directly toward us. He brought the boat in until it was about six feet away from the rock I was standing on.

"You people lost?" he yelled. He looked to be in his late forties, maybe early fifties. He wore a thick, down-filled Gore-tex coat with the hood up over his head.

"No, we're just admiring the view," Nico said to him with a smile. "Are we on your land?"

"Almost," the man said.

"Is it okay that we're out here?" I asked.

He cut his eyes to me and took his time answering my question. "Depends on what you're doing." He pushed the hood back from his face. I thought I recognized him from somewhere.

"Like I said, we're just admiring the view," Nico told him. "We know people who got married at that lighthouse. But we like private affairs. So we thought we'd just go around the lake and see how many people are out here."

"You thought people'd be out here today? You getting married in the winter?"

"No," I chirped in, smiling at him, trying hard to recall the face. "We just didn't know if there were many houses out this way."

"You looking for people or houses?" he asked, and I realized I'm not good at this sneaking around business.

"Both, I guess." I continued to smile. "You know, you look familiar to me."

"Yeah, I've been told we all look alike." He turned in his boat and reached for a long pole with a hook on one end.

Horrified at what I'd just implied to an African-American man, I flailed my arms and almost fell off the rock. "That's not what I meant!" I insisted. "I just thought maybe we've met before. Do you ever go into Atlantic City?"

He took the pole and swooped in a plastic grocery bag from the shoreline before answering me. "I go in every now and then." He put the bag into a larger trash bag in the boat with him.

"Maybe that's how she knows you then," Nico said.

"Actually, are you familiar with the Blackman farm?" I asked without thinking. Both men snapped their heads to me. "I mean, Isaac Blackman and his sons. They own a farm near here." I waved my arm behind me toward Isaac's land and wobbled on the rock again. Nico's face suggested I should probably not talk anymore.

"Yeah, I know them."

"Are they your neighbor?" Nico asked.

The man stowed the pole in the hull of his boat and looked hard at Nico. Unlike me that morning, he was thinking before he spoke.

"I know that family. And you wouldn't know me from them," he finally said to me.

"Oh," was all I could produce, but I knew why he looked familiar to me. I remembered him approaching Isaac a few years back when I was there with my dad. He and Isaac had fierce words. Isaac aimed his gun at the man, and the man pulled out one of his own. My dad promised me neither would shoot the other. I still didn't know why he was so sure.

"Well, to tell you the truth," Nico said, "Actually, they're the real reason we're here. We used to do business with that family, too. This is Lucy McCool. She's a great chef."

I nodded at the man.

"Are you a farmer?" Nico asked.

"I'm someone out here in my boat cleaning up trash people throw in the lake," the man said. "That's all you need to know about me."

"Oh, well, we were hoping to find another source for our tomatoes," Nico said. "We really don't want to deal with the Blackman family anymore."

"I thought you were getting married."

"We're doing a number of things," Nico grinned at him. "Don't mean to take you away from cleaning up the lake." He reached his hand toward me.

"You really a cook?" he asked me.

"She is." Nico's eyes told me to smile and nod only. "She's fed a lot of people. In fact, we have an eggplant parmesan back in my truck, we need to take down to Avalon right now."

"Yeah? You make deliveries that far?"

Nico grinned. "It's personal. Her uncle had a colonoscopy yesterday."

"Ouch."

"It's a special treat for him." Nico grabbed my hand. "It was good to meet you."

"The name's Jonathan Green," the man said. "And I have tomatoes of my own. If you're interested, come season, you can look me up."

"Great! We'll be in touch," I braved to say. Nico pulled me off the rock and practically dragged me back to the Land Rover.

"What are you doing?" I asked as I kicked the sandy mud off my feet. "You almost ruined my boots."

"I wanted to get out of there before you said too much to that man. Mr. Green might be able to help us with Isaac's weak link." He opened the SUV door, and I got in.

"How can he help?" I asked when he was sitting next to me.

He put his finger to his lips, and I heard a phone ringing through his Bluetooth. Nico spoke to one of his muscle-bound men, asking him to research John Green and his property.

"That's one of the neighbors I mentioned earlier," his henchman said.

"Interesting." Nico winked at me. "Good work. See what else you can find on the Green man."

"Got it."

"What's interesting?" I asked as he turned the SUV back to the road.

"From satellite images, we discovered the Blackmans weren't just farming on their own land. They've been encroaching on neighboring properties and have even drained off wetland areas where they shouldn't be doing anything. That's information we can use on him if we need to, but it would help if the neighbors were on our side. By the sound of it, Green is the owner of some property that Isaac's taken over, and it didn't seem to me he was on good terms with them."

I told him what I remembered from seeing Green and Isaac fight.

"Again, interesting." He leaned over and pecked me on the cheek, making the Land Rover zig on the road. "You make a good partner."

I smiled and inhaled deeply. The interior of the car smelled delicious. "I'm getting hungry," I said. "We better get to Uncle Sid's without any more pit stops."

Uncle Sid has a giant house a couple of doors down from the Yacht Club in Avalon. His place sits on the water, and there's a dock out back with *Sid's Other Woman* tied to it. He doesn't captain her himself anymore, but his sons, Anthony and Julio, still take her out quite a bit. She's a beautiful boat. They would bring her up to AC for my barbecues and dock behind Angie's place. They used to stay the weekend and take us all out on the water.

I only had fun and happy memories of my cousins, who were just a few years older than Angie and me. But as we pulled into Sid's driveway, I wondered if they were in the process of being made, too. I wondered if binoculars were ever trained on us as we zipped through the inlet going out to the ocean. I wondered if they'd ever dumped a body into the sea off the side of *Sid's Other Woman*. I also wondered, no, I decided, I really *did* need to stop watching TV.

I made myself at home, heading right to Sid's kitchen to warm the eggplant parmesan in the microwave. Aunt Lydia had passed away from breast cancer when my children were babies. Sid took it hard and never remarried, though he's very close to the housekeeper he's had for years. She wasn't there, but her presence was obvious: the place was immaculate, the refrigerator was stocked, and there were no dirty dishes in the sink.

We settled around the end of a very long table in the dining room. Sid poured us wine. I made eye contact with Nico over my glass. He raised his eyebrows and tilted his head sideways.

"I'm not going to get drunk," I said. "I want to be conscious— well, I don't *want* to be awake for this conversation, but I will be."

"*Salut!*" Uncle Sid said. We clicked glasses and drank. "Now then, Lucy, what is it that you don't want to be awake for?" He stuck a forkful of the eggplant into his mouth, closed his eyes, and smiled as he chewed.

"I think you have a gift for me? My father left some notes..." I couldn't figure out how to explain what I didn't understand. So I ate.

"The eggplant is divine, my dear, simply divine," Uncle Sid said. "And you already have your gift."

"I do? The note said you had it. What is it?"

"It's your freedom. Or is your divorce not final? I was going to force it if I needed to, that's what the note implied." He continued eating as if he made complete sense.

"I don't understand."

Uncle Sid leaned back in his chair and smiled at me. "It's no mystery your father hated your husband."

"Right."

"Sean made Les agree to file for a divorce after the summer was over, that way he wouldn't ruin your favorite season. He figured by the time the next summer rolled around, you would be over Les and maybe have moved on to someone he'd approve of. Like this left-handed Italian, here."

"How do you know Nico is left-handed?" I asked, maybe because it was a safer topic than why my father made my husband leave me.

"*Mancuso* is Italian for left-handed," Nico said. "It's just one of those real coincidences that I'm," he raised his fork in his left hand, "a southpaw. But that's not really the question you wanted to ask him, is it?"

I dropped my fork and put my head in my hands. Both men were patient with me, or maybe they were just hungry. After a few minutes of me listening to them eating, I looked up and shoved my plate away.

"This is a first," I said. "I've never lost my appetite before." I didn't even want to drink anything. I wanted only to go for a long, long walk down the beach and not stop until I hit Cape May. Maybe then I could hop on a ferry to Delaware and continue walking until I made it to the tip of Key West. Perhaps by then I'd have enough perspective to understand what was going on in my life.

"Darling Lucy," Uncle Sid said. "I mean it, the eggplant is divine. Simply divine." He reached over and took one of my hands into his. "Now then, what is it you really want to know about? Your divorce? Your parents' situation? Your father's sickness? Why Angie gets the necklace?"

"All of the above! Wait! My parents...my dad sick? He wasn't sick."

"He was very sick. He had brain cancer," Uncle Sid said.

"What?" I felt my jaw hang loose. "Daddy had brain cancer? Why didn't he ever tell me?"

"He didn't tell anyone," Sid said. "Except me, of course."

I stood, but didn't know where to go, so I sat again. "Uncle Sid," I said. "I came here for answers. And you seem to have them, but for different questions."

"You start then." Uncle Sid poured himself more wine. "Ask away."

I forced my breath to stay regulated and my voice to be in therapy mode: soft, controlled, soothing. The effort was for my benefit. "I found these notes my father left, and they pointed me to you. Why? Angie is supposed to get a necklace, but I think it's the same necklace Les needs to give to some Sal Pul-something. Do you know about that? And I came here because there are some men, some cousins named Enzo and Aldo Finarelli, who are after me. Do you know them? They want me to connect them and a crazy tomato farmer. But, but now you're telling me my father had brain cancer. And that my parents had a situation. What's that about? They are all different issues, different problems, and I have no idea how to fix any of them. Which one do you want to tackle first?"

Uncle Sid held his wineglass up and smiled at me.

"Lucy, doll, actually, they are all connected." He sipped and leaned back in his chair. "And I have answers for everything, except maybe the tomatoes. You might have to tell me more about that. But first, a story."

MIA FAMIGLIA

The story begins when your grandmothers were little girls," Uncle Sid said. He resumed eating. I looked at my plate, then glanced at Nico.

"It's not a good time to lose your appetite, babe," he said. "I don't think there will be any leftovers."

I moved the dish back in front of me and picked at the food with my fork. "I'm ready to hear it, Uncle Sid." I nibbled the eggplant.

"So, do you remember them, your grandmothers, telling stories about when they were young?"

"A little. They were both orphans, right?"

"Right."

"Their parents had immigrated to this country just before the Depression," I explained to Nico. "Both sets of parents came down with a deadly flu and died shortly after their arrival. The girls were put in an orphanage run by nuns in Philadelphia around the same time." I turned to look at Uncle Sid. "That's all I got."

"And I have the rest." Uncle Sid nodded. "So, there they were, two young girls, alone in the world. Luciana, your mother's mother, my mamma, your namesake, received her first Communion before leaving Italy. Siobhan, your father's mother, was seven, Irish, and equally steeped in Catholicism.

"Though they came from different countries, they bonded through their loneliness, their fears, and their faith, which was reinforced by the nuns. When they were old enough, Siobhan took a job in a bakery, and Luciana in a nearby food shop that the two women later were able to convince their husbands to buy and turn into a delicatessen. They were the best of friends."

I handed him my empty wineglass. "Daddy did tell me that. When we were little he told us that's how he met Ma. Their mothers were close."

"Very close." He tipped his glass to me before drinking. "Those women were closer than the best of friends. They were at each other's sides when each married. They made their husbands become business partners. They were godparents for each other's children. And they promised at least one son would marry one daughter." He stood. "I think we need another bottle of wine."

"Are you all right?" Nico asked after Uncle Sid left the room

"Yes, I guess so." I shoved some eggplant onto my fork. "Thanks for making me eat." I smiled at him. "I'm dying to hurry Uncle Sid along. I want to get to now. I want to know what he meant by my 'parents' situation.' I want to know why no one told me Daddy was sick."

"All in good time, my dear," Uncle Sid said, coming back into the room. "All in good time. This story is an old one; it cannot be rushed. Rather like the aging of this wine, I would guess." He set the open bottle on the table next to Nico.

"Now then, poor Siobhan had a devil of a time getting pregnant and carrying a baby full term. Your father, Sean, was the only one she was able to birth and raise. Luciana had me around the same time, then four years later, she had her twin girls, your mother, Octavia, and your aunt Julia. Octavia was first by about twenty minutes. And the matriarchs immediately decided that Sean and Octavia would eventually marry and bond our families together permanently."

"In this country? In the middle of the twentieth century? They made an arranged marriage?" Nico asked.

"In this country, as immigrant women who were tough as nails and adamant about doing things their way. No one said *no* to them for any reason. You have no idea how formidable those women were."

"I do," I snorted. "Every time my mother would browbeat my father into doing something, he'd tell me she was just like both my grandmothers. She always got her way."

"Only when it was in accordance with *her* mother's wishes," Uncle Sid corrected me. "She never did anything her mother wouldn't approve of. None of us did. As long as Luciana and Siobhan were alive, everyone bided by their wishes."

"Which probably explains why my parents were in a less-than-perfect marriage. Did they ever like each other, Uncle Sid?"

"They liked each other just fine when they were younger," he smiled at me as he nodded his head. "But your father and Julia were wildly in love." He sipped, oblivious of me staring at him. My father had never mentioned her.

"I had just married Lydia when it was announced Sean and Octavia would wed," Uncle Sid said. "Sean and Julia were devastated. They had hoped, since it was only by twenty minutes, their mothers would let them be together and not force Sean and Octavia. But once those women made up their minds, there was no changing it. Besides, there was a handsome man, a well-connected Italian named Salvatore Pulsoni, in the mix. Julia had taken his eye and his heart, too. He was much older than Julia, but had more money than Luciana had ever thought of having. So when he approached her, Luciana gave him permission to marry Julia."

"That's so sad." I felt sorry for my father. This was all news to me. He had never hinted that he was unhappy with his lot in life. My mother was always angry, but Daddy was the one to teach me to make lemonade. I sipped my wine and made eye contact with Nico. He winked at me. "It was just a sip," I insisted.

Uncle Sid leaned back in his chair again, smiling at Nico teasing me. "It was agreed, Sean and Octavia would marry in August, and Sal and Julia in September. The night before his wedding, Sean and Julia snuck out together for one night of love. She asked me to help her escape, which is how I knew back then. He gave her a beautiful necklace made from his paternal grandmother's rosary chain to keep him close to her heart. Sean had a medallion of St. Cecelia put on it because Julia was quite musical and played several instruments. She wore the necklace every day, even the day she was married."

"Which is why Daddy wanted it back," I said.

"Not really. Lucy, my darling, I'll get to why he wanted it back soon enough. Please be patient. Do you need more wine?" Uncle Sid went ahead and topped off my half-full glass before I could answer.

"So the girls get stuck in arranged marriages in the early 1970s when most women are burning bras?" Nico asked.

"Not many of those bra burners were good Catholic girls terrified of their mothers," Uncle Sid laughed.

"But my dad?" I asked.

"Was madly in love with Julia. Your mother was the next-best thing and a way that he could stay close to her," Uncle Sid shrugged.

"He didn't trust Sal."

"Daddy did have a strong protective streak." I took a last bite of eggplant. "Okay, the girls marry. What happened next?"

"Sal immediately moves Julia into a new house on the western side of Philly, where they expected to live with his three sons from a previous marriage. Sean and Octavia move in with his parents in their row house near the deli. October comes, and Sal must go down to Miami on business. He plans to be gone for several months, and because his boys were in boarding school, he did not want Julia to be alone in the big house. So she moved back into our family home, which is in the same set of row houses as Sean and Octavia." He paused to drink.

"By November, Julia discovers she is pregnant. She is very sickly, and she is worried. My mother thinks she is worried about Sal. No one had heard from him. By January, we thought perhaps he was dead. However, in February, we get word that he had been arrested for trying to facilitate smuggling guns into Cuba. But, again, he was well-connected and would be released and returned home by the end of April. Julia refused to let anyone tell him she is pregnant. She claimed it was because she feared losing the baby."

"Oh," I said. I gripped my napkin in my lap. "But that's not why she was really scared, was it? Did she think Daddy was...?"

Uncle Sid nodded.

"Was he? Or is he? She didn't have kids, right? I think Ma said she died shortly after she married."

"You're trying to get ahead of me again, my dear." He smiled at Nico. "How do you handle this impatience?"

"The way you do, I torment her by taking even longer," Nico clinked wineglasses with Uncle Sid.

"I'm not thinking this situation is very funny," I said.

"And you're right, my dear," Uncle Sid sighed. "Frankly, it's somewhat tragic. But isn't that what you and your father handle best? Aren't you the ones who find ways to make everything more bearable for the rest of us?"

"I guess."

"Then you'll appreciate your father's role in this story, if you would just be patient." He pushed his chair away from the table. "I wish I had a cigar. Damn housekeeper keeps throwing them away."

"Maybe she wants you to live longer."

"Bah."

"So, Julia is pregnant and scared to tell Sal..." I urged, hoping I didn't seem impatient.

"Yes. Pregnant, sickly, and scared. And then she goes into labor in March. The baby is very, very small, but the grandmothers don't care. She had barely been married six months. It didn't matter how small the baby was; they were convinced she had conceived it before her wedding day. And they suspected someone else was the father because the baby was fair, not olive like Julia and Sal. They demanded to know who the father was. Julia and Sean agree to tell them about their one night together. Julia desperately tried to point out that the baby is tiny, so tiny it could be Sal's."

Uncle Sid closed his eyes and sighed. "You see, my sister was just as scared of your grandmother's thinking she had a baby by another man as she was of her husband thinking it. I remember her begging and pleading with them to believe it was Sal's. I remember the doctor saying it was very possible, because it was so tiny. And then I remember my mother saying it really didn't matter, because the baby would probably die before Sal got home anyway. They would never tell him."

"How horrible! Poor Julia! Did they at least try to help the child?" My stomach clenched up.

"The baby stayed in the hospital and, contrary to all expectations, grew and lived. By mid-April, it was healthy enough to go home. No one knew what to do. The child hadn't even been legally given a name yet. Julia had gone every day to the hospital to be with it. She threatened to commit suicide if her mother put her up for adoption. So my mother and Siobhan got together and came up with a solution. Since the child was apparently Sean's anyway, he and Octavia would raise her as their own, and they would do so away from any tongue that could wag the truth to Sal. They had a friend of my father's take care of the birth certificate and, just a few days before Sal's arrival home, Sean, now-pregnant Octavia and baby Angelica, as Julia had been calling her, moved to Atlantic City, where my father's cousin got Sean a job on the police force."

The bomb dropped from my Uncle Sid's lips with such casualness, it took a full thirty seconds to land in my awareness.

"Oh my God!" I clutched at my throat. "But...but that was a different baby, right? They named my sister after her? Right? I mean, something happened to that baby, and she died anyway. And when they had my sister..." I stopped because Uncle Sid was slowly shaking his head.

"No, my dear. Angie was the baby."

I fell back into my chair. Nico came around my side. After a few minutes, I took a deep breath and sat up again.

"Angie doesn't know, does she?" I asked.

"No." Uncle Sid sipped his wine. "She turned out to be fair-haired, like your father, so no one ever thought she was another woman's child."

"And Sal never found out?"

"No. Sal returned. Julia moved back in with him and became pregnant with another baby soon afterward. That baby was premature, too, and she died with it when she went into labor the following fall. Sal was grief-struck. He literally lost his mind for a short while and never truly recovered from losing her. He did really love her. He kept everything that belonged to her."

"Including a necklace with a medallion of St. Cecelia," Nico said.

"Including a necklace with a medallion of St. Cecelia," Uncle Sid repeated, nodding.

I tried to process what my uncle had just said to me. Things were making a little bit of sense, but so much was still a mystery.

"So, life goes on for Sean and Octavia," Uncle Sid said before I was ready for him to. "They have another baby, you, shortly after they settle into Atlantic City. Their girls grow up, the grandmothers pass away, and the number of people who know the truth is down to three: your parents and myself. You get engaged to Lester, and against your father's wishes, you marry him. Sean decides to keep close tabs on Lester's activities. He kept an eye out, constantly looking to find Lester in a position to hurt you."

"What does that mean?" I asked.

"That means your dad spent his entire career as a cop waiting for his son-in-law to screw up. After his retirement, when you were worried about his 'wandering' as you used to call it, he was really pretending to be out of it so that Les wouldn't know Sean was spying on him."

"Did you know what was going on?" I asked.

"Not in the beginning," Uncle Sid said. "But, when your father was diagnosed with brain cancer, he was given—"

"Stop!" I slammed my hand on the table. "Why did you say that? Daddy wasn't sick. I would know!"

"He wasn't sick in a way that you could easily tell. For a while, the symptoms were just dizziness."

"He suffered from vertigo," I insisted. "That was probably some kind of post-traumatic stress from his years as a cop."

"The vertigo was a story he wanted you to believe. Really, the dizziness was from an inoperable tumor pressing against his brain." Uncle Sid tilted his head and looked at me with such compassion, I knew he was telling the truth. But that didn't mean I had to believe him. "Remember his frequent headaches?" he asked.

"Yes, but—"

"And there were three seizures that only your mother and I know about."

"What? Why the hell didn't she tell me? Why...I might have been able to help him! Why didn't she give me a chance to help him?"

"She didn't know it was cancer, either. He convinced her the seizures were from the vertigo medication that she thought he was taking. He insisted that neither you nor Angelica know. He didn't want to worry you. He told me the truth when he felt his death was imminent. He needed my assistance with his plans with Lester and with his game with you."

"Game? No! Nothing new right now. I can't handle another new subject. Lester. Tell me about Les." I gripped so tightly to the stem of my wine glass, I was surprised it didn't snap.

"Your father thought he'd hit the jackpot when he discovered Les was connected to a robbery Sal had requested. He had been watching Sal for all these years, too. He always wanted to get the necklace back and give it to Angie so that she'd have something that was her mother's. The chance to screw Les over *and* get the necklace felt like divine intervention was guiding his movements."

Uncle Sid stopped to drink. I drank with him. Nico refilled all three of our glasses. "That's your third one," he whispered into my ear.

"Two and a quarter," I corrected. "Over an entire meal. I'm okay."

"Sean photographed Les with the Finarelli boys," Uncle Sid continued. "He discovered Les owned a condo—the one I believe your friend here put you in—and he had a sit-down with him last spring. Sean told Les he knew he'd hired the Finarellis to rob Sal, and then he blackmailed him into divorcing you. Either divorce you or go to jail. Sean insisted he do it after the summer was over, though. He wanted you to have a good summer, like I said.

"Lester agreed to the divorce. Sean then came to me to ask for my help. By then, he was having symptoms that suggested the time was close for his death." Uncle Sid stared into his glass and sniffed. "He was beginning to get very weak on his left side, and he'd been catching himself saying things he didn't mean to say. He was worried he would tell all the family secrets."

"Why not tell us?" I asked. "Angie and I are adults. Why not tell us when he knew...why not tell us that he was dying?" *We might have been able to help him*, I wanted to scream. But the person who needed to hear it was not among the living.

"I asked him that very same question." Uncle Sid closed his eyes. "And when he was first diagnosed, he almost did. But then, by chance, he ran across a brochure on DNA testing at the neurosurgeon's office. He decided to sneak a DNA test on Angie so he could prove Octavia was not her mother. He felt it would be easier for everyone to accept the truth if he could provide some kind of proof. He did the DNA test himself, too, to prove he was her father. But that's when he learned he wasn't. He wasn't her father, which meant Sal had to have been. And Sean became very ashamed." Uncle Sid leaned over and touched my arm.

"You must know this, and Angie, too," he said. "Your father was disappointed in himself when he learned what he'd been keeping from Angie. Your mother was never as good to her as she was to you. He felt horrible about that. He worried that once Angelica knew the truth, she would hate him for keeping her away from her real family and for forcing her to live with a woman who resented her existence."

"But Angie's not like that! She's so—"

"He loved her, always, like a daughter. And having her close to him was almost like having Julia close to him. The thought of her being upset with him was too much to bear. The guilt for lying to both of you was almost too much for him to live with."

"Is that why he...he..." I still couldn't say *committed suicide*.

"No. He took his own life because the symptoms were telling him he was getting close to the end of his time. He thought it would be easier for you, Angie, and your mother if you didn't have to handle him going into hospice or see him in a state of dementia. I agreed to help him in whatever way I could. He liked to gamble, remember?" Uncle Sid smiled at me.

I could only nod. My dad loved blackjack, in particular. But he was cheap at the tables. He preferred to bet on things like a Guinness if the last leaf from my maple tree fell before December 1st.

"He decided to leave whether or not you knew about Angie's parents up to chance. He did, after all, live in the city at the center of a famous board game, right? And he always loved a good pun. He thought it was only fitting. During the last couple of months of his life, he set about writing the notes and hiding clues." Uncle Sid grinned and sipped. "It was all a matter of chance, a gamble, whether or not you'd find them and figure them out."

"What if she had found them prior to the divorce?" Nico asked.

"That last note told her to come to me so that I would be the one to tell her about it, and then she'd have to make the choice whether to leave him or stay."

"I'm not sure how I feel about that," I said. "I was so upset with his passing, I don't know if I would have been able to handle it too soon."

"So everything worked out for the best. *Salut!*" Sid hoisted his glass and drank.

"But what about Angie?" I asked. "Who is to tell her?"

"You. If you want to and you think it's wise." Uncle Sid said.

"That's just wrong." My grief and shock were replaced by anger at the unjustness of my position. "As much as I love my father...as much as I admired him...how could he justify doing this to her? And to put me in the middle of it?"

"Because, as I said, he was afraid she would hate him. He couldn't go to his grave knowing that he'd hurt her. But he could go knowing the one person who knows her best, the one person she wouldn't hate after she learned about it, you, told her."

I rubbed my face with my hands. When I looked up again, Uncle Sid had left his chair and was opening a china hutch.

"Here it is." He placed a white jeweler's box on the table and lifted the lid. I reached in and removed what could only be a St. Cecelia medallion on a beautiful rosary chain.

"Now what do I do?" I asked, turning my face to Nico. "It's

Angie's. I feel like the right thing to do is to give it to her. But what about Les?"

"What about him?" Uncle Sid asked.

"Sal gave Lester until tomorrow evening to return the necklace to him," I explained.

"I see," Uncle Sid said. "And you're interested in Lester's safekeeping because of why?"

"He's the father of my kids."

"Well, if you need my help with Sal, call me," Uncle Sid said. "It's my fault Les and Sal even know each other. I guess I could step in and help the bastard if you want me to." Uncle Sid smiled. "Now then, you remained awake. How are you doing?"

"I honestly don't know." I closed my eyes and collapsed my head into Nico's chest. "My head is reeling. I don't know what to tell Les. I don't know what to tell Angie."

"I think the truth should be told to them both," Nico said.

"Yeah, so do I, but..." I sighed and leaned back in my chair again. I needed to rouse myself to clean up the dishes. I looked at the remnants of eggplant on my plate. The eggplant cooked in my gravy. "Oh, the tomatoes! Uncle Sid, I'm not done."

"I got this one," Nico offered. I cleared the table while he told Uncle Sid about Enzo and Aldo and the tomato issue.

"Ha! Oh, Lucy!" Uncle Sid's eyes squinted as he chuckled. "You do keep things fun! Just like your father."

"Yeah, well, it wasn't fun when those two took me at gunpoint into Angelo's." I sat in my previous chair. "What do we do?"

"They're buffoons! But they'd be better off in a kitchen than back in jail. Ha!" He laughed again. "Why didn't you know about this, Mancuso? Sean admired you. I'm surprised he didn't ask for your help with the smugglers. That sounds like something you would have been good at."

"Frankly, I'm a little insulted he didn't."

"Oh, he probably enjoyed the adventure. How do you plan to handle this?"

"I was going to have Lucy put the squeeze on the Blackmans over their land and farming habits. She could tell them they have to take on the Finarelli boys as clients or else she's going to report them to the authorities for farming on neighboring lands and draining wetlands."

"I like that. You're much nicer than I am, Mancuso." Uncle Sid nodded. "But if it doesn't work, tell the Finarelli boys they'll have to deal with Sid Davio if anything happens to my wonderful Lucy. Got it?"

A LITTLE LESS OF LUCY

Iwas silent on the way home. Nico seemed to sense my need for a lack of stimulation and let me sulk or ponder or do whatever it was I was doing. He contacted his men and spoke quietly to them about the Blackman land on his Bluetooth. I let myself eavesdrop and learned that one had already gone out and met with Mr. Green to get his involvement and approval to use his property to spy on Isaac.

The men had also printed aerial shots of where Isaac had been farming and had retrieved plot records from the county and information from the New Jersey EPA. All the documents and photographs were waiting for us in a large file with the doorman at my condo.

My landline was ringing as we entered. Thinking it was my mother, someone I didn't have the strength to talk to, I didn't answer. But it was Mona's voice that echoed through the answering machine.

"Hello, Lucy," she said. "I know you're taking the week off, but I was hoping—"

"I'm here," I said, picking up the receiver.

"Are you sober?" she asked.

"Yes, Mona, I'm sober. Why?" I made eye contact with Nico's grinning face. "Did something happen to one of my people?"

"No, no. Nothing like that. I keep reading that e-mail you sent. I think I read it several times now, and I can't wait until Monday to ask: what's with the 125 big ones?"

"I came into some money—"

"When people say it that way, it sounds as if they don't want you asking where it came from."

"It's legitimate, but it's a long story."

"A long story, huh?" she paused. "Well, I can take a long story as long as the money is legit. If you actually have 125 thousand, this place can get a line of credit and stay open longer."

"I actually have it." I wondered if Uncle Sid would like to donate more. He was loaded and had no problems with vanity. If I said a wing of the building would be named after him, he would probably open the checkbook. "But let me get through the rest of the week, okay?"

I felt the need for a shower. I wanted to wash the day off me. Nico offered to join me, but I refused without an excuse, and he was okay with that.

"I think I'm going to make Angie a vegetable Napoleon casserole," I said, once I was clean and good-smelling again.

"You really feel up to cooking?" Nico was sitting at the dining table with all the paperwork from his men spread beside his laptop.

"I do. This is an easy thing to do for her. Besides, I have a little eggplant leftover that needs to be used." I smirked. "And it'll get rid of some of the angst I'm feeling right now. I'm so sad. I'm so...so worried for Angie."

"Worried?" He looked at me over his monitor.

I nodded and dumped the vegetables on the counter.

"She loved my father as much as I did. He was our only hero for years. Probably still is her only hero." I put the zucchini and tomato in the sink to wash. "How will she take it when I tell her he's not her father? Who will be her hero now?"

"Her Uncle Sean." Nico came to the pass-through and reached across the sink to touch my face. "Who, for all intents and purposes, was her father. Just as you are her sister and your mother—"

"The jury's still out on her." I smiled at him.

His cell rang. He reached for it and glanced at me. "It's Les."

"What are you going to tell him?" I peeled a shallot.

"What do you want me to tell him?" The phone stopped ringing.

"That we have the medallion but can't do anything with it until tomorrow," I said. "I don't want him doing something stupid if he panics thinking the medallion is nowhere to be found. But I kind of think it's Angie's call on whether it gets returned to Sal." I banged the knife on the cutting board. "Or am I pushing off on to her what my father pushed off on to me?"

"Why don't you make the decision together, with her?" Nico asked. "I'll call Les back now."

Angie came for dinner around seven thirty. She bounded into the condo with a beautiful smile on her face, gushing about how well she and Rick had been getting along.

"It's so amazing. He's just about perfect! We should go out together tomorrow night," she said at the table. "What do you think? The four of us. It'll be like in high school." She laughed hard. "Oh, Nico. I didn't mean that at all. I could never convince her to go out with any boy who wanted to hang out with the boys I went out with. You should have seen the poor things she dated."

I smiled. Then tears fell from my eyes. I leaned over and hugged her.

"What the hell's going on?" she asked. "Are the kids okay?"

I sat up and sniffed.

"Here," Nico handed me a tissue.

I blew my nose. "Oh God, Ange! I have the craziest thing in the world to tell you."

I gave her the whole story as Uncle Sid told it to me. Her face remained impassive. Unlike my reaction, there were no tears, no signs of anger, no attempts to get up and leave. She just sat and listened quietly as she drank her wine and ate her vegetable Napoleon. I finished the tale and retrieved the necklace in its box from my purse.

"That's so messed up," she finally said when I placed the medallion in her hand.

"I know." I sat beside her and put my arm around her shoulder. She leaned her head against mine.

"I guess that explains why it always felt like Ma held a grudge against me. It was because she actually held a grudge against me."

"Yeah, I guess so."

"And it explains why we get along so well and like each other so much. Sisters don't act like that."

"True." I gave a quiet laugh.

"Now what do I do?" she asked. "I mean, do I go on like before?" She stood and walked to the glass doors. We let her stare into the darkness while she processed everything. After a few minutes, she twisted around and grinned at me. "Am I exempt from Mother's Day brunch with her now?"

"Absolutely not! *I* need you there." I smiled at Nico. "You know, when I was trying to figure out how to tell you, a wise man said to me that I am your sister and Daddy was your father because that's the way we were all our lives, so I guess that makes her your mother, if you still want us."

She turned fully around. Tears were in her eyes. "I can't imagine not having you in my life," she said. She looked at Nico. "Are you the wise man?"

"I think so."

"Thank you. And you're right. Daddy was my father, so I guess Ma is my mother."

"I hate to bring this up now," Nico said. "I don't mean to be insensitive or anything, but there is this issue with Les. He's supposed to get that medallion to Sal by tomorrow."

"Do you know how to contact this Sal person?" Angie asked him, returning to her seat at the table.

"Of course."

"Will you arrange for me to take the necklace to him tomorrow? We should probably get to know each other."

I realized I'd found another real-life hero to replace my dad: Angie. She was so damned brave.

Nico wrote a script for me to use when I spoke to Isaac Blackman on Friday morning. His guys had dug up another phone number, a landline that went directly to Isaac's house.

He answered politely, like a normal, sane human being would answer a phone: "Hello."

I introduced myself, and he went off the rails.

"How did you get this number?" he shouted into the phone.

"I have all sorts of people doing things for me these days. When my father passed away, he left me all his contacts, you know."

"What do you want?" He continued to yell.

"I told you before. I want to connect you with some friends. They're opening a restaurant and—"

"NO! And I'm not doing business with you again either! Don't ever call me back!"

"Then I'll hang up from this call and contact the zoning committee, the EPA, and the FDA. I'll tell them all your secrets. I even have a contact with Monsanto."

He was quiet for a minute.

"I have no idea what you're talking about, lady. You don't know who you're dealing with." His voice was calm.

"I do know who I'm dealing with," Nico whispered. That response wasn't in my script.

I repeated it and, grinning at Nico, I added: "But you have no idea who *you're* dealing with now."

Again, Isaac Blackman was quiet a long while before responding.

"When can we speak in person?"

"This afternoon," I told him. "I'll come to your property. And I'll be very protected."

Nico left to meet with some of his men. I phoned Enzo and told him what they were to do, and then I decided I needed to take a walk. I couldn't help but appreciate the irony of how I used to hate power walking to lose weight, and yet I longed to do it whenever I wanted to clear my head.

Outside, it was in the upper forties and overcast, but not too windy. I walked north on the boardwalk, heading to the mall at Trump's Pier. Inside, I bought a bottle of perfume. Just as I went past Boardwalk Hall on my way home, my cell phone buzzed.

Lester was calling. I almost didn't answer. The kids would still be in school. He could only be calling about the medallion.

"Yes?" I answered anyway.

"Lucy, can I talk to you?"

"Now? I can barely hear you. I'm out on the boardwalk."

"Can I meet you at your place? Without him?"

Funny, he couldn't say Nico's name. I wondered if he had forgotten what it was.

"Not at my place, but on the park bench on the boardwalk in front of it." I glanced at my watch. "I should be there in about five minutes."

I chose an end spot on a bench in front of my building and placed my large purse with the perfume inside it in the spot next to me. With my arm protectively draped over the bag, I ensured Les would have to sit in the spot next to it and not directly beside me. Though it was cloudy, I wore my sunglasses and people-watched while I waited for him to arrive.

I saw him walking up the boardwalk before he saw me. I couldn't help but notice how very handsome he still was. His thick blond hair perfectly framing his boyish face. When he found me, he smiled and sat on the bench, on the other side of my purse.

He placed his hand over the one I held on my bag. I didn't want to take it off the bag, but I also didn't want him touching me. But if I moved the purse, he could come closer. I left my hand where it was.

"What did you want to see me about?" I asked.

"It's crazy, Lucy. When I called you, it was for one thing, but on my way over, Angie called and said she was on her way to see Sal and that she had the medallion. Why the hell would Nico get you two involved in that?"

"He didn't get us involved." I half snorted, half laughed. "Angie is Sal's daughter."

"What the hell does that mean?"

"It's a long story. And it really doesn't have anything to do with you anymore, so you don't need to worry about it."

He frowned at me.

"So are you done?" I asked.

Les reached up and took my sunglasses off. "No, that's not all." He squeezed my hand.

"It's bright, Les." Really, it was so cloudy I wouldn't have been surprised if it rained. But the sunglasses prevented him from looking in my eyes. I was still trying to work through the fact that Les had been forced to leave me, that he didn't do it on his own. The knowledge weakened me when I was next to him. "Please, can I have them back?"

"I like being able to see your eyes when we speak. Can I hold them for a minute, just a minute, Lucy?"

"What do you want?"

"I want you back."

"Oh Christ."

"That wasn't the response I was hoping for."

"Did you really think I'd go running into your arms, Les? Honestly?" Though I would have had to lie to myself that it wasn't a tempting proposition. Yes, he'd behaved like an ass. He'd kept secrets that endangered me. But my life was so stable and comfortable when we were together. Once I healed from all the craziness I'd just been through, is it possible I'd want that again?

"I'd hoped you'd been thinking about us," he said. "Lucy, we were together a long time. A long time. And we were happy for a long time."

"And you fucked it all up." The anger I'd felt that cold, gray day in the rain on the beach came back to me. My dad was dead. Les could have come forward with the truth instead of divorcing me. Why didn't he?

"So Joy gets that mouth from you." He chuckled.

"She gets it from both of us." I jerked my hand away. "How can you come up to me, now and—"

"Because I still love you. I've never stopped loving you. I didn't want to get a divorce." His voice shook, and his face was uncertain.

"Uncle Sid told me, just yesterday, that Daddy made you divorce me. I get it now."

"So you know it wasn't my fault?"

"I know you've been screwing around on me for a long while. *That* was your fault." Actually, I didn't know it. I'd only guessed it.

He put his head in his hands, elbows resting on his knees. I covered my bag with my arm again. *Can't be too careful on the boardwalk*, Daddy's voice echoed in my head, *Purse thieves never look like bad guys*.

"I know," Les said after a few breaths, his voice shook hard. He gasped. "I know."

"Les." I don't know why, perhaps it was another old habit, but I removed my hand from the bag and put it on his shoulder. He looked at me. Tears rimmed his eyes. I feared that if I spoke, I'd cry too, so I sat silent.

"What can I do, Lucy?" He sat upright and took my hand in his. "How can I fix this?"

"I don't know, Les."

"There's nothing you want back? We had a pretty good life, didn't we? We can get it all back! I swear to you, Luce. It'll never happen again. I got caught up in a lifestyle, but I wasn't happy there. I was happy with you." He wiped his eyes with his sleeve.

I still couldn't talk. My eyes felt wet, and there was a lump in my throat. We could have our old lives back.

"You know, one of the things I miss most," he continued, still holding my hand over my bag. "When I'd come home in the middle of the night after working the late shift, I'd put the light on in our bathroom but shut the door almost all the way so that I'd have just enough light to watch you sleep without waking you. I'd stand there for a long time and just think about you, about how much I loved you, about how badly I wanted to wake you and make love to you like I never had before."

"But you never did." Would things have been different for us? If he allowed himself to express that passion?

"I..." he gave me a sheepish grin. "Because you were too perfect. I didn't want to do anything that might make me take you off the pedestal. I didn't want to taint you with me."

"What?"

"You ever hear that expression 'an angel in the kitchen and a whore in bed'?" He wiped his face with his free hand again and leaned back. "Well, I rephrased it with you: an angel in the kitchen, an angel everywhere. I didn't want to taint you with my aggressive needs and wishes."

"I still don't understand." I thought about how Nico, with no inhibitions, had made love to me in the mornings, evenings, afternoons, whenever, wherever he, we, wanted. That didn't make me less of whoever I was. I was stronger than that, had Les never noticed?

Les looked me in the eyes. "You're perfect, Luce. And I'm not. That's the way I saw it. You always had the answers. You always had the laugh. You always made everything all right." He reached up and twirled a strand of hair around his finger. "I wasn't happy with the life I was leading. I was trying to figure out how to get out of it. I explained that to your dad. I explained how I wanted to recommit myself to you...I was happy with you. You were happy, too, right?"

I couldn't answer him. I wanted to take another walk.

"What do you say, Lucy? Let's try all over again. You, me, the kids. Let's get our old life back."

I blinked away tears and inhaled long and deep. My phone rang before I could say anything. It was Nico. The man who wasn't afraid to show me his ugly, tainted side. The man who realized I was strong enough to accept and love him anyway. The man who didn't need me to make him happy.

If I didn't answer, he'd worry. I looked at Les and his pleading face, then pulled the phone out of my pocket.

"Is it time?" I asked instead of saying *hello*.

"Yeah. I'm at the condo, where are you?"

"On the boardwalk, with Les."

"We need to leave soon if we're going to be on time."

"I just need a minute longer," I said, realizing what would make me happy. "I'm trying to explain how there's less of me now."

"Good to hear."

We clicked off, and I looked at Les again.

"Was that him?"

"Who?" I wanted to make him say his name.

"Nico. Are you really happy with him?" Les asked.

"I am."

"He's a mobster, Lucy."

"And you would know because you met in the conference room?" I laughed. "He's not, Les. I know that for sure." I stood.

"Lucy!" Les leaped in front of me. "Anything, please. Just tell me. What do I need to do to get us back to where we were?"

"You can't. It's impossible. There's just not enough of me anymore."

"What?" He took my hands in his.

"I can't go back to where we were before. There's not enough of me left to handle it." I kissed him on the cheek and was about to ask for my sunglasses back when some little shit came running by and snagged my unprotected purse off the bench.

"Hey!" I shouted and took off after him, not knowing or even caring if Les was trying to help me.

I'd had enough of people taking advantage of me. Enough of people thinking I'm too weak, too nice, or too whatever to take control. For the first time in my life, I was ready to take care of myself full charge, and that skinny, little punk kid felt my resolve firsthand. I tackled him and bashed his face into the boardwalk.

IT'S NOT JUST ABOUT TOMATOES

We drove to the Blackman tomato farm in Aldo's van.

"Get ready, Aldo," I said. "You thought I had some crazy seniors at the center. You haven't seen anything yet. Get ready for one of the craziest senior citizens of all time."

The plan was for Nico to drive, and then he and I would get out of the van to chat with Isaac. On cue, Enzo would send a text to one of Nico's men to bring round another car. He and Aldo would then step out of the van. I would make the introductions, and Nico and I would leave in the newly arrived car.

The plan sounded like a good one to me. It made sense. It was logical. One step led to another. I was confident in it. I just wished I were confident in myself. The burning scrape on my chin that I'd received when I tackled the purse thief on the boardwalk made me feel bad assed at first. But the closer we drove to the farm, the less of an impact it had on me. And being armed with an encyclopedia of blackmailing information wasn't as empowering as I'd imagined it would be.

We drove down the long driveway and stopped in front of the farmhouse. In typical Queen Anne style, there were several steep pitches to the roof, white wooden walls, tall and narrow windows, and a porch that wrapped around one corner of the house, featuring gingerbread decorative trim. My former house on Maine Avenue, though only around ten years old, echoed the style of the one in front of me, which was probably built in the 1800s. I could picture a happy family relaxing on the porch, playing in the yard, maybe eating farm-fresh watermelons and peaches on a hot summer day. I could also picture children running from it as bats flew out of cobweb-covered, broken windows on a late October night.

The clouds had grown thicker, and when Nico and I got out of the van, the air was damp and heavily scented with pine. We were in a clearing in front of the house. Pine trees flanked the muddy drive coming in and formed a border of sorts separating the house from the farmland behind it. No one was in sight. That wasn't part of the plan; Isaac was supposed to be waiting outside for us.

"What do we do now?" I asked and took hold of Nico's hand. We stood in front of the van.

"We wait." He leaned against the bumper and took my other hand. "You okay?"

"I was until we got here."

"It's just tomatoes, Luce."

"I hope that doesn't mean you're not taking this seriously."

"I'm wearing two guns and a knife. I have armed men hidden all over this property. I think that means I'm taking it seriously. But really, it's just tomatoes. What's the worst that can happen?"

"Well, for starters, Isaac is probably also armed. So we could get shot by a tomato farmer. Second, he's a paranoid nutcase. So we could get shot by a paranoid, nutcase tomato farmer. Third—"

Bang. The screen door on the porch slammed, and I think I might have peed myself a little. I jumped and spun around. Zeke had come outside. He stood on the porch with his legs spread, one hand on his hip, the other holding a big gun. He wore camouflage fatigues, black boots, and had smeared black face paint under his eyes the way a football player does to keep the glare from the sun at a minimum. It was still cloudy out.

"Hello," Nico called to him.

"I thought you knew the rules, Lucy McCool," Zeke said, striding down the steps that led off the porch. "Thought you knew how important it is to stick to them. Especially the rule never to bring someone here without prior permission." He stopped at the bottom.

I stared at his gun. I don't know one kind of gun from another. Zeke's was long and dark brown. Unlike Rambo, he didn't have bullets strapped over his chest in an X, so in my mind, that meant his gun was a hunting gun, not a combat one. I thought maybe it was a rifle. I allowed myself to be confused enough to think a hunting rifle was the least scary variety of all guns. And I wondered if the gun meant there would be no sharing of wine.

"Lucy just thought you'd like a new friend or two," Nico offered.

"We got enough friends and acquaintances. Don't need any

more." Zeke leaned on his gun like a walking stick.

Because I was pretty certain mental illness wasn't contagious, I figured he either inherited the same synaptic misfirings that afflicted his father or that he was sane but had drunk too much of the family Kool Aid. I wasn't trained to deal with the certifiable kind, but if he was just misguided due to a dysfunctional family life, I stood a chance of making headway with him. I remained mute as I contemplated how to tell the difference.

"Sometimes it's the friends we make by accident that we wind up enjoying the most," Nico said with a cocky grin.

"Who are you?" Zeke asked him.

"Lucy, would you mind making formal introductions?" Nico asked.

I blinked a few times, not sure what he was doing. I guessed he was playing some kind of mind game with Zeke. I wished he had gone over those rules with me before he started.

"Lucy?" Nico encouraged.

"Um, yes." I cleared my throat. "Nico, this is Zeke Blackwood." I waved my right arm as if presenting a new car to a game-show contestant. "And, Zeke, this is Nico Mancuso." I waved my left arm toward Nico.

"Mancuso?" Isaac's voice shouted from inside the house.

Before anyone could answer, shots rang out. With tiger reflexes, Nico ripped me around the van. He popped the driver's side door open, but didn't let me get in. That's when I noticed the gunfire had stopped.

"So maybe it's not just tomatoes we need to worry about," Nico grinned at me. "We have backup, though, so no need to panic."

"Then what else am I supposed to do?"

"Um, excuse me," Aldo said. He had moved the driver's seatback up and poked his head out the open doorway. "Could you try and not let them shoot my van anymore? I've only had this baby for a couple of months. And we're going to need it to make deliveries from the restaurant. It'll look bad with buckshot in the sides."

"Not if you call it violent violet gravy," Nico said. "Think of how you can work it into the brand of the place."

"Are you kidding me?" I yelled at him. "You're joking right now?"

"Mancuso!" Isaac yelled. "When I fired your family as a customer, I told you never to show your asses here again. Angelo's is cut off!

OFF!"

"I'm not one of those Mancusos," Nico yelled back to him. "I'm not affiliated with Angelo's restaurant at all."

"Then why are you here?"

"As a bodyguard and an ombudsman." Nico texted madly on his cell phone. I strained my ears but couldn't hear backup coming from any direction.

"A what?"

"I'm here to make sure this meeting goes smoothly between you and Lucy." He tucked the phone away into a pocket and pulled out a handgun from inside his jacket. I closed my eyes and took a few steps back, toward the rear of the van. My ears rang. I bent over and put my head between my knees to keep from fainting.

"I'm not in the mood for making a deal," Isaac said.

"Well, I wasn't in the mood to get shot at," Nico replied. "So now you have no choice. Lucy is going to introduce you to a few friends, and you will make arrangements for them to buy your Afghan tomatoes."

"Don't say those words out loud!" Isaac screamed. "No one is to know."

"Which is another reason why you have no choice but to make a deal," Nico replied. His voice, though loud enough for Isaac and Zeke to hear, was calm and steady. "Lucy has in place several contacts who, if they don't hear from her within a certain time frame, will release paperwork to particular authorities. Those authorities will be very upset to learn that you drained wetlands, you violated easement agreements with your neighbors, and that your plants have never been inspected. Do you understand?"

"I understand she will go to jail for knowingly buying my produce," Isaac said. "I can implicate her with the original plants."

"I think we all understand we need to have a chat, a very respectful chat." Nico glanced at me as I slowly stood straight again. He lowered his voice. "You okay?"

"Of course," I said. "I mean, I don't really have another choice now that you told me I can't panic, right?"

"Right." He grinned. "I take it that's Isaac?" I nodded. His phone vibrated in his pocket. With his gun remaining in one hand, his other reached into the pocket to get the phone. I watched him look down at the screen, and the next thing I knew, someone took my arm in a tight grip and rammed a hard thing in my side that felt remarkably similar to the gun barrel Aldo had shoved into my kidney.

I tried to say something. All that came out was a morphed sound, something between a gag and "ow."

Nico looked at me again.

"Now then," he said. "That's a bad move. A very bad move." He whistled. A large, burly man with a gun of his own pointed in our direction came out from behind a pine and slowly walked toward us.

"Isaac," Nico called. "I don't know who just came out to flirt with Lucy, but I'm not liking it much. She's my girl, you know. In return, I invited a pal of my own to keep an eye on your guy. Let's consider him a chaperone." He tucked his phone back in his jacket, looking directly at the man at my side. "We're all going to walk to the other side of the van so we can see each other," he continued in his loud voice. "No one is going to do anything on impulse. If anyone moves quickly or does anything I don't like, I'll have another good buddy come out of the wilderness to get even. Just so you know: I have a whole troop of bored men with their eyes trained on you and your house."

He walked around the front of the van. My captor dragged me around the rear. I had yet to see his face, but I figured it was Isaac's other son, David. The big man from behind the trees moved forward and out to the side as another man joined him. I was sure he really held David in his crosshairs, but it looked like Mr. Big's gun was leveled at me. The second man had a gun pointing beyond us toward the house.

Once we went around the van, I braved a look at the porch where Isaac stood. He, too, was in combat gear and football paint. His gun, larger and meaner-looking than Zeke's, was lowered, and his trademark machete was strapped on his back, the hilt poking up behind his balding head.

"Hello Lucy," he said to me.

"Hi, Mr. Blackman," I squeaked out. "How are you?" I'm not sure why I asked. I knew the answer. I knew how he was: crazy and dangerous.

"I'm not happy," he said, instead.

"Sorry to hear," Nico said to him. "But you could be again, real soon, right, Lucy?"

"Huh?"

"Right? He could be happy again soon, knowing he has another customer."

"Oh, right." I was desperate to rub my face, or pull back on my hair; to do something that would give me a tactile sensation and ground me. But I was terrified to move. David stepped more to my side, keeping a tight hold on me. I saw it was definitely a gun he had shoved against my ribs. The sight was grounding. I inhaled. "Um, well, I have some friends who ate some gravy my father made from your tomatoes."

"It's sauce. I don't know why you crazy people keep calling it gravy!" Isaac shouted. "Have you ever read the words 'tomato gravy' on a jar? It doesn't even sound right."

I looked at Nico. He sucked in his lips. Seeing him holding back laughter in the face of what I assumed was imminent death made me realize why Mr. George smiled the way he did. I think I gave Nico that smile, the one that said the world is so absurd, you might as well laugh.

"Mr. Blackman, whatever you want to call it is fine by me. I don't really care. I just want to make sure I keep getting enough tomatoes to feed my family every year and that my friends get enough to run a successful restaurant."

"And you really think I'm interested in helping either of you?"

"I think you'd be interested in what I have to say to the EPA and the Zoning committee if you don't." I sounded so brave, I almost believed I was.

"Like I said, you'll go to jail, too."

The man had a point. And it was one I hadn't thought of. I looked at Nico. Had he thought of that?

"But Lucy has more connections than you," Nico said. "She'll be safe."

"Not safe from the angry chefs who will lose business all along the coast. Not safe from the angry farmers who let me violate the easement because I was letting them violate my easements. That will end. And I'll make sure every one of them knows she was at fault."

Nico grinned outright at the man. Either he was playing another mind game, or he had anticipated this turn in the conversation. I never learned what was going through his mind, though, because before he could say anything, I glanced down at my feet and blew up.

"I don't fucking think so!" I yelled and jerked hard away from

David. He fell. His gun discharged in the air, cutting into the top of Aldo's van.

"Hey!" Aldo jumped out of the van. "Enough of that!"

"Yes, it is enough." I stormed over to the porch in a way that Joy could admire. "Look what your son did to my boots!" I screamed at Isaac. "You will have the wrath of my mother on your head if I can't get these things cleaned! Do you know how hard it is to get mud out of suede?"

I think everyone was too stunned to speak but it didn't matter to me. I was only peripherally aware that anyone else besides Isaac and me existed. I stomped up the steps and barged into his personal space.

"I've had just about enough of everyone, including you, Mr. Blackman. Enough of your crazy antics. If you think you can fuck with me anymore, you're even more insane than I thought you were. And if I can't get the mud off these boots, Octavia Davio McCool will be on your doorstep because *I'm sick and freaking tired* of taking the heat from my mother *when other people mess up!* You'll be making a deal with the devil to get away from her. Do you understand me?" My burning face was inches from his. My blood pounded in my temples, and my eye sockets strained to hold my eyes in.

I saw him swallow, and then I heard a gargling, snorting sound and came back to my senses. I froze in place, suddenly too scared to take my eyes off Isaac's. My heart backed off from my head and pounded in my throat. I breathed in deep and eventually realized the strange sound was one of someone trying to hold back laughter. Isaac's face broke into a smile and he, too, started laughing. I turned around and saw Zeke leaning heavily against the railing on the porch steps, roaring with laughter.

"Please, Dad," he said, wiping tears from his eyes. "Give her the Goddamned tomatoes. She can have all she wants. Just make sure she doesn't tell her mommy on us."

He fell, laughing on the steps.

"Deal, Lucy," Isaac put out his hand. "Just don't tell anyone about the charades, okay? We like keeping people scared and confused. Keeps us in control that way."

WHEN ALL IS SAID AND DONE

I'm taking a nap," I said after Nico put a fresh layer of Neosporin on my chin. "Wanna join me?"

"I always wanna join you in bed."

"I'm seriously taking a nap."

"And I'm sure you will, eventually."

He had my clothes off before I even made it to the bedroom door. I did eventually sleep for a little while. I woke when Angie called to ask if we were still interested in going out for dinner. We weren't, but still wanted to see her and learn how things went with Sal.

She showed up with two pizzas. A small cheese one for herself and a large pepperoni for Nico and me.

"Everything okay with you and Rick?" I asked when she came in.

"Yeah. Everything's great. It's just that...you know, I really, really like him. And I've seen him every day this week, but this whole...whatever. This whole situation with my newly discovered father...I just don't think I know him well enough to include his opinion on how to figure it out."

"You want me to leave, Ange?" Nico asked. We'd spread a blanket on the floor in the living area. I put a throw pillow against my leg where Dasher would have lain.

"Not at all, Nico. You feel more like family to me than Les ever did." She dropped to the floor. I opened the pizza boxes. Nico doled out napkins.

"What happened to your chin, Lucy?" Angie asked.

"Today was the day. I finally got control of my life."

"I'm not sure I understand."

"I'll tell you the whole story another time. Tonight it's all about you. How did it go today?" I asked, taking the first bite.

"Well, we're not going to a father-daughter dance anytime soon, but I can't rule it out for the future." She chewed. "Though he's a little old. He was like fifteen years older than Julia, my mother."

"Did he ever suspect anything?" I asked.

"About having a kid? No." Angie laughed. "He thought I was you at first. When Nico told him Angie McCool was bringing the medallion to him, he thought it was Les's wife. When I showed up at the restaurant, he made this face like he was surprised. He told me I looked like someone he once knew." She sipped her wine. "I handed him the medallion and told him I expected to get it back from him one day. He asked why, and I explained that it was because I was his and Julia's daughter. He didn't believe me at first. He thought it was some kind of scam. So I told him what you'd told me. He had some thug get Uncle Sid on the phone, who confirmed it."

"Was he angry?"

"Oh yeah. He started railing against Sid, then against Daddy, well, your dad...no he railed against Daddy."

I reached out and touched her arm. "What did you do?"

"Nothing. I waited for him to finish. That guy, Micah, that you sent with me, Nico, he came and stood behind my chair. I think he thought Sal might try to hurt me somehow." Angie paused and nibbled at the crust of her pizza. "By the way," she grinned. "He's really hot. If things don't work out with Rick and me, maybe you could persuade him my body needs protecting again?"

"Jesus, Angie!" I laughed. "Is that why Rick's really not here?"

"No!" she laughed. "I just needed some comic relief. And the guy really is hot. But I'm probably old enough to be his mother." She drank her wine. "So, anyway, he calmed down and stared into my eyes for a second, hard. That's when *I* got scared. But then he slumped, put his face in his hands, and cried. I waited him out. Eventually, he looked up again and told me he was an old man, and he hoped there was time for us to get to know each other."

"Wow! So what happens now?"

"Well, I'm going to his house on Sunday. He wants to introduce me to my brothers. I have three half-brothers from his first wife. How weird is that? I'm not sure what happened to her, but Julia was his second. Anyway, he wants to tell me about my mother and said he had a couple of old photographs he thought I should see. He showed me a tiny picture of her on their wedding day that he keeps in his wallet. She was wearing the necklace in it. She was really pretty."

"Just like you," I said.

She smiled at me. "Anyway, I asked him where my blond hair came from. His mother was Swiss, and she was blond. So that explains that."

"Interesting." I nodded. "Well, I guess that means all the family mysteries are solved. What do we do for fun now?"

"Not all of them," Angie replied. "There's one more. And I don't think anything fun will come from it."

"What?"

"Ma's surprise birthday party," Angie replied. "How do we pull that off?"

"That's so easy." I poked Nico in the side with my toe. "We should have it at Angelo's. I think I remember the food being good there."

Thank you! I hope you enjoyed your romp with Lucy in Atlantic City. I truly appreciate you joining the caper. If you have time, I'd love a review. I hate asking. I know you're busy. But reviews are beyond important, especially on Amazon. They help other readers find new books, and they encourage Amazon to take writers seriously, which I need them to do. I am working on sequels and other projects.
~insert drumroll~

...I have a new book launching in early 2026!

Coffee with Vodka

Three women. Three secrets. One unravelling summer.

Funny, compelling, and suspenseful—*Coffee with Vodka* is a story about friendship, trauma, reinvention, and the truths we hide even from ourselves. Sign up for news about when it comes out here: https://lisashiroff.com/coffee-with-vodka/

Again, thank you! Thank you for reading!

If you'd like to read another work by me, Show up Dead and Revenge Café are both available now. An excerpt from *Show up Dead* follows my bio on the next page.

Cheers!

ABOUT THE AUTHOR

L
isa Shiroff is a ghostwriter and developmental editor who has helped shape dozens of memoirs, business books, and women's fiction titles. With more than two decades of experience in publishing, she brings a sharp editorial eye, a love of layered storytelling, and a deep understanding of women's inner lives. When she's not writing or coaching authors, you'll find her crafting, cooking, or tending her garden. *Coffee with Vodka* is her latest novel.

www.lisashiroff.com.

Excerpt from

SHOW UP DEAD

Best Interest

I'm pretty sure my eyes had been open for several minutes before I realized I could see. I remember darkness. Then light. Then blurred masses of color. Eventually, the colors became distinguishable and detailed enough that I knew I was staring at the foot of a table leg: the foot of a highly polished, mahogany, ball-

and-claw foot of a table leg, to be exact. The points of the claws were painted with red lacquer. The table leg was standing on a Persian rug. The same Persian rug that my face appeared to be resting on.

It was Mr. Wooley's Persian rug, which made sense since I was pretty sure I had gone into Mr. Wooley's house that morning.

The good news was that it didn't seem as if I was alone. A woman's stilted voice pierced the air, someone was tapping my cheek, and I sensed movement around me.

I rolled onto my back and found a man hovering over me, his blond head only about a foot above mine. Even though his face was upside down from my perspective, it was still quite pleasing to look at. His sapphire blue eyes peered at me with such intensity, I wondered if I was asleep and dreaming. Traditionally, I'd never been the kind of girl with charming knights at the ready for her rescue. Though I'd never thought it a detriment to be one.

"Are you okay?" he asked. The unimaginative question disappointed me.

"I don't know." I leaned up on one elbow. "What happened?"

"I was hoping you could tell me," my handsome hero replied. He glanced up as another man, a dark-haired one who wasn't all that delicious to look at, knelt opposite him. He took my free hand.

Looking around me, I confirmed I was in Mr. Wooley's townhouse, as were several of Philadelphia's finest men in blue. They were keeping company with a few other sundry people whose presence, I learned later, was useful whenever a dead body was found.

"Are you in any pain?" asked the man holding my hand. It turns out he was in an EMT uniform and was actually taking my pulse.

"I don't think so," I said. "I—"

"Peri!" shrieked Mr. Wooley's daughter. She ran across the room and dropped to the floor, bursting into my personal space before I was ready to deal with her. I fell back against my blue-eyed guardian angel. He righted me.

"What's going on?" I asked.

"My father!" Jacqueline's breath shot in and out. She shoved the EMT away and then gripped my arms as if she were preparing to throw me over a balcony. "He's dead!"

"What?" I pulled my face back. She leaned in closer. My blond defender put his hand on her shoulder as if to shove her back.

She released her hold on me and flung her long, wavy brown hair over her shoulder. "My father." She placed the back of her hand on her forehead. "He has passed."

"Is this...are you rehearsing?" I asked. I still wasn't sure whether I was awake or not. If I was, the only thing that could rationally explain the situation was if Jacqueline—pronounced with a soft *Zha* at the beginning and a long *eeeeen* at the end—was holding an acting workshop in her father's home. She did that periodically. She called them *impromptu performances*. Anyone who happened to be in the vicinity would either be forced into a nonspeaking role or expected to provide thunderous applause, complete with *encore!* calls at the end.

"What have you done to him?" Jacqueline clasped her hands in a prayer position. Her eyes pleaded with mine.

"To who?" I asked.

"I need to look at her." The EMT bent in front of Jacqueline to shine a light in my face. "Your vitals check out okay. Do you think you can stand?"

I nodded.

"It wouldn't hurt to get evaluated at the hospital," he added.

"I don't like hospitals," I said.

The EMT smirked as he stood. "I'm done here," he called out before walking away.

Jacqueline had disappeared, leaving me alone with my mystery man.

"I have a few questions for you, if you're ready," he said as he helped me up.

We stood before the never-used wingback chair in Mr. Wooley's dining room. In the chair sat Mr. Wooley. A team of people separated him from me. They appeared to be inspecting him at a very close range.

"Oh…wait!" I pressed my fingertips against my temples, almost able to remember why I was in Mr. Wooley's townhouse.

"Do you need the EMT again?" the man asked.

"No. I'm, I think I'm okay." My face scrunched as I looked at him. "Did I already ask what happened?"

"You did." He nodded. "Where did you come from?"

I inhaled deeply while I thought about his question.

"The back door." I pointed to the rear of the townhouse. Mr. Wooley's home stretched a half block. The front door opened to the street, the back to a narrow alley. "Yes, that's right," I continued. "I parked behind the townhouse…I knocked." I tucked my hair behind my ear. "Mr. Wooley didn't answer. He was expecting me. So I waited. Then I just came in. He lets me do that. I just like to knock first. Anyway, I had flowers for him."

"Are you the one who brought the funeral flowers?" His eyes took on a steely quality, somewhat akin to how my accountant's look when he challenges my claims for deductible expenses.

"Yes." My voice cracked. Stark memories from the morning emerged from the fog in my brain. "Is Mr. Wooley really dead?" I asked, although I knew the answer.

"The body of Shelby Wooley was found by his daughter this morning. She notified the police and then waited for us at the front of his home. When she brought us to him, you were lying on the floor next to him. How did you get here, and why are you here?"

"Like I said, I knocked—"

"I got that. How did you get in? Do you have a key?"

"I do, but I didn't use it. The door was unlocked."

"I see. So you came in. Then what happened?"

"I put the flowers on the counter and called out for Mr. Wooley. He didn't answer. So I went to look for him. That's when I saw the wax figure. I mean, I thought it was the wax figure. Then I, I…touched…his cheek and it…" My ears rang. "I think I need to…" was all I got out.

I awoke in the man's arms as he dragged me to a sofa at the front of the house. Mr. Wooley was out of sight.

"Do you need water?" he asked.

"Please."

He left me for a few minutes and returned with a glass of water. The EMT was on his heels.

"Thank you." I accepted the glass. "I feel silly. I haven't fainted in years."

The EMT took my pulse again. "Do you think it's possible someone hit you over the head earlier?" he asked.

I reached around to feel the back of my skull. "I'm not tender anywhere. I'm sure I fainted."

"Do you have a history of fainting?"

"Yeah. I used to do it a lot as a kid."

He looked into my eyes again. "I think you're okay. It would still be a good idea to get looked at by someone at the hospital."

"It's not necessary," I insisted. "Really. I'm allergic to hospitals." I sipped the water. "Actually, I'm allergic to their bills. They give me hives. Make me hyperventilate.

"I hear that's a common side effect," he said as he left.

"Sure you feel better?" Mystery man asked.

"No, but I'm conscious, so I guess I must be."

"Good. I have to ask you a couple more questions. I am Detective Collin Beatty. This is," he tilted his head toward a man who had just joined us, "my partner, Detective Micah Jameson."

"Hello," I said.

Detective Jameson nodded.

"And you are?" Beatty asked.

"I'm Peri Milano," I said.

"Why are you here, Peri?" Jameson asked.

"I was bringing flowers for Mr. Wooley."

"The ones in the kitchen with the ribbon that says *In Sympathy,*" Jameson said, or maybe asked.

"Yes," I offered in case it was a question.

The men exchanged a glance.

"How did you know Shelby Wooley was dead?" Beatty asked.

"I didn't." I set the glass on a coffee table, suddenly aware of how bad the situation looked for me. "I'm organizing a funeral-themed party for him. He is very particular about the details. I brought the flowers to get his approval on the red tips of the callas. The florist has been having a tough time getting the right shade of red dye."

"Who is the florist?" Beatty asked.

"Pearl Slack at Custom Floral Designs." I gave them poor Pearl's number. She'd found this event to be more of an artistic challenge than she was prepared for. I had a feeling her stress level would see a cliff-dive once she realized the pseudo-funeral was off.

"Why did you come through the back door?" Jameson asked.

"I always do when I'm bringing props. Mr. Wooley wants everything to be a surprise. No one is supposed to know all the details. Not even Jacqueline." I glanced toward the back of the house, to where Jacqueline stood speaking with someone. Her head was tilted. She held a hand over her heart.

Together, the men grilled me over the events of the day, about my relationship with Mr. Wooley, and then took my full contact information. I answered their questions all the while straining my ears to hear what the others in the house were saying. It seemed they were under the impression Mr. Wooley was put in the chair after he had passed away.

Eventually, they sent me on my not-so-merry way, advising me it would be in my best interest to stay in town.

Outside in the back alley, I sat behind the steering wheel of my ancient Ford Explorer while I called my mother. The woman was a bit of a nutcase, but she never failed to have some kind of help or advice. Granted, it wasn't always useful, nor was it ever offered with a cookie, still, she did her best to act like a normal mom, and she was the only mom I had.

"I touched a dead body," I said when she picked up.

"Really? Why?" she asked.

"I thought it was a wax figure."

"How did it feel?"

"Spongy." I dropped my head back to rest on the car seat.

"What part did you touch?"

"The cheek."

"Butt or face?"

"Yuck!" I straightened to look out the front window. It was late April, but being in the back alley, there were no blooming flowers, nothing cheery to be seen. "Why would I touch a dead butt?"

"Why would you touch a dead face?"

"Like I said, I thought it was a wax figure. I touched the face."

"Was it grimacing?"

"Uh…I don't know. Why?"

"Just wondering how dead it was."

"Oh God." I sighed. "Why did I call you?"

"Maybe that was the wrong choice of words. I was just wondering if you could tell if rigor mortis had set in. It begins with the face before stiffening up the rest of the body. Then it all reverses. What most people don't know is that the body gets soft again."

"Do I want to know how you know that?"

"*Criminal Minds.*"

"Who?"

"A TV show."

"Oh." I think I sighed again. "Do you have any cookies?"

"Of course not. I do have some delicious grain-free muffins. I made them with almond meal for a change instead of almond flour. How's *that* for living dangerously?"

"You're on the edge, Ma."

"Want some?"

"I don't think so." I wanted bright flowers. Bright flowers and cookies made with wheat gluten and sugar.

"You sure? They have walnuts and coconut flakes," she sang.

"Sounds tempting," I lied. "I have too much to do today."

"Don't get so busy you don't allow yourself to grieve."

"I wasn't that close to him, Ma. I'll be okay."

"That's what everyone says before they self-destruct in unresolved grief."

"I'm fine, Ma."

"Then why did you call me?"

"I can't remember." We clicked off.

Get the book today to find out whether Peri is the next to Show up Dead.